dirt
music

tim winton

dirt
music

A NOVEL

COMPASS PRESS
AN IMPRINT OF WHEELER PUBLISHING, INC.

Published in Large Print by arrangement with Scribner, a division of
Simon & Schuster, Inc., in the United States.

Compass Press Large Print book series;
an imprint of Wheeler Publishing Inc., USA

Set in 16 pt Plantin.

Library of Congress Cataloging-in-Publication Data

Winton, Tim.
   Dirt music: a novel / Tim Winton.
     p. (large print) cm. (Compass Press large print book series)
   ISBN 1-58724-246-X (hardcover)
   1. Western Australia—Fiction. 2. Alienation (Social psychology)—
Fiction. 3. Middle-aged women. 4. Hitchhiking—Fiction. 5. Fishers—
Fiction. 6. Large type books. I. Title.

[PR9619.3.W585 D57   2002]
823'.914—dc21   2002067522
                                                  CIP

Denise
Denise
Denise

There is a solitude of space
A solitude of sea
A solitude of death, but these
Society shall be
Compared with that profounder site
That polar privacy
A soul admitted to itself—
Finite infinity.

Emily Dickinson

one

ONE NIGHT in November, another that had somehow become morning while she sat there, Georgie Jutland looked up to see her pale and furious face reflected in the window. Only a moment before she'd been perusing the blueprints for a thirty-two-foot Pain Clark from 1913 which a sailing enthusiast from Manila had posted on his website, but she was bumped by the server and was overtaken by such a silly rush of anger that she had to wonder what was happening to her. Neither the boat nor the bloke in Manila meant a damn thing to her; they were of as little consequence as every other site she'd visited in the last six hours. In fact, she had to struggle to remember how she'd spent the time. She had traipsed through the Uffizi without any more attention than a footsore tourist. She'd stared at a live camera image of a mall in the city of Perth, been to the Frank Zappa fan club of Brazil, seen Francis Drake's chamberpot in the Tower of London and stumbled upon a chat group for world citizens who yearned to be amputees.

Logging on—what a laugh. They should have called it stepping off. When Georgie sat down before the terminal she was gone in her seat, like a pensioner at the pokies, gone for all money. Into that welter of useless

3

information night after night to confront people and notions she could do without. She didn't know why she bothered except that it ate time. Still, you had to admit that it was nice to be without a body for a while; there was an addictive thrill in being of no age, no gender, with no past. It was an infinite sequence of opening portals, of menus and corridors that let you into brief, painless encounters, where what passed for life was a listless kind of browsing. World without consequence, amen. And in it she felt light as an angel. Besides, it kept her off the sauce.

She swivelled in her seat, snatched up the mug and recoiled as her lips met the cold sarcoma that had formed on the coffee's surface. Beyond her reflection in the window the moony sea seemed to shiver.

Georgie got up and padded across to the kitchen which was separated from the living space by the glossy rampart of benches and domestic appliances. From the freezer she pulled out a bottle and poured herself a serious application of vodka. She stood a while staring back at the great merging space of the livingroom. It was big enough not to seem crowded, despite the fact that it held an eight-seater dining table, the computer station and the three sofas corralled around the TV at the other end. The whole seaward wall of this top floor was glass and all the curtains were thrown back. Between the house and the lagoon a hundred metres away there was only the front lawn and a few scrubby dunes. Georgie slugged the vodka down at a gulp. It was all sensation and no taste, exactly how a sister once described her. She smiled and put the glass down too loudly on the draining board. A little way along the hall Jim was asleep. The boys were downstairs.

She pulled back the sliding door and stepped out onto the terrace where the air was cool and thick with the smells of stewing seagrass, of brine and limey sand, of thawing bait and the savoury tang of saltbush. The outdoor furniture was beaded with dew. There wasn't breeze enough yet to stir the scalloped hems of the Perrier brolly, but dew this time of year was a sign of wind on the way. White Point sat in the teeth of the Roaring Forties. Here on the midwest coast the wind might not be your friend but it was sure as hell your constant neighbour.

Georgie stood out there longer than was comfortable, until her breasts ached from the chill and her hair felt as though it was shrinking. She saw the moon tip across the lagoon until its last light caught on bow rails and biminis and windscreens, making mooring buoys into fitful, flickering stars. And then it was gone and the sea was dark and blank. Georgie lingered on the cold slate. So much for the real world; these days it gave her about as much pleasure as a childhood dose of codliver oil.

On the beach something flashed. At four o'clock in the morning it was probably just a gull, but it gave a girl a start. It was darker now than it had been all night; she couldn't see a thing.

Sea air misted on her skin. The chill burned her scalp.

Georgie wasn't a morning person but as a shiftworker she'd seen more than her share of dawns. Like all those Saudi mornings when she'd arrive back at the infidels' compound to loiter outside after her colleagues went to bed. In stockinged feet she would stand on the precious mat of lawn and sniff the Jeddah air in the hope of catching a whiff of pure sea breeze coming across the high perimeter wall. Sentimental attachment to geography irritated her, Australians were riddled with it and West Australians were worst of all, but there was no point in denying that the old predawn ritual was anything more than bog-standard homesickness, that what she was sniffing for was the highball mix you imbibed every night of your riverside Perth childhood, the strange briny effervescence of the sea tide stirring in the Swan River, into its coves, across the estuarine flats. But in Jeddah all she ever got for her trouble was the fumy miasma of the corniche, the exhaust of Cadillacs and half a million aircon units blasting Freon at the Red Sea.

And now here she was, years later, soaking in clean, fresh Indian Ocean air with a miserable, prophylactic determination. Sailor, diver and angler though she was, Georgie knew that these days the glories of the outdoors were wasted on her.

There was no use in going to bed now. Jim would be up in less than an hour and she'd never get to sleep before then unless she took a pill. What was the point in lying down in time for him to sit up and take his first steeling sigh of the day? Jim Buckridge needed no alarm, somehow he was wired to be early. He was your first out and last in sort of fisherman; he set the mark that others in the fleet aspired to. Inherited, so everybody said. By the time he was out of the lagoon and through the passage in the reef with the bird-swirling island on his starboard beam, the whole bay would be burbling with diesels and the others would be looking for the dying phosphor of his wake.

At seven the boys would clump in, fuddled and ready for breakfast, though somehow in the next hour they would become less and less ready for school. She'd make their lunches—apple sandwiches for Josh and five rounds of Vegemite for Brad. Then finally they'd crash out the back door and Georgie might switch on the VHF and listen to the fleet while she went through the business of keeping order in a big house. And then and then and then.

Down at the beach it wasn't a gull, that blur of movement; there was a flash of starlight on wet metal. Right there, in the shadow of the foredune along the bay. And now the sound of a petrol engine, eight cylinders.

Georgie peered, made a tunnel with her hands to focus in the dark. Yes. Two hundred metres along the beach, a truck wheeling around to reverse toward the shore. No headlamps, which was curious. But the brake-lights gave it away; they revealed a pink-lit boat

7

on a trailer, a centre console. Small, maybe less than six metres. Not a professional boat. Even abalone boats had big yellow licence markings. No sportfisherman launched a boat with such stealth an hour before Jim Buckridge got out of bed.

Georgie grabbed a windcheater from inside and stood in the hallway a few moments. The plodding clock, a snore, appliances whirring. The vodka still burned in her belly. She was shaky with caffeine, and restless. What the hell, she thought. A moment of unscripted action in White Point. You had to go and see.

Underfoot the lawn was delicious with dew, and warmer than she expected. She crossed its mown pelt to the foredune and the sand track to the beach. Even without the moon the white sand around the lagoon was luminescent and powdery. Where the tide had been and gone the beach was hard and rippled.

Somewhere in the dark an outboard started. So muted it had to be a four-stroke. It idled briefly and as it throttled up she saw for only a moment the hint of a white wake on the lagoon. Whether it was surreptitious or merely considerate, the whole procedure was extraordinary in its quiet and speed. A bird's wings whopped by, invisible but close as a whisper; the sound prickled Georgie's skin like the onset of the flu.

Along the beach a dog blurred about. When she got closer she saw it was chained to the truck. It growled, seemed to draw itself up to bark then hesitate.

The big galvanized trailer was still leaking seawater when she reached it. The dog whined eloquently. Steel links grated against the Ford's barwork. An F-100, the 4x4 model. Redneck Special. The dog yanked against the chain. It launched itself into a sprawl, seemed more eager than angry.

Georgie bent down to the shadow of the dog and felt its tongue hot on her palms. Its tail drummed against the fender. She saw seagrass trailing from the driver's step, black shreds against the talcum sand.

Hmm, she murmured. Are you a nice dog?

The dog sat, got all erect and expectant at the sound of her voice. It was a kelpie-heeler sort of mutt, a farm dog, your garden variety livewire fencejumping mongrel. All snout and chest and balls. She liked it already.

Good dog, she murmured. Yeah, good fella.

The dog craned toward the water.

Feel like a swim, eh?

Bugger it, she thought, why not.

She stripped off and laid her clothes on the truck. The blouse was past its use-by date; she picked it up, sniffed it and tossed it back.

Unleashed, the dog flashed out across the sand in a mad tanglefooted arc. Georgie belted down to the water and ploughed in blind. Her reckless dive brought to mind the paraplegic ward. She felt the percussion of the dog hitting the water behind her and struck out in her lazy schoolgirl freestyle until she was amidst moored lobster boats with their fug of

9

corrosion and birdshit and pilchards. Behind her the dog snuffed along gamely, snout up, with a bow wave you could feel on your back.

Stars were dropping out now. A couple of houses had lights on. One of them had to be Jim. Puzzled, perhaps.

Out on the seagrass meadows where the lagoon tasted a little steeped, she trod water for a while and picked out Jim's house on the dune. It was a bare white cube, a real bauhaus shocker and the first of its kind in White Point. Locals once called it the Yugoslav Embassy but these days nearly every owner-skipper had himself a trophy house built with the proceeds of the rock lobster boom.

Jim would be in the bathroom now, holding himself up against the tiled wall, scratching his chin, loosening his back, feeling his age. Despite his reputation he still seemed to her a decent man, decent enough to spend three years with, and for Georgie Jutland that was a record.

She imagined him back in the kitchen, boiling water for his thermos, doing a room-by-room, wondering. He'd step outside to scan the yard and maybe the beach and take in the state of the sky and the sea, gauge the wind while he was there. He'd go inside and get his kit together for eight or ten hours at sea. And if she didn't arrive? When his deckhands turned up in the old Hilux in their beanies and fog of brewer's breath, with the dinghy lashed across the tray like a cattle trough, what then? Did she really give a toss anymore? A few months ago she would

10

have been tucked up in bed. Not swimming nude in the bay with some stranger's cur entertaining mutinous thoughts. But recently something in her had leaked away. Vaporized in a moment.

The dog circled her patiently—well, doggedly, in fact—and in every hair and pore Georgie felt the shimmer of water passing over her body. After weeks of the virtual, it was queer and almost painful to be completely present.

Georgie thought of that afternoon a few months ago and the meek puff of steam she had become in the boys' playroom. She could barely believe that a single word might do her in. As a nurse she'd copped a swill of curses, from dying men and girls in labour, from junkies and loonies, princesses and smart-arses. Patients said vile things in extremis. You'd think a woman could withstand three simple syllables like *stepmother*. But the word came so hot and wet and sudden, screamed into her face by a nine-year-old whose night terrors she'd soothed, whose body she'd bathed and held so often, whose grief-muddy daubs she'd clamped to the fridge, that she didn't even hear the sentence it came wrapped in. She just lurched back in her seat like a woman slapped. Stepmother. The word had never been uttered in the house before, let alone fired in anger. It was fair in its way; she understood that. Along with his need to win, his desire to wound, Josh was merely clarifying her status. She could still see his face wrinkled and sphinctery with rage. It was his geriatric face waiting for him.

11

For the sake of a moronic video game he was defining her out of his life while his brother Brad, who was eleven, looked on in silent disgust. As she got up to leave Georgie was ashamed of the sob that escaped her. None of them had seen Jim leaning in the doorway. There was a universal intake of breath. Georgie left the room before a word was uttered, before she let herself break down completely. She ducked beneath his arm and scrambled upstairs to bawl into a teatowel until she was steady enough to slop chardonnay into a glass. Jim's voice was quiet and ominous rising up the stairwell. She realized that he was about to hit them and she knew she should go down and put a stop to it but it was over before she could take herself in hand. It had never happened before, none of it. Later Georgie wondered if it really was the S-word that had broken the spell or the knowledge that she might have spared the boys a belting and hadn't even tried. Either way nothing was the same.

That was late autumn. Within a few weeks she turned forty and she was careful to let that little landmark slide by unheralded. By spring and the onset of the new season she was merely going through the motions. Another man, an American, had once told her in a high, laughing moment his theory of love. It was magic, he said. The magic ain't real, darlin, but when it's gone it's over.

Georgie didn't want to believe in such thin stuff, that all devotion was fuelled by delusion, that you needed some spurious myth to keep you going in love or work or service. Yet she'd felt romance evaporate often enough to make her wonder. And hadn't she woken one heartsick morning without a reason to continue as a nurse? Her career had been a calling, not just a job. Wasn't that sudden emptiness, the loss of some ennobling impulse, the sign of a magic gone?

In her time Georgie Jutland had been a sailor of sorts, so she knew exactly what it meant to lose seaway, to be dead in the water. She recognized the sensation only too well. And that spring she had slipped overboard without a sound.

That's how it felt sculling about in the lagoon this morning while the sky went felty above her. Woman overboard. With nowhere to swim. What was she gonna do, strike out for the fringing reef, head on out into open water, take on the Indian Ocean in her birthday suit with a liberated mongrel sidekick? Stroke across the Cray Bank, the Shelf, the shipping lane, the Ninety East Ridge? To Africa? Georgie, she told herself, you're a woman who doesn't even own a car anymore, that's how mobile and independent you are. You used to frighten the mascara off people, render surgeons speechless. Somewhere, somehow, you sank into a fog.

She lay back in the water wishing some portal would open, that she might click on some dopey icon and proceed safely, painlessly, without regret or memory.

The dog whined and tried to scramble onto her for a breather. She sighed and struck out for shore.

IN THE WRECKYARD behind his roadhouse a bear-like man in a pair of greasy overalls had a last toke on his wizened reefer and shifted his weight off the hood of the Valiant which some dick had recently driven off the end of the jetty. It was his morning ritual, the dawn patrol. A piss on the miserable oleander and a little suck on the gigglyweed to soften the facts of life.

The light was murky yet. You could feel a blow coming on, another endless screaming bloody southerly. He snuffed out his tiny roach-end on the Valiant's sandy paintjob and shoved the remains through the kelp-laced grille near the radiator.

From the beach track, between the dunes and the lobster depot, came a trailer clank and a quiet change of gears. There was plenty enough light to see the truck and the boat behind it spilling bilgewater as it pulled out onto the blacktop.

Fuck me sideways, he said aloud. You bloody idiot.

The V8 eased up along the tiny main drag, fading off in the distance.

Beaver slouched off toward the forecourt to unlock the pumps. A man could do with a

14

friggin blindfold in this town. And get his jaw wired shut while he was at it.

Inside at the register he tossed the padlocks down and pawed through his CDs. Tuesday. Cream, maybe. Or The Who *Live at Leeds*. No. *Fiddler on the Roof*, it was.

He opened the register, closed it, and gazed up the empty street. You silly bugger.

WHILE THE BOYS ATE breakfast Georgie went about the morning routine in a sleepy daze. She was passing a window with a wad of beefy male laundry when she saw that the Ford and trailer were gone from the beach. Right under her nose.

Of course it might be nothing. But really, in a town like this, where crews regularly pulled their pots to find them unaccountably empty, a non-fleet boat going out under cover of darkness and slipping back at first light was not likely to be an innocent occurrence. There was something shonky about it. Some fool with a taste for trouble.

She went downstairs and stuffed the washer full and for a few moments she paused, overcome with weariness. Beneath their lids her eyes felt coarse. She probably should have reported what she saw this morning, told Jim at the very least. Whoever it was, even if he wasn't pillaging other people's pots, even if he was just taking fish it could only be as a

15

shamateur, the fleet equivalent of a scab. That was no recreational angler. Local families mortgaged themselves into purgatory to buy professional licences. This bloke was taking food from their mouths.

Georgie slapped the lid down and smirked at her own righteous piety. God, she thought, listen to me! Bread from their mouths? Once upon a time, maybe, in the good ole bad ole days.

She caught the reek of burnt toast rolling down the stairwell. How did they manage it? The toaster was automatic.

In earlier times, when arson was a civic tool and regulatory gunfire not unknown at sea, the locals sorted poachers out with a bit of White Point diplomacy. Back in the fifties it was a perilous, hardscrabble life and crews protected their patch by whatever means came to hand. Georgie had seen the photos in the pub and the school, all those jug-eared men with split lips and sun-flayed noses posing barechested in tiny football shorts with their eyes narrowed against the light. Returned soldiers, migrants and drifters, their stubby plank boats with masts and sails, stern tillers and tiny, gutless diesels looked impossibly slow and cumbersome.

The only safe anchorage for many miles, White Point was then just a bunch of tin sheds in the lee of the foredune. A sandy point, a series of fringing reefs and an island a mile offshore created a broad lagoon in which the original jetty stood. The settlement lay wedged between the sea and the majestic white sandhills of the interior. It was a shanty town whose perimeter was a wall of empty beer bottles and flyblown carapaces. Before the export boom, when most of the catch was canned, rock lobsters were called crayfish. They were driven out in wet hessian bags on trucks that wallowed the four hours of sand tracks to the nearest blacktop. The place was isolated, almost secret, and beyond the reach of the law and the dampening influence of domesticity. It was the boys' own life. On the rare occasions when the coppers and the bailiff did their rounds, somebody radioed ahead so that the pub-shed might close and the alimony cheats, bail absconders and nervy drunks made it into the surrounding bush. For the bulk of the time men worked and drank in a world of their own making. How they loved to run amok. And when, in time, their women came, they did not, on the whole, bring a certain civilizing something. True, they conferred glass and lace curtains upon the windows of shacks. Geraniums appeared in old kero tins and there was an exodus of idealists who were driven north into the tropics, but, male and female, addicted to the frontier way, White Pointers remained a savage, unruly lot. Even after the boom when many families became instantly—even catastrophically—rich and the law came to town, they were, in any estimation, as rough as guts.

Nowadays rich fishermen built pink brick villas and concrete slab bunkers that made their fathers' hovels look pretty. The materials were long-haul but the spirit behind the construction was entirely makeshift, as though locals were hard-wired for an ephemeral life. Georgie, who rather liked the get-fucked Fish Deco vibe of the place, thought it remarkable that people could produce such a relentlessly ugly town in so gorgeous a setting. The luminous dunes, the island, the lagoon with its seagrass and coral outcrops, the low, austere heath of the hinterland—they were singular to even her suburban gaze. The town was a personality junkyard—and she was honest enough to count herself onto that roll—where people still washed up to hide or to lick their wounds. Broke and rattled they dropped sail in the bay and never left. Surfers, dopeheads, deviants, dreamers—even lobster molls like herself—sensed that the town was a dog but the landscape got its hooks in and people stayed.

Just because you became a local, though, didn't mean you were a real White Pointer. Georgie never really qualified. Socially she had always remained ambivalent. Not because she came from the world of private schools and yacht clubs but because there was something dispiriting about hearing the wives of illiterate millionaires complain of the habits of crew families, at how squalid their women were, how foulmouthed their childen. These were women maybe five years out of the van park themselves, who hid their own shiners beneath duty-free makeup and thought of themselves already as gentry. Georgie had always held back and she knew what it cost her. There was always some lingering doubt about Georgie. She wondered if they felt her faking it.

A real fisherman's woman wouldn't have hesitated about reporting something suspicious. Georgie knew what a shamateur was, what was required. A simple call to the Fisheries office. Or a quiet word to Jim. Either way it would be dealt with and she'd have done her civic duty. But stealing bread from their mouths—really! People with a million dollars' worth of boat and licence, a new Landcruiser and six weeks in Bali every season, families who owned city pubs and traded in gold, whose TVs were the size of pianos? Even the lowliest deckhand earned more than the teacher who endured his children six hours a day. Not that Georgie begrudged anyone the money. Men worked seven days a week for eight months of the year at something dangerous and their families had endured the bad times, so good luck to them. But she wasn't about to go running out to protect millionaires from one bloke and his dog. She had two boys to get off to school and she felt like shit. Besides, she never had been much of a joiner.

UP IN THE BRIDGE it was all Roy Orbison and bacon farts. Jim Buckridge was still thinking about that radar blip from earlier on and as he eased the boat up to the next float he

19

looked out across the broken sea. He didn't notice the deckie go down.

Rope coiled through the winch and the steel-based pot tilted on the tipper a long time without anybody opening it up. The boat heeled and twisted in the chop and down there on deck no one was skinning the pot. It was bristling with feelers, choking with lobsters, he could see it from up there, but no bastard was pulling them out. Boris, you lazy, stoned prick, what are you doing?

Someone began to yell.

He slammed her out of gear and went down to see.

Georgie woke on the sofa with the phone trilling beside her. On TV fat-arsed Americans were braying about their addictions, their satanic memories, their Lord'n Saviour. The light in the house was a headache lying in wait.

Georgie? You awake or what?

Half her face was numb. She pressed the device to her ear.

Yep. Yes.

Christ, it's ten o'clock.

Oh? Georgie unglued her tongue and lips.

Look, we need the ambulance on the jetty in half an hour. And find me another deckie. Boris is out to it, blood from arsehole to breakfast. Jim's voice came from within a roar of diesels; it gave him a creepy, industrial sound.

Um. You clear his airway?

Packed him in ice, too.

All of him?

Listen, don't use the radio. I've only pulled two lines and I don't want this pack of nature's gentlemen pillagin my pots, orright? You awake?

Yeah, she croaked. Half an hour.

In the stairwell to the garage Georgie was queasy with fatigue. She hauled the Landcruiser door open and climbed in barefoot. The plush interior smelled of pizza. She hit the roller remote. In the mirror she saw that she was no triumph of middle-aged womanhood; she chided herself for even looking. The turbo diesel gulped a moment while the door cranked up and as she reversed out into the blizzard of summer daylight she heard the pistol crack of a skateboard under the rear wheel.

OUT IN THE SHED with the dog at his shins he leaves the boat smelling of bleach. Everything squared away. Ices up the truck. The dog leaps into the cab before him, reads his mind, knows the routine. Its tail whacks his elbow as he goes through the gears up the long sandy drive, through the blighted paddocks to the highway. The mutt licks salt off his thigh. Through the window the smell of dead grass, banksia, superphosphate, the hidden sea.

♦ ♦ ♦

IN THE BLINDING limestone yard of the depot Yogi's bait truck stood empty, its two-way squawking. Georgie leapt up onto the loading dock. The office cubicle, permanently makeshift and ripe with sweat, was empty. On the scarred desk was a depleted bottle of ouzo and a Buddy Holly tape in a visceral tangle. *Penthouse* centrefolds, girls waxed to the point of martyrdom, were taped to the ply walls. From the back of the shed, beyond the growling freezer, came the surprisingly lovely voice of a man crooning. Yogi was a shambles of a man. Georgie figured his singing pipes were God relenting, a moment of mercy.

Yogi! she called. You there?

The singing gave out. Whossat?

Ah, Georgie Jutland.

Who?

Jim Buckridge's—

Jim's missus? Jesus, hang on, I'm in the shower. Won't be a tick.

We need the ambulance.

Just get the soap orf!

Georgie retreated to the office and glanced at the pinups. Well, she thought. Age shall not weary them, nor the years condemn. She looked at her watch. Twenty-five minutes in which to find three sober, competent people. In White Point. Two volunteers for the ambulance and some unlucky conscript to work the deck in a rank southerly. Without the strange power of Jim Buckridge's name at her disposal she doubted it was possible.

22

Righto!

Yogi Behr came out wrapped in a Simpsons towel. He was small and round and, so dressed, he was a potato burst from its jacket.

Instinctively, Georgie's hand went to her mouth.

Rachel's rostered, said Yogi. His bare feet were cracked and hard, brown as his face and arms. The rest of him was spud flesh. Hairless. The toenails like iguana claws.

Don't spose you know a free crew?

Who's hurt?

Boris.

Try the surfshop, eh. I'll just get me strides on. Have to get someone to deal with me... affairs here.

He scuttled behind some reeking crates a moment and came back shirtless in a bib and brace overall.

Sundy best, he said.

It's Tuesday.

I won't let on if you don't, he said giving her a view of the windswept teeth in his smile.

Keys. Phone. Shall we?

In the cab, as she gunned the Cruiser across the three blocks of town, Georgie could smell more soap on him than ouzo; a good sign. He punched digits into his mobile and put his feet up on Jim Buckridge's dash.

Rachel, he said to Georgie. She knows her shit from shavin cream. Went to the university and what-all. Jerra! he yelled into the phone. Oy, you lazy, fat hippy bastard, get ya missus down the ambo shed and tell her to put

23

her teeth in!... Well, mate, excrement occurs and this is ya small community arrangement. She's rostered on... Yeah, yeah, wash ya mouth out, ya cheeky prick. Five minutes.

Georgie swept them into the yard in front of the volunteer service shed.

Slick drivin, Georgiana. Should join up, drive the bloodtruck for us.

Thanks, but I'm more your fire brigade type, Yogi.

Yairs, well there's more bells and whistles, I spose. And a yellow hat.

That's it.

Bloody helmet. Gets em every time. I'll put in a good word.

She left him there and drove off with a smile. She understood why the fishermen loved him. The God-given laugh. The sunny outlook. After a day at sea in a miserable slop and the hammering wind they came in to heave their catch onto his truck and his happy bullshit was balm. He was no gift to womanhood but he probably took the edge off a few homeward tempers.

Pulled up in front of the surfshop, she saw several dreadlocked boys and girls come to wary attention. Piercings, coldsore lips.

She had ten minutes. Wished she'd brushed her teeth.

COASTAL HEATH. Sheep pasture jagged with limestone. Banksia thickets. A couple of

24

sterile pine plantations before the farmlets and crappy subdivisions. The empty two-lane hums and the dog slumps across its forepaws, eyeing him. He does it in two hours. Wonders about the dog and time.

Did he who make the Lamb make thee, mutt?

The dog lifts an eyebrow.

I'm talking fearful symmetry.

The dog coils up and settles in to lick its balls.

Behind the vast terracotta roof plain of Perth a clutch of mirrored towers rises in the bronze band of sky.

Jerusalem, he mutters.

Luther Fox pulls into the greasy funk of the rear courtyard at Go's. A kid bagging bottles by the dumpster looks up through his black fringe and stalks inside. The yard smells of burnt oil and rotting vegetables. The dog whines a little.

Stay put, mutt, or you'll find yourself on a bed of steamed rice.

The city hums with the white noise of traffic and airconditioning. Somewhere a car alarm whoops endlessly.

Go comes to the door in his crisp white apron. Fox gets out, extends a hand.

You got abalone, Lu?

I'm fine, Go, and thanks for askin.

We do business, Lu. No time for fuck around.

Fox grins. Go strides to the rear of the Ford.

25

His manner never alters. The Vietnamese has purposeful intensity down pat.

No abs, says Fox.

Ah, that's bad.

You could buy it legit, you know.

Two hunnerd dollar a kilo? You fuckin crazy?

Imagine so.

What you have, then?

Some good fish. Jewies, snapper, cod.

Fresh?

When did you ever get anything from me that wasn't fresh?

Jokes, all your jokes stale.

Okay, you got me there.

The restaurateur gives the dog a wide berth and leaps up onto the truckbed. The two big steel boxes look like tradesmen's toolchests. They even have the obligatory stickers—Stihl, Sidchrome, 96FM. Go motions toward the larger of them and Fox unfurls a hand in a gesture of permission, their little moment of civility. A cold mist rises when Go cracks the lid. The fibreglass liner is packed with ice slurry. The Viet digs out a pink snapper. Death has robbed it of most of its blue spots yet its body is still firm, scales laid back in perfect cobblework from lucent eye to taut anus. Iced the moment it hits the deck, Fox's catch would still be considered prime this time tomorrow but it's a matter of personal pride to have it here within three hours of leaving the water.

Beautiful, eh?

Fresh is beautiful, Lu.

But fresh *and* cheap—

Tha's berluddy beautiful!

The ritual laugh.

Go burrows further into the slurry, grunting thoughtfully. Fox doesn't mind not bringing abalone. He knows most of it will go to the Triads. It's a shitload of trouble.

Okay. Good fish.

While Go and his brothers unload the fish, Fox counts the cash. After fuel and bait he's miles ahead.

Still lucky, says Go, wiping his hands on his apron.

Fox shrugs. He hasn't felt lucky in a good while.

So, Lu, who you sell abalone to?

Didn't get any, mate. I said that.

Someone pay more, huh?

No, there wasn't any.

I do good business with you all year one year.

That's right.

Hard for me. Big family. Too many restaurants here.

Most of em buy their seafood at the market, Go. They're paying twice what you are.

And not fresh!

Yeah, you're a man of standards, Go.

I don't call cops.

Me neither. We're both in the same position, you know.

Bullshit! I been through a war. And then South China fuckin Sea and Malaysia camps and Darwin. And fifteen people looking up to me, Lu. Not the same!

Go, there weren't any abalone, orright? It was too rough to dive.

Best jewfish today.

Yes.

Next time abalone.

We'll see.

No *we'll see*. Gotta be absolutely.

I'll be tryin.

Shake hand now.

Fox takes his cold hand. The family retreats inside. Out in the street the car alarm finally blips off.

JIM'S BOAT was called the *Raider*. Georgie figured it was a pretty mellow name in an anchorage full of boats like *Reaper*, *Slayer* and *Black Bitch*. A couple of younger crew had vessels called *Mull Bus* and *The Love Shack* but apart from your standard ethnic saints' names the labels were generally aggro-extractive. When Jim came steaming into the lagoon with his bow wave up like a rippling flag, there was something of a gathering on the jetty. Yogi and Rachel had the ambulance light flashing.

At the sandy end of the jetty Georgie met the sorry youth she'd lured from the bowels of the surfshop and together they walked out to where the crowd waited.

Jim'll be in a nice old shit, said the boy.

Think of the money, she said.

28

Raider pulled in with a histrionic reversing of screws. GM diesels, she thought with what remained of her fishwife self, cheap and loud. Whatever he saved at the dealers this season he'll be spending on hearing aids in the next.

They brought Boris up conscious and muttering. He was never pretty but today he sported a head like a spoiled mango. His wound was a ragged exclamation mark from scalp to nose and Georgie saw that he needed sutures.

The *pupils* on him, said Rachel as they loaded him in.

Pissholes in the snow, said Yogi.

You've never bloody seen snow, Yogi, said Rachel.

Seen a few pissholes, though.

You see what I have to work with, Georgie? said Rachel mildly. I'll have hours of it.

Least you're in the back with Boris.

Some alternative.

Who's up? Jim yelled from the bridge of the lurching boat. There was blood on his shirt and he looked ornery behind his reflector shades. Who's comin?

Me, said the kid beside Georgie. His dejected voice barely carried above the idling diesels.

Well, what're you waitin for—a printed fuckin invitation?

The boy swung aboard to stand beside the other crewman and Jim had them boiling away before the lines even hit the deck.

He'll wish he was never born, said Yogi. Poor little cunt.

Hey, driver! called Rachel. You thinking of taking this bloke to hospital any time soon?

He'll be orright. Torn upholstery, thasall. Keep yer rubber gloves on, girlie.

Girlie me I'll kick you fair up the date.

You'll put a hole in me ouzone layer.

Yeah, that'd hurt.

Scuse me, George. Must convey a chap to his physician.

Yogi waddled around and climbed into the 250's cab.

Rachel paused from swabbing and smiled.

Yogi's forgotten the doors. Would you mind?

Sure.

Georgie liked Rachel. Word was she'd been a social worker. Georgie had the impression her bloke might be the local dope dealer. Despite having stayed ten years, Rachel wasn't a genuine White Pointer either. She wore peasant scarves and didn't shave her legs. Her face was plain and honest and open. Georgie wondered how it was they had never become friends, but even as she asked herself the question she knew the answer. She just hadn't taken the trouble. For three years she'd kept entirely to herself.

She swung the doors to. Rachel winked. The big Ford eased up the jetty behind a rolling wave of gulls.

AN HOUR OUT of the city Fox sees the ambulance come bawling and flashing round the
bend, its white duco flecked with the shadows
cast by lemon-scented gums. Grips the wheel.
Clocks the sight of Yogi Behr at the helm, elbow
out the window like a bloody hot-rodder.
Sees his eyes widen in recognition as they
pass in a slam of slipstream. The moment
rides by. He's okay but chilled to the teeth.
It takes a breath or two to digest the fact that
Yogi, the little bugger, crossed himself going
by as if warding off the evil eye.

JOSH HELD the two halves of his skateboard and
looked at Georgie in disbelief. Not that such
a thing could occur but that it might have been
accidental.

That's it!

Georgie had begun patient and contrite, as
upbeat as she could manage to be so late in the
day. Brad looked on with an air of disinterest
she no longer believed in. The fridge hummed.

Maple top, Georgie.

I know, love.

My birthday present.

From me. Yes.

Well that's *it*!

Leaving bag and shoes and shirt on the
kitchen floor he flounced down to his room.

Bummer, said Brad with the faintest hint of a smirk.

He knows I'll buy him another one, she said, a little shaky. So how's school?

Sucks. New teacher wants a choir.

Great. You used to sing so much. You've got a lovely voice.

Not anymore.

Oh.

And no *woman*'ll make me.

Georgie felt it somehow directed at her, was stung as he grabbed up an apple and sloped off. Within a few moments the hateful, lobotomized music of some Nintendo game rose from the stairs. The usual explosions, yelps of pain, murderous laughter.

Late that afternoon Jim came in bloodshot and silvery with salt.

Ah, she murmured, pouring him a glass. Captain Happy.

Ahoy. As they say.

How was it?

Shithouse.

The kid?

Worked his ring gear out.

Good for him.

Three hundred kilos.

Not bad for a day of disasters.

I'm a day ahead of em, I reckon. Maybe tomorrow we'll kill the pig.

Hell, that's what, seven thousand dollars?

Before bait and fuel. Wages. Tax.

Yeah, destitution, eh.

He grinned.

Called the hospital, she said. Boris took fifteen stitches. Concussion. He's okay. What hit him?

Snapper sinker big as a hotdog. It was all fouled in the pot. Came up swingin off it. Kerblam. Coulda killed him. Some bloody wood-duck up for the weekend got his line snagged on the gear and just left it there. Hey, nice goin with the skateboard.

You know already?

He was waitin on the front lawn for me, the little dobber.

He knows I'll buy him another one.

Bugger him, he can save for it. Told him often enough about puttin the damn thing away.

No, I'll get it.

Not this time. He needs to learn. After a certain point everybody's on their own.

Georgie sighed. He didn't see the politics of it. But she was too tired to argue.

At dinner Jim quizzed the boys about their day at school. Like most kids they'd blotted it from consciousness the moment they flew from the classroom door, so their responses were vague and guarded and Georgie felt the ghost of the broken skateboard hanging over her end of the table. Although Jim had started there himself, he had misgivings about the local school and Georgie could sense his restraint in not launching outright into a test of what they had learnt in six hours. He was a curious man. At forty-eight he was weatherbeaten but still attractive in a blunt, conventional antipodean way. His eyes were grey and his gaze steely. There were scars on his forehead and sun lesions on his hands and arms. His lips were often chapped and he had coarse, sandy hair whose curls, no matter how short the cut, seemed incongruously delicate for a man whose rumbly voice and physical presence altered the atmosphere of a room. There was something resolutely sober about him, a ponderous aspect. He was emotionally reserved. His features were impassive. Yet he had a weary humour that Georgie liked and when he did laugh a network of creases transformed his face, dividing it so many times as to render the whole less daunting.

At White Point Jim was the uncrowned prince. People deferred to him. They watched him and took his lead and hung on every word. Several times a week men and women alike would drop by for a moment in confidence and he'd retire with them to the airless little room he used as an office. Even his perennial presidency of the regional branch of the Fishermen's Association couldn't account for the breadth of his authority. Some gravitas seemed to have been inherited from his legendary father, years dead. Big Bill was, by all accounts, not merely a man's man, but a bastard's bastard whose ruthless cunning was not confined to fishing. The Buckridges had been successful, acquisitive farmers in their time but as fishermen they were profoundly, prodigiously superior, and others in the fleet were in awe of Jim's success. To them it was almost supernatural. They lived and died by chance, by fluctuations in weather and ocean current, by momentary changes in spawning patterns and migration. Crustacea was a fickle kingdom. And Jim Buckridge seemed touched. He simply refused to admit to it or even discuss it but Georgie knew this was the nub of his effect upon them: they thought he had the gift. Although he lived like a man without a past, never reminiscing—not even with the kids—and always seeming to look forward, Georgie knew there were painful secrets there. He was a widower, and he'd lost his mother as a child. He refused to discuss either loss and sometimes Georgie detected a suppressed rage in him that she was glad to be spared. It was rare; it came and went in brief flickers, but it unnerved her. Watching the caution and deference with which townsfolk treated him Georgie wondered if they thought his fishing luck was special because it was the obverse of his domestic life, if they believed that his freakish touch had come at a high personal cost. She knew they came around to stay in with him socially, but also in the hope that his luck might rub off on them. He endured it but he seemed to hate it too.

Jim loved to fish but he wanted his sons to do something else. He didn't want them to follow the standard White Point trajectory which meant bumping out of school at fifteen to

35

end up in seaboots or prison greens. Bill had sent him to board at an exclusive school notorious for its alumni of politicians and white-collar criminals. Neither Josh nor Brad would ever need to work a day in their lives if he didn't insist upon it, but Jim was a stickler for hard work, for education and upright behaviour. All of which made him even more an exception at White Point. Down off the rooster perch of the bridge he was a fair, articulate, thoughtful man. And he'd always been kind to her. He was capable of, sometimes compelled by, a special, almost fearful physical tenderness. He was blokey and, yes, a little dull, especially of late, but he wasn't a narcissist or a whiner. She'd had her share of supposedly reconstructed males, and after them Jim was a breath of fresh air. They were an unlikely pair—she'd always enjoyed that. The shame of it was that recently, each time she catalogued his virtues like this, it left an odour of self-persuasion, and she feared that as a couple they grew less likely by the day.

After dinner Jim stepped out for a bit. He came back with a video from Beaver's garage. Georgie and Jim were on a Bette Davis bender. The great, hairy retired biker specialized in the campest years of Hollywood. Beaver was the closest thing Georgie had to a friend in this town.

All About Eve, Jim said. Her last really good one. And Marilyn Monroe.

Aha.

So sue me—I'm a bloke.

Georgie helped him put the boys to bed. Josh, his face softened by the nightlight, looked at her imploringly.

Dad says I have to save for a new board.

I'm sorry, love, she murmured. But it was an accident and you know we've been trying to get you to put it away.

A hundred and fifty dollars, but.

I'll help you out.

Yeah?

Are the wheels okay?

Think so.

Then it's just a new deck.

Josh pulled at his buttons thoughtfully.

We'll have a look at the surfshop tomorrow.

Don't tell Dad.

Why, love?

He's mad at me.

Well, you were mean to me. It hurts, Josh. I have feelings, too.

The memory of the S-word lingered between them. Things had been rocky these past weeks in its wake.

Night, he said abruptly.

Josh?

Yeah?

Thought you might say sorry.

It wasn't me who did it.

Georgie got off her knees and left him. Up in the livingroom Jim was asleep with the weather fax and the TV remote in his lap. The southerly caused the windows to shudder.

The house felt like a plane powering up at the end of a runway. Or maybe that was wishful thinking. She sat down and watched the movie anyway. Marilyn Monroe came and went without him, twitching those lips fit to beat the band. Georgie worked through the bottle of chardonnay hating Anne Baxter, wondering how Miss Davis seemed forever old, raising her glass to the deliciously cold George Sanders.

The tape played out and rewound automatically and when it was done she sat in the ambient hum of other domestic machines.

She got up unsteadily, checked her email in vain. There was only rubbish: perverted strangers, hawkers, the usual dreck. She padded downstairs and looked in on the boys. Brad slept with his head flung back like his old man. He'd lost his infant cuteness. She supposed Josh was in the process of shedding his. You could see why women teachers retreated into the pleasing compliance of the girls in their care. After nine, from what she could see, boys didn't care to please. In his room Josh slept with his sheet off. He lay in the starfish position, a gentle nickering in his throat. She wanted to touch him while he was disarmed but she resisted the urge.

What was it with him? Did he sense her withdrawal? Was his behaviour some kind of pre-emptive strike? God knows, he'd been through a storm of grief as a six-year-old. Did he feel it instinctively, this change? Had he really caused her to drop her bundle this winter, or did he just pick up on her beginning to let go?

And where was his toughness now? Not that she could hold it against him. A bit of grit was useful. As a girl she'd had it in spades, hadn't she? She despised her sisters' girly meekness, the cunning, desperate way they strove for cuteness out of fear of losing favour. They were strategically pliable. And Georgie was not. Yet she *was* the loner in the family. An uncle once said she had more balls than her father. He was the one who felt her up when she was fifteen. She went upstairs to her father's desk and showed him a business card which caused his eyes to widen. His boss, the editor of the newspaper he worked for, was her father's sailing partner and here were his private numbers. If her uncle ever entered a room she was in without another adult present, she told him, she would make the call. That certainly pepped up Christmas gatherings in the Jutland house. She learned to steel herself. Georgie took that martial bearing onto the wards of a dozen hospitals. Along with a sense of humour, it helped when you were extracting a Barbie doll or a Perrier bottle from some weeping adventurer's rectum. It immured you from the sight of your favourite sister's nails bitten down to the quick. Or the gunshot sound of a camel's legs breaking when run down by a speeding Cadillac. It mostly protected you from the sensation that you were making do, that your own soul was withering. But having a child turn away from you, nothing could steel you against that.

Georgie trawled about in the wee hours. Cyberspace was choked with yearning, with fantasies and lust and bad spelling. The chat rooms were full of pimply boys from Michigan or the daughters of Indian diplomats who wanted to converse like Lisa Simpson. They drove her out into the real night again.

She walked in the dark hollow between sandhills listening to her own breath as she went. Long before dawn she saw the shadow of a man easing his boat into the lagoon while his dog skittered along the shore. For a moment the dog paused, propped, as though sensing her crouched in the dune behind them. She heard the cough of a four-stroke behind her as she scrambled low in the direction of home.

AFTER A WEEK of watching the shamateur launch, Georgie knew that she'd let it go too long. She couldn't tell Jim or anyone now without condemning herself. A couple of times she'd even fed the bloke's dog; unleashed it again and swum in the lagoon. Somehow she felt complicit and it left her exposed, nervous.

Acting out of some oblique guilt about this, she sneaked Josh the money for his skateboard, but Jim found out and made the kid take it back and return her money. He could not believe, he said, that she would undermine his authority like that. She could barely credit it, either, but she did not feel contrite. They worked their way through Bette Davis with a funless determination.

Georgie considered speaking to Beaver about the bloke with the boat. She loved their pumpside talks about the Golden Age. Beaver was gross in a comforting sort of way. His beard had gone the colour of steel wool and his tatts gave his chest and arms a bruised look. He favoured black 501s and blue singlets which displayed his bum crack and his monster gut. Overalls, when he conceded to wear them, hid the arse but enhanced the pot. He was short a front tooth and the remainder weren't long for this world. A Dockers beanie hid his balding pate but from its rim a plaited rat's tail dangled the length of his sweaty neck. His steel-capped boots were scarred and blackened with oil. Georgie tried to imagine him taking them off at night—what strange, naked things his feet must be in the moments before bed.

There was some mystery to his retirement from bikerdom. She couldn't get him to talk about the stripping of his patch, the loss of his colours. He was, on his day, a scream, but there was something sad about him.

Today the forecourt was empty. She found him in the workshop with someone's shit-bucket Nissan up on the hoist.

Petrified Forest, he said without turning around.

41

Well, you rented it to us, she said.

Leslie Howard. Fucksake, eh? What an ugly bastard. How'd he get there with Bette, you reckon? To make her look better? Was that the best the English could offer the big screen between the wars? You can't even blame rationing for a runty bugger like that.

Well, said Georgie. Now they have Jeremy Irons.

Cher-rist!

Oh, he has his moments.

Don't they *feed* the pricks? And Ra-a-a-fe Fiennes, fuck!

Beaver wiped his hands on an old tee-shirt in order to receive the video she was returning.

You ever, she began, you ever see anything odd round here, Beaver?

Getcha hand off it, George! This is White Point. Odd? That's me job. Doing odd-ometer readins and windin back the dial.

She laughed. Oddometer.

Seriously, though, she continued. In the mornings, I mean. On the beach. Before dawn.

Not a thing, love.

Never?

Ever.

She watched him degreasing his hands. Noticing her interest he spread the cloth for her to see. It was a Peter Allen tour shirt. Beaver wriggled his eyebrows. She didn't ask.

HIGH ON THE PROPERTY, beyond the ruined melon paddocks where the quarry gives onto the riverbend, Fox stands amidst the limestone pinnacles smelling the baked dryness of the land and the tang of abalone slime on his skin. The briny southerly rushes, full of crow-song, across the hill and the upright stones whistle. He pulls out the wallet. Looks at the dud licence and fake papers. Slips out the fold of notes. Steps up to the leaning stone and shoots his arm into the fissure. Finds the square tin with his fingertips and pulls it out in a shower of dirt fine as baby powder. A tea tin, Twinings Russian Caravan. Pops the lid, sniffs again. Regrets it.

In the tin is a thick roll of money bound in a perishing rubber band. Also a few sand dollars, an abalone shell the size of a child's ear, some dried boronia blossom, two cloudy marbles and the beak of an octopus. Beneath them some tiny wads of paper folded into pellets. Fox considers putting the shell to his ear, thinks better of it. He adds his money to the roll. The rubber band contracts without conviction. He snaps the lid on and replaces the tin in its hidy hole. Doesn't linger.

BORIS WENT BACK to work. Georgie slept badly, prowled, drank and did not go down

43

to the beach in the dark. Outside the post office one afternoon she saw a woman in a bikini with a child on her hip tear the wipers off a Hilux. In the cab another woman gave her the finger, wound her window up and locked the door.

Georgie found herself courting Josh. She felt like some bimbo wheedling her way back into a fortune. She despised herself. And the kid wasn't having any of it anyway. He returned his school lunches uneaten, avoided eye contact, left rooms when she entered. You had to admire his grit.

Eventually she cornered him in his room where he lay on the bed with a photo album. She sat beside him with an arm across his shoulder to detain as much as to comfort.

What about we organize some jobs you can do to earn back the dough?

It's Christmas soon anyway, he said.

True.

I'll wait.

It took her a moment to process what he'd said. Georgie spluttered in her effort to stifle a laugh at the child's nerve, his certainty. But instantly she felt him tense up, his whole body recoiling at her laughter. He took it as ridicule. She could have bashed her head against the wall.

Josh ripped back the adhesive cover of the album page and scraped off a photo of his mother. He held it at her face a moment and then raised it over her head in some awful priestly gesture she didn't understand. His arm trembled with fury. The image felt like a jug of something he might tip over her at any moment.

Stranger danger, he said through his milk teeth. Stranger. Danger.

Georgie compelled herself to meet his gaze and he began to swat her with the photograph. It wasn't forceful, just a casual batting about the ears and mouth and nose, a contemptuous motion that brought tears to her eyes.

Then both of them became aware of Brad in the doorway. He seemed galvanized by the image of his mother.

You don't even remember, he said to his brother.

Do so.

Put it back.

Josh returned the photo to its gummy space and pulled the cellophane sheet back across. A tear drop appeared on the surface.

And you better say sorry.

He's sorry, said Georgie. I know he is.

Josh breathed, closed the album.

Brad stepped aside to let her by. He smelled of oranges. He looked away as she passed.

At dinner that night the four of them paused a minute to watch a boy on the jetty reeling in a gull.

It was sometime after midnight when, out of some ancient reflex, Georgie looked up from the computer to see Jim's expressionless face reflected in the window. He was across the room behind her and, unaware that she could see him, he stood there some time with his hip against the corner of the stairwell, scraping his chin with the back of his thumb. His expression was not the indulgent look of a man secretly observing his lover. He looked closed and intense, impossible to read, and a ripple of uncertainty, of fear, even, went through her.

Hi, she said at last, startling him.

Late, he said. It's late.

WHILE HE COILS droplines back into the tubs and racks up tarpon hooks by their crimped traces, the diesel generator drones behind the wall. He stows the gear up on the boat, checks his batteries and steering, tilts each motor up and down before wiping off the screen and console. Already the wind is in the east. Tomorrow will be hot as buggery, the sea flat, the water clear.

He climbs down from the ladder at the transom and scratches the dog's head as he passes. The long shed wall is festooned with tools—shears, shifters, scythes, saws, stirrups—most of them the old man's, which is a laugh when all the coot ever used was a pinchbar and a roll of fencewire. A twitch of wire was his answer to every conundrum, mechanical, agricultural, theological. Above the bench in its jacket of dust is the plaque that once hung in the kitchen.

Christ is the head of this house,
The unseen Guest at every meal,
The silent Listener to every conversation

Alongside it a stringless mandolin, a stove-in Martin dreadnought and a fiddle case covered with stickers and stains.

From the wide doorless entrance to the shed Fox sees the shadows of roos in the melon paddock. Behind them, all the way to the river, tuart trees roar in the wind. The dog stiffens, growls, and Fox grabs it by the collar. Confounded by the wind the roos turn their heads and after a few moments, they gather up their haunches as a company and retreat into the darkness.

He can't admit it to himself but the sight has jolted him. Four figures suddenly out there across the yard with its perimeter of gutted vehicles. He walks barefoot back to the house with his mind knocked out of neutral. The light feeling is gone. He resumes the discipline. These days he lives by force of will.

He fries the dog's fish first, a marbled slab of morwong that the mutt lowers itself upon lustfully. Fox watches it shunt the tin bowl across the dirt then goes back inside to cook himself a few fillets of sweep which he eats at the sink, standing. Rinses his dishes, racks them up. Opens a bottle of homebrew. Considers a shave. Reminds himself to buy a few drums of fuel in the city tomorrow. Drains his glass. Feels restless. Should just go to bed for the four o'clock start.

Out of ritual, he goes through the old timber house room by room. He doesn't know what the impulse is. Checking he's alone, maybe. When he knows he's alone. Doesn't want to think about it.

The library empty. Keats open like a gull on the seat of the rocker. Wind moans in the chimney.

At the door of the kids' room he stares at the half-packed cartons. A gruelling collection of dried fish heads on the windowsill. Made beds. Crayons on the floor.

Launches down the hall past his own room to the one with the double bed. All day he holds up. Living in the present tense. Only to come to this.

Sits on the bed. The smell of stale linen rises up around him. Looks at the beaten-up Levi's slung across the pine chair and touches the frayed hem with his toes. Hair rises along his arms. He reaches out and feels the denim which burrs beneath the calluses of his hand as he squeezes it between thumb and forefinger. Fox pulls the jeans from the chair and sees how they hold the imprint of her body. Held by the belt loops, the denim falls open, fills out as though it's her very skin. And Fox, again, is powerless before her shape, can't help but have his hands upon it, to hold it to his face till the zipper bites his lip. He falls back on the bed ground down by the weight of her, writhing up against it until he comes, in a miserable, shaming sweat, and lies there ruined.

You can't do this, he tells himself reeling for

the door, and as he goes he stumbles into the dented steel guitar and leaves the bastard thing falling in his wake to crash to the floor and ring discord at him on his way down the hall.

And it's hours before he sleeps, ages of lying there in a fever of composure, denial, recrimination. When sleep comes it undoes him again: no grip, no purchase, no defences.

At him come flickering jabs of memory that stew his blood and bones as the house creaks on its stumps and his trees groan.

Gulping creek. Stones alight and ahum. The yellow sand jitters with the chime of that National guitar. It drones, drones in the metal bedframe and at his ear the hot Vegemite breath of a child. Rosin. Brass-wound strings. Campfires, campfires. Spill of dirty blonde. Feral beard up at the end of a pole and his mother crouched amidst a paddock of melons which drink silent as hunkered birds. Basket of eggs: chinking, holy brownshelled bumnuts. And that boyhood feeling, the conviction that nothing bad will ever happen, that things will always be the same.

WITH THE BOYS GONE to school and the morning crashing white from every window Georgie came into the bedroom to dress. She threw the damp towel down beside the clothes laid out on the bed—shorts, knickers, tee-shirt—and was struck by how limp, how bleached, how small they were. As if any of that could be a surprise. They were hers, weren't they? This morning those three adjectives were bang on the money.

She hated mirrors but she felt enough self-loathing to reef back the robe door to expose the full-length glass behind it.

Georgie grew up in a house blighted with mirrors, amongst females who simply couldn't pass one without turning. Jutland women went to mirrors the way prisoners sought windows. They tottered, it seemed to her, from one to the next, sidling up, confronting, storming them to hold their frames and scowl or beckon, to simper and leer. Her sisters took the lead from their mother who hitched her eyebrows and bared her teeth, drawing them somehow into comparison, even competition with her beauty. At fifteen, the eldest and still a virgin, Georgie swore off the dreaded looking glass and mounted a sniping campaign. As a full-time engagement against her mother it lasted twelve weeks, during which time Georgie lost her cherry but not her guerrilla smirk. She was never quite one of them again.

Now she stared at her body in a manner she hadn't employed for a long time. Okay, she was small. *Compact*, that used to be the word. *Petite* handed you an Alice band and a cardigan, for Chrissake. So, short. *Small*. Dark hair, thick and glossy, cut straight above her eyes in a way that now looked abrupt, even severe. A little helmet of hair. She was pretty enough, she'd always known it. Dominant upper lip, smallish nose, tanned skin with crow's feet from the sun and shadows from everything else. The eyes? She had the stare of a cattle dog. No wonder she'd scared people at school and on the wards. On her shoulders the straplines in her tan ran into the silly whiteness of her breasts. For goodness sake. Even without them your clothes shaped you. She had an inverted navel and an unmarked belly, though veins showed in her legs from years of trudging the wards. Unruly pubic hair.

It was three years since the morning she first saw Jim Buckridge and his kids on the beach at Lombok. From her room at the Senggigi Sheraton, with a tiny pair of salt-stained binoculars, she had picked him out in the crowd and watched him pace along the volcanic sand of the shoreline while his little boys snorkelled in the shallows. She only noticed him because she was hiding from another man. Holed up in her hotel she had nothing to do but keep watch with those daggy little binoculars for somebody she should have left behind two months ago— Tyler Hampton. After sailing all the way from Fremantle with the crazy, seasick Californian—right up the western coast of Australia, enduring hell's own storm beneath the Zuytdoorp Cliffs and the two-day grounding in the islands off the far-north Kimberley—she should have called it quits at Timor. The man was a handsome, glamorous fraud, a day-tripper who was a danger to himself and others, and Georgie had deluded herself too long. And then, finally, came the ignominious collision with another boat a mile out from the beach at Lombok that tore a hole in the hull and made her mind up. As Tyler Hampton dropped anchor a hundred metres out with the pumps failing she had gone over the side in the last light of day with her wallet, shoes and passport. The binoculars had still been around her neck when she swam in.

From any distance you could have picked Jim Buckridge as an Australian. He had crow's feet like knifecuts. Handsome in a blocky way, of the sort she usually avoided, he was forty-five and looked it. Georgie gravitated toward lounge lizards, men with pointy sideburns and a cocked eyebrow. Whereas this bloke was a citizen. Although he was an imposing physical presence he looked hesitant, even fearful, as if he'd just woken to a different, a harder world. He shouldn't have rated a second glance, but that charming desolation so intrigued her that Georgie decided to find a way of bumping into him. She wasn't interested in a man of any description. At the very least, she needed a breather. But she was curious despite herself. She told herself she just wanted to hear his story.

Back in Perth, a fortnight later, she scandalized her sisters with the news. On hearing that her eldest daughter was moving in with a widower, a lobster fisherman from White Point, their mother laughed with that special trill of disappointment she reserved exclusively for Georgie.

Georgie often thought of that laugh. She wondered whether the fear of that cool trill had kept her here these past months, given her the determination to stay on when it was clear that things had dwindled away to nothing.

She turned from the mirror, stepped up into the cavernous wardrobe and pulled down the Qantas bag.

THE WHINING DOG wakes him. He checks the luminous dial of his watch and sees that it's after four. So much for the timelessness of animals. Hauls himself up. Showers, feels the sun-baked towel rough as bread. The dog rasps at the back door. It knows the rules but lives in hope, as though paradise awaits indoors. Should break tradition, he thinks, and let it in one day. See lino and die. Piss the place slippery in mortal excitement. Break its heart, too. For somehow the dog believes the others have just been indoors all this time, that they're here in their beds having a bit of a lie-in. Be cruel to let it inside now. He pulls on some shorts, lights the kettle, and goes out to console the mutt with a few playful slaps around the chops. In the dark, with the easterly stirring, the land smells of fresh biscuits.

There's a shirt on the seat in the cab and he pulls it on while the truck warms up. He eases out, no lights, with the boat clunking behind him down the white ruts of the drive. Through the gate and out onto the blacktop. Bush and paddocks are indistinct. There's no one about. He's got the jump on them but he's as twitchy as the dog for the twenty minutes it takes him to reach White Point, where, from the downhill run into town, he sees the bone-yard of surf that marks the outer reefs. He coasts through the empty streets to the beach and pulls up a moment to scope the lagoon. Not a soul. He's got the jump.

Pulls in past the jetty, backs down to the water and slips the boat in. Tosses the pick, lets the boat hang back on the rope and drives the truck out before it sinks. When he's run the rig up against the foredune he chains the dog to the roobar and drops a chunk of ice into the tin bowl at its feet. The mutt settles, miserable but stoic, onto its belly in the sand.

Fox pushes the boat out till the breeze catches it. He steps up onto the transom, tilts a motor in and starts it. The righteous sound of a four-stroke Honda. He slips it into gear and slides out across the seagrass banks through moored crayboats, keying up his instruments, radio, echo sounder, global posi-tioning system. The lagoon has the same old enigmatic smell of sour milk that carries over the brine and the bleach and the bait.

He begins to feel good. It's what he lives for, this feeling, knowing they're all still ashore in their beds sleeping off the Emu Export and the bedtime bong while he has the sea to himself. Let em sleep till dawn, he thinks. Give em their coffee and crank in the wheelhouse, their ZZ Top on the stereo. The Foxes still have the jump.

In the passage, nearly a mile out, he pauses to find his marks and starts the second motor. The deck vibrates as he throttles on to send the hull up onto the plane. Picking up speed he senses as much as sees the straight lines of waves converging on the gap in the reef. He blasts out in a welter of spray and hoots as he goes.

Before first light, on ground that he's left fallow since May, he gets in two good sets. The lines come up so heavy he uses the winch. Blackarse, jewfish, snapper. He kills them quickly and ices them down. A remnant school of southern bluefin rolls by in a killing swathe. He lets them go; they're a rare enough sight as it is.

There's still no one out this way so he presses his luck and moves into shallower ground to anchor where he knows there's abalone. Pulls on a wetsuit, mask, fins.

The water is warm, though blurry with plankton and silt and dim in the half-light. On his way down he equalizes with a little dolphin chirp that exits his ears in a pleasurable fizz.

The blood runs thin as copper wire in his veins. The bottom looms and there it is, a long reef crevice just wide enough to reach into, and inside, hidden from casual view, a stippled colony of molluscs. He pulls the small lever from his belt and opens his mesh bag. Fifteen minutes' work. Everything so vivid, so present, so clear. And sunlight spearing down now, ploughing the water.

Just as he hears diesels on the easterly, Fox gets the boat up off its haunches and steers into the rising sun. He's obscured by lumping swells but he knows that anybody alert will have picked him on radar by now. Men and boys he knows. Kings of the ocean wave. Likely as not they'll be steaming out on autopilot with their heads thrown back in a snoring funk of bad breath. Not much to worry about. Still he drops a few points south to be safe and passes without even seeing them.

From out here the land looks like a badly baked cake and all those sandy white gouges in the khaki scrub like random gobs of icing. Fox winds his way in through floats and ropes, veering from the path of every outcoming vessel, until the great undulating white field of dunes marks out the only town for miles. It's cheeky, coming in this late, and stupid too, but what can he do now but scan the beach for anything unlikely and come through the passage like a regular civilian back from a few hours' recreational angling?

• • •

On the highway, just outside the town limits, his elation peaks like a shimmering mull-hit before the hot wind dries him and a mortal gravity presses down once more. Fox bites into the apple that's been baking on the dash in the sun and the juice sizzles in his mouth. He steers one-handed. The dog licks salt from his thigh. Wind sears in through the windows; man and dog narrow their eyes against it. The land is jellied with heat. Above the low, grey heath a few Christmas trees seem to swim upright. They tread the current of the mirage to hold their gorgeous orange blossoms aloft. Higher still, hawks throw figure-eights in the octane sky.

At the bend, when he sees the vehicle pulled off onto the shoulder with its hood up, he throttles off instinctively but only a second later he comes to his senses and fangs it. A Land-cruiser, for Godsake! Fisheries! Shit!

The dog sits up blearily. Fox scans his mirrors for anyone behind but there's nothing. Too narrow here to turn around with the boat on. Besides, where can he go but back to White Point? Without the boat he'd have a chance—no one knows the bush tracks and firebreaks better than him—but by the time he unhitched the trailer with its incriminating load he'd be surrounded, buggered well and truly.

The Ford's V8 purrs with feeling as he approaches. But he's done and he knows it. Never outrun them on the blacktop with this load. The Cruiser looms, pulses with glare. Your own fault, he thinks, you cocky bastard, you had to lairize around like you owned the bloody bay.

As he blows past, rigid with anticipation, he gets a glimpse of a woman's bare legs hooked in the polished steel of the roobar. She's head down bum up beneath the hood. In denim shorts. A civilian. He hits the brakes.

Jack-knifed onto the gravel shoulder, Fox sits there a while, craning at the nearside mirror. The woman hauls herself out from beneath the Cruiser's bonnet and looks his way across her shoulder. She climbs down onto the gravel and waits. Hands on hips if you don't mind.

The dog tenses up. It rises onto the windowsill and whines. Fox sucks his teeth. Damn, damn, damn. He knows he should drive on. There'll be other cars by before too long. She'll be okay out here for a while; it's not that hot. And it could still be a set-up. That banksia thicket beside her might be full of khaki shirts. He puts the Ford back in gear. Sorry lady.

Then the dog launches itself out onto the gravel and takes off. Fox stalls the truck in surprise and chucks his gnawed apple after the mongrel in disgust. God Almighty.

In the mirror he watches as the mutt bounds up to the woman who bends to greet it. She has short, dark hair, wears a white tee-shirt, denim shorts and tennis shoes. No one he knows. A tourist maybe, but the big, metallic gold, luxury-edition 4x4 is no renter. And the dog is all *over* her. He pulls properly off the highway and gets out to face the music.

The gravel is hot and sharp underfoot. He has to high-step it to keep going and he wishes to fuck he had some shoes to lend himself a bit of dignity.

He who hesitates is lost, she says, shielding her eyes from the sun.

Yeah?

G'day.

Got trouble?

It just choked and cut out like it was out of juice, she says. Gauge shows half a tank but it's like there's nothing getting through. I've nearly killed the battery turning it over.

Fox hitches his shorts nervously.

Ah, injectors maybe?

Dunno. It's one of these turbo diesel thingies. Even the cigarette lighter looks computerized.

Ah.

Fox looks from the trophy Cruiser to the gravel and then to her. Shadows under her eyes. Sun enamels the thick bowl of her hair. She pulls the sunglasses down from her brow and he sees himself reflected. Not a reassuring sight; he looks feral and fidgety.

Sorry to be a pain, she says.

I spose I...I spose I could run you back into White Point, he utters with difficulty.

Just the prospect makes his head light. What a cock-up.

Thanks, she says, but you see, I've gotta get into the city.

Well, I can't tow you with the boat on. Don't spose you've got one of those mobile phones?

Sorry.

The dog presses itself against her legs. Fox could kick it in the slats. He hops from foot to foot, as the woman pats the mutt.

Listen, she says, I'm not fussed about the car. I can call someone later to come and get it. I'm supposed to be in Perth.

Right.

Shit a brick, thinks Fox, this really isn't good. No towns between here and the city, not even a fuel stop until the outskirts. I can't abandon her in the sun, can't take her to White Point without a bloody scene and anyway she won't go, and I can't drive her to Perth without getting rid of the boat and that means taking her home first. She's leaving an eighty-thousand-dollar Tojo by the roadside. So maybe it's stolen. She's in a hurry after all. Looks kind of strung out. And here's me with a shitload of illegal seafood.

Look, I'm really sorry, she says. You look busy.

No, no, I've just been fishin. Day off.

Get any?

Oh, this and that. Nothin you'd brag about.

It's hot, eh.

Fox smiles. The weather, yeah. Listen, I gotta go into Perth as it happens.

You're not from the city, then?

Fox looks at her, wondering if that's a smile fading off her face or a twitch caused by the flies.

No, he murmurs. I'm from down the highway a few minutes. Gotta unhook the boat and stuff but I guess I can take you after that.

60

She sighs. That'd be brilliant. Thank you. I'll just get my bag.

Fox stands there in the murdering sun while she leans into the Landcruiser and grabs things. He feels sick at the idea of taking her home. He hasn't even tried to start this woman's engine but he'll look like a prick if he doesn't take her at her word. He'll need to think how to get the catch from the boat and onto the truck without her twigging to anything. She doesn't look like Fisheries. Sunglasses not polarized. Silly straw hat she's pulling out. But that's a dive watch on her wrist. She hoists a Qantas bag out and a linen jacket.

Right, then.

You gunna lock it?

Oh. Yeah. She points a gadget at the 4x4 and the lights flash. Well, she murmurs, that much of it works.

Get off her, dog. Sorry, he's a bit familiar.

Oh, we're old mates, she says. He's a friendly dog.

He's bloody craybait, thinks Fox, fire-walking back to the Ford.

GEORGIE SAT in the withering dogfunk of the shamateur's cab and tried not to smirk at the irony of it. God knows she was glad he stopped but, given his situation, had the shoe been on the other foot, she'd be blowing on down the road and to hell with simple decency. She couldn't believe he'd take the risk. He hadn't the least idea who she was, who she lived with. She had to be, through no fault of her own, his living, breathing nightmare. Was he cocky or just soft in the head?

She stared at the crushed beercan sprouting from the mouth of the cassette player. It was the sole trashy touch in a truck so clean and shipshape. No crap on the floor, no classic mire of tools and receipts and wrappers rolling across the dash. He was fastidious.

There was no conversation. The shamateur looked too mortified and she had a headache that felt like a trepanning. Ten minutes passed, fifteen. She couldn't work up the effort to shove the dog's head from her lap.

Eventually they slowed at the skeleton of an old fruit stand which seemed dimly familiar from all those roadtrips to the city, and turned up a dirt drive through the lumpy paddocks of some sunblasted farm. It wasn't much: bellying fences, uncut hay, a few olive trees. As they bumped down the ruts, you could feel his discomfort intensify like an ear-popping change in altitude.

Georgie took a look at him while the dog rose and made a fuss. He was tall, lean, brown from the sun. His hair was short and light brown but bleached by weather at the ends. He had small ears and a boyish face with blue eyes. The outdoors had taken the shine off him but he still had his child's face. What a wide-eyed thing he must once have been.

He drove to a wide sandy yard surrounded

by casuarinas and junked machines, and as he wheeled about to reverse the boat toward an open shed, she saw the unpainted weatherboard house that hunkered on its stumps in a parched field of melons. The dog raked her with its claws on its way through the window and the shamateur got out without a word.

Georgie sat there a moment, uncertain as to how to proceed. The heat was killing. A tap creaked and there was the sudden blurt of an outboard. Bugger this, she thought, getting out.

Before she even got into the shed he was in her path.

There's shade over there, he said, pointing to the trees across the yard.

I'm fine, she said, pulling on the straw hat which suddenly felt a bit Laura Ashley. Wouldn't have an aspirin, would you?

Better come over to the house, he said reluctantly.

A few hens bustled out from beneath the verandah as they approached. He paused at an aluminium bin by the step and threw them a handful of pellets.

The kitchen was cool and dim after the blinding yard. It smelled of cooking oil, fried fish. Everything orderly and simple, a woman's kitchen if ever she saw it.

From the old Arcus fridge he pulled out a bottle of water and poured two glasses. Opened a drawer. Shook out two pills. Georgie thanked him and looked at the label and then at the tablets themselves. Paracetamol. What she felt

like was codeine phos. And a tall glass of
Margaret River semillon. She drank the pills
down with the water, whose metallic chill
caused her headache to flare horribly for a
moment.

Rainwater, she murmured.

Shit-free, he said.

He led her down the hall a few doors to a
big room lined with books.

Cooler here, he said. Just be a few minutes.

Yes. And thank you.

Georgie didn't move until she heard the
screen door clap shut at the other end of the
house. The room was walled with jarrah
shelves that looked to her like recycled floorboards. And they were real books up there,
serious books. George Eliot, Tolstoy, Forster,
Waugh, Twain. She saw a fancy collected
edition of Joseph Conrad, big quarto volumes of natural history, art books, atlases. On
a small table lay a heavy scrapbook of pressed
botanical specimens, each leaf and blossom
annotated in mauve ink with a calligrapher's
nib. On a sea trunk under the window, beside
a sunbleached upright piano, was a stack of
yellowing sheet music.

The only wall without books was taken up
by a brick fireplace on whose mantelpiece
were some old black-and-white photos in
cheap frames. A formal wedding shot from,
say, the fifties, and two studio portraits of the
same pair. Handsome people. The man shorter
and more intense. Stacked beside these images
was a wad of fading colour snaps of kids

64

swinging in a tyre across a muddy river, babies with chocolate-smeared faces. The shamateur with a kid in the seat of a tractor.

Georgie flicked through till she came upon a shot of a woman in her twenties with ropy blonde plaits which fell across her halter top. She had a glossy complexion and a thick mouth. The way she leaned like that in a doorway, hands in the pockets of her jeans, gave Georgie a jolt. Such lazy, native confidence. Like girls she'd seen on the train on her way to school. Honeys in hybrid uniforms blowing gum and sunning their legs in an effortless sexual arrogance Georgie once associated with state schools. As a teenager she'd grown a crust and tried to be fearsome, but how she envied those girls their slutty self-possession. It stirred men and boys like the smell of food.

The outboards went silent. Georgie lifted the book from the rocking chair and sat down. Keats. Yeah, right. Though she never did read him. Jesus, when was the last time she'd read anything? The family bookworm, her father called her. She tried to read a poem. It went on for pages, dense as her headache. No use.

The back door whacked again. Georgie put the book down, heard another door slam, a tap running. This wasn't a good idea. Being here. Alone with this bloke so far from the highway. God, she knew better than to get into a situation like this.

Christ, if only she had her own car. After a

few tax-free years in Saudi it wasn't as though she couldn't afford one. It was just laziness. For the entire Jeddah posting she'd been forbidden even to drive a bloody car and now here she was still dependent. What kind of passive fog had she subsided into? What a triumph for the mullahs she was, what a rattled scatty thing she'd become.

She went through the kitchen and eased the screen door shut behind her. The dog was delirious to see her again. The truck's keys were not in the ignition.

SHAME YOU DIDN'T BRING your dog, she says, still breathless.

He just drives. Capstone. Banksia. Tuarts.

Does he have a name?

Fox shakes his head and strives to be nonchalant.

Seagoing dog like that. Should have a name.

He sweats in his jeans, thinking five things at once. She's having a dig or sniffing around. Yes, it's a disgrace having a nameless dog but it was never his to name. And it's no use explaining that the mutt doesn't come on the boat because it leaps overboard to tackle fish and he's gaffed the prick twice already. Besides, he doesn't buy this new tone. She knows more than she's letting on. That friggin dog.

Had the place long?

Been there all my life, he says.

66

Great library.

He nods.

Big reader, then?

Yeah, it passes the time.

So tell me, she persists. Tell me who you read.

Fox sighs.

C'mon, she says. It passes the time... Okay, I'll shut up.

The empty road feels like a tidal race he's working against, its surface dimpled with mirage-current.

Steinbeck, I'll bet. And Keats, obviously. What about Conrad? I see you have a set.

Fox squints neutrally.

Never could stand Conrad, she says. Too...strangled, or something. And *earnest*.

He purses his lips to defend the old Pole. Holds off.

The horror, the horror! she declaims. Is it a bloke-thing, you think?

It stays with you, he murmurs, that's why.

Fair point, she says with a smile that strikes him as gloating. It's one thing I remember from school. Mr Kurtz, eh? So you *are* a fan.

I spose.

What is it? The sea? Manly honour? The heartless heart of nature?

He shrugs.

Well, it seemed like a lot of huffing and puffing to me.

Specially *Typhoon*.

Ha. So what about women writers?

What about them? asks Fox, a little disoriented. For a year his conversations have been procedural exchanges only. It's making him giddy.

I mean, do you read them?

You live at White Point?

You're changing the subject, she says. Yes, I live there.

A teacher.

What makes you think that?

Books.

No.

Fox wonders what dream he's been in. No teacher can afford a rig like the one she just left on the road. She stinks of lobster money. The sideways knowing look. What possessed him?

Nurse by trade. Oncology, she says. Know what that is?

Yeah. As it happens. Get out and walk, he thinks, ever heard of that?

Sorry.

And your old man's an exporter or a fisherman.

Ah.

They drive in silence for a while.

I really am sorry, she says. For everything. Just being there. Having to be picked up like this. I know it's not easy. In your situation.

My situation.

You needn't worry. I'm not a very loyal fishwife.

Geez, there's a recommendation, he says, sounding more bitter than he means to.

I see you go out some mornings.

Oh?

And I swim with your dog.

Well, that's *really* unfaithful.

My name's Georgie Jutland, she says turning in her seat toward him.

The name doesn't ring a bell.

And, look, it's none of my business or anything but can you imagine what the locals will be like when they catch you? I mean, take up something safer, like bomb disposal.

I don't think I'm catching your drift, Fox says evenly. You'd swear she can hear the pulse in your throat.

I just can't see how it's worth the risk. The law's one thing, but Jesus.

Fox gives his dumbshit farmboy look and she turns back in her seat and crushes the straw hat across her knees.

Sorry, she murmurs.

Not as sorry as I am, he thinks, wishing he'd settled for the fish and left the abalone for another day. If he'd gotten up on time and stuck to the routine this would never have happened.

There followed an hour's silence in the truck. An entire hour. Paddocks segued into pine plantations then market gardens and finally the hobby farms whose flybitten, shaggy ponies marked the farthest outposts of suburbia. Georgie toughed it out. It was, after all, a ride. Besides, you had to admire the shamateur's resolve. But it gave her too much time to think, to feel how the morning's events had robbed her of momentum. A couple of hours ago her mind was full, if not clear. Everything told her to bolt. But now she didn't know what she was doing. She only knew that love was impossible. It arrived and moved on like weather and it defied pursuit. Not just romance—any kind of love. The emotion itself was promiscuous and not to be trusted. She'd thought all this before and failed to learn from it. The story of her life.

Pillars of dust rose behind dozers and graders scraping out another subdivision. The perimeter walls were already up as were the limestone plinths at the sweeping entry. TUSCAN RISE. Beyond it stretched the treeless plain of terracotta rooftiles.

Georgie checked the contents of her Qantas bag. A single change of clothes. What did that say about resolve? She needed a job, was overdue for a pap smear, could do with a tall glass of something cold.

Emily Dickinson, said the shamateur.

Georgie zipped up the bag. I beg your pardon?

They entered the miserable throughway of Joondalup. It was like a landscaped carpark with all the franchises that passed for civilization.

Woman writer.

There you go, she murmured.

The freeway loomed.

Anywhere is fine, she said. The train station would be good.

Just missed it, he said merging into the stream of traffic. Sorry.

70

No worries. Anywhere's good.

Where you headed?

Right in. The Sheraton.

I'm going right in. But you'll have to give me directions.

To the *Sheraton*? she asked before she could catch herself.

The look on his face was a mixture of embarrassment and defiance. Never been there, he said. The five-star thing isn't—

That was rude. I'm sorry. Again.

He shrugged. At a sedate metropolitan speed you could smell Pears shampoo on him.

About that Landcruiser.

I'll call Beaver in White Point, she said crisply. She caught the smile before he turned aside but she decided not to pursue it. The best she could do now was to leave things be.

As he pulls into the hotel setdown, amidst the windtunnel of the business district, the woman waves him on toward the declining ramp of the basement carpark, but he brakes at the crest.

I don't need to park, he says. Here's good.

Behind them another car honks.

I'll buy you a beer, she says. I owe you one.

Thanks but I gotta be somewhere.

Fox slips the truck into reverse but the vehicle behind honks more insistently.

It's all one-way, she says.

Shit.

● ● ●

'The Girl from Ipanema', she says, ushering him from the lift.

I know it, he murmurs, face still hot from the shame of being declined service in the bar on account of his attire.

Essential part of the five-star experience.

I'm not really that thirsty, he lies.

Almost as essential as the minibar, she says, rattling the key on its plastic tab. C'mon. It'll prove I have some manners.

Honestly.

Fox is exhausted by all this, the talk, the sudden proximity, the threat she poses. She hands him the bag while she rifles through her wallet, and he finds himself tramping down a plush corridor. He lags behind her until she slows and they continue shoulder to shoulder. She's small. She seems unaccountably happy. He just wants to piss off out of here. Thinks of all that fish and abalone sweating on ice in the basement. It'll keep, he thinks, but is it safe? The muzak is unbearable.

They come to the door she's looking for and as she leans in to turn the key in the lock Fox notices the curve of her neck. She pushes the door open. He holds her bag out. She smiles. She has an impish face. Shit.

She grabs a fistful of his shirt and drags him inside.

Beer, she says.

Listen, he murmurs, staggering from the momentum, tipping against her.

The door clunks shut.

God, she says, you're shaking.

No, he says with a laugh. There's a weird hysteria in his voice that he doesn't recognize. You bloody idiot, he thinks. You blind fucking idiot.

She kisses him; he stands there and lets it happen while a spasm like a hunger pang shoots through the meat and bones of him, and although he still grips the bag as a barrier between them, he feels her leg against his and her hand firm in his back. The feel of a living body. Like some obscure force of physics. He hears the rasp of denim, the hoarse whisper of it, in this placeless downlit room. The woman swims against him, despite the Qantas bag, and he feels himself coming unstuck.

Don't, she murmurs.

Fox recoils into the door as if kicked.

I mean... I'm sorry, I meant don't cry.

He puts a hand to his cheek, realizes and says, Oh.

It's all right.

No.

Don't go.

Fox puts his head against the door. She's a merciful blur now but he turns away even so.

Come here, she whispers kindly. Sit.

He lets himself be steered to the bed. She brings a wad of Kleenex. He mops his face, gets a few breaths.

Oh, God, he murmurs with a shudder and lies back to ease the smarting muscles of his chest.

The woman sits cross-legged on the king-size bed beside him.

You wanna talk?

No.

He turns, puts his lips against her knee. She unfolds like a wing against him. She has her hands on him. She looks into his face and pulls up his shirt to touch him, kiss his neck, his nipples, his belly. Then she sits up, reefs off her top and falls to him, grinning.

Georgie Jutland didn't know why. She'd started out trying to make amends and now this. Stupid to walk into the bar dressed like that, cut-offs and tennis shoes. The look on the shamateur's face—like he'd been shot. So vulnerable. Was it then or after, the way he held the bag out like a good boy for his mother?

She pressed him to that great paddock of a bed and felt his heart banging away beneath her hands and his cock trapped against the prow of her pubic bone. She ground slowly against him, saw his blue eyes go sleepy, felt sweat prickle her all over. She felt completely there, within herself, in the acid rash of heat that began to scald her scalp and belly and thighs. She was neither trying now, nor pretending. She felt his fingers in the loops of her shorts, the downward force of him, their legs snarled and snagging. The smell of shampoo. The hot shout in her throat. She fell across him as she came and felt the terrible fluttering of his chest. It was laughter.

The five-star experience, he said.

Didn't you...make it?

Fraid so.

Then, what? she said, crestfallen.

We have our clothes on.

FOX LIES BACK A MESS. He tries to swim up through pangs of guilt, his unfocused sense of betrayal. But betrayal of whom?

He glances about at the generic furniture of the room, the wood veneer, the floral fabrics, the hulking TV. Probably shouldn't have laughed.

So how does it feel to be a poacher? she says rising onto one elbow beside him.

Um. Can you repeat the question?

You got away without telling me your name, she says. He likes the straight line of the hair across her eyes.

Lu.

I'm Georgie.

Pleased to meet you.

Very bloody pleased, I hope.

Fox kicks off his elastic-sided boots and looks at her. She's older than him. No rings. Those shadows beneath her eyes.

I'm trying to figure it out.

What? he murmurs.

Why you do it. Don't you feel you're ripping off the sea?

No.

But you're breaking the law, you admit that.

Why would I admit anything to a stranger?

Well, ouch for that. It's just that...there are rules. You know, to protect the environment.

You honestly believe that?

Well, yes.

Fox rolls aside, gets up and goes to the window. Out there in the shimmering heat of the city, the river sprawls into Perth Water with its butterfly swarm of spinnakers.

It's never about the environment, he says hotly. Fisheries law is about protecting all that export money. To save all those rich bastards from themselves. None of them give a shit about the sea.

Those toolboxes on your truck. They're full of rock lobsters, aren't they?

No, he says truthfully.

But they're iceboxes.

I only take what I need, he says. I'm one pair of hands.

Without a licence.

He shrugs and leans against the glass to feel the plangent heat of the outside world boring into his shoulder. She sits up against the bedhead, cross-legged in her shorts, and grabs a few tissues.

So, she says, enlighten me.

You don't need it.

How d'you know what *they* think?

I went to school with most of em.

I detect the smell of revenge.

Maybe.

You just like getting away with it.

He smiles despite himself.

Aha.

Got me there.

Let's have that beer, she says, her green eyes shining. I did promise you. The fridge is there beside you.

He grunts and roots around for two beers. He cops the price list.

Gawd, he blurts, they should be wearin a mask.

Well, you'd know, Lu.

He opens a bottle and passes it to her.

You cried.

Spose so.

What about?

I can't say.

Can't or won't?

Fox gulps his beer. After his homebrew it tastes so thin and industrial.

You're not what I expected, she murmurs.

I wasn't expecting anythin.

I must have some perversion that involves Sheratons.

He stares at her.

Geez, she says. You don't have much small talk.

Out of practice.

Come here, she says. And get those jeans off.

For a long time afterwards and even while he slept Georgie felt the heat of his body in hers. She liked him; she knew she liked him and yet she couldn't say why. Here was this weird reverberation still with her. He was fresh somehow, there was something pure about him. And despite her record of impulsive assessments, a string of failures that stretched all the way back into the mire of adolescence, she was certain she would never need to fear him.

She spooned up to him, held him by the belly, and nursed his buttocks in the hollow of her lap. Across his biceps the line of his tan was sharp as a painted mark. Georgie felt his respiration in the pillow, in the kingsize mattress, and her breathing fell into a hypnotic synchrony with his until the whirr of the minibar and the muffled barking of car horns and the aircon hiss receded to leave her consumed by the sensation of his sperm trickling out of her like some implacable process of geology. So slow. Stately, almost. With a cooling trail in its wake, the ghost of itself. Georgie felt her skin trying to absorb it, to drink it before it rolled away for good, and when it did finally spill to the linen beneath her folded thigh, she half-expected to hear a crash, a hiss upon impact. She lay there a while feeling her skin contract and dry. A sadness descended on her, a sense of loss. She took a hand from his belly, slipped it between her legs and brought the damp tips to her mouth. It didn't feel reckless or even gross. It left her peaceful.

When she woke he was lying there with his hands behind his head.

You didn't call about the Tojo, he murmured.

78

Oh. Yeah.

You were in a hellova hurry.

Georgie hesitated. I don't know what I was doing. Leaving, I suppose.

Who is he?

Jim Buckridge.

Fuck!

Yes.

Fuckin fuck.

The shamateur sat up so fast it reefed the sheet off her. She grabbed it back and covered herself.

You should go, she murmured.

Yes.

He got off the bed in the failing light and dressed quickly.

All night in the room she could smell him. Pelicans hung over the freeway like billowing newspapers. She watched the darkness fall with a vodka in her hand. She worked her way through the minibar: miniatures of brandy, bourbon, scotch, liqueurs, champagne. She ate the Toblerone and scarfed the peanuts while strangers fucked on pay-TV. How they shouted and grunted in their perfect bodies. Georgie toasted them and was, now and then, reconciled to how things really were.

AT THE BACK STEP the dog sniffs him a little too fastidiously. The night is hot and salted with stars and on the easterly breeze you can

79

feel the wheatlands of the interior and even the deserts behind them. He goes inside and scrubs at the sink then goes ahead and showers anyway. The water is tepid; he can't get it cold enough.

Back in the kitchen he makes a meal yet can't bring himself to sit down and eat it. He walks into the library but the air feels gritty and oppressive and somewhere in the room a moth struggles against a smooth surface, frailing, hidden from view.

He goes out onto the verandah and lights a couple of mosquito coils. The dog comes around the stumps of the house and mounts the steps. The paddocks thrum with cicadas, crickets, birdwings. Up from the creek comes the chirr of frogs. He sits and lowers his head to the battered table, queasy as a man with a hangover. Yes, that's the feeling, a diffusion of anxiety, disgust and regret.

Jim Buckridge, he thinks. Could it be any worse? Could I be any more stupid? A whole year without even a close call and now this. He thinks of the way she lay there looking at him, studying him while he shucked off his jeans, how she pulled him to her by the cock like a rider leading her horse. Had she been doing nothing else from the moment he pulled over on the highway this morning? Leading him into something? Was it Fox paranoia or was this some kind of set-up? He'd as good as admitted to poaching. But Buckridge and his lackeys wouldn't bother with a confession. They'd be filling their jerrycans before asking any questions or having someone ask for them. Boats scuppered at their moorings, sheds alight, he's seen it all.

Had he run today or did she turn him out? It bothers him. That and the fact that he liked her. Smart. In your face. In control yet strung-out somehow.

Fox feels the air chafing at him. He knows what it is, knows the feeling and why. You put up a tent to make a space you can deal with. You know the whole night's still out there— the land, the sky and every creeping thing— and you understand how thin the fabric is, what a pissy pretence you hold to, but with your tent blown open you feel more exposed than if you'd lain down on your mat beneath the stars. You can't see what's coming.

Fox wakes to the sound of someone in the kitchen. It's late morning by the feel of it and the dog hasn't made a sound. He scrambles out of bed and grabs a pair of shorts, all the time looking for something to defend himself with.

Morning, the woman says, suddenly in the doorway.

Shit!

Only me.

Fox covers himself with the shorts he hasn't had time to pull on. She's barefoot in a short black skirt and a sleeveless blouse. She gives him a washed-out grin.

Got any coffee?

You look awful.

Don't be familiar with me, young man. I require coffee and aspirin.

Again.

Yes. Again.

How...how'd you get here?

Hired a car. Something small and red. As one does.

You know where the kitchen is.

I could only find instant.

You strike me as the instant type.

Oh, cheap. Let me look at you.

No, he says, holding the shorts to his lap.

I'm still a bit pissed. A real citizen wouldn't have driven.

So, Fox murmurs. Why did you?

See if I imagined you. Mind if I lie down?

She flops onto the narrow bed. Confusing, isn't it?

Yeah. That'd cover it.

She rolls over and buries her face in his pillow. Sit down, she says.

Fox hesitates, sits on the edge of the bed, his shorts in one hand.

Didn't sleep, she says, muffled by the pillow. And now it's so hot.

Fox looks at her. The skirt rides up on her thighs. There's an old vaccination scar high on her arm. A smear of vermilion lipstick brightens the pillowslip.

You left your dinner out, Lu. Waste of linguini.

The dog'll get it.

When I'm better will you cook something for me?

When will you be better?

When you've touched me.

I'll make some coffee, he says.

After.

Sleep, he says, watching her lift her head with a smile sliding off her face.

Oh, be a sport.

Geez, how much did you drink?

See, you sound all concerned. Actually I drank everything. It's less than you'd imagine. For the money.

Fox puts his hand on her leg. She sighs.

What?

Just gloating.

He slips his hand beneath the elastic of her pants. She sprawls a little and murmurs approvingly.

You don't mind if I just lie here, do you? Tired. And you could do with some initiative-building.

Only if you shut up, he murmurs.

No promises.

Fox slides his hand into her. She feels like hot, wet earth. Her pulse beats in his hand. She lifts against it, enfolding it. She twists on it, muttering, clenching. He climbs onto the bed properly and kneels to her with his hand clasped.

Don't run away, she says. You don't have to run away.

He doesn't mind her talking. It reminds him that she's real and not something he's dredged up from longing.

Fox pulls his hand from her with a sound like a gasp and slowly, joint to joint, as he holds her by the hips, they rock in his creaking child's bed, slippery with sweat, while the dog scratches beneath the window outside.

Georgie found him out on the verandah with a split watermelon. It was after midday. He stared at the melon whose seeds, she noticed, ranged in curves.

Is it like reading tea leaves?

He started. Geez, you're a creeper. Here.

Georgie took the half-melon he offered. She could barely hold it. As she bit into it she thought she could feel the sun still in it and the sugar sent a ripple through her.

I'm used to it out of the fridge, she said, dripping some on her rumpled top. Spose it's like wine. When it's cold you only half-taste it. You look sad.

He shrugged.

This sort of compounds things, doesn't it?

In for a penny—

In for a compound.

He smiled and Georgie felt her hangover lift as though it had only been a mood.

What're we gonna do? she asked.

It's hot. How about a swim?

I meant about our...situation.

I know, he said. So what about the swim?

In the river?

The sea, he said.

Well, we can't go in to White Point.

I know. C'mon. Grab a towel.

Georgie quickly knew she'd been optimistic about the demise of her headache. The paddocks were white with heat. The truck rattled and lurched toward the highway and when they got out onto the smooth relief of the blacktop he only drove a few seconds before pulling off onto the other side.

Get the gate, will you? he murmured.

Whose place is this?

You mean you don't know?

Georgie shrugged. Flies came in through the open door.

Jim Buckridge.

You're kidding, she said.

Don't dawdle.

It was more a firebreak than a track. They swayed and jounced uphill in four-wheel drive along a fenceline between grasstrees and acacia scrub.

This is the northern tip, said Lu. Most of this end was never cleared. Goes right through to the coast.

I thought the farm was long gone.

The original place, yeah. They sold in stages to some developer. This end still hasn't settled.

Is...is it safe?

There's a house another kay or so south. Got a manager in but the place's in limbo. He'll be inside watching the cricket, don't worry.

Georgie held on, absorbing this news until the sand of the trail turned white. They slalomed up the back of a dune and came drifting down onto a hard pan of beach behind a scrubby headland. He just got out and walked into the surf while she sat there watching. The sea was still smooth in the offshore breeze and in the calm beyond the breakers where he lay it was sandy green. It was too hot to sit in the cab so she stripped off and scuttled down to join him.

This strikes me as somewhat reckless, she said, hearing the attempt at irony transmit as prissiness.

He spouted water, lay on his back.

You enjoy it too much, she said. What's the history here?

Just neighbours, you know.

A feud, I take it.

Nah.

What then?

My old man. He wasn't the deferential type.

All that stuff in your house. You were married?

He shook his head.

The kids' stuff, all the photos.

Lu rolled over and stroked away. He was good in the water. Georgie looked back at the truck on the beach and the wild scrubby country that ran down to it as far as you could see. She wondered what else she didn't know about Jim Buckridge. She was sober now and jittery. She stood on the sandy bottom and waited for him to turn back to shore. The melons, the fruit stand, they rang a bell but she couldn't think

86

of the connection. He swam back and dived. He surfaced beside her with his eyes open.

My family, he said. There was an accident.

Jesus, she blurted. You're *that* family? The musicians, she thought. The rollover.

As they stood there the sea changed colour and the wind died. Within a few moments the first cool breath of the southerly was upon them.

I don't know what to say.

You'll think of something, he said.

Georgie remembered the party at Gilligan's, one of those rare occasions when she'd bothered. The keg hissing on the verandah. The groom's father rolling his eyes at the endless delay. The band, the bloody band. Someone rigging up a stereo in the meantime. The beery vibe rising, the celebration going on regardless. The bride throwing someone through an asbestos wall. Coloured lights raining onto the yard amidst all that laughter. Just White Pointers running amok. She remembered Yogi ostentatiously taking a call. Shoeless in flares. Sidling off with the keys to the ambulance. And then, so much later, on their way out, with Gilligan and his bride gone and the first real fights brewing, the news rolling up the lawn. The musos. Right in their own bloody driveway. In a ute. Three of them dead and one of the kids critical. People sat around on cars to drink and speculate. Jim took her by the hand and was silent all the way home.

C'mon, said the shamateur. Time to go.

I never heard you play, she says, still towelling off from the shower. People say you were good. The three of you.

Fox slides the omelette onto her plate and proceeds to wash the few dishes on the sink.

Don't keep shrugging like that, she says. It's infuriating.

I didn't notice, he says.

You rolled down the shutters, Lu.

Sorry, he says unapologetic.

I've crossed the line, then?

Fox catches himself smiling, thinks: Lady, you're all over the place, you've never seen a boundary in your life.

I guess I should go?

Eat your omelette.

Yes, Dad.

Tell me about his kids.

Jim's? she says only pausing a moment from loading her fork. Nine and eleven. Boys. Nice kids, really.

Really.

I've...been very fond of them.

So you're the one after Debbie.

Yes. That's me.

Ever want any of your own?

Georgie Jutland chews for a while and swallows. No.

Fox wipes his hands.

My sisters, she says, had all the babies. It looked to me like accessorizing. I'm the wild aunty.

With stepchildren.

Exactly.

Fox looks at her. Even fresh from the sea and a shower she looks spent, as though she should go to bed with a fan until tomorrow. Despite the sweet, tousled hair there's a wound-up look to her that gives you the idea she's forgotten *how* to rest.

And you don't work anymore? he says.

Ran out of puff.

Be a hard job, nursing.

She smiles.

You're the first man I ever met who can scrub a bath properly.

Well, it took years of study. Did it all by correspondence.

Good omelette. And look at that stove. Christ, you're completely domesticated.

Even shit in a sandbox.

Play me something. Just to ice the cake.

I don't play anymore, he says.

Not at all?

He shakes his head and takes the empty plate from her. All this talk feels dangerous, worse than the stuff about fishing. Like being caught in a rip. Half of you knows it can't kill you but the rest of you is certain it must. You stay calm, swim across it not against it. Sooner or later it'll spill into placid water.

So what did you play?

Guitar.

I mean, what kind of music.

Oh, I dunno. All kinds, I spose. Anythin you could play on a verandah. You know, without electricity. Dirt music.

As in...soil?

Yeah. Land. Home. Country.

You *can't* mean country and western?

Nah. Though we'd play Hank and Willie, Guy Clark. Plenty of bluegrass and some Irish stuff. Whatever felt right with a guitar, mandolin, fiddle. But mostly it was blues. Country blues, I spose. You know—Blind Blake, Doc Watson, Son House.

Um, she says blankly.

Rootsy stuff. Old timey things.

Folk music.

I spose. No, not really. Well, I dunno.

My mother made me do piano lessons, she says, scrutinizing him.

Same. We had to take turns. Darkie used to lift the lid and pull the strings. The old man brought home a guitar he found in a pawn shop in Midland. That was it. Borers got the piano. He was the *real* player. Darkie.

Your brother? That was his name?

No. William.

So where did Darkie come from?

Dunno. That's what we called him. Except Mum.

Where's she?

Dead. When we were kids.

And your father?

Mesothelioma. I was seventeen. He was at Wittenoom before we were born. Mining asbestos.

Jesus, she murmurs, I probably nursed his mates. Him, even.

All dead. Weird, you know. He was dyin our whole life. But we didn't know it.

Did he?

I did wonder. Later.

It's his library, then?

Mum's. The old boy didn't care for books that couldn't show you how to fix an engine or save your soul. Bumfluff, he called it.

Was...was Darkie a reader?

Nah. Could hardly even read music. But you'd play him something and he could crank it back at you.

That's a gift.

Fox finds himself uncoiling somehow, as though he can't pull back once he's started. He babbles at her about how they practised to tapes and LPs on the verandah instead of doing their homework. How they taught themselves from liner notes, how they played J. J. Cale and early Bowie at high school bong parties in empty rope sheds, after which Sally Dobbins began to hang around with a mandolin and an old Rod Stewart record. And suddenly there were three of them. Endless afternoons of tuning and de-tuning, of arguments and sudden breakthroughs. They got hold of bootlegs—Skip James, Robert Johnson, Blind Willie—and found a Taj Mahal record at the White Point rubbish dump. Darkie taught himself banjo and then the fiddle. They found a washboard in the shed and made guitar slides from the necks of plonk bottles. Sudden watersheds, like the first time they made it all the way through 'Cripple Creek'; the moment they heard Ry Cooder. Deckies heard them play on somebody's porch and then

they played for beer at parties. Skippers'
wives began to book them for twenty-firsts when
everybody expected punk or disco. They
played a few country halls where farmers
wanted Glen Campbell. But in the end, despite
the fact that they were Foxes, there came a
grudging respect. Not everybody liked the
music but people admitted that they played
like demons.

He tips back against the sink appalled at this
outburst.

Always envied people with languages and
music, she says with a wry grin.

I need a walk, he says. Feel like a walk?

Not really.

Think I'll go. You mind?

Will I need shoes?

No.

Georgie followed him across the ragged paddock where runty melons grew wild. The grey
sand was hot underfoot and the afternoon
sun roasted the back of her neck until they came
to a grove of tuarts whose shade and pad of
fallen litter offered some relief. From there,
with the dog trotting between them, Lu led her
down the rutted yellow riverbank, mottled by
the shadows of melaleucas.

You had a market garden, she said joining
him in the lee of a cantilevered paperbark.

Just watermelons.

God, there must be money in it; that's a nice
boat you've got.

Lu smiled.

In melons? Nah. Not at the rate we were growin em, not after the old boy got crook. Even before that things were pretty lean. The old fella used to cut through that Buckridge land, slip out with the dinghy and liberate a few lobsters from the pros' pots. Boil em up, sell em on the sly down the highway.

Like father, like son.

Anyway, he must have suspected somethin about the cancer, cause he insured himself. We didn't know until afterwards. Darkie got the pay-out. He was the eldest. Blew most of it on sixties Holdens and Fords, vintage guitars. We lived for years on what was left. That and melons, and the occasional gig, but playin never paid much. Last summer I sold everythin up, a whole shedful, and bought the boat. Figured I could get by.

So. The disreputable Foxes.

That's us.

Georgie looked down into the shallow tea-coloured water. It was cool here. The southerly shivered the leaves and hoary bark.

I don't understand what you're doing, she said. Living like this. I mean, why stay on?

Things, places, they're hard to shake off.

Georgie tried not to grimace. She had never understood the grip that places had over people. That sort of nostalgia made her impatient. It was awful seeing people beholden to their memories, staying on in houses or towns out of some perverted homage.

I did think about goin north, he said. Just

wanted to leave everythin and bolt. You know, disappear. I already felt like a ghost.

A ghost?

Like I was dead anyway but the news still hadn't got through to my body. Like in a bushfire that rolls over you so fast you're cooked inside but still running.

Jesus.

But then I thought, I'm gone already. Why not disappear without leavin?

You've lost me, Lu.

I came back from that last funeral and burned all my papers. Licences, any ID, school reports. Never had a tax file number anyway. Just go off the grid, you know. Live in secret. *Be* a secret.

But what's the point?

Privacy. Privacy. Sooner or later your secrets are all you have.

The Ghost Who Walks.

That's me.

So you poach on the high seas and read books and play music out here on your own.

Music, no.

You really don't play anymore?

Don't even listen.

You can't or won't?

Both.

What, never?

Ever.

That's terrible.

Lu gave her a pained, defiant smile and she could see the boyish refusal in him. It was hard to hold it against him but you could only sense it bringing trouble down on his head. He was stuck. And all the more endearing because he reminded Georgie of herself.

You ever have that dream, he said, when you were a kid, that everyone's got back in the car and driven off and forgotten you?

I know exactly the one, said Georgie bitterly.

He smiled and Georgie couldn't account for it; she had no idea where a smile like that could come from.

How about a place? he said. Ever have a special place?

As a kid, no. Though I liked the river where we lived.

Where?

Ah, Nedlands.

But no special spot.

Georgie felt as though she was failing a test of some kind. He obviously had no notion of how different they were. He was some autodidact farmboy and she was a refugee from the winner's circle, a girl who chose nursing to thwart the old man's dreams of a doctor in the family.

I'll show you something, he said.

The dog rose from its belly and looked at him.

She caught herself looking at her watch.

Fox takes her up the hill above the quarry. The dog rifles through the dry grass chasing something unseen.

I should have worn shoes, she says.

You want a piggyback?

95

No.

I don't mind. You're only little.

I'm forty bloody years old! By the way, how old are you?

Thirty-five.

How old did you think I was?

About that. You getting up or what?

Fox hoists her up with his arms through the crooks of her legs. God, the weight of another living body. She holds him round the neck and presses into his back.

Won't take long, he says.

Who's in a hurry?

You can be back before dark.

Who says I'm going back at all? she says sharply.

You are going back. You're just testin the water.

Bullshit!

Little bag full of lipstick and credit cards, come on.

Put me down.

You were on the way back, he says. Be honest. You needed time to get yourself straightened out.

Let me down! she yells, tugging at his hair and ears. He stumbles and the dog barks and they go sprawling into the dirt.

Jesus Christ, it bit me!

The dog retreats a metre or two to look doleful and contrite.

You scared him, Fox says, trying not to laugh.

Has he had his shots?

Only shots around here come from a rifle, lady.

Don't fucking lady me.

Orright.

He picks her up and kisses her hair. She wipes her eyes on her arm.

Georgie followed him up to the clump of stones in silence. The yellow sand was soft and cooled by the shadows that streamed from the pinnacles. The stones were encircled by grasstrees whose fronds twitched in the wind.

Came here as a kid. Bird liked it too. My niece. Here, look.

He stepped up to the tallest stone and pulled something from its side. Then hesitated.

Just a tin, he said. Her secrets.

He put the container back without opening it and looked at her confused, embarrassed, it seemed.

There *was* somewhere once, said Georgie, from pity as much as solidarity. A place I got stuck in. Up north.

Stuck how? he said.

In a boat. Aground, no less. There was an island and mangroves, boab trees, birds. I had this feeling of déjà vu about it, that it was a place I'd always known.

You're a sailor, then?

If I was a sailor I wouldn't have got stuck on a mudbank for two days.

Show me sometime. In an atlas.

Coronation, she said. Coronation Gulf.

97

And it's way up north?

In the tropics.

He smiled again and Georgie knew, even though she *was* headed for White Point any moment, that she wanted him. You couldn't trust an impulse like this.

What'll we do? she said.

Who knows.

We should be sorry we met.

Yeah.

You can trust me.

I will. Fuck, I have to, he said. Just be careful.

But what'll we do?

It's a long life.

What does that mean?

I'm not goin anywhere.

The stone shadows interlocked now like a maze at their feet, and the dog panted over the sound of crowsong while Georgie considered the unlikeliness of anything working out between them. It was futile even to think of it as anything more than an interlude, a simple accident you had to leave behind.

WHEN SHE'S GONE Fox heads back along the river with the dog in tow. He doesn't understand the impulse but he feels driven out of the house, compelled to retrace his steps, the path they took this afternoon. What is this lurching, plunging sensation, this panic that alternates with a new fatalism descending upon him? And this return, is it some kind of purifying ritual which some part of him thinks might reclaim the safety and solitude he had until twenty-four hours ago? All that work, the hard exercise of discipline unravelling even as he stands there.

Wind ruffles the water. Trees groan and lock horns above him.

How might he have told her that the way he lives is a project of forgetting? All this time he's set out willfully to disremember. And some days it really is possible, in a life full of physical imperatives you can do it, but it's not the same as forgetting. Forgetting is a mercy, an accident. So it's been no triumph, but it's got him here, hasn't it? Through a whole year without burning up.

He stares along the dappled bank. As a boy he thought the place was alive somehow. At night in bed he felt the ooze of sap, the breathing leaves, the air displaced by birds, and he understood that if you watched from the corner of your eye the grasstrees would dance out there and people wriggle from hollow-burnt logs. Those days you could come down here and stand in the water on the shallow spit and clear your mind. Stare at the sun-torched surface and break it into disparate coins of light. Actually stop thinking and go blank. It was harder than holding your breath. You could stand there, stump-still, mind clean as an animal's, and hear melons splitting in the heat. A speck of light, you were, an ember. And happy. Even after his mother died he had it, though it waned. Later on only music got him there. And now that is gone there is only work. It's a world without grace. Unless the only grace left is simply not feeling the dead or sensing the past.

The dog looks on puzzled but patient. It follows him up to the stones in the weakening light.

Fox pulls the tin out and looks at Bird's shared secrets. Amidst the shells and blossoms the little folded bits of paper. Each piece bears a single word—SORRY—in blunt pencil. He'd found them beneath the house. Fallen through the boards perhaps, or posted through cracks. He's since found them too in the crook of the peppermint tree in whose shade they plucked roosters at Christmas. Also in the freezer. And one night on his pillow. He'd slammed the dado above his bed in a fit of grieving rage and had it fall in a pellet beside him. SORRY.

Bird was perfect. Funny, fey, sharp. What does a six-year-old have to apologize for? And who was she writing to? Did she know something? See her death? And his failure?

So much that he nearly, almost said to Georgie Jutland. He stands there in the last light divided by relief and regret.

A SMALL WHITE CAR pulled out of the drive as Georgie coasted in to Jim's place at dusk.

The glare of lights obscured its driver and Jim turned from the step and watched Georgie park the renter.

What is it with women and red cars? he said as she climbed out and locked the door.

What is it with men and fishnet stockings?

You orright?

Who was that?

Some local pissant.

Georgie followed him up, conscious of the Qantas bag over her shoulder. In the kitchen he had a pot boiling. He dropped peeled potatoes into the steaming water.

Saves cooking time if you chop them, she said.

Jim simply looked at her and she knew she'd overstepped badly.

I'm sorry, she said. I was a bit stir-crazy, that's all. Did you fish today? Did Beaver pick up the Tojo? I don't know what came over me, Jim. I feel awful about the boys, not being here. Are they downstairs? I just needed a breather.

You only had to say so, he said unwrapping some chicken pieces.

Unnerved by the calm, Georgie poured herself an orange juice.

It won't happen again.

You sound like a governess. Like an employee. I was worried, that's all.

Georgie reached into the freezer for the Stoli. Plain orange juice just wasn't going to cut it tonight. She'd prepared herself for fury, not this mournful understanding. You can hide in someone else's rage—it blinds them.

101

But this. He was right, though. Her life was reduced to an arrangement. On the drive back this afternoon hadn't she resolved to tell him she was leaving, that she planned to do it gradually, placidly, for the sake of the boys? Now the idea sounded like nothing more than a month's notice.

Obviously, he said, flouring the chicken awkwardly, we need to talk.

Yes, she said. I suppose we do.

But not tonight. Let it go tonight.

Bloody Cruiser. I don't know what it was. They can get us to the moon but can they get us to the shop?

You look awful, Georgie. Get an early night.

No video?

The Star. It's pretty bad.

Did Debbie like Bette Davis?

Jim looked up at her. I don't know, he said. I never asked.

Georgie downed the vodka and orange and felt a twinge of apprehension. At the mention of his dead wife's name, Jim's eyelids had lowered somehow and his posture bespoke an anger she rarely saw. She poured herself another drink while Jim fried the chicken. Jesus, she thought, maybe I should leave tonight.

There were a lot of things I didn't ask, he murmured.

The moment passed. Georgie knew she wouldn't leave tonight.

Later, in bed, she lay beside him almost certain he was asleep, and thought how cheap it was, bolting for someone else. She'd left men before but they were always bastards and she'd gone without a pang. But she'd never abandoned anyone for another man. It robbed you of the high ground, clouded the purity of your purpose. And, choosing one over the other, that felt bitterly close to shopping. Could be she was her mother's girl after all.

IN ANOTHER LIFE he's going barefoot up the old sheep track in the wake of his shadow. Wind curries the brown grass uphill in waves, spritzing the broken skin of the land. It blows hair across his mouth and buffets the cockatoos whose passing blackens the sky a moment. At the top of the hill he finds her among the limestone pinnacles doodling with a stick in the yellow dirt.

Tea's up, Bird.

She glances at him, her little knees knobbed in a squat. He hunkers down beside her. The tall white stones radiate the day's heat. He digs his toes into the sand.

Lu? she murmurs.

Hm?

I saw God today.

Fair dinkum?

Was him orright.

How'd he seem?

Eh?

Er, what'd he look like?

A dot. A dot in a circle, sort of. When I close me eye and poke it with me thumb he floats across the sky. Right into the sun, even. No one else can go in the sun, right?

Smiling, he puts his hand in her hair and picks out a burr. She grimaces enough to show where her front teeth have been.

Tea, he says.

Gis a piggyback?

Yer getting too heavy.

Carn, Lu, ya weak or somethin?

Get up, ya cheeky bugger.

He hoists her up, thinking that if anyone saw God it would likely be her. Bird's the nearest thing to an angelic being. He carries her downhill. Already, over their shoulder, the moon is blundering up amongst the tuarts. The house tilts on its stumps like a tide-stranded boat in the twilight and from it come the sounds of mandolin and guitar.

'Irene Goodnight', says Bird.

Sounds like it. Where's your brother?

Down the creek.

Fox skirts a crate of melons half-covered by a tarp and lowers Bird onto the back step.

Thank you, fair beast, she says.

Fox smells ganja on the breeze. The mandolin burrs dolefully through the house, where doors and windows stand open to the coming cool of night. The dog barks off in the distance.

Get in the shower, Bird.

You said tea.

You stink.

Well, thank you.

104

Good advice and free. Use soap front and back.

Soap in the front hurts.

I'm just a bloke, what would I know?

He follows her through the house, adjusts the hot water in the shower for her and goes on into the kitchen to check how the crabs have cooled. He makes a salad, pulls out some bread. The screen door slaps back and his nephew comes in smelling of dog.

Crabs!

Bullet, wash your hands. Better still, fall through the shower.

Aw.

Go on, get your sister out. And no teasing! he yells after the boy.

Fox takes the meal out onto the verandah where it's dark already but for the moon catching in the tarnished steel face of Darkie's National guitar. He lights the kero lamps and sees his brother's head tilted back, his feet on the jarrah rail, chair tipped so the guitar lies flat to his belly. Sal sits against the cornerpost, skirt up her thighs, feet white in the lamplight. She plays with her eyes closed. Cape-like, her hair falls down around her arms. Then she opens her eyes, sees Fox and smiles. For a few minutes he leans against the table to listen to the intricate improvs that they weave around the old standard. After a while he goes inside and gets some beer. The hall has filled with steam.

Fox whumps the wall to rouse Bullet from the shower and goes back outside to dinner.

Darkie and Sal are into a tune he doesn't recognize, a striding bit of bluegrass that has mandolin and guitar calling and answering. Fox pulls on his beer, stands there smiling, getting the feel of the changes.

The kids come out, hair towelled askew, and set upon the crabs. Bullet is nine and rangy as a roo dog. Even in sleep he twitches and whimpers as though dreaming on the run. Cracking crab claws with his teeth he inhales more food than he chews. Bird is a methodical eater. She strips the shells of meat and piles it on her plate. At night she sleeps in total immobility, like a diver enraptured. Most nights she wets the bed as though unable to swim up through the weight of sleep. Fox knows the sound of her footfalls on the boards in the dark. It's him she comes to for the sponge bath and the change of linen. A thousand nights they've stood silent together in the bathroom, her head on his arm as warm water runs in the sink.

Fox loves the kids as his own. Sometimes it surprises him to remember they're not. Now and then he still catches himself watching Sal. There are nights when the low rumble of her laughter stirs him awake in his bed.

They've more or less grown up together, the three of them. He doesn't mind. He's his brother's brother. That's how it is.

Come get some crabs, he says to Darkie and Sal. You'll be late for the gig.

Crabs don't wait, says Bullet.

Well, these ones aren't goin anywhere, says Bird. Not anymore.

Except down me neck.

They playing tonight? asks Bird as though her parents aren't there.

White Point, says Fox.

We go?

You got school tomorrow.

Darkie and Sal leave off playing, wipe their strings and lay the instruments in their tatty cases. They come to the table shining with sweat.

Saw an eagle today, says Bullet with flecks of crabmeat all over his face. Wedgetail, it was.

That's a beautiful bird, says Sal.

Not as good lookin as *our* Bird, says Darkie swilling a cracked claw in vinegar.

I saw God, murmurs Bird.

Well, that's hard to beat, love, says Sal with a grin.

Bullet, you been aced, mate.

The boy goes back to eating. If he wasn't so hungry, he'd likely pursue it, thinks Fox. Bullet doesn't fancy being bested.

For a while they eat and talk with the warm night closing in and the house creaking on its stumps. The air is sharp with kerosene and vinegar.

Anyone for a hunk of watermelon? asks Fox.

Fox is the only one not sick to the guts at the idea of melon. Darkie calls them vineturds.

Don't know what you're missin out on, youse blokes.

You just go ahead, Lu, says Sal.

Fox steps down off the verandah with an old

butcher knife honed away to a crescent. He rolls one off the crate, strikes it with his knuckles and rejoices at the healthy sound it makes. He slips the knife in and feels the melon sigh as it falls open. It gives off a sweet musk which causes the hair to rise along his arms. The sigh, that musk, like the breath of God.

Tear into it, Lu, says Darkie, laughing.

Fox brings the halves back up to the verandah, one in each arm, like a midwife with glistening twins.

Go, boy, says Sal.

Yeah, go hard or go home.

Fox sets his teeth into the flesh, sees the very cells of the stuff turgid, bright with moisture. Sugar cool in his mouth. He chews a moment, spits a few seeds across the rail into the dark.

Spittin blackfellas, says Darkie.

Give over, Darkie, says Sal.

Somethin your grandad used to say, Lu explains to the kids.

If a man can number the dust of the earth, says Darkie, *then shall thy seed also be numbered.*

He said the seeds were like blackfellas hiding in the melons, says Lu.

What blackfellas? calls Bullet.

Abos, Darkie says.

Oh. Them.

Used to be a mission, says Lu. A camp. Out the back of the river there at Mogumber.

And who was hiding? Bird asks, lost.

Kids used to run away from the camp, Bird.

Lookin for their families. Your grandad used to let em stay down the creek where no one would find em.

Then what happened?

They went south. Got caught mostly. Back to the camp. Before my time, Bird.

The girl looks at the seeds buried in the melon.

They only made one of your grandpa, says Sal. Just as well, eh.

Bullet saunters over to the melon and buries his face in it for the laughs.

While Darkie and Sal get ready Fox does the kids' school reading. Bullet lies on the library floor intoning until released. Bird insists on sitting in Fox's lap to read *Possum Magic*. She's already halfway through the Narnia novels but the picture book, a hangover from infancy, retains a ritual hold over her. She nestles into his neck smelling of Pears shampoo and fresh pyjamas.

Lu, how come water lets you through it?

Um. Good manners? he says.

That's not the answer.

Darkie comes in wearing a clean shirt, his hair tied back and shining, eyes bloodshot.

You blokes comin to the Point?

Yeah! cries Bird.

I told you, Darkie, it's Sunday. School tomorrow.

We're playin one short. It's a weddin.

You'll be fine.

They booked us.

I've got the kids. Told you when they booked it.

They can sleep in the ute, can't you, Bullet?

Bullet has come in with Sal who's finishing the plait in her hair. It's the colour of short-bread. Sweat glistens on her neck. Bird launches herself toward her mother and Fox rocks alone, pissed off that they've done it again. He'll be to and fro all night from the car, playing with only half his mind on the music. By midnight Darkie and Sal will be wound up tight and the party will move on to someone else's place and they'll get blasted. He'll either drive the kids home himself or doss down with them on the tray of the ute. In the morning they'll be slit-eyed and cranky and likely miss school.

Carn, mate, says Darkie. Don't be such an old woman.

Well you've told em now. The genie's out of the bottle. I'll bring some sheets.

Whew, says Sal. Too hot for jeans. Where's that dress again?

When Fox gets out to the yard they're all waiting. The dirt is pink from brakelights.

Carn, Lu, says Bullet from the tray of the one-tonner.

Want me to drive? he calls to his brother. You probly shouldn't.

Get in, says Darkie lazily.

Fox throws some bedclothes and his old

Martin in the back and climbs up with the kids. He kicks a few furry melon stalks aside and sits back against the cab window with the kids snuggled up to him in their pyjamas. He smells the sweet, dry grass and watches their dust rise pink and white into the starblown sky. In front Sal's laughter is just audible over the squelch of gravel and the old Holden motor. Even in the dark the amber blossoms of the Christmas trees hang vivid at the track's edge.

Bird begins to sing.

I love a sunburnt country
A land of sweeping plains

They pick up speed, Darkie lairizing a little at the wheel to make the kids giggle. Fox cranes to see Sal cuddled up against Darkie, kissing his neck. He turns back, sees his olive trees, the ones he planted as seedlings, fall by in a dusty procession in the front paddock.

Fishtail! yells Bullet.

Darkie gives the old Holden some throttle and the tray slides into a drift, kicks back while the kids shriek with pleasure. Behind them the ruts of the drive yaw in and out of view.

And then there's dirt in his mouth. The sky gone completely.

For a few moments Fox thinks he's gone to sleep, it's been a long, hot day and the travelling air is cool. But dead grass rasps against his cheek and a queer red light washes over the earth. Strange, but he thinks first of his mother, that he's there again on the ground

111

beside her. And he considers the olives which fall to the dirt, season after season. He smells fuel, rolls over and is rent with the most abrupt pain like a hatchet high in the chest. God Almighty, he's out in the paddock. He feels a sudden panic that he's been left behind and scans the dark swathe of the highway beyond the gate. He gets to his knees and quickly understands that his collarbone is broken. Upright, arms crossed before him, he tries to take it in. Light pours up out of the ground and a red cloud of dust rolls along the drive until it overtakes him and billows out onto the blacktop.

He shambles across stony dirt to the drainage ditch where the ute's headlights burn into the ground. Fencewire twitches in the hay stubble, hissing, snagging as he stumbles. He blunders down to the upturned one-tonner calling their names, all their names, revolted by the beetle-like underbelly of the vehicle, the evil turning of the rear wheel.

There's no sign of the kids; they must be safe, but before he can call out for them he spies Darkie half out of the cab and he goes to him, kneels to see that his arm is pulp and the rest of him feels like a kitbag full of loose tools. God Almighty, he thinks, how long have I been out? The earth at his feet is tarry with blood and his brother is so gone. He can hear Sally now but not see her in the darkness of the cab. She's just a horrible wet noise in there. Fox crabs around to the passenger's side and on his belly and crying with pain, he burrows in through the bent hatch of the window frame. The undulating cab roof is hot and slippery beneath him. He smells shit and Juicy Fruit, gropes one-handed until he finds her wedged under the steering column, bits of metal protruding from her trunk.

Lu?

He feels her lips under the palm of his hand.

It's okay, she says, I don't feel it. Sing, Lu.

He feels the breath go out of her before he can pull his hand away. The hot rain of her urine sluices his face. He comes to again out on the dirt. The same night, perhaps the same minute.

Goes searching up the track, crosses himself for relief, nursing hope.

But he finds Bullet in the stony edge of the paddock, his head rent like a cantaloupe, still smelling of soap, pyjamas clean.

The National in its case, right there in the ruts. The mandolin dusty. A folded rug full of burrs.

From way back up the house the chained dog barks.

And finally, across the track in the soft dirt, luminous beneath the moon, Bird. Like a fallen kite there in her nightie, breathing, breathing but there's no way he can lift her. His collarbone grinds like a broken joist. When he tries again her weight rends him almost in two and he falls back into the blood-varnished oats. His back goes into a fierce spasm through which he still feels the child's breath hot along his arm. He fights to his feet and pants a while and then with his good arm he takes the small, warm foot and proceeds to drag the child along the white rut of the track, resisting the pain for several paces until the wheatbag noise of her on the dirt shames him and he relents. He knows he should never have moved her. Stepping back, he stumbles into the broken belly of a guitar which cries out, and for a few moments he makes horrible vaudeville shaking the bastard thing from his boot.

The moon hangs above the house. He limps up the track. He creeps, he shuffles. He leaves all of them out there under the moon. There is no wind now but the wire of the paddock fence sings and a hiss is abroad in the weeds. Just behind the ruined fence the heavy orange blossoms of the Christmas trees shiver in the night and beyond them the beetle backs of melons shine. At the house he takes the verandah steps in increments of pain and as his hips lock up he staggers against the doorjamb and smears someone's blood across the timber frame.

The verandah table is loaded with crabshells and sodden newsprint and already the ants are into it. Plates, beer bottles, a roach end. On the jarrah boards a child's rubber thong.

Inside the floorboards shine. The telephone has a dial tone. The house smells of life, but he knows he has seen the end of the world.

◆　◆　◆

THE WALK BACK up the hill does nothing to settle his mind. Fox comes back in the dark with his whole outlook in ruins, his thoughts sprayed in all directions at once. The wry, throaty sound of her laugh. The miserable prospect of children involved and, worse, the probability of it all ending here tonight, that it could all have been merely an adventure for her. At least she won't be stupid enough to brag about it at his expense. Nobody would be that reckless, not anybody who knows the Buckridges. Even the idea of them, of falling into their orbit again, makes him agitated. It's hard to be specific about why. Big Bill is long dead, there is nothing to fear from him anymore but even he was mostly legend to the Fox boys. They understood that White Point was his town and that before the shacks were built there the coast was considered his fiefdom. Fox has never seen a burning or a sinking with his own eyes and he's never got the straight story about those Jap boys who disappeared after the war. The old man wouldn't speak of it but the stiffness that came over his father's body at the mention of the name said plenty.

Fox can't help but think of Jimmy Buckridge at school, his brooding presence at recess. He was untouchable; his word was law, but some days he turned up with unexplained grazes and once or twice a shiner even. Still you'd never pity him—even if you could feel such an emotion you wouldn't dare admit it, not even to yourself. There was something frightening about him, something spoiled in his nature. Poisoned was the old man's verdict, but he never would elaborate.

He remembers best a single boyhood day on the White Point jetty. Jimmy Buckridge when he must have been eleven years old. One of the big kids, it seemed to him then, and a townie as well, out to impress the visiting city girls with feats of cruelty. Stomping blowfish, ripping the jaws from live trumpeters. Fox remembers looking on, coiling his own handline with an absentminded intensity while the finale unfolded. A live boxfish, harmless and silly-looking, about the size of a softball, was shoved beneath the back wheel of the idling depot truck. The spray of gore, the laughter. And then some brave mother who'd seen it from the beach striding up to give the Buckridge kid a high mouthful in front of the entire holiday assembly. Later, while she was back on the beach attending to her toddlers the boy tipped whale oil through the open window of her car. King of the kids, Big Jim even then.

Back at the house the dog is already panting on the step and it leaps against him for comfort, as though the whole day has been a confounding of routine. Fox sits a moment to ruffle its ears and consider that he's well out of it if Georgie goes back to Jim Buckridge and puts the whole episode behind her. She's impulsive, sure, but smart too. She knows which way the wind is blowing. They're both better off

116

letting it go. But the entire business has rocked him. He cannot believe the ludicrous hopes he's entertained these past few hours. In her presence he was all over the place; it was a kind of madness.

While the night deepens he lets the dog mug up to him, licking his hands and face for all it's worth. He's too disgusted with himself even to bother pushing it off and eventually the dog grows bored and slopes off under the house.

GEORGIE KNEW within the first half-hour that neither the vodkas nor the ten milligrams of Temazepam would get her over the edge tonight. She felt mind and body holding sleep at bay. The anxiety reminded her of those nights in Jeddah when she was afraid to sleep lest she dream once more of Mrs Jubail stalking her down the hospital corridors. The nightmare pursued her from Saudi Arabia and on to the States, to Indonesia and home to Australia. For a long time at White Point she thought she'd shaken it off but it had reprised itself of late. She recognized the creeping sense of dread. She thought of how epileptics and vertigo sufferers could feel episodes approaching. That's how she felt tonight with Jim Buckridge lying so still and quiet beside her. His breathing was too reserved. He was feigning sleep.

She didn't dare move. She understood what

it took during the lobster season to keep him awake after midnight. So why not just front him with it? Why lie there pretending alongside him? Unless he really was asleep. But that stillness felt like restraint. And somehow that holding back, the force of it—it unnerved her.

Georgie considered how little money she had saved. She thought of working again. Of the boys. That house out in the bleached paddocks. The hire car. The towing fee. The hotel bill. The things she'd miss.

At four-thirty Jim sighed and rolled out of bed. She half expected him to say something. Lying there doggo she thought he lingered a moment before padding into the bathroom. She wished she'd said something, told herself it wasn't too late, but she let him dress and make his coffee in the kitchen while she lay there. The Hilux rattled into the drive.

She was almost asleep when the blurt of *Raider*'s diesels rose from the lagoon.

FOX STANDS OUT in the hot, still morning dark with the dog whining at his feet. It's totally calm. The air is thick. It feels as though somewhere over the horizon two opposing systems have stalled momentarily and cancelled each other out to leave this peculiar stillness. You can tell already that the day will be breathless. Gift weather. Last night he resolved to keep his head down a while, to stay ashore until things settled down again, but how can you pass up weather like this on a coast where a howling wind is the only constant? Some days you just have to be out there; it'd be a sin to waste it.

Problem is, it's already a little late for a proper fishing run. He's unprepared with no bait ready. But he figures there's fuel enough in the boat's tanks for a quick foray. Out and back, maybe. Just time for a quick dive, a hit-and-run job on his favourite coral lumps to the north. What the hell.

Fox strips the boat of special tackle and all instruments. No echo sounder, no GPS, nothing fancy. Without droplines and beacons, with not even a decent icebox aboard, who's to say he's anything but just another barebones amateur hoping to spear himself a jewfish? Even the most suspicious Fisheries crew will have nothing on him. And the White Pointers? Well, he'll always have the jump on those dozy bastards.

By the time he's left the dog on the beach and broached the northernmost limits of the White Point lagoon it's almost daylight, but Fox feels protected by this weird meteorological dispensation. He absorbs the perfect calm into his very being. He skates out on a motionless sea. Hair beating at his neck. Pearly dunes at the corner of his eye as he hugs the uninhabited empty coast. Warm air. Lurid calm. Flashing daubs of seagrass and reef underfoot. And not a damn boat in sight.

A few miles north he anchors and goes over the side and right away he wishes he hadn't bothered with the wetsuit; days like today you want to feel it barebacked. There's a delirium in the water, something special in the way the reef morphs and throbs below. He hangs at the surface a few moments to hyperventilate and then he kicks down through the enfolded layers, the unseen byways of current and the changes of temperature that lace the clear water. From a hole in the reef a groper slides out into the open in a blue-green blast of light. Fox doesn't even load the spear. The big fish rolls aside to watch him. He hovers motionless over soft corals and sponges, across hard yellow plate and rifts of purple-blue. There's staghorn and brain coral, eels and blennies and blackarse cod and the feelers of a hundred wary rock lobsters. The sea is thick with clicks and rattles, the encrypted static of the silent world speaking. Pressure tightens his skin and current roots through his hair. You could stay here, he thinks. On a single breath you could live here on a God-given day like this when plankton spin before your eyes and fish leave their redoubts in phalanxes to swim to you. The thread of heat inside him trickles back to a thudding core. There's no discomfort now, no impulse to take another breath. Way up there his boat hangs from the anchor rope like a party balloon. It looks so buoyant, so beautiful, that he has to go back and see. He kicks up lazily. From too far and too long down. Poisoned and happy. A distant part of him knows how close he's come to shallow water blackout, but as he crashes through the glittering surface where his body still does the breathing for him, the rest of him settles for simple ecstasy. He lies half in the world. Tingling.

JUST AFTER EIGHT Georgie walked the silent boys to school, kissed their averted heads and walked on to Beaver's to see about a car.

He seemed surprised to see her. She put the Bette Davis cassette on his counter.

Not her best, he mumbled.

So what's the gossip?

Industrial deafness, Georgie. Blame Harley-Davidson.

Can you sell me a car?

Not before Christmas. You wanna lift somewhere?

No, I've got a renter for the moment.

Jesus, George.

What?

Be careful.

That's why I came to you, she said brightly. I wouldn't buy a used car off just anyone.

I'll let you know. When something comes in.

You're a mate, said Georgie.

He laughed his rumbly laugh.

Well. Aren't you?

Oh, I'm everybody's mate, George.

121

She was halfway home when she heard what sounded like gunshots. God, she hated this town.

THE SEA is so flat and cerulean that clouds seem to founder in it. Planing through their reflections Fox feels more skybound than waterborne as he bears in toward the lagoon.

Nothing moves ashore at White Point. There's only this prevailing painterly stillness. Deserted beach. Norfolk pines immobile. And boats languishing at their moorings.

Throttling down across the seagrass flats he feels watched but he knows he's home free—there's nothing to be caught with, no fish, no lobsters, no abalone. He cuts his motors and tilts them to glide in to the shallows. His wake folds on itself like poured treacle. He thinks of the curve of her neck. Smells saltbush, pigface, iodine. The world feels becalmed and dreamy.

The bow grinds gently against the sand. The dog doesn't get up to greet him. The truck windows have no sheen. Cicadas. The boat wake arrives; it laps up a desolate crescendo while he begins to see what he's looking at.

He vaults from the boat in his wetsuit and walks up to the dog which lies in a stain of itself on the chain's end. Fragments of hair and meat discolour the sand. There's blood underfoot but

122

no flies yet. The truck windows are blown out and the iceboxes are ragged with holes. Fox fishes the keys from beneath the sidestep and shoves them into the ignition through the ruined door-frame. He doesn't expect a spark; doesn't get it. He pops the hood, sees the V8's blasted entrails and knows it's useless.

He walks away before he falls, walks to the boat. Washes his feet of gore. Steps up onto the transom. Pushes off.

ABOUT NINE Georgie made herself a stiff coffee and stood at the kitchen window to drink it. Down on the beach she saw a boat trailer and the curve of a vehicle roof mostly obscured by the foredune. She put the cup on the sink and snatched up the house binoculars. Oh, Jesus. Lu. What was he doing going out? Today of all days, and in broad bloody daylight?

She went down across the grass at a half-trot and came over the dune to see the Ford's windscreen blown out and the pink spray of dog on the sand. The sun beat into her head.

The first thing Georgie did was shower. She couldn't help herself; she had to wash and, no matter how hot the water, she couldn't get warm. She had a drink. For half an hour she looked for the keys to the rental car but they were nowhere about. She found a cardboard removal carton in the garage and took it upstairs. She threw open the wardrobes and looked at her clothes. Most of them were rubbish. Apart from a few toiletries and a handful of CDs, that'd be it. Christ, she'd barely fill a single box with her life here. Everything else was Jim's.

The phone rang. She let it ring out. Georgie sat on the bed and held her face. The phone started up again.

Out in the livingroom she took up the house binoculars and scanned the lagoon, the reef, the passage. A couple of boats were steaming in already and a terrible panic took hold. She was cut off, encircled. She thought about the kids at school. The highway. The watchful quiet of the town. She picked up CDs. Wondered if the Joni Mitchell was really hers, told herself that if she calmed down she might find the keys to the rented car; it was due back in Perth at noon. How could she lose them? She was high and dry. She needed another drink. Then she'd calm down.

The Stoli burned in her neck but the warmth didn't spread. And she didn't find the keys. Sometime during the day she just stopped looking. Even stopped packing. She just curled up on the sofa feeling cold.

When Jim came in Georgie wasn't yet too pissed to notice that he was hours early. His face looked boiled. Hers felt frozen.

Found your keys on the drive, he said, lobbing them onto the sink beside her.

You fucking liar, she said following him unsteadily to the bathroom.

Christ, the boys'll be home in a few minutes.

I can't believe you'd do it. You vicious bastard, I don't know how you could.

Georgie, sober up.

He closed the bathroom door on her and the lock fell to with a sullen plunk.

Open the door!

Cool off, for Chrissake, he said muffled by the door. The shower ran.

Georgie went back to the kitchen and took up the binoculars. A mob of kids milled at the jetty already, their school uniforms in puddles on the landing. The bravest of them shinnied up the crane to jump from the top and send gouts of spray into the air. The water was bronze and their bodies backlit. There was still no breeze. People made their way down to the beach for relief from the heat. She watched them drive down to the water's edge in Patrols and Cruisers. It was turning out to be a sociable afternoon. Big women in merciless lycra shorts hefted toddlers into the shallows. Men brought out beers in neoprene holders; she watched their lips move. Nobody seemed curious about the truck and the dead dog a few hundred metres up the beach.

The phone rang again.

Georgie scanned the sea. She couldn't think where he might come ashore. There was nowhere else you could bring a boat safely to shore on this coast. It was all surf beach north and south and there wasn't another anchorage for seventy kilometres. Maybe he had fuel enough for that. She doubted it. Still, the conditions were perfect.

The boys came in. She tried to assemble herself.

FOX GOES and goes across the flat sea. The wind in his teeth. The tinnitus whine of the Hondas. He's numb with speed, nearly mindless with going. Eventually the outboards falter and lose revs. They cut out with their throttles wide open and for a few moments the boat surfs its own momentum before settling onto its chines and lagging to a halt. He stands at the helm, blank as the afternoon sky. The boat's wake finally catches up; it tosses him about a little and stirs him from the stupor. He stares at the fuel gauge. Tries to calculate how far he's come. The compass has him bearing nor-nor'west but without sonar or GPS he can only estimate how far out he is and guess how far north he's come. White Point is out of sight and the landscape is just a dun smear. He stares at the seaward horizon. The binoculars are home in the shed with the navigational instruments. He takes a punt. Five miles out? Maybe ten miles north?

He kneels at the gunwale and retches up a little tea-coloured stain. The sea's surface is silver but underneath it's black.

From the dive crate he takes a bottle of half-frozen water and drinks until his throat burns. He considers the radio, the packs of flares beneath the console. But he knows who will come looking. He'll be out here alone on the open sea armed with nothing better than a speargun. The old White Point story. No witnesses but White Pointers. It'll be another tragic accident at sea.

He sits on the gunwale. The deck is hot underfoot.

Fucking Buckridge. He tries to think back through yesterday. Did someone see them on the highway? Or was it the swim? Could have been the caretaker on the old farm; he might have been about after all. Unless she'd just gone home and fessed up of her own accord, made a clean breast of it. Shit, he doesn't know what to think.

And now they'll burn the farm. That's how it'll go. The end, amen. You bloody idiot.

He pulls off his shirt and hauls the wetsuit back up hot over his shoulders. Drags his fins from the crate and works up enough bily spit to prep his mask. He takes time to pick out the darkest patch in the hazy rumple of the land and makes it his bearing. He drops anchor though it doesn't make the bottom. Reaches over the stern and opens the cocks. He goes over the side and leaves the boat rocking. Least you've picked a good day. In a chop you'd never do it. But today you've a chance. Either way you're gone.

Beneath him the water is purple and blank.

He tries a measured crawl and breathes through his snorkel. Long gone.

JIM BUCKRIDGE FELT the plastic phone creak in his grip as he tried to control his fury. Was the whole fucking world populated with cretins?

From the doorway of his office he could see her down in the kitchen making herself another vodka martini. The only thing she was cutting the Stoli with was an olive. Her face looked peeled. The boys were off somewhere, thank God.

So have someone come and collect it, he hissed into the phone. Okay, when you have two people available, then. Yes, I know it'll cost and I said I'll pay. Do I need an interpreter, or what? White Point. On the map. Yeah, at the roadhouse. It's red. Well, it's your car, mate.

He hung up and watched her slug the drink down. The phone rang. He sat in the office and let it ring.

FOX CRAWLS through the sunstruck water. Feels it part heavily across his skull. The sea is caramelizing in the heat of the afternoon. It's harder to move through all the time. Like a landslip; the more you dig the more there is to be dug. The wetsuit causes him to sweat but he knows he'll never be able to take it off with his limbs as heavy as this. Besides, the neoprene gives him buoyancy and very soon he'll need all the flotation he can get.

After a long time he gives up stroking and just kicks with his trembling arms free. Beneath the surface the water is transfixed by bars of sunlight which ripple and twist in the misty aqua blur below him. Now and then a startled garfish snoots away. Jellyfish float amidst the clouds reflected on the water. They are cumulous, their tentacles like strings of rain.

Looks at his puffy fingertips. The guitar calluses all but gone.

Thinks of lettuces prostrate in the heat. Silver flash of olive trees. The snorkel cuts his gums now. Eardrums tight as banjo skin.

Crawls on. Air hot in his throat. Can't look at the giddy deep below. It's giving him vertigo. He rolls onto his back and kicks along with his face in the sun, his eyes pressed shut.

Later. He finds himself stopped. Face down like a dead man. His hands have dune wrinkles. You could lie here and grow old. Like a kite, that's how it seems. Suspended between worlds. It makes him laugh. Bill Blake did not a fisherman make but still we're both suspended. Mad as hell, your head a bell, like an angel's arse up-ended. You're a poet but you'd never know it and the laugh coming from your snorkel doesn't sound human.

Keeps the light behind him, the laughter in his legs. Swims on.

Can't believe he's getting cold. Cold as hospital air.

Sees the dog pitching against its chain, pink in the brakelights, pink in the sand. And then there's no light. He swims out of habit. The water, a dark, dreamless sleep. His limbs trail phosphorescent auras. Makes him look all saintly. St Luther of the molten melon. Fuck me dead, it's the fishin felon. Laughs creepy with chills.

No lights ashore.

No shore at all until the moon rises.

JUST ON DUSK a gentle nor'wester sprang up. It barely shifted the curtains, the kind of breeze that brings some relief but too little too late. Georgie propped herself in the sofa. The vodka bottle stood on the glass table in a pool of its own sweat. A pile of olive seeds sat in the pretty blue butterdish.

Down on the beach a few lamps burned. Locals cast for tailor or sat in folding chairs with their feet in the shallows. Georgie took the bottle and navigated the distance to the door and the terrace. Jim and the boys sat out on the buffalo grass in a plume of barbecue smoke. Their heads turned as she sat heavily. Those upturned faces, they were hardly the same faces she remembered from Lombok. They turned back to their meal, their voices just murmurs. The air was briny.

Two big boats started up simultaneously. Their diesels blubbed across the lagoon and they eased out of the bay under lights. Lobster boats don't work at night, she told herself. Could be dropliners. Could be anybody.

NOW THAT HE HEARS them breathing in the dark he's not afraid. Doesn't Bird breathe warm in his ear every other night and isn't that chair rocking before he gets to it sometimes? He hears cheeps and snores now, even in God's own Indian Ocean. He feels the noise of their movement in his chest. Smells their breath in the still air. All about him, in the blackwater world. Singing.

Enchanted, he stops kicking. He pulls off his mask and feels the sudden chill of air on his face. Works the fins off too and feels his feet burn with a surge of freed circulation. Bubbles of talk burst against him. He slips back in a swoon, could go down happy into sleep right now. But the water is all bellies and hips like a packed dancefloor. It holds him up. There are rolling white clouds ahead. The air is full of leaping bodies. Fox tumbles headlong into the clouds and surfs them onto the sand. He gets to his feet and hobbles up into the savoury smell of saltbush.

WHEN SHE WOKE on the terrace the yard was dark and inside only a table lamp burned. Georgie blinked and wet her lips, trying to take it in. The town was asleep. The beach looked deserted. She had the terrible feeling that she'd slept through something important.

Someone had thrown a cotton blanket over her. She tore it off. A torchbeam flickered up through the foredune; it threw shadows across the scrub. Georgie tried to get up but her legs were asleep. She floundered and fell. The bottle dropped and rolled unbroken across the slate. The balcony was washed for a moment in the torchbeam. She picked herself up, wracked with pins and needles.

Ahead of the torchlight she saw the swinging blade of the shovel. Jim's legs. His feet. The light went out. He crossed the lawn and a few moments later he was on the steps.

What have you been doing? she asked.

Go to bed, Georgie, he said coming past.

It's a simple question, she said knocking the torch out of his hand. It bounced and glanced off her shin.

Jesus, he muttered. Get outta my way.

We need to talk.

You need to sober up to talk and stop wastin my time. I've got children. And a boat to run. Sleep in the spare room. And don't spew on anything.

Where's my car keys? You've got them again.

They're safe.

I want them.

Not a chance.

Jim slid the door to. Georgie held onto the back of the sun-lounge. She wanted to follow him in but she looked at the big orange plastic torch at her feet. Inside the toilet flushed.

She took the torch and went down the stairs and followed the beam to the beach where the truck still stood on its rims in the sand. The dog chain was gone and so were the poor animal's remains. There was a smooth, packed area where Jim must have just buried it.

Water lapped eerily against the shore. She wanted to swim. She wanted to set houses alight. She wanted to drive until daybreak. She wept until she was sick on herself.

He walks rubberlegged for a while. Comes upon wheel ruts in the heath and follows them south. The heat of the day is still in the sand and it's a warm night but he shivers in his wetsuit. A couple of roos float by. He pads on until he sees the glint of a tin roof. He goes in closer to find several squatters' shacks in a hollow. Two beach buggies. A pyramid of beer-cans. A rough-hewn filleting bench and a rope strung with clothes. He looks for a dog but reaches the closest watertank without rousing anything. On his hands and knees he drinks from the tap. The water runs cool

133

and brassy into his throat. He lets it sluice his face of salt and sand.

From the clothesline he takes a pair of shorts and a tee-shirt which smells of dish-washing detergent and when he's a good way off he shucks out of the wetsuit and pulls them on. Down the track he finds a big dune gully with a thicket of acacia. He crawls in where there's a bed of leaf litter and lies down amidst the fidgeting noises of small creatures.

When he wakes it's midday and hot. He crawls out but the light is too hard, the white sand blurs and the air is woollen in his throat. His legs are tight and painful. He squirms back in to wait for sunset. Sleeps again.

At dusk he feels better and after he's walked a while his legs feel fine. In time he sees the yellow dome of light in the sky. White Point. He approaches the town from the beach. Keeping to the shadow of the foredune, he makes his way along the bay. Boats yank like curs at their chains. The floodlit jetty is wild with gulls. He sneaks past in the hollow between dunes until he's well clear and can walk on the beach again.

Where his truck and trailer stood there's nothing but tiny cubes of laminated glass underfoot. It's no surprise. This is how it will be, as though he never was.

He bellies up to the perimeter of Buck-ridge's place. Within an arm's length of the lawn he lies watching the windows flicker with television. In the dark, the town sounds benign enough: music, laughter, doors clacking.

He rubs the cramp from his legs. Eventually the house goes dark and quiet.

On his way to the garden tap he smells meat on the barbecue. He levers a couple of blackened chops from the hotplate and crouches on the lawn to tear the burnt meat from the bone and drink greedily from the hose.

He thinks of Georgie lying inside. Just up those steps. Sees the form of the shovel against the wall. He picks it up as he takes the stairs to the terrace. The glass sliding door is unlocked. Jim Buckridge asleep in his bed. But his kids too.

He kisses the glass and slips away.

IT WAS A DAY and a half before Georgie surfaced. The previous day was a miserable feverish blur, but from the soiled linen and the towels on the floor she could see only too clearly how she'd spent it. Her head hurt and so did her throat and chest. She had never sunk so low. It killed her to think that the boys might have seen it.

The empty house was in disarray and afternoon light lay in blocks on the livingroom carpet. She went unsteadily to the window to find that Luther Fox's truck and trailer were gone. She looked about for the keys to her rented car. Downstairs the garage was empty. She came back lightheaded and jittery and stood in the livingroom a while.

It took her a few moments to see the weird smudge on the glass door. Right there at eye level. The greasy imprint of a pair of lips. Georgie shuffled over to the sliding door and stared. With the filthy sleeve of her housecoat she tried to rub it off and when nothing happened she grew panicky until it dawned on her that the mark was on the other side of the glass. She stepped out into the heat and hurriedly did the job.

Then she showered and put herself together as best she could. She knew she needed to eat but she was queasy and her throat so sore she could only manage vitamins and a can of Sprite. Back on the wards a big toke of O_2 might have done the job; it was God's own pick-me-up. She thought about the cops but decided against it. Not while there was a sniff of hope.

Back in the garage she pulled her bike from the tangle of weightlifting gear and reticulation pipe. The seat felt like a fist between her buttocks. She thought of the supermarket, the post office and the school she'd need to pass. She pedalled feebly out into the hard light of day.

To say you look shithouse would be brown-nosin, said Beaver as she pulled up beside him at the pump.

Sell me a car?

Mate, there's nothin to sell ya.

I'll rent something.

Jesus, George. I gotta live here.

136

Just some old banger from out the back.
You sober enough?
Yes.
You bloody promise?
I bloody promise.
He wiped his hands and glanced at her critically. I need me truck, he said. You can take the EH. But—
I'll be careful.
Yeah, one day, George.
I really appreciate it, she said. I can't tell you.
No, he murmured. Best if you don't.

FOX WAKES AT DAWN to see that White Point is only a mile or so behind him. He doesn't even remember lying down and now he has to walk on in the heat of the day. So slow, so weak and sleepy. He presses on along the soft, empty beach with the roar of surf in his head. The sand is white, blinding, endless. Figures ten miles, no fifteen to go. Now and then he comes upon a bit of vegetation hanging from a blown-out dune and he lies in the precious shade a while to take sips from the plastic bottle he scored from a bin last night and filled from a yard tap.

At the lonely cove beneath the old Buckridge boundary he stares at footprints until he realizes they're his own. And Georgie's too—so small. When *was* this—two days ago? Longer?

He follows his own tyre tracks a short distance up into the hinterland before it occurs to him to keep wide of firebreaks and bush tracks, but the scrub here is savage underfoot. Heady smell of saltbush. The insect hum of acacia. The only trees are rare huddles of coastal morts whose bark hangs like torn bandages. Heat shudders upon the land. A fenceline. Then a nasty belt of banksia country—all sharkskin trunks and serrated leaves—and it's like wading through barbed wire.

And finally the highway, quartzy as a river. He can't walk down it in the open. He'll have to come around the back way. As he limps across he sees a dead roo with its legs in the air on the gravel shoulder. The stench pursues him across the road and into the capstone country and grasstrees beyond.

Drinks the last of his water. Comes into pasture and remnant clumps of tuart trees. A few startled sheep that must belong to a new neighbour he hasn't even met. And at last there is the strangling ditch of the brackish river. Paperbarks within whose shadows are wagtails, wattlebirds, honeyeaters.

How they flutter and scream and loop; they net the sky across him, stitch him in. He creeps south in shade. Emus step away solemn as yuppie bushwalkers.

At the home bend, where the tyre still hangs from the tilted tree, he soaks his feet. His shadow falls across the water. Past noon. No smoke nor smell of ashes. Eventually he climbs the rutted bank to look.

Prostrate on the baked earth, with wild oats rasping dead at his ears, he clocks the vehicle parked in the yard amidst the puzzling flutter of feeding hens. A 1964 EH Holden utility all buffed in gleaming monkeyshit brown. Tonneau cover and spoke wheels. A real lair's wagon. And familiar. But he can't place it. Can only wait and see. Half expects the dog to come bounding down any moment.

Retreats to the shade of the riverbank whose open veins are ropy with shadow. Feels bound to the earth by them. They pull his cheek to the soil.

When he wakes it's dusk already. There's light across the farm but behind him it's dirty dim. Shadows flit across the sandbar below. It takes a few moments for his eyes to adjust. Figures. Boys. Two. One stoops at the water's edge, commotion at his feet. Suddenly he stands with something silver in his hands, something that flickers and shakes. The earth vibrates.

Fox scrambles up the bank toward the house.

GEORGIE SAW the movement in the trees and stood ready. She was afraid; no use pretending otherwise. She hadn't heard a vehicle. She had nothing but a blackened firepoker to see them off with. The house phone looked like it'd been ripped from the wall some time ago. Could be a dog, she told herself, some stray cur from a farm across the river. But too upright.

I can see you! she yelled. It sounded prissy, the voice of an eldest sister at hide-and-seek.

He limped up to the steps like a flogged animal.

Me, he said wheeling skittishly as she dropped the poker. Georgie?

Yes.

And who else?

Just me.

I...

Only me, Lu. Come inside.

He stood there a while, his face obscured in the gloom, until Georgie realized that he needed help. When she touched him he recoiled. He felt jammy with blood and sweat. He smelled terrible.

There's food, she said leading him up the steps. He had a geriatric tremor and the sleepwalker gait of the post-op patient. At the threshold his eyes glittered.

Georgie sat him at the kitchen table and tried to assume the old professional mask in order to conceal her horror at the state he was in. Lacerated, sunburnt, crusty with salt and dirt, his lips split, his eyes red above bruises of exhaustion. His hair was full of grass seeds and cobwebs. His flayed thighs and feet shook. She took his pulse surreptitiously and thought about an ice bath to bring his body temper-

140

ature down, but his heartbeat was regular and strong and she was afraid to leave him alone to go in search of ice.

You fed the chooks, he said beatifically.

Yeah.

Was that today?

Couple of hours ago. Here, drink.

She got water into him. He swallowed methodically. It struck her as maddeningly characteristic; it made her eyes sting with tears.

There's food, she said. I cooked some things. The potatoes were here. The chicken I had to borrow. I'll run a bath. You'll stay?

Luther Fox looked at her in complete incomprehension. She left him reaching for a cold baked potato and when she returned from the bathroom he had hiccups. He tried to smile but they sounded painful, sob-like.

Drink, she said.

They comin?

I don't know.

No fire.

No.

He tore a drumstick from the chicken she'd roasted and ate it haltingly. He struggled to get it down his neck. He seemed puzzled.

The EH?

Beaver's. It's his chook, too. I'm stretching the friendship.

Georgie felt his brow and neck for clamminess, for any change of temperature. He seemed stable enough.

I'm gone, he said with a tone that sounded to Georgie like satisfaction.

In the bathroom he was dazed enough to let her strip the shorts and shirt from him. She sat him in the old clawfoot tub and sponged his wounds. He had ticks on his arms and neck. He sighed as she washed him down and Georgie wondered how long it had been since anyone had knelt here and bathed him. When he closed his eyes the lids were translucent.

After ten minutes or so he seemed to revive a little. He told her what he'd done, where he'd been, what it took to get home, and she was thankful he wasn't alert enough to ask her how she'd spent the intervening period.

When it came time to get him out she braced herself for the lift but he got up under his own power. Georgie thought of the swabbing and bathing she'd engaged in over the years. The men she'd kneeled to comfort, to clean, to save. This impulse she had. God, she thought, is it any different to the feeling you had looking at Jim the first time and seeing someone bereft, in need of saving? She'd quit the job but it was still Nurse Georgie to the rescue.

She wrapped him in a towel and walked him to the kitchen where she burnt the ticks out of him with a safety pin heated in a gas flame. She felt, she said, like the Grand Inquisitor torturing him for heretical secrets. He smiled drowsily. All secrets, he murmured, are heresies. Georgie painted him with antiseptic cream and rubbed oil into his sunburn. She put him to bed and sat a while, trying to figure out where to go from here. The car first. Somehow she needed to find one of her own.

You don't have any secrets? he asked, eyes fluttering.

You're my secret, she said trying not to think of Mrs Jubail.

He smiled. Well, we've blown that out of the water.

Yes.

I didn't tell you. About Bird. That she lived for a while. On machines. They kept shovin all these forms into my hands. I wasn't gonna do it. I stayed and stayed. Think I just got tired, you know. They wore me down.

It was mercy.

He shook his head. A convenience.

No, Lu.

You don't understand, he murmured.

Believe me, she said, I do.

He sighed.

Do you have an atlas? she asked.

In the library, he said. Why?

Show you my other secret. My island.

By the time she returned with the great dusty tome Luther Fox was asleep. Those eyelids were petal-like, marbled with capillaries like those of a child. She kissed his brow and drank his chickeny breath a moment before pulling the curtains.

Georgie thought of herself a couple of days ago sprawled on this bed, languid as a duchess. With his hand in her, warm and startling.

She stooped and took his hand. Held it to her cheek. Listened to the night beyond the insect screen.

SWIMS IN A WINY SEA. All around him, in a mist, the piping breaths of the dead; they surge and swirl and fin beneath, roundabout, alongside him. It smells of soil, their breath, of soil and creekmud and melons. He hauls himself along with his face out, his limbs butted and glanced by slick bodies, one insistent at his hip knocking again and again in bunting enquiry as he goes on like a metronome, a beat without a melody. The water grows thick with limbs, too tangled to swim through and streams of kelp-like hair snag in his teeth, catch in his throat.

He wakes in the dark room. Curtains spill against the dado wall. Ah. Here.

He pushes the sheet back and winces at the tightness of his hamstrings. He shuffles to the bathroom and then to the kitchen. The house feels emptier than it ever has.

Georgie?

When he turns on the light he finds the atlas on the table. A grubby envelope protrudes from it and he opens the book to read the message written neatly on it.

Promised to return the car.
LOVE, G.

He slides Georgie's note onto the table. It sticks to his damp fingers but his eye is drawn to the page between his hands. Australia. The continent is a craggy frown and half that

144

frown is Western Australia. He's never left the state, never crossed even that lowly a frontier. He traces the faintly mottled deserts that separate his coast from the remainder of the country. It makes for a pretty austere chart. Compared to Asia or the Americas it looks short of names. White Point does not appear; there's a nip of satisfaction in that. Fox anchors his thumb where he estimates himself to be and considers the vast space around him. Such isolation on the page when every bugger in the world is breathing down your neck. He checks the scale and out of boyhood habit lays the short side of the envelope along the map's key to measure units of two hundred miles. South, there's only four hundred or so to the rainy granite coast. Forests, fresh water, people. And to the north? Well, it's all north, isn't it. A thousand miles of the same state. Mostly empty. Until it peters out in the tropic swamps.

Fox follows the coast all the way. The far north looks fractured. So many bays and islands. And he gives a little snort of surprise to see it named. Yes, right at the top near the Timor Sea. Coronation Gulf.

He turns the light out and goes back to bed but he doesn't sleep.

two

BEAVER CAME to the door wiping his mouth and beard on a hank of toilet paper. The service station was shut and dimly lit and from somewhere in his lair behind the office a forties showtune surged and eddied. Beaver's overalls were open to the navel to reveal the droop of his breasts beneath a thin-stretched tee-shirt. He unlocked the glass door and opened it enough to poke his head out.

Who's singing? asked Georgie.

Ethel Merman.

You're a mystery, Beaver.

I am at that.

Sure you won't sell this car? she said handing him the keys to the EH ute.

Written in stone.

I'm desperate, you know.

You'd better go home, George.

Jesus, where's that? she muttered.

Jim's been round twice this arvo already. Says he's got bad news. You should go.

Beaver, he *is* bad news. You don't know him.

Oh, I know him.

The evening air was heavy with the iodine stink of seagrass. A few gulls skirled in Beaver's forecourt lights. The sea sounded like nothing so much as steady traffic. Georgie thought of her modest box of chattels up at the house.

Here, said Beaver holding out a hairy fist. Keep the keys a few days. I'll look around for somethin you can buy.

Georgie stepped up and kissed his hoary cheek.

One day, she said, you'll have to tell me the story of your life.

Well, gimme time to go over me notes.

On her way upstairs Georgie saw Jim's Cruiser parked in the bright-lit garage and she flipped the light switch off as she went. Jim sat in front of the flickering television with the newspaper and a weather fax in his lap. His face looked blue—you couldn't tell if it was the TV or exhaustion. Despite all the open windows the house smelled of eggs and bacon. The sea shimmered with moonlight.

Sit down, Georgie.

I'll stand.

In truth she felt weak enough to lie down right here and sleep.

Sit.

I'll never forgive you for it, she murmured.

Well, I won't be hangin out for *your* forgiveness.

I want you to call it off. Let him be.

I already have, he said.

How did you know?

Know what?

About me and Lu Fox.

Well. Jim folded the papers on his knee and threw them to the floor. It was hearsay until tonight.

150

And who told you tonight?

You did.

As Jim got up she felt herself backing toward the kitchen. He passed her on his way to the office.

Call your sister.

Don't worry, I'll go.

Call Judith, he said over his shoulder. She's been trying to get you all day. Your mother's dead.

GEORGIE'S EARLIEST childhood memory was a shopping expedition with her mother. Herself a toddler in a white nylon harness. The smells of roasting cashews, of doughnuts, cut flowers, steely tinsel. A baby in the pram at her heels. The memory was so crisp—she could see herself plunging at the end of her leash in Hay Street like a Jack Russell terrier surrounded by the retail cheer of Christmas in the city. Both the image of her straining at her bonds and the nature of that expedition struck Georgie as prophetic; they summed up her character and her relationship with her mother.

She'd been a willful little girl, and the older Georgie got, the more people said it. Wayward. If everyone wanted to go north Georgie Jutland went south. She was divergent as though by compulsion. At school she was regarded dubiously as 'a bit of an individual', the kind

151

of phrase Australians still uttered with their mouths set in an uncertain shape, as though sensing something untoward. Nowadays Georgie wondered how self-conscious her maverick attitude had been. In class and in the quad she was recognized as a type and assigned a role that, instead of resisting, she'd embraced and embellished. Within the narrow confines of the prissy private school she became something of a tough nut. On the train in the mornings she knew she was just another princess from the lady-mill. But in her own circumscribed world she made people anxious. She considered herself popular and never understood until years later that girls and teachers disliked her. She read fear as respect. She didn't see how lonely she was.

At home, however, she was under no such illusions. There it was clear. She was the odd one out. She loved her mother—Georgie supposed it should go without saying—but she said it to herself a lot because from an early age she realized that she would never please her. After a certain age she went out of her way to defy the old man—it was food and drink to her—but disappointing her mother was a source of ongoing misery to Georgie.

She was the eldest of four sisters. Georgie, Ann, Judith and Margaret—the Jutland girls. She had felt loved in her way but it puzzled her to see the immense satisfaction her sisters gave her mother as they grew from infancy into girlhood. Their sheer ability to please was unnerving. Their very teeth and hair caused

152

their mother happiness. The enthusiasm with which they wore their frocks and pinnies and their hunger to wear *her* clothes and paste on *her* cosmetics made her queasy. They were ladies in the making. Gels. Georgie's tomboy streak was instinctive and unconscious but by the age of ten her resistance to girlydom had a bitterness to it. She began to dig her heels in. Besides grooming and deportment, her mother's only passion was shopping. It was the shopping that finally cut Georgie off from the other Jutland women. Somehow it drew her sisters together and it kept them close to their mother. Twice a week the four of them laid siege to the boutiques.

Every few years, out of a grimacing loyalty, she made herself go with them, but these interminable outings were indistinguishable from the excursions of girlhood when she'd tramped heavy-lidded behind her mother and hung in doorways stifled by competing scents, bored beyond reason. The swirls of fabric, the clack of nails on registers, the racks and tags and bargains, all made her want to lie down and sleep. Her mother was hurt by her lack of excitement and, long ago, her sisters took Georgie's refusal to shop as a rejection they found hard to forgive.

She left home early, bombed out of Medicine, trained as a nurse and remained a bad example the others were supposed to rise above.

Georgie was in Saudi Arabia when her father, Warwick Jutland QC, left their mother.

So she wasn't home for the tears and the confrontations, the hand-holding, and this too told against her. Within a week of the divorce the old man married a woman only nine days older than Georgie. Cynthia—a nervous, decent woman with a beauty that must have reminded him of Georgie's mother at the same age. She wondered what Cynthia saw in *him*. As a girl Georgie had adored him for his zest and his fun. They sailed together in river regattas and spoke as equals on the water. Yet one day she simply didn't believe in him anymore. She'd thought that he enjoyed her company, that he liked her. But quite suddenly, there on the yacht club dock one Saturday evening with all those back-slapping scions climbing up from their boats, she saw that she was a display, a piece of his success. The feisty sailing daughter destined to be the first woman doctor of the clan. She was a bit of spin, some shine on the Jutland ball. So she'd turned against him.

And now she was parked behind his Jag in Beaver's ute on the glistening lawn, delaying the moment. Angled there beside the Saab and the two Beemers, the EH looked like a statement of the sort she might once have strained to make. She wished that she'd pulled in to the Fox place on her way.

The night was balmy. Before aircondi-tioning, when she was a girl, you could have *heard* the river on a night like this and not simply smelt it.

Ann's husband Derek opened the door with his sad family face on and Georgie heard her-

154

self sigh. Derek was tall and a little stooped and sincerity wasn't his strong suit. In the river suburbs of Perth he was notorious as a bit of a pants man. Even had he not been a dermatologist, the word *squamous* might have come to mind. He greeted Georgie with an embrace of consolation from which he took more than he offered.

They're out on the terrace, he said. Drink?

No. Yes. Vodka martini. She thought: *My mother's dead.*

On the carpet in the livingroom was a long damp patch with an electric fan oscillating across it. It smelt of Pine-O-Cleen and very faintly, despite it all, of urine.

Cerebral haemorrhage, said Derek handing her a glass. Quick at least.

And how long was she there? she asked, realizing he'd put vermouth in with her vodka.

Twelve, eighteen hours.

God.

The pool man found her about lunchtime. Saw her through the french doors.

Where's the body?

Gone.

Oh, she said strangely deflated.

We couldn't get you. Jim said you were going through some kind—

I would've liked to see her.

To dispute the diagnosis, no doubt, he said with a smirk.

She wanted to chuck her drink in his face.

It's a human thing, Derek. You wouldn't understand.

There's a viewing tomorrow.

Sure.

Well. I'll be out with the others.

Georgie stood thinking of her mother tottering around alone in her high heels in this big house. She felt guilty for not being here. Again. Letting it happen. Her lying there all night and half the day with no one but a stranger to find her.

Jude found her crying. She took the drink, hugged her, patted her back. You shouldn't have favourites but Jude was the one. Georgie pressed her face into the soft bulk of her sister's shoulder pad. The linen jacket smelt of lavender, their mother's smell.

How are you, sis?

Under-dressed, she said, noting that Jude was in Dior while she wore Cargo shorts. Where's little Chloe?

We got a sitter. And she's not so little. Ann's kids are asleep upstairs.

How is she?

She's okay. It's Margaret who's the mess.

Still the baby sister.

Christ, she was thirty-two last week.

Oops. I forgot her birthday. Gimme that drink back.

Well, a drink certainly cheers *you* up.

Got to set a bad example.

Oh, God, Georgie, Jude said crumpling. She's really gone.

They stood clinched again for a while until her husband Bob came in and broke it up and steered them outside. Georgie watched how he moved Jude with a firm hand between the shoulderblades.

The yard was a series of terraces that descended toward the river. Lights in the trees looked weirdly festive. The pool was emerald. She thought: I grew up here.

Georgie? cried Ann, already peeved. What are you staring at?

The yard, she said. Seems bigger. I was here for Easter but I'd forgotten. How big it is.

You and your lapses of memory, said Ann. Come and meet Margie's new bloke.

Georgie let herself be propelled from exchange to exchange. None of her sisters had much happiness from men. Ann seemed to endure Derek for the money, and Judith, who looked bombed on Valium again, was miserable with Bob but afraid to leave him for fear of somehow losing her daughter. Margaret's ex was serving time for tax fraud. The youngest of them, Margaret specialized in a kind of petulant neediness that had served her well since infancy, but Georgie, who still remembered having to change her nappies, was finally inured to it. Her new squeeze wore a fez and satin slippers—what was he, an arts bureaucrat?

During every conversation Georgie was aware of Himself QC lurking by the pool, awaiting his sententious moment.

And the conversation—Jesus what was it? There was talk of the *arrangements*, but little about Vera Jutland. What can we say? thought

Georgie. A compliant if distracted wife. A competent and distant mother. Feminine. Good skin, nice manners. Yet how did she distinguish herself? What stories could you tell? It was awful. Even so, it was worse, this suddenly not having her, much worse than not knowing how to be with her.

In the end the old man cornered her by the pool.

Georgiana.

Learned Counsel.

She pecked him on the bricklike cheek. Beneath the stink of his cigar you could smell Bulgari, Cynthia's scent. He had his tartan socks on with the tux. He'd come from something else the moment he heard. Cynthia, out of deference to sensitivities, had stayed on.

Good God, he said. Look at the tan on you.

Life of the fishwife. Got a bit of colour there yourself, she said tilting her glass toward his florid complexion.

Ah. The Tipperary Tan, he said. Every drink you ever had decides to take up residence in your nose. Still, some of it's probably sunburn. We take the boat out to Rottnest most weekends. You still get out?

Georgie shook her head. Think my sailing days might be behind me. Turned forty, you know.

Yes, he said as though he remembered. I know. Shame your mother never liked it. Sailing, I mean.

Well.

But you were a demon for it. I'd love to see

you back on the water. Christ, girl, you sailed to Indonesia.

That's what cured me of it, she said with a hollow laugh.

But, still.

Georgie sensed it coming, his closing address on the subject of her mother. It hung there like a southerly on the horizon. You look well enough, she said, stalling him.

Cynthia's got me on a treadmill.

Then Cyn's been good for you.

Sin? He looked horrified.

Georgie laughed. Look at *you*. Sin? Moi? I meant Cynthia, you drongo.

Oh.

Mum's dead, Dad. You don't have to say anything.

He smiled then, his face a picture of heroic indulgence. I understand.

Georgie sighed. There were actual tears on his cheeks now.

God, I can still see her at Freshwater Bay, 1957. Some university bash. Mauve cashmere sweater, hair flying. So fresh and beautiful. Could have been Audrey Hepburn.

Well you'll have to console yourself with Kristin Scott Thomas.

Who?

I just don't want to hear it again, Dad. Can't you see?

I have my memories, too, you know. What are you *doing*?

Undressing, she said kicking off her shoes and shucking her shorts.

Jesus Christ Almighty! he bellowed as she got out of her smalls and her sleeveless top. Have you lost all decency?

Georgie fell into the pool and lay on the cool smooth bottom beyond the sound of his voice, all their voices.

GEORGIE WAS BARELY twenty-one, a trembling trainee, when she'd first handled a corpse. The charge nurse called her in and explained the administering of last offices, the tidying up of the deceased. Think of it, she said, as housekeeping. Georgie knew the patient, an old bloke called Ted Benson whom she'd nursed for weeks. His death was expected but Georgie was aghast all the same. She was required to bathe him and to plug his orifices and to bind his limbs before he went downstairs to the morgue. Soon after Georgie began the task, the charge nurse was called away and she was left alone with the body. The room felt awfully quiet and the corpse too big for the space. Already it was cool to the touch and she began sponging briskly as though the dome of the belly was a Volkswagen roof, but as she did so she remembered Ted's uncomplaining presence on the ward, his soft voice, his gentlemanly deference, and the memory shamed her a little and calmed her down. She began to pay a different attention to his remains. She rinsed his face and patted it dry as delicately as she had when he was alive. She found herself whispering to him soothingly as you do to a patient who's submitting himself to your care. Georgie was no longer sorry to have the job; she was just sorry she'd been unable to save him. I liked you Ted, she said. I admired your dignity, you know. I miss you already. She wadded him, bound his ankles and jaw tenderly and knew when she was finished that she had found a pure part of herself. The room felt holy.

To the surprise and consternation of the others, Georgie refused all offers of a bed for the night and stayed on in her mother's house when everybody left. The place felt desolate. It was just her, and her mother's stain. In the morning she had an urge to swim naked once more in the pool. She began with a few lazy laps for the sensation of it, for the clean fizz of bubbles against her belly. Then she settled into a firmer rhythm, a hard stroke that caused her muscles to burn until she was swimming in a state of rage. It was that ghostly damp patch on the carpet. The sign of a final opportunity gone begging. None of them would understand but she really would have cherished just half an hour alone with her mother before the undertakers arrived. To undress her, yes, and wash her, to sponge away the cosmetic crust that had disguised her in life, all that lippy, the foundation and rouge, the pencil and eyeshadow. Gently. With reverence. Not in anger or triumph, but as a daughterly offering. To relieve each of them of their burden. All you ever wanted was to show her what you did best, to have her understand something about you. And to prove that you could love her. In a quiet room, alone. Before the essence of her was gone. Before your heart finally shrank to the size of a dried fig.

Georgie heard her name in the water. A hand appeared in the spotty blue haze.

Georgiana!

It was Ann. She was kneeling at the end of the pool, wriggling her hand in the water like a dolphin trainer.

For Godsake, Georgie.

Georgie stood with her head against the tiles and tried to breathe. She felt hot and faint in her sister's shadow. Her body felt poisoned. She began to shake.

Wasn't last night enough for you? Ann cried. The kids are here. It's Saturday, the day of your mother's funeral, and you're skinny dipping like a teenager in her pool?

Georgie looked up at Ann in her Chanel suit.

And wipe your nose. God, here they come.

Hello Aunty Georgie, chimed Blake from the steps. Her sundress made her face look yellow. Her new teeth looked too big for her mouth. Beside her, young Jared smirked.

You're a nudist.

The rudest nudist, Jared.

The kids covered their mouths and looked sideways at their mother as if for permission to laugh.

Jim called, Georgie.

Oh.

He's coming down.

No.

I just assumed.

Oh, God.

I don't understand you, Ann said. It's noon already. Get out.

Georgie climbed up the ladder and stood a moment looking about for the towel she'd forgotten to bring down. After a moment she registered the kids' eyes wide as anemones and she was just turning to Ann when her sister grabbed her in a blanketing hug that felt for a few moments like love but was, she realized, nothing more than shame.

Later that day Georgie sat in the baking black limousine while the others trooped in to view the body. Nobody spoke when they rejoined her in the funeral car.

The service itself was a model of discretion and taste. The presence of Warwick Jutland QC put the vicar into an obsequious tizzy and it seemed to Georgie that her father was eulogized as much as her dead mother. As she mouthed the tepid, tootling hymns familiar from school, she wondered why it fell to Derek to speak about their mother. During the sermon it dawned on her that she'd suffered a terrible sunburn to the buttocks and the longer the service went the tighter her skin became until, near the end, she had the feeling her arse had blown up to twice its usual size.

Later, at the crematorium, which had the décor and atmosphere of a three-star hotel lobby, Jim and the boys appeared in the upholstered pew beside her as though by arrangement. Jim's suit fitted him perfectly but he still managed to look too big for it. The boys looked bewildered. Georgie wondered whether they'd been at their own mother's funeral. Conversations of that sort had always been tacitly out-of-bounds. As the coffin descended through the marble floor, a handkerchief appeared in Georgie's lap and she looked up, startled, to see Josh lean back into place beside his father. She knew the hanky—she'd once ironed it into its little square—but she'd never seen it leave Josh's drawer before. She stared at it while the crematorium filled with the sound of Barbra Streisand.

The wake was at Derek and Ann's. Jude lay on a bed and sobbed. Afterwards Jim drove Georgie back to her mother's, and the boys sat downstairs to watch TV while she and Jim went to her old bedroom to talk. She felt numb. She didn't know why he was there or why she'd consented to have him drive her. She felt conspired against and her backside hurt.

You've been talking to Ann, she said standing at the window while he sat on her narrow bed with its dire pink coverlet.

Hard not to, he murmured. Funeral and all.

She sighed. You could see the river glittering through the boughs of the lemon-scented gums. The flame tree was twice the size she remembered.

164

I didn't realize you still kept your stuff here, he said.

When she looked back he was surveying the mountain of gear her mother must have been dusting all these years. He was right. On the rare occasions that she'd come up here in the past few years it just looked like furniture she'd acquired somehow. All this stuff accreted with her barely aware. The room felt progressively smaller but now she saw that it was the simple volume of junk not the passage of time that caused it. The suitcase with its sticker scabs, the rucksack and crates of souvenirs and knick-knacks. Poster tubes, boxes of LPs, the stereo. On the little desk the piles of postcards and photographs and a *jambiyya* dagger which Jim drew from its scabbard, to gaze solemnly along the blade the way men will. She looked away and saw the shelves with their rows of textbooks. *Patterns of Shock, Key to Psychiatry, Oncology for Nurses and Health Care Professionals* (in two volumes), *The Lippincott Manual of Nursing Practice*. They were thick and hard as hospital mattresses, and probably long-outdated. On the wall were framed photos that her mother must have put there. Georgie in school uniform with the Charlie's Angels hair she had before she hacked it off and dyed it purple. Her in the Saudi desert somewhere with camels, her eyes like postal slits against the glare. And her in a miniskirt and Oakleys on the hood of a convertible in Baja California.

Your whole life's here, he said.

165

I haven't lived here since I was eighteen.

But you keep everything here.

She shrugged.

What's happening to this place?

Who knows. I guess there'll be a will.

Be worth a packet.

I suppose.

Georgie—

The boys have been good.

Yeah. Listen, I want to talk about the sha-mateur.

I can't.

Fair enough. But sometime.

Maybe.

You'll be back?

I need to think.

Right.

He got up from the bed. She looked at the Axminster and saw the furrows of the Electrolux still there. Her mother's presence.

I'll get going, he said. Before dark. Don't fancy dodging the roos.

Thanks for coming, she said.

She went down for the sake of appearances to see the boys off. She stood on the neat lawn verge and waved like a relative. Before they'd rounded the corner she turned for the house but was ambushed by the sprinkler system.

About eight that evening she was sitting by the pool with a tall glass of mineral water and a few citronella candles when Ann came down the steps in her heels. The night was stifling hot and the garden heavy with the scent of frangipani and the stink of chlorine.

There you are.

Here I am.

Bob had to call a doctor. Jude was beside herself. Gave her a tranquillizer.

Poor Jude.

I half thought you'd be gone. Christ, it's hot.

Have a swim.

No.

They sat at the table, their legs lit by the pool and their faces by the candles whose murky lemon odour rose into sweeter smells overhead.

I can't bear to think of her gone, said Ann.

I know.

But you wouldn't come in with us to see her. I just don't understand you, Georgie. We wanted to go in together. Like sisters. And you're doing this tough-girl thing, acting as though it's all a bit of an inconvenience.

I didn't want to see her like that, said Georgie, knowing that it was impossible to explain. If Jude didn't understand she stood no chance with Ann.

You're a nurse! Even Margaret managed.

I'm sorry, Ann.

Is that vodka? Ann asked, pointing at the glass of water.

Yes, Georgie lied.

Do you have a problem?

I have a number, as it happens.

Does Jim know?

Jim knows all, believe me.

I saw you talking to Dad.

What's wrong, Ann? You look like you've come here for something specific. Honestly, I don't want a fight.

So why are you staying here?

I've got a few things to sort out, sis, I just needed one night's breather.

You've seen the will, haven't you?

What are you—

It just makes me wild. The cool attitude. You suddenly hanging around our mother's house.

Ann?

It's just so...brazen. Sitting here by the pool as though you already own it.

As she uncrossed her legs Ann's stockings crackled with static.

You're just tired, sis.

Some of us have responsibilities.

I know that, love.

No, you don't. You don't know what it's like to be trapped.

In a marriage, you mean.

No, Georgie. Financially.

You and Derek have money trouble? Georgie asked in genuine surprise which probably sounded to Ann like amused disbelief.

Me.

You mean debts?

Try not to sound so blinking superior.

How did this happen?

I went into business with Margaret. Well, I was the silent partner.

Oh, no.

You want us to beg you?

And that's why you came to see me tonight?

You hardly even knew our mother. And we need the money.

So have the money.

Ann began to sob.

Georgie found herself unable to comfort her sister and curiously unwilling as well.

I'll be gone in the morning, she said.

WITH ALL THE SYMPTOMS of a hangover that she hadn't earned, Georgie packed everything she wanted from her old bedroom into Beaver's ute and drove down through the dress circle suburbs to the river at Crawley where she pulled in for a moment to see an old bloke dive from the jetty and set out in a gentlemanly crawl across the shining water. In their pens the boats at the yacht club were a scene from a Sunday painting, their masts a thicket of silver and white.

She thought of the mirrors and moths she'd sailed from there. The Australs and Robertses and Farrs the old man's friends raced. The Swarbrick they once had. The twilight meets. The mad, ploughing reach in from Rottnest.

As she wheeled the EH back onto the road, she glimpsed the arches and ovals of the university and wondered if those two years when she blew Medicine were the sabotage she presented to her father or the real failure she privately suspected.

She drove down Mounts Bay Road and watched the river between the date palms. At the old Swan Brewery site the Aboriginal protesters seemed to have packed up and gone back to their camps. Around the bend the commercial district loomed. There was nothing left in this city for her. She should never have come back from abroad. She'd never live here again.

It was noon when she pulled in off the highway at the old fruit stand and her mood began to evaporate as she thought about Luther Fox and all her chattels in his house. They needn't go into White Point anymore. They could shop in the city once a week and use the short cut to the beach. And there was the river. The peaceful silence of the place. And music. A houseful of books. She needn't rescue him; she'd just be *with* him. They'd plant trees and he could grow melons again. It was a real chance, wasn't it?

The chooks fluttered from beneath the house when she got out. We'll compare sunburns, she thought, feeling her butt. The hens threw themselves at her shins in a way that startled her. She saw the back door closed behind the insect screen. She caught her breath a moment and stepped up. It was locked. She went round to the front, blood ticking in her throat, and saw that it too was bolted. Before she even began to call and knock she knew he was gone.

On the verandah table a couple of riverstones stood in the dust left by mosquito coils. Crows gave out single syllables from the clump of casuarinas. Georgie took the sounds as irony. How else could you hear it?

She took up a stone and pitched it out into the paddock and then followed up with its companion. They made little thuds in the dirt. Pats, really. Tiny, taunting pats. She stood at the rail and held it and did not cry for some time.

She hadn't pride enough to resist a tour of the sheds and the riverbend. She checked the hill above the quarry despite the certainty of his not being there. She told herself it might be temporary. But where does a man without a car go to for a day or so? He doesn't pop off to the shops, for Godsake. She knew he'd bolted. He'd left her to the wolves.

A last, sputtering hope stayed with her until she pulled in to Beaver's. It was faintly possible that he'd hitched in to look for a vehicle, could even be waiting there. But Beaver didn't say a word. He seemed disinclined. She drove to Jim's because she had nowhere else to go. She had a car full of junk and no clean clothes. She could not think.

The house was empty but, as ever, unlocked. She saw that the squalid remains of her night in the spare room had been cleaned up. Between the exercise bike and the recliner-rocker that was forever about to be re-upholstered, a bed was neatly made and at one end of the mattress stood the carton she'd half packed days before. She went down and unpacked the car.

It was two hours before Jim came in. He dropped a plastic bag of something in the sink and saw her there on the sofa.

Took the boys trolling for tailor, he said.

Any luck?

Yeah.

Where are they?

Down the jetty. Hot as hell.

I'll cook, she said.

If you like. I'll fillet them out.

Yeah.

You orright?

Georgie shrugged.

Want a drink?

No.

How your sisters takin it?

Fighting over money.

Already. Gawd.

Who skippered today? Who took *Raider* out?

Boris.

Oh.

I didn't really expect to see you, he said.

You want me to go?

You don't have to.

Georgie watched the big boats snuffle up to their moorings bronzed and silhouetted by the westering sun.

I think I'm quite within my rights in not being prepared to beg, though, he said.

Beg?

You can stay on your own terms. Really. I don't mind.

Georgie looked at the dry white skin on her knees.

The boys and I, he murmured, we appreciate what you've done for us.

Sounds like you've had a team meeting.

Sort of, he said turning to wash his hands. Josh feels like he's been giving you a hard time and he's feeling bad about it.

Because my mum died?

Jim rinsed his hands and wiped them. Even from where she sat you could see how huge and brown they were, how burled with scars.

They're not stupid. They pick up on stuff. They're hearing things already. Every kid in town has a father or brother on the boats. I don't want them to feel like it's their fault.

What?

How you are. What you're doing. I'm busting my nuts to be reasonable, Georgie.

Sounds like ambivalence to me.

I woulda thought you'd be grateful for complete bloody indifference, he said flaring up at her stupid, flip tone. Anyone else in this town would have knocked your teeth out and put you on the step like a sick cat.

Here it comes, she thought. This is what you've always feared. Deep down.

Well, she said, her heartbeat right there in her voice, a girl should be grateful she's in the hands of a gentleman.

Fuckin right.

So the Buckridges close ranks. Pull in the washing. Show them we've sorted out our differences?

You wouldn't even recognize the differences, Georgie.

Oh, I might.

Why do you do this? Jesus, your sisters are right. You think you're too good. You turn things to shit.

She got up, more stung than afraid, but when he came across from the sink she backed away.

Sit down, he said.

Go to hell.

Sit the fuck down.

You think you're so bloody civilized, she said with her last gasp of defiance. Because you went to some snob-factory school and read Shakespeare and *rowed* like a champion. But I know what you are. I know now.

Sit down!

He came at her so fast she sat down without thinking.

I'm trying to tell you, he hissed. I didn't do it. I didn't approve it or organize it. I don't have a fucking firearm and I'm not happy that it happened. Are you hearing this? I'm saying stay or don't fucking stay because I feel bad about it and because I'm *trying* to be decent. I have children. My life is bigger than you and who you play with and what you think. But you might consider how decent you've been. You might like to think about that. You don't know what I am. You can't even see what you are.

Georgie closed her eyes. She felt the sun find her there on the sofa, its heat creeping down her face to her chest. She wouldn't have been surprised to discover that in its glare her bones showed clear beneath her skin.

IN THE WEEKS before Christmas, while the fleet pursued lobsters on their annual migration west into deep water, Georgie stayed on at Jim's in a state of sober, confounded lethargy. Within a day or so of returning she resumed her household duties which she discharged with a competence that belied the mess she was in. She felt cauterized inside. After the funeral and Ann's outburst, after lobbing up to the empty farmhouse and then enduring Jim Buckridge's withering homily, she had the sensation of having been pushed outside herself. The routine was a kind of shelter. She didn't even think about her daily offices; they just happened to her. They were what she lived.

She kept to the spare room and Jim to his office. The boys were subdued, even solicitous. Georgie felt reduced to a working house-guest. The skin peeled off her sunburnt arse and gave her a shabby look that, as the fog began to thin in her head, she began to see as emblematic.

Jim rose hours before dawn now that the deepwater run was on. He was travelling between twenty and forty miles to get to his lines and each pot lay in darkness at the end of a rope the length of the Eiffel Tower. It was something he used to joke about, winching crays from touristic depths, but now in those few hours he was around and awake, he said little. He was courteous, almost courtly, but not familiar.

Some afternoons, when she found herself without chores to occupy her, Georgie sat out on the terrace and watched trucks come and go from the jetty, bait trucks, live trucks, freezer trucks. Some trucks were piled high with coils of orange and yellow rope. She could no more imagine all that rope in the water than she could take in the idea of the tonnes of lobsters arriving alive in Tokyo that night.

She stayed away from the beach. She shopped for supplies in the city. The only time she ventured outside was to hang washing, and then the light felt too bright.

What finally roused Georgie from her state of suspension was anger, but it was, for a time, hard to identify the source of this fury which persisted morning and night like heartburn. Ann's griping calls about the secrecy over the will were merely an irritant, and Judith, whose emails seemed to fluctuate from whimsy to misery within the space of a single day, had begun to worry her a little. It was driving by the old fruit stand on the highway on her first trip back into the city that brought this anger into focus. It was Luther Fox. His cowardice. And the humiliation of being abandoned. She had torched her whole life in White Point for his sake and he couldn't wait a couple of days while she buried her mother and gathered her wits. It was the misery of knowing that she'd done it to herself again, been suckered by her own stupid urge to rescue lame ducks. This time, though, she'd really exposed herself to someone. She'd been more than intrigued by Lu. She was gone on him the way she never had been before and he turned out to be just another self-absorbed prick. What had she been thinking anyway? He was a farmboy, some creepy, secretive thief with a death wish. A grieving mess. She was no better than those bourgeois princesses who fall in love with tattooed prisoners. You had to ask yourself if this entire sordid episode of finding yourself caught between a big-knuckled fisherman and his hillbilly rival was anything more than a pointless and embarrassing per-petuation of her adolescent rebellion. At forty did a woman still need to go to such extremes to define herself against her family? She was furious with herself about it, but it was only simple stupidity. It's not as though she'd cut and run. She wasn't like Fox; she was no coward.

For a while she felt sorry for Jim and guilty for shaming him before his peers. But she began to see that his wounds were hardly mortal. When things settled down she could see that he was pained but not devastated.

His reaction puzzled her. It was not that he was without emotion. She had seen him hurt, ruined, incapacitated—that was the state in which she first knew him. Debbie's death had all but killed him. You could tell he'd loved her; and, in truth, the afterglow of that devo-tion was part of what attracted Georgie those early days on Lombok. But it was chastening now to see the difference. Georgie saw that his feelings had never run so deep for her. Not even in the ballpark. She supposed she'd always known—after all it was mutual. The heat of her interest had been as much for his situation as for him. Yet it stung to realize that Jim Buckridge had been merely...well, fond of her. And now she had nothing while he was visibly re-grouping. She had no idea of where to go or what to do.

Jude's emails became more weird and insistent. She posted things which might be jokes but they made no sense. Georgie stopped trashing them. After a few days they racked up in the mailbox like an anthology of demented koans. Georgie knew she should call her.

She began to venture onto the beach. To avoid sticky meetings with White Pointers she kept clear of the jetty and favoured distant stretches of the lagoon. On the point itself windsurfers from out of town rigged up on the bonnets of their clapped-out stationwagons, among them Swedes, Danes and Germans who came every year for the wind that drove others mad. In their fluoro wetsuits they looked like übermenschen. She felt invisible in their midst. Out on the bay and against the towering surf of the outer reefs a hundred sails raced and flew. Georgie walked the lonely beaches south where she saw nothing but windblown cuttles and the pounding relay of the shorebreak. Some days she hiked for hours but like a domesticated creature she eventually turned back to the enclosure she knew best.

• • •

One afternoon, almost home, she lay in the pig-face blanket between dunes and wept for her mother. She had only stopped to rest and escape the breeze a moment, but the long fingers of the succulent groundcover brushed against her face and suddenly reminded her of her mother's hands on her cheeks. How long had it been since her mother'd done that, held her face and really looked at her the way a mother will? She missed the plainness of early childhood, the years when you lived without a mask, without acting your part. Those days Georgie just wanted her; hadn't learnt to hide her child-hurt by pretending she didn't care.

Georgie sobbed till she was hoarse, until there was nothing left but a spent calm. There in her hollow between the dunes she looked up and saw specks and bubbles in the air. The sky was a sea, blue as a coma. Around her, bees toiled in the pink blossoms, their drone soporific, musical. The shadows of dragonflies fell across the bared skin of her belly. Sand creaked beneath her. The dune, now she listened, seemed to thrum like a boiling kettle. Georgie lay there for some time in a sort of over-heated swoon while the world teemed.

That night Jude called. She seemed in such high spirits. It turned out that all their mother's savings, her shares, the house and a yacht that nobody had the slightest knowledge of had been left to Warwick Jutland QC. It was

179

astounding. He was already wealthy. He was her faithless ex-husband, for crying out loud. It was hilarious. Georgie found herself laughing for the first time in a while. Our sisters, said Jude, aren't taking it quite so well.

BEAVER SAW HER some days. There were times he wished he could say something to her. She was like someone who didn't realize they'd wandered into the cinema during the third reel. There was so much stuff she didn't know about this place, about Buckridge, even about himself. Christ, things she couldn't imagine. She might have made a confidante, an ally, and God knows he could have helped more than he had but there was so much frigging backstory it was hopeless. He liked her. Fancied her, if he was honest. But she'd be gone soon. Like a bloody sub-plot. He kept his eye out for a decent car. It was best she went. He didn't need Big Jim breathing down his neck a moment longer than was necessary.

Shame, though. She had the sort of face you only saw in wank mags. The fuck-*you* look. Must have been a firecracker once. Like Jennifer Jason Leigh.

◆　◆　◆

GEORGIE BEGAN DREAMING once more of Mrs Jubail. She woke in a panic and went through the house and turned on lights.

Mrs Jubail was from a middling merchant family in Jeddah. She'd probably never been beautiful but you guessed she had mild features to suit her gentle disposition. Before the fungating sarcoma colonized her face she'd probably suffered the veil as all women did in Saudi, but by the time Georgie encountered her the poor woman craved concealment so much that you could barely get at the horrible tumour for shrouds of black linen. She held the veil to her chest fearful and ashamed. The cancer was so advanced and so bewilderingly aggressive that the staff all knew the moment they saw her that this was a purely palliative situation. The woman's family was strangely absent. Every week or so an emissary from the Jubail clan came to reception twitching his *thobe* nervously to ask after her condition, the sorry details of which were usually delivered by a fellow male.

The miserable patient writhed and sweated beneath her cover while that mask of vegetative tissue consumed her day by day. From out in the corridor you could smell her, foul and sweet as compost. The surface of her cheek was like a rotten cauliflower and only one eye, compressed into a slit by the pressure of swelling, could follow you round the room while you prepared her pissant treatments on the

181

trolley. Her English was quite good. Once, before the analgesia and the heavier tranquillizers took over, she said she would like to see Australia. She asked was it true that Arabs imported camels from there. Georgie told her of the wild herds in the north that were the legacy of the Afghan traders. Early on in her time in hospital, Mrs Jubail was afraid. Before long she was reduced to addled puzzlement.

In order to deal with that face up close Georgie found that she had to make a monster of herself. Her bedside dialogue had a flippancy to it that felt spiky as a carapace. Tough and tender, that's how the girls in oncology saw themselves. But you knew when you'd lost the tenderness. She'd seen people suffer and die before and a few who suffered and lived for what that was worth, but she'd never struggled with simple visceral disgust to this degree before. It built to the point where you could barely perform the most basic clinical procedures on her without giving in to a kind of hysterical convulsion which threatened your competence as a caregiver. One time, after supervising the irrigation of Mrs Jubail's tumour, Georgie stood in the corridor beyond her room wracked with giggles. Her laughter turned heads along the ward. It must have been audible to the patient. And while her junior colleague looked on, Georgie bent double with shrieks and peals that degenerated into gulping, horrible sobs.

Mrs Jubail, of course, died. It seemed to Georgie that she'd been well cared for. Short of killing her, they'd spared her as much suffering as the law permitted. Had Mrs Jubail asked, Georgie knew that she would probably not have euthanased her. It was madness in a country like that. She had a career to think of.

Georgie was away when Mrs Jubail died. She was skin diving up at Sharm Abhur with two doctors—a couple of Brits she didn't mind. They got back to the compound late in the day where a radiologist friend gave her the news. Instantly Georgie could tell that her contented sigh seemed inappropriate. She didn't even feel the smile on her face, but she saw it in the reaction of her friend, who wheeled in confusion toward the pool, and she heard about it later that week around the compound, about what a callous bitch she was. It was there that she lost the magic, the belief she had in herself and her chosen path.

At White Point, in the lead-up to Christmas, Georgie had Mrs Jubail come visiting in her sleep. Down hardlit corridors with her veil thrown back and her grisly face out-thrust behind those arms. Sister! Sister? Georgie ran and used the steel trolley to batter her way through stone and glass in a shower of paper cups and ampoules. The sweet smell blew on her. And there was always a wall, a blind alley she couldn't broach.

♦   ♦   ♦

GEORGIE HAD ALWAYS LIKED to cook but now she felt herself pitching toward mania in the kitchen. It felt counterfeit in a way, but there was some satisfaction in the companionable silence they all enjoyed at dinner. She rendered them speechless with the variety and the quantity of food she cooked. It became a form of management. She didn't know what else to do.

She was cooking osso buco one afternoon in the last week of school when Brad came in to snaffle a piece of celery.

What's that? he asked.

Bone marrow.

Cool.

Georgie looked at her hands to avoid looking into his face. It was the first non-essential conversation they'd had in a while.

Zoë Miller likes me, he said.

Cool.

But I don't get it.

What, mate?

What she wants. I don't even talk to her. I mean *you're* a girl.

Um, yeah.

What is it, then? That youse want.

I don't know, she stammered. What does anyone want?

Well, boys just wanna be left alone. With our mates. Anyway she's Monkey Miller's kid. He's a greenie. They're rubbish.

I thought she was so nice, she said in a small voice.

He shrugged and looked hungrily at the shanks she was browning.

Beaver found her a car. Some Norwegian sailboarder had to fly home in a hurry and Beaver had bought it with her in mind. It was, he said, a cherry. When Georgie got down there, though, and looked at what lay behind the door that he hauled up so laboriously on its chain, she saw that it was more jellybean than cherry. The little Mazda was canary yellow. It was so tiny she wondered why he'd gone to the trouble of cranking up the roller when it would have been easier to bring the thing out under one arm through the office.

Sons of Thor, he chuckled. Can they pick a colour or what?

A bubble car.

Like a ju-jube with jaundice, eh.

Georgie shook her head ruefully. You had to smile.

Does it go, Beaver?

Runs like a kid at bathtime.

This Euro had boards and masts and sails strapped on it?

Beaver laughed. Well, he had the car strapped to the gear, put it that way.

Okay, she said. I'll take it.

But we haven't haggled.

You do both sides, Beaver. I'll pay whatever you wear yourself down to.

Oh. Righto.

You got the keys and papers?

Yeah, yeah. Listen, sorry about your mum.

Georgie realized that Beaver had probably known about her mother's death before she did. That and plenty besides, she imagined. More than she cared to think about.

Tell me something, Beaver.

No worries, he said patting his pockets, licking his lips.

Had she imagined the tiny tremor of wariness that came over him?

Did you tow the truck and trailer? she asked.

Keys must be in the ignition.

Beaver? The F-100.

Whose?

You know whose. Lu Fox.

Ah. Melon boy. Nope.

Georgie followed him inside across the oily floor to the tiny yellow car. He had to squat to look in the window.

I don't know what I'm doing, Beaver.

You'll be gone soon. Don't worry about it.

Why d'you stay?

He shrugged. It's somewhere.

You know anything about shotguns?

Plenty, he said resting his elbows on the roof.

Did you help him?

He didn't do it, Georgie.

Least you both got your story straight.

It was Shover.

Shover McDougall?

He's a fuckin loose cannon.

Georgie considered it. Shover McDougall

was not an unlikely prospect. He was paranoid and litigious, universally despised as a cutter of ropes and spoiler of potlines. He was a teetotaller and hated drugs. Last season he'd rammed another vessel. He was a supremely successful lobsterman. He had a kid in Josh's class.

How do you know? she asked.

That's the word.

From Jim.

That's the word, Georgie.

But why?

Aw, don't be wet. Havin a shamateur flittin about on the water's bad enough, but there's poachin and there's poachin, love. Shover probly thought he was doin it for honour. Thinks the fisher kings've gone soft in their old age. Figures Jim didn't know or didn't have the balls anymore. He always idolized Jim, you know. Bet he did it out of love. Christ, don't you ever see his missus drivin up and down like a fuckin spy satellite? The satanic white Camry?

Georgie considered it. Yes, it rang a bell. The car leaving Jim's the night she returned.

Shover McDougall, she said.

And don't get any ideas. Loves a feud. He's the good ole days, Georgie. Not even Jim could see him off anymore unless he killed him.

Georgie blinked at this.

Relax, I'm jokin.

Yeah.

That bloke, he was somethin out of the box.

Shover?

No, your mate. Fox. He could really play. They all could. I towed the wreck, you know. The cab, inside the cab, it was like a friggin slaughterhouse. No belts, I spose. But you never seen anythin like it. Four dead in one rollover. People said it was too freaky, like an act of God. Their kind of luck.

Suddenly so forthcoming, Beaver, Georgie said, unable to listen to any more of this.

You know me. Ingratiatin under pressure.

Georgie drove home via the McDougall place, where she pulled over a moment to stare at its fortress façade. Behind the high steel fence and the avenue of cocos palms it hulked on the foredune, all electric window shutters and security alarms.

Shover McDougall. She'd seen him at school concerts, tall and balding with the perpetual sidelong glance of the maltreated pet. His wife Avis was a dumpy, intense woman with an underslung jaw which Brad likened to that of a potato cod. Shover and Avis. Two more reasons to leave. After Christmas. She'd wait until then. It was only days away.

At dinner that night nobody mentioned the little yellow car in its slot downstairs beside the Cruiser. They hooked into their lamb fillets and thyme-roasted potatoes and watched a yacht motor in through the passage and drop anchor directly below them. Georgie was grateful for the distraction. She admired the boat's lines. It was a Dufour, she decided, a nice piece of work. A man and woman went about the business of making fast for the night with a weariness she understood too well.

Good tucker Georgie, said Brad.

She picked up her knife and fork, a little startled, and caught the exchange of glances.

Next morning, on a whim, she swam out to the anchored yacht in the hope of striking up a conversation, perhaps being invited aboard. She needed respite and the vision of the lovely long white boat brought on fantasies she was still not immune to.

She stroked languidly across the seagrass flats. Mooring chains clanked in the water. Sculling closer she saw the kevlar hull stained with rust and spilt oil. The steelwork was dull and wet-gear was strung in the lines like a party of flogged matelots. The steering vane looked battered out of shape and a familiar mouldy locker-smell hung over the water. A rough passage. This time of year you'd be heading south away from the monsoon storms but you'd be punching into southerlies all the way. Georgie thought of offering the use of her washing machine, a meal perhaps. But as she glided within reach of the boat's transom, the woman rose from the cockpit with such a fierce stare that she swam by as though she hardly noticed the boat was there.

The bleached, strawy hair. Face burnt and peeling. Shadows like kohl-smears beneath the eyes. The thousand-yard stare. Georgie knew all about it. She wondered if, beneath that stare the woman was thinking of her luck, protecting it, even disbelieving it after her passage. Only three years ago Georgie had felt that her crossing of the Timor Sea was a feat of luck from which she might never recover. There were times when she suspected you could use up your allocation of good fortune in a single massive stroke like that. Now she was certain of it. But where did that leave her? How did you live a life knowing you're arse-out of luck?

ONE AFTERNOON, without any warning or precedent, Georgie's sister Judith turned up at the door in a sundress, mascara in wretched streaks down her face.

Josh looked on horrified as Jude fell into Georgie's arms and wept in the hallway. After a few moments he retreated to the games room and Georgie took her sister out onto the terrace where the sea breeze was only just stirring.

I just. Miss. My mum, Jude said between awful gulping sobs.

I know, sis, Georgie murmured. I know.

Jude was scalding to the touch. Her lavender scent had a cooked smell about it and the back of her neck was livid with a pimply rash. When Georgie brought her sister's face up to hers she saw that there were blood vessels burst in her eyes from force of weeping. It was a chastening sight. Georgie had only ever achieved red blots like that from kneeling at the toilet bowl, poisoned with booze. It made Georgie feel low: she'd never cried that hard in her life.

Where's Chloe, Jude? School's out, isn't it?

She's at a friend's. Her friend Angela has such a *happy* family.

She pulled her sunglasses down over her eyes.

Aha, said Georgie.

What is it with us, Georgie? Us and men.

Georgie hesitated.

I mean, Jude went on, look at Ann. She's married to a—

Shit.

Well, yes. He doesn't *love* her. She's an incubator for his offspring. He makes her feel so small and inadequate. It's like watching Mum all over. Dad was such a pig to her and she couldn't see it.

Georgie knew that this talk of Ann's marriage was little more than Jude's veiled confession about her own.

What about Margaret, though, Jude? She's no victim. She eats men.

That's just insecurity.

Georgie laughed at this. Her sister seemed surprised.

How bout a swim, sis?

Jude shook her head. I didn't bring anything to wear.

Borrow mine. I've got spares.

Jude looked mortified at the idea.

191

So, just go in your smalls.

What, like you in Mum's pool? In front of the kids, Georgie—I don't think Ann'll ever get over it.

It's not in Ann's nature to get over things, Jude. Anyway, I paid for it. Out of my own hide, no less.

The sou'wester began to stir the cotton palms. Jude knitted her lips. She looked out across the brilliant lagoon as though it were no more interesting than an eight-lane freeway.

This is about Bob and you, isn't it?

I just can't *believe* she'd give Dad everything.

Have you thought about counselling? Georgie persisted.

You know I always admired your spirit of adventure.

Oh, Jude, stop it. You always thought I was bringing the family into disrepute.

That was Ann. She thought you might be...playing for the other team.

A lesbian?

It was that photo you sent from America. You and the other girls with that big car. Like *Thelma & Louise*.

Geez, I *hate* that film.

But Brad Pitt.

Jude—

Anyway, you sailed to Asia with that bloke.

Brad Pitt?

Near enough.

Jude, that guy was a dickhead.

Gorgeous, though.

He couldn't even navigate.

Dad's going to give you the boat, you know. The yacht she left him.

Hell, said Georgie, aghast, I don't want it.

We haven't talked like this in ages, said Jude airily. Have you got a glass of water?

Georgie fetched her a drink and watched her swallow a couple of tablets.

I was the one who loved you, George. But you never took me along.

Oh, Jude.

No matter. Must fly.

Georgie found herself trailing her sister to the door as Josh sidled out from his room. She kissed Jude fiercely and felt her sudden stiffness, the self-consciousness returned. As she swayed across the buffalo grass in that sundress Josh stood at Georgie's side.

That your sister?

Yeah.

Oh. She's pretty.

Yeah.

They watched her fold herself delicately into the black Saab.

She's gonna back into the tree, said Josh.

You could be right. Don't look. Ow!

Josh shook his head the way his father would and their eyes met, but the boy sensed that it was best to say nothing and Georgie was glad of it. Jude had made a five-hour round trip for a fifteen-minute chat. She'd never been here before. The pills were Valium, she was certain, and Jude was blasted. She was totally stuck; they both were. They'd gone in opposite directions to the same end, to become their poor hopeless mother.

•   •   •

With the Bette Davis festival suspended by tacit agreement, Georgie sat out on the terrace to watch the masthead light of the yacht anchored below and think of the adventures that Jude pretended to envy. Chances were she'd gilded the lily in the recounting of them at miserable family barbecues, and now she felt like a phony. She had driven down the west coast of the States and into Mexico but it wasn't as glamorous as it sounded, even after the austerities of the Arab world. And Tyler Hampton was beautiful in his bermudas and open silk shirts but there was less to him than met the eye. That wild drive through the States had been mostly bitching and collapsing friendships, and the voyage with Tyler from Fremantle to Lombok had been marked by fear and confusion. Yet some things lingered untainted in the imagination. Like the gulf they had come to as they ran before a squall at the extremity of the Australian coast. It was a long gut of milky-blue water edged by beaches and belts of mangroves. Around its mouth was a rash of islands and at its end loomed a great steamy plateau. In the lee of the biggest of the islands, only half a mile from the mainland, they had anchored in the late afternoon, silenced by fatigue and relief. Across the water dry stone ranges rose in grand disorder into the smoky distance. The country here looked like cured hide. It was wilderness of a sort that Georgie had not encountered before and the island they

194

sheltered behind was a wilderness within a wilderness. The moment she saw it Georgie felt that she'd seen it before.

It was a great red rock skirted by rainforest, like a mesa grown up through a garden. On its white shelly beach were boabs and vines and from its cliff faces where the late sun flared yellow, pink and purple, came the looping echoes of birdsong. Georgie couldn't understand this feeling of recognition. It was iconic Australian landscape but not even twenty years of nationalist advertising could account for this sensation. It even smelt right, as familiar as the back of her arm, like a place she came to every night in her sleep.

Before dawn they were in trouble. By eight that morning they were high and dry.

They spent two days trying to motor and then winch off the mudbank that they'd stupidly anchored over during the spring tide. Tyler and she bickered and fought, knowing they were hundreds of miles from help. They were screaming into each other's faces. And from deep in the belly of the gulf came the unlikely sight of a boat. A fishing guide in an aluminium punt with two sunburnt clients and a barramundi flapping on the deck. You couldn't forget the name or the face. Red Hopper. He was a pugnacious bloodnut with a droll wit and a rollup fag on his lip. The only man for an unimaginable distance and they'd come aground a few miles from his camp.

He was anxious to see them on their way; in fact he had them gone inside twelve hours, but heading out into the Timor Sea Georgie felt regret as much as relief. She couldn't get the image of that monolithic island out of her head. The memory of it there in the milky gulf surrounded by a wilderness you couldn't conceive of for space and distance. She marked it on the chart and in her pocketbook. She thought about it now and then. It gave her a warm, uncertain feeling.

She was still on the terrace staring out at that masthead light in the lagoon when Jim appeared with a beer beside her. She noticed that he had an old Joe Cocker album playing inside.

Nice car, he said.

Didn't think you'd noticed it.

Nearly tripped over it, he said smiling. What's it run on—fairy dust?

I wish, she said unable to match his tone.

She looked out across the water until the music expired.

THE BUBBLE CAR remained an unsettling presence in the garage. It was parked against a pile of cartons that contained the life she'd never unpacked here, the stuff she'd hauled up from the city. Each time she drove to Perth—to buy groceries or presents for Christmas—Jim and the boys seemed mildly surprised to see her back. But she did return. Passing the fruit stand on the highway gave her a few bad moments but Georgie managed to think

Luther Fox back into a dim corner where he belonged. He was just another symptom of her weird attraction to suffering. He'd done her a favour. She was, she decided, the kind of person vulnerable to the sexiness of pity. A child's hot tears against your breast, the delicious collapsing weight of a man bereft—they gave you a power that you couldn't resist. And there you were, crashing through the overcast as hot as the sun itself, determined that you were the cure. White Point considered Fox gone. Officially he already seemed not to exist—he didn't appear to be in anyone's database, he had no tax file number. Well, let him be the ghost of his ambitions. He could stay gone. She was over it.

On Christmas Eve Jim came in with a whopping haul but he seemed strangely subdued. A big shark had followed the boat all day, its snout visible every time they pulled or dumped a pot. Jim told the deckies it couldn't be the same animal because the distances they covered and the speeds they steamed at between lines made it impossible. Yet Boris insisted that it was the same shark and by noon Jim had to admit that it seemed to be so. It was a tiger, a good twelve-footer and ugly as an in-law. By the middle of the afternoon Boris was all for killing it and Jim confessed that, had there been a weapon aboard he'd have consented. It gave him the creeps. Boris said it was an omen. But Jim didn't know what to think. Did Georgie believe in omens? Not on Christmas Eve, she said, giving him a beer.

That evening, before setting out the gifts beneath the plastic tree, they drank a few toasts to the *Raider*'s good fortune. The air was mild and there was laughter on the beach. Tomorrow nobody would fish, no one had to get up in the dark to ram bait into baskets or pull the heads off occies or heave pots around the lurching deck, and there was a palpable sense of release in the air, an atmosphere so infectious that Georgie and Jim stayed out late to share a bottle of sparkling burgundy. When the hot desert wind sprang up they lingered undeterred, listened to music, even told a few jokes. That night Georgie left the spare room empty. Their lovemaking was gentle, almost circumspect.

On Christmas Day the four of them took the dinghy out to the island to lie in the shade of an umbrella and snorkel about the fringing reefs. All of them were wary but amicable and that day a puzzled détente seemed to set in. It felt fragile, artificial even, but after recent events it came as such a relief that Georgie convinced herself that this new mood was a return to something like the life they'd had before spring.

White Point was feral at the best of times but during the Christmas holiday the place went mad. As the van parks and beach shacks filled, the population quadrupled. The pub was always full and the little shops gridlocked. There were boats and trailers, jetskis, 4x4s, trailbikes, kites, boomboxes, collisions, altercations, near-misses. The locals were obnoxious and the sun was brutal. At night the air was thick with the smoke of barbecues and the stink of scorched meat, and from Jim's terrace when the wind got around to the east you were overwhelmed by the greasy stinking vapour of deep fryers.

In the middle of it all, on Boxing Day, no less, Beaver disappeared. He was only gone the one day but he left pandemonium in his wake. Nobody could get fuel. When he returned, amid tumult and sensation, it was as a married man. His wife Lois was a tiny dark woman with a silver incisor. She was Filipino or Taiwanese, depending on who you asked. For days Georgie tried to catch his eye across the throng at the pumps. She saw Lois through the window puzzling at the register and staring bewildered at the stamping mob and she figured that by New Year's the worst might have subsided and she'd get her moment.

Georgie noticed the national flag go up on the white pole in the McDougalls' yard. She'd never seen it there before.

On New Year's Eve the traditional brawl at the pub evolved into a riot as a rave party on the beach was driven indoors by the wind. It was, simply put, a clash of cultures. By midnight youths were pulling rooftiles off the White Point tavern and throwing them into the crowded carpark as the place began to burn. Thirty minutes later, the White Point vollies (a little worse for wear themselves) had a firetruck in and were pitching young people from the roof into the very same carpark.

Jim came ashore New Year's Day with a paper nautilus. Boris insisted that it was a good omen.

The day Georgie finally met Beaver's wife Lois, she discovered that she was Vietnamese. Beaver was sombre with the effort of restraining his pride. Lois, he said, had a thing for Abbott and Costello, though her English was sketchy. The way White Pointers used the language made it a challenge even to those born to it, so Lois really had her work cut out for her. The locals who knew how Beaver had found his bride were already calling her Mail Order to her face. Georgie noticed the way Lois glanced between her and Beaver as though sniffing something suspicious about their friendship. She didn't quite know to reassure the poor, struggling woman, so she felt it wise to keep her distance. One evening as she cycled past the workshop she heard dishes breaking and the high, tiny shriek of Lois expressing some doubts. She felt like a rat but she figured she was best out of Beaver's way.

One humid January day while the remainder of a cyclone brought low cloud and brooding air down across the central coast, Georgie rode back from the post office with a sheaf of bills for Jim and a letter addressed to her in a hand she didn't recognize.

At the kitchen table she glanced at the grubby envelope.

Georgiana Jutland
c/o Post Office
White Point
Western Australia

She opened it with a butter knife and drew out a blank fold of notepaper. There was nothing written there. Just faint blue lines and the torn holes of the spiral binding from your bog-standard notepad. As she tilted the envelope up to make sure, a trickle of dust fell between her fingers onto the scrubbed table. It looked like dried paprika or chilli powder but when she dipped a finger in and put it to her tongue she knew it was nothing more than red earth.

The envelope with its boab tree stamp was postmarked Broome a few days before. Two thousand kilometres away by road. The far north, the edge of the tropics. She recognized the pink dirt of the pindan country; it wasn't the sort of natural colour you forgot once you'd seen it for yourself. With the paper's edge she scraped the dust into a little pile. There was more here than she first thought—perhaps a teaspoonful. It was no accident; it was some gesture.

She screwed up the envelope and tossed it into the kitchen bin. Then she stared at the little mound of dirt a while until, wetting a finger, working dab by dab, she ate it.

She wiped the table clean. On the VHF Jim announced he was only ten minutes out. When Georgie rinsed her mouth at the basin it was like spitting blood. She brushed her teeth and wiped the basin down. Gone.

three

HE WALKS the narrow blacktop in the warm dark. The sea is miles behind but he feels it at his back. Above the murky hinterland, stars hang like sparks and ash from a distant bushfire. By dawn his hamstrings are tight and his feet sore in their boots. The pack is snug enough in his back but the swag lashed across it teeters with every stride and butts the top of his head. He trudges into the rising sun until an old truck eases up beside him and an arm motions him to get in.

The man is long and thin with a shapeless hat and stringy grey hair to his shoulders. He looks tired, waits for Fox to speak and then sighs a suit-yourself sigh and just drives. Fox glances behind at the flatbed where several olive trees lie wrapped and lashed beneath a tarp.

They drone through floodplain country and into the beginnings of rich soil where late crops stand brassy in the sun. They veer north into the midlands wheatbelt where harvesters raise clouds of chaff and dust across the rolling hills.

This is it, says the driver at New Norcia.

Thanks, says Fox.

That Darkie could play.

Fox climbs out.

Headin north?

He drags his pack and bedroll off the rusty truckbed.

Fox cinches himself in. The sun is in his face.

It was only a matter of time, the man says. You would've buggered off eventually.

Thanks again.

Worth it for the conversation.

Fox walks through the old Spanish monastery town with barely a glance. Town cars and farm utes roll by but he doesn't even bother sticking his finger out. At the outskirts he shrugs his load onto the gravel shoulder and waits. Flies suck the sweat around his eyes, along his neck. In the paddock's remnant stand of gums, cockatoos stir. Eventually a Kenworth hulks up in a gust of airbrakes. He throws his kit up and climbs in.

G'day, says the truckie.

G'day.

This man is the colour of a boiled crab. His nose is thin and ruined. His ears are crisp with lesions.

Great Northern Highway, says the driver.

That's it, says Fox settling back into the smell of sweat and old socks and fried food.

Get yeself a hiding?

Fox grimaces. Hasn't thought how he must still look after swimming and walking home.

Face says everything, dunnit.

Yeah.

They ride in silence the rest of the morning with the cricket trickling in like water torture from the radio. The aircon dries the perspiration then chills him. As they lurch inland, the trailers swaying behind them, the country grows dry and low and wheat gives out to sheep paddocks which seem thinner and more marginal until only squat mulga scrub remains; just olive dabs of vegetation spread over stony yellow dirt.

Wildflower country, says the truckie, failing to suppress a fart. Should see it in September. Flowers as far as ye can look.

Fox can't imagine it. He hasn't expected this sudden absence of trees. He's hardly been on the road five hours and already it's just flat dirt out there.

So, what you pissin off from?

People, says Fox.

People in particular, or people in general?

Both.

The truckie takes the hint and contents himself with the cricket match on the radio. It's hard to think of anything more dreary but at least it spares him music.

A steer lies with its legs in the air like an overturned table at the road's edge. Rippling black sheet of birds.

Out of the low scrub a gum rises in the distance and as they pass Fox sees a white cross and a pair of elastic-sided boots. A scene from a Burl Ives song. Old Burl. How the old man loved him. Wrap me up in my stock-whip and blanket.

At the Paynes Find roadhouse Fox sits up in the Kenworth's cab while the bowser pumps diesel into its enormous tanks. He looks out in search of a settlement to go with the name but there's only scrub and stony ground. Eventually the smell of diesel drives him out. He buys a Coke and sits in the sweltering shade while his driver, having made it plain he wants to eat alone, hoes into a bacon-burger at a table inside.

Caravans towed by Pajeros and Range Rovers pull in from the north and line up for fuel. Old people with baggy shorts and leathery tans cross the oil-tamped dirt of the fore-court to the reeking bogs.

A young bloke in khaki work gear and steel-capped boots comes out of the roadhouse dragging a gust of refrigerated air and ciga-rette smoke with him.

Sads, he says disgustedly.

Sorry? says Fox finishing his Coke.

Sads, the bloke says, jerking his head at the retirees emerging from the toilets to com-pare mileages. See Australia and Die.

Fox shrugs.

Some of em do the whole trip. North, then across the top to the Territory. Queensland. Drive south. Come back across the Nullarbor. The big circle. Then they start again. I blame private superannuation. They clog up the road. Where you headed?

Oh, says Fox, up.

Hitchin?

You can tell?

Practice, mate.

Fox looks at the embroidered logo on his workshirt. A gold miner.

Headin back to Magnet in a sec. Give you

208

a lift if you don't mind ridin in the back. Me mate's takin a dump.

Thanks.

The diesel bowser continues to roll its eyes at the Kenworth. The luckless motorists caught behind the truck's trailers wait it out. Fox hauls his gear down from the cubby behind the cab and humps it to the miner's trayback Cruiser.

All afternoon from the windblown tray of the Landcruiser he watches the mulga country gradually transformed by the emergence of granite breakaways. The rocky escarpments come as a relief from the horizontal monotony. Convoys of vans and towed dinghies blow by southward. But for the occasional northbound roadtrain, the traffic is all headed the other way. In the cab they're playing Judas Priest; it's mercifully muted by windrush.

At Mount Magnet the young blokes set him down at a corner that feels like a crossroads of some moment. This is the end of the south. Farm fences are gone and soil has long been replaced by dust or grit. The Indian Ocean is hours to the west. On the roadsign, towns have three- or four-digit distances. He tries to imagine the gibber plains and red dunes to the east, the impossible amplitude of the continent. They say it's empty and the idea draws him but he can't get his mind around it. Thinks of the north the old man spoke of with pride and fear in his voice, the rugged stone ranges, the withering heat, the ceaseless blasting and digging, the epic drinking that made the boozy south seem temperate, the cattle herds pounding red dust skyward and the seasons discounted to plain Wet or Dry.

He hoists his kit and considers his options. It's not too late to steer seaward to Highway 1 and head north along the coast, but he has momentum now and he knows the inland route will take him past Wittenoom and the mine that orphaned him. He plumps for pressing on.

He pulls the bankroll from his pack and stuffs a few notes into his shorts to buy food. He crosses the wide, empty street to the BP station and orders himself a meal. While he sits black kids come and go. They buy Cokes and icecream and stand out on the tarmac to tease each other and mug at him through the window. Later he straps himself to his load and they follow him a little way, giggling, cheeky and loud as cockatoos.

Nobody stops so he walks to burn the time. The sun gets low but the heat seems to abide in the land. On the other side of town at sunset with no chance of a lift in such gloom, he veers into the scrub to find a place to camp.

He heads for a granite outcrop that he spies over the mulga and there he finds a decent patch of dirt. He unrolls his swag and collects sticks before the night closes in. The fire he lights is more for illumination than anything else. Having eaten not long back he doesn't bother to cook. By the glow of his little fire he examines the contents of his pack, the dried food, the billycan, lighter, torch, two changes of clothes, spare socks, waterbottles, pocket knife, a boning knife and steel, the floppy hat he's forgotten to wear all day, sunscreen, repellent. He carries a few first aid supplies. Band-Aids of course. Tweezers, Betadine. But no book, not a one. It's a bad oversight. He wants to be alone, God knows, but not without something to read.

He's sore now and his skin itches all over where scabs have formed. His nose is peeling and his lips cracked. He pulls his boots off and feels the blisters on his toes where the skin is still soft.

He doesn't think of Georgie Jutland. She hovers, of course, like something you can't quite believe in, but he doesn't let himself think of her. Stretched on his swag with the sheet half off, he thinks of himself in the paddock this morning kneeling with the knife to cut the end from a melon and slide his hand in, his arm to the elbow. It was hot from the sun and sweet, winy as the sea he'd been dreaming of, and days past eating. He took a mouthful to feel it fizz a little on his tongue. Even now he imagines he tastes that fermenting sweetness. It was the last thing he did before pulling his money from the stone on the hill and setting out. He doesn't know why he did it, though it was true that his mouth was parched from the night and day before and from what he'd decided to do. It was the sacrament he couldn't admit to. Just goodbye, that's all. A spitting of seeds, a quick turning for the hill.

Neither melancholy nor creeping anxiety keep him awake tonight. The farm could be burning but he sleeps. Last thing he hears is the curlew.

THE SKY is still layered pink and grey when the seventies-model Bedford van pulls over in a gale of dust and music. He steps up to the door and pulls it open and the aircon and the thumping bass blast him head-on. The driver is in his twenties with sunbleached dread-locks and flat blue eyes, the very picture of a surfer.

Got any juice money? he yells across the music.

I spose.

Orright, then.

Fox reefs the side door open and throws in his gear. It's pandemonium in there. A naked foam mattress with bites out of it and a sheet skewed halfway across it. On top are cheap PVC stuffbags, a fishing rod, jaffle iron, Igloo esky, camp oven, wank mags, a bong made from garden hose and a Mr Juicy bottle. A carton of Victoria Bitter has burst and cans lie all about.

He climbs into the passenger seat and feels the van surge away. Holden motor, you can bet on it.

Where you goin? says the driver, turning the tapedeck down a notch.

Wittenoom.

Fuck. Ghost town, innit?

Fox shrugs.

I'm not a tidy packer, says the surfer who catches him looking back at the shambles in the back. Only bought it last night. Well, won it as a matter of fact.

How?

By bein better than the other bloke, of course, he said with a hoarse laugh.

The van stinks of mull smoke and dirty clothes and the chilled air pouring from the vents smells mouldy. Fox's boots settle into a snarl of junk-food containers, beercans, crushed maps, and plastic bags. At the uncommon bends in the two-lane, a half-full Southern Comfort bottle rolls against one ankle.

Rusty, says the driver.

Lu, he offers reluctantly.

The music hammers at him; he feels it at the back of his throat. Steely Dan, their best album. Full of angular licks and slick changes, lyrics that peck at you. But he doesn't want to hear it. Music unstitches him now; he can do without it.

They drive hard into the morning. The tape restarts itself over and over. Rusty, it seems, hardly hears it. The country spreads out into salt lakes and vast baked pans wherein tiny islands of mallee hold up. They blow through the old mine-town of Cue where diggings and slagheaps become landscape.

At Meekatharra the earth is red. It stains the tar streets and the vehicles and buildings

213

along them. Rusty veers into a service station and looks expectantly at Fox. It takes a moment to realize he wants money.

You fill it and I'll buy breakfast.

I've eaten, says Fox, though his billy tea and muesli bar are long behind him.

Rusty takes three twenties from him and limps inside while Fox pumps the tank full. There's something about Rusty that strikes him as odd. Sees him limp from the restaurant to the toilets. On the way back to the glass doors his gait seems milder. When he comes back he hands Fox a burger and a bag of doughy fries and he drops a carton of similar delicacies onto the seat. Fox registers the clonk of Rusty's shin as he climbs in. Rusty looks at him with a sudden ferocity.

Artificial, orright? I'm a fuckin pegleg.

Oh.

Yeah, friggin oh.

Rusty pulls a monster rollie from his pocket, a roach the size of a turd. He lights up and wheels them out into the street.

Some dickhead in his Range Rover backed into me, says Rusty. Out the front of the Margaret River tavern. I was sittin on me car. He reverses up, pins me at the knee, totally friggin crushes it. Some fancypants lawyer from Cottesloe.

I spose you were surfing at Margaret River.

Not anymore. And that prick gets himself a bunch of hot-shot mates and they do me out of a decent pay-out.

Out on the highway Rusty opens it up and the Bedford's transmission gulps.

Automatic, he says. Cripple-friendly.

The van gets up so much speed that it floats, seems to hydroplane across the water mirages on the road.

Ever felt bitter? says Rusty not noticing that Fox has killed the stereo. You look the contented type.

That's me.

Fox watches him toke on the joint with all the pleasure of a man siphoning petrol. The van fills with smoke but it's too hot outside to crank down a window. Right at the dag-end of his smoke he offers Fox a puff but he declines.

Chuck me that Woolworths bag behind the seat, will ya?

Fox pivots and pulls the bag onto the seat between them.

Got some good gear in Geraldton.

Fox nods.

Well, take a look.

He opens the plastic bag and sees a jumble of tubes, bottles, cellophane sachets. There are boxes of prescription drugs in there and several syringes.

Starting a pharmacy, says Fox.

My oath.

All day Rusty grips the wheel but his pace is erratic. The breakneck speed of the morning gives out to fitful surges and lulls by midday. Now and then they pull over so he can stuff a morphine suppository. In the afternoon

215

Fox offers to drive but he's rebuffed and Rusty pilots the van at a pace that has triple-trailer roadtrains honking as they overtake in slipstream blasts that shove the Bedford aside.

Almost without noticing the transition, Fox sees that the country has become vivid, dramatic. The midwest is behind them. This is the Pilbara. Everything looks big and Technicolor. Ahead the stupendous iron ranges. There are trees again. This land looks dreamt, willed, potent.

Fark, says Rusty apropos of nothing.

At Newman they drive, lost for a while, through the big mine-town's circuitous streets. There are lush lawns here and flowers, mists of pumped water that soften the lines of neat bungalows and company shops. On one corner a Haulpak truck towers over the suburb. Water, iron ore, money.

Eventually Fox coaches Rusty back out onto the highway which climbs into the Opthalmia Ranges whose bluffs and peaks and mesas rise crimson, black, burgundy, terracotta, orange against the cloudless sky. Gully shadows are purple up there and the rugged layers of iron lie dotted with a greenish furze of spinifex. You sense hidden rivers. Your ears pop with altitude. Closer to the road, on scree slopes the colour of dry blood, the smooth white trunks of snappy gums suspend crowns of leaves so green it's shocking. Mobs of white cockatoos explode from their boughs. The colours burn in his head. Wide bends reveal the country behind darkened by the shadows of late afternoon. Fox feels his head slump back on his neck. He comes from low, dry, austere country, limestone and sand and grasstrees. Apart from the sea itself the only majestic points at home are the sculpted dunes. Even the graceful tuart tree seems dowdy up here.

Jesus, that's me done, says Rusty veering off into a roadside scrape where a snappy gum and a few tufts of scrub mark a rough lookout.

Fox realizes that twilight has fallen. He's a little stoned from the smoke in the van. The sky is puce, the peaks and crags of the iron ranges black against it.

Rusty kills the motor, throws the door open and hot, clean air rushes in. It feels velvety. Rusty pisses on the dirt.

Fox climbs out into the still heat of evening.

They break up dead wood for a fire and by dark the billy is boiling. Fox throws tea leaves into the water but lets the tea stand so long Rusty picks it up and takes it to the van where they've left the mugs. Fox feels tired and passive; he doesn't care.

Spose you want me to cook, too, eh? calls Rusty.

I don't mind.

Need a pep-up?

Just a cuppa. Maybe a beer later.

No worries!

When Rusty brings the tea back it tastes coppery, worse than stewed.

Here, says Rusty, almost jovial. He tips a bit of Southern Comfort into each mug. Rusty's chronic tonic.

Fox sips his bitter tea and stares at the dance of flames. The drone of the road seems to vibrate in him still. The night is thick as a blanket.

Why Wittenoom? asks Rusty.

Fox tells him about the old man and the asbestos mine. The mesothelioma and the monumental bastardry of the cover-up.

There was a Midnight Oil song, right?

Fox nods. He doesn't mention the dying, the actual way he went. The yellow slaughteryard eyes, the horrible swelling trunk. The falling down and liquid shitting and desperate respiration. In the end it was hospital. Lying there like a man being held down in a tub of water. Neck straining at the end of him as though he might get his head out and take a clean breath if only he pushed hard enough. But he was drowning anyway. And Fox sitting at the bedside too young to drive legally. Darkie and Sal waiting down in the carpark.

For revenge, says Rusty, I could understand it. But from what I heard there's nothin there, no one.

Rusty seems a long way off.

He said it was God's own country up here, says Fox. And I was headin north anyway—

What, *further* north?

Yeah, all the way.

Take you to Broome if you shout me the juice.

Fox shrugs. Orright, he murmurs. Spose it'd give the trip some shape.

Shape. Yeah. That's what I'm after. I'm gonna get shaped up in Broome.

Yeah? How's that?

Rusty starts grilling a couple of T-bones on an old fridge rack. Fox feels like he's looking at him from the other end of a drainpipe. Out beyond the firelight there's only blackness.

My fella in the Range Rover. He's in Broome this month.

How d'you know?

I paid someone.

Shit.

Mate, he purrs conspiratorially. I'm all organized. Gonna give *his* trip a new shape.

My lips are numb, says Fox at the very moment he thinks it.

Rusty snickers.

You put something in the tea.

Relax.

Shit.

Fox listens to the thousand tiny sounds of the hissing fat, the throbbing coals, the beef bones expanding in the heat.

Here.

Fox suddenly contemplates a hot steak on a torn strip of cardboard. His leg burns. He feels it, feels it.

Rusty's gnawed bone drops into the fire before Fox picks his up to begin. A sprinkle of ash settles on him as he eats.

When he's finished he turns to see Rusty in the open door of the Bedford with his jeans around his knees and a needle shoved into his thigh.

Morphine made me an orphine, says Rusty. So what's your excuse?

From a long way off the sound of a car. It's more road roar than engine noise; it rolls against the gorges and returns like backwashing surf. Fox sits and listens, watches Rusty as if through the wrong end of a telescope until lights bleach the mesa ahead and a motor eases into a coasting deceleration and a vicious grate of gears. In a blaze of headlights something pulls in nearby. As it wheels around on the gravelly pad Fox sees it's an old stationwagon, an EK. Someone, a woman, calls out.

Mind if we camp over here?

Suit yourself, says Rusty.

The car pulls away a few yards and the engine dies and the interior light appears yellow and feeble as doors open.

A man and two women wander over to the fire stretching and groaning as they come. The man has wild hair and a beard. Elastic-waisted pants, a shimmery waistcoat over his bare chest. They're barefoot. The women wear baggy cotton dresses, and jangly bangles.

G'day, says the man.

Where you headed? says Rusty.

Perth. Comin back from Darwin.

Long way.

Fox looks carefully at each woman's face. The fire twitches in their eyes; it lights up the studs in their noses and brows. They seem young, eighteen, twenty.

Quiet, isn't it? says one. Her arms in the sleeveless dress look downy.

Can we cook on your fire? says the other. Her hair is thick and tight with curls and it hangs down to her elbows and glistens in the fire-light.

They bring a cast-iron pot already full of rice and vegetables to the edge of the coals and stir the slurry with a long steel spoon. Fox watches with a tired detachment.

Woman crouches, stirring, hair lit in flickers. Someone offers him the bong but he barely notices. Steely Dan in the Bedford. Lips tingle with pins and needles.

You don't say much, says the man.

Superior being, says Rusty.

We can dig that, says the girl with all the hair.

Fox gets up with infinite care and pukes his steak into the dirt behind the Bedford. When he straightens himself he discovers that he still has the greasy bone in his hand and he hoiks it into the darkness. Unsteady and slimed with sweat, he hauls his swag out of the van and drags it a little way beyond the firelight where he lies on the canvas and watches the dandruff drift of the sky.

The earth thrums beneath him, stirs with a thousand grinding clanks and groans like the deck of a ship in heavy weather. He feels it twist and flex and murmur and, deep down, between rivety stones, there's an endlessly repetitive vibration like a piston-chant foghorn drone. *Whorr, whorrrr, whorrrrr.*

He surges in and out of darkness, sleep, stupor.

●　　●　　●

Two of them—Rusty and the girl with all the hair—backlit by the fire. On her knees in the dirt. Something glitters on her tongue. The surfer's dry crow laugh. Her hair in his fists.

Fox lies back with his throat scorched. The ground purrs against his skull. The dark, the hiss of static.

Sometime then, later perhaps, the girl or a girl is over the fender of the stationwagon, hair and arms lolling with Rusty upright and jerking like a shot man. Then so much yelling.

A small creature with eyes ablaze trembles beside his swag a moment and flees.

Silhouettes blur past the fire with screams propelling them. Fox rises incrementally to an elbow and summons a cry that never comes. Convulsion and confusion in the flickering half-light. The bearded man shirtless. Great gout of sparks as something crashes into the fire.

My pack, Fox thinks. I should have kept it by me.

The sound of breaking glass. Men and women screaming. And in the last seeable moment of the night, the sight of Rusty beating the station-wagon with his unstrapped leg like a madman flogging a dog. Fox falls back with flares and flashes beneath his eyelids. They crackle and buzz like neon. He sleeps, it seems. Lights out.

Fox wakes with the hot sun on his face, and when he shifts onto his side he sees a girl facedown in the dirt beside him, her cracked heels, the down on the back of her thighs a mist in the morning light. She smells of patchouli and sweat. The pattern of her cotton dress is a field of tiny shells in purple and white. For a long time he considers touching her but is afraid of what he might find; she's only half an arm away and his hand flutters back and forth until she finally breaks into a snore and his hand falls in relief. A posse of cockatoos passes shrieking overhead and the girl stirs. Her small, crushed and dirty face emerges.

Hello.

Hello, he croaks.

She rests her head on the edge of his swag. There are sticks in her hair and smears of red grime across one cheek. Her breath is bitter.

I'm Nora.

He nods and sees beyond her that the other car is gone. Rusty's arm hangs from the open door of the Bedford and his leg lies on the dirt nearby.

All around, the country is high and red. When Fox gets up he sees stars and his lips prickle. He finds a drum of water at the rear of the van and drinks greedily from it. He reaches into his pack, to discover that he hasn't been robbed.

Fox drives them through the gorge country. He feels like he's driving through a movie. A western. Mesas, buttes. Cliffs, gulches. Nora sits with lips parted, breathing through her mouth, only half awake. They don't talk. He feels queasy and anxious, uncertain about last night's proceedings but alive to the fact that she doesn't want to talk about it or anything else. From the moment they got up she's just acted as though she's along for the ride. He drives while Rusty sleeps in the back. The surfer wakes when they hit the rugged corrugations at the turn-in to Wittenoom.

In the gutted old settlement Fox steers them up paved streets with footpaths and remnant gardens but no houses. Almost everything has been pulled down and carted off to stop people living here. Front steps and concrete pads lie bare. Here and there a set of house stumps, a driveway. A forlorn school sign. Sections of low neighbourly fence, exotic trees, trellises with bougainvillea and jasmine wound through. A few people seem to have persisted but mostly it's just empty streets and health warnings. At the end of the last bare lane Fox pulls up on the cracked blacktop and gazes out at the canyon wall. Back up in there, he supposes, was where they mined the blue asbestos with it billowing in drifts all round them. When the old man was a sandy-haired young fella with a bookish wife at home and some land down south he had an eye on.

The Bedford idles. Above them the gorge rises like a breaking wave, red, purple, black.

Didn't expect it to be beautiful, says Fox, not meaning to say it aloud.

It's not, says Rusty. It's fuckin hot and dusty and the coons are welcome to it.

The girl looks back at Rusty then at Fox; she blinks.

Fox realizes he's seen enough; more to the point he wants to go now.

The girl opens the door, climbs out and squats. Her piss bores against the stony earth.

Fucksake, growls Rusty.

Fox turns to look at him but says nothing. Rusty lies back on the foetid jumble in his leopard-skin jocks with his stump blunt and angry looking.

I'm hungry, says Nora climbing in and shutting the door on the heat. I could eat a horse.

Eat me, says Rusty.

You're a pig.

And it's my truck you're in, so fuckin watch yer mouth.

Fox turns the van around and winds his way back down the empty streets, busy driving to keep himself from saying anything.

What? yells Rusty. That's it? You come this far and that's all you wanna see? This is the place that killed his father and five minutes and a dose of hippy piss is all he gives it?

The girl looks at Fox, he can feel it but he doesn't meet her gaze as he drives on past the remnant dwellings of the diehards and out onto the corrugated red track to the highway.

Yer ole man must be proud.

Shut up, will you? says the girl over the battering of the suspension.

Suck my stump.

Yeah, sure.

And I'll fuck your big hippy rump.

God, you're low.

I'll pump and I'll pump and I'll pump and I'll pump—

Fox stuffs Steely Dan back into the deck and drowns Rusty out. After a time he sees the surfer in the rearview mirror with a syringe stuck high in his leg again, lurching with the sway of the vehicle, and ten minutes later he's lolling back with his hand on his cock mouthing the words to the music.

Through the deep red ranges they clatter, below stony foothills stippled with snappy gums whose limbs are mere whiskers on the jowls of the great bluffs and buttes above them. Up there the clefts harbour shadows black enough to unnerve him. Sit here looking long enough, he thinks, and those shadows'd suck the mind right out of you. Just one indrawn breath from all those gill-like fissures. These ranges look to him like some dormant creature whose stillness is only momentary, as though the sunblasted, dusty hide of the place might shudder and shake itself off, rise to its bowed and saurian feet and stalk away at any moment.

His thoughts reel on until at a sharp bend in the road Fox sees a solitary termite mound whose black shadow beats a path to its door. A moment later there are others, a whole colony of them. He brings the Bedford to a sliding halt.

You all right? says the girl Nora as he climbs out.

I just want to see this, he says as their pastel dust wake boils up and overtakes them. I'll only be a sec.

The hot air is thicker than dust. He strides out through bunches of spinifex to stand among the red monoliths. He puts his hands on the first one he comes to and feels the rendered form of the thing, traces the creases at its sides, hot to the touch. A spinifex pigeon takes wing nearby. The Bedford's horn begins to honk.

At the huge, bleak roadhouse the girl asks for rice. The woman behind the counter smirks. Back out on the highway Nora eats her pasty with a look of martyrdom. Back on his mattress Rusty sits with a silver thread of drool suspended from his chin.

They come down out of the brilliant gorges onto a vast savannah. They cross the Fortescue River, and iron nubs and boulders begin to jut from the grassland.

Fox wonders if he should have made more of the stop at Wittenoom. He could have gone up to the minehead. But the old man would have thought him a bloody idiot. All that asbestos puffing up at every step. Be like an insult. Let the dead bury their dead—isn't that what he said?

For a long time he wants to talk to the girl, figure out what's what, but she seems impervious as a lizard to his frequent looks. Eventually when he's given up, she speaks.

He your mate?

You must be jokin, he says. I was just hitchin.

She nods and puts her bare feet on the dash. Air balloons her dress. She pegs it down with her hands.

You orright? he murmurs.

She shrugs.

D'you know where your friends went?

Perth, I guess. Amber had to get her kid.

Is that where you're headin?

Yeah.

Well, you're goin the wrong way. You know that?

She doesn't move.

Shit, he says.

A windblown tear rides off her cheek into her hair.

How old are you? he asks.

Sixteen.

God.

God? she laughs bitterly. God is sixteen. And she's a girl.

Well.

And men fuck her to death every day.

Look, he says, bewildered. We'll drop you at the next town. You can get a bus. Port Hedland, I spose. You'll probably catch your mates.

The girl says nothing. Fox begins to notice graffiti on every outcrop.

The Great Northern Highway finally ends at the junction with Highway 1. Fox makes the turn. The low flat floodplain is bleached yellow, the colour of a dried biscuit. It feels coastal but the sea is not in sight. This stretch of road is festooned with shredded radials, beasts, beercans.

Welcome, Nora says, to the land of the big white bogan.

What?

Rednecks.

They plough on but the van feels motionless on the shimmering plain. Boredom eats at Fox. He writhes in his seat.

After the longest time, maybe half an hour, the saltpiles of Port Hedland rise above the plain. In the desolate outskirts of the iron port, a badlands of power pylons, railyards, steel towers and smokestacks, they pull into a roadhouse whose dirt forecourt is black with spilled diesel. Disassembled roadtrains. Pre-fab buildings stained with iron dust. Hitchhikers sleeping beside cartons of Emu Bitter.

Fox pulls up beside the pump and peels off some money.

Here, he murmurs to Nora before Rusty stirs. Just hitch into town if the bus doesn't stop here.

She nods. She smells of mouldy towel. She takes the money and climbs out. The door closes with a thump.

Fuck, I need a piss, says Rusty. Where are we?

Hedland.

Shithole.

Been here before?

Nah. Where's the chick?

Gone for a leak, says Fox. Want me to fill it?

I'm not keepin you on for the company.

Fox gets out and pumps petrol while Rusty straps his leg on. They meet at the register.

Get some of that steak, says Rusty pointing out a whole vacuum-sealed fillet behind a beaded glass door. She likes meat, that chick.

Buy it yourself, says Fox, wishing he'd been the one to hide in the toilet. If it wasn't for the girl he'd be bailing out here. A child with a steaming plate of chips before her stares at Rusty's prosthesis. Under fluorescent lights it gleams a shocking pink against his floral boardshorts.

No money.

It's too big.

Rusty scratches his scalp through the musty furrows of his dreadlocks. Through the window Fox sees Nora climbing back into the Bedford. The miserable dumpy girl behind the register sighs dramatically.

We'll have the porterhouse, love. Ring it up.

Fox pays and carries the meat out cold against his chest.

Nora doesn't even look at him as he climbs in.

He drives, his anger giving out to desolation. The two-storey roadsigns don't help. Perth is 1650 kilometres south and Kununurra the same distance north. Halfway feels like no way.

For a while there is the consolation of the grand mesas that rise from the ravaged floodplain but they give out onto the same dreary flatlands with grim, narrow creeks.

Fox drives with odd flashes erupting behind his eyes.

The De Grey River, brown and wide on its tree-strewn banks, gives a moment's respite as they fly across the bridge.

Rusty rolls a joint and shares it with Nora. She tokes on it with feeling. Fox's lips tingle and for a few minutes one of his legs trembles. No one speaks. The fungal smell of dope fills the van.

Fox drives.

The two in the back rustle in the stash bag.

The plain, the plain, the plain.

Rusty begins to sneeze.

Fox knows it's cattle country by the dead bullocks, but he hasn't seen a live beast yet. This far north there are no fences. He has cramps with the flashes now.

All along the roadside are the remains of campfires, strewn empties, rubbish. From the north the Landcruisers and Cherokees drag their loads. It's like a column of well-heeled refugees. Fox needs to stop. He has to get out.

At Pardoo he pulls in. It's just a fuel pump and van park. He climbs out and reefs his kit from under the surfer in the back. Rusty lolls, slit-eyed. The pack smells of him as Fox pulls it on.

You wamme to fill it? asks a crewcut woman through her teeth.

That turn-off go to the coast? says Fox.

Yeah. You want petrol or not?

Ask him.

Thanks for nothin, says Nora.

Fox walks fast until he finds a rhythm. The air is woolly. Sweat leaves him purblind. He thinks of the hat but the sun is low. The mulga scrub is thin and burnt on the gravel track either side of him. There are no trees in sight. He is the tallest thing on the plain.

After a long time he hears a motor and the sound of spitting gravel. He moves over, doesn't stick his hand out. Hears the vehicle slow behind him.

You forgot something, says the girl from the driver's window.

It hits him in the belly and knocks him winded to his knees and when the van finishes its dirt spraying U-turn and its brief wallow in the mulga scrub on its way back to the highway, he finds the vacuum-sealed parcel of porterhouse in the dust by his knees. He gets his breath back. He picks it up, hauls himself upright and presses on into the sunset and the gathering mosquitoes.

JUST ON DUSK he comes to a mangrove creek reduced to a trickle by low tide and he presses on past it to a stony, treeless cape from which the Indian Ocean is still visible in the twilight. He picks his way down to a basin of coarse sand above the tideline and throws his load. He drinks a litre of water and sheds his shirt and shorts to climb over into a rockpool and wash the sweat away. He has a momentary shiver wondering about crocodiles but that's as cool as he gets. The water is tepid.

For a moment before he dresses he feels refreshed, but the heat makes him clammy again by the time he's unrolled his swag in the thickening dark.

A little higher on the cape he sees a camp-fire and his spirits sink. Then he thinks of the beef fillet there on his pack. He pulls his baking boots on.

Only the pale sand track guides his way up the rocky ridge.

Hello the house! he calls from a discreet distance.

Gawd aggie! someone says.

There's the clang of something dropped in surprise.

Sorry to startle you, Fox says, walking toward the fire which lights a pair of legs.

Scared the tripe out of me!

It was a man's voice. Older. Fox shields his eyes from the fire. He makes out a caravan and vehicle.

I'm from down the beach a bit.

Orright, the man said cautiously.

Where's that lid gone? said a woman.

Fox is suddenly blinded by a torchbeam.

Everythin orright there, sport? What's that you got?

Meat, says Fox proffering the parcel. He tries to explain that he's got too much and that he's happy to share it with them or they can even take the lot—he doesn't mind. But the man and woman behind the light are doubtful. He tells them it's vacuum-sealed, that he didn't steal it, that it's perfectly all right, that he doesn't want it going to waste.

Spose it does look a bit suss, he concedes.

Beware Greeks with freebies, says the woman in a tone of amusement.

Well, says Fox. Troy just spoiled it for the rest of us.

The woman laughs. They switch off the torch and invite him in. A fluoro strip sputters to life above the caravan door. Fox sees an old man in a white singlet with a pair of stubbies hanging off his bum. In a folding chair a silver-haired woman holds a glass of white wine. Firelight catches her specs and the chain that hangs from them. They introduce themselves, Horrie and Bess. Fox hands them the beef. Horrie passes him a beer. He drinks it in one gluttonous swallow and then stands there suddenly embarrassed.

Thirsty, says Horrie.

Oh. Yeah.

You want somethin for this meat?

No. Maybe a few litres of water.

No worries. Easy.

Here, Lu, says Bess. Sit down and put on some repellent. You'll be eaten alive. Sandflies are worse than the mozzies.

Fox takes a seat. They have a folding table and esky out here on the sand beside the fire.

You're a student, then, says Bess.

No, he murmurs. Unemployed.

Headin south to the cool weather, I imagine.

North, actually.

Horrie, he's as mad as us.

Every sensible bugger hit the road south weeks ago, says the old man. No one heads north this time of year except the knuckleheads.

And those on a mission, says Bess. Which are you, young man?

Fox laughs. The knuckleheads, I'm afraid.

Same as us, says Horrie.

I beg to differ.

She differs but I've never seen her beg, the old boy pronounces with a laugh.

Here are those others you used to prize, says Bess, *But why go further we?*

Here she goes!

The future?—Well, I would advise you let the future be, unshown by me!

Oh, says Fox taken aback. That's...isn't that Hardy?

Get him another beer, Horrie.

She taught English, the old man says. Forty years.

What university did you go to? Bess asks.

Ah. I didn't finish school.

But you read.

Well, yeah.

Actual books? Actual poetry?

Oh boy, mutters Horrie.

Not just *information*, then?

Leave the boy alone, Bess.

Fox laughs uneasily. No. Just books.

Who?

Bess.

Fox tries to think.

Hemingway, I imagine.

He shrugs.

Byron, by the look.

He wrinkles his nose.

Blake, perhaps?

Aha, says Fox.

Aha indeed. Then Wordsworth, of course. But not Shelley.

You got me, he smiles, amazed.

So who do you *identify* with?

This week? Keats.

Oh, you sad boy. A name writ in water.

Let's eat this bloody meat, says Horrie.

Fox stays and helps them grill steaks from the fillet. They have a tossed salad and cold potatoes. Although he can't keep up with Bess's banter he enjoys sitting there with them. He thinks wistfully of his parents, the idea of them growing old together like these two. He was young when his mother died but he remembers the fiery talk, their combative devotion.

After a couple of hours he gets up and thanks them, wishes them a good trip north. The old couple rhapsodize about the vast Kimberley country ahead while he stands there, inching away by degrees.

This state, says Horrie, is like Texas. Only it's *big*!

Fox laughs and seizes the moment.

That night he coats himself in repellent and lies on his swag to watch the stars and listen to the tide fill the bay. He still has flashes behind the eyes now and then but not enough to keep him awake. At dawn he sees a wallaby observing him from the scrub, eyes bright, ears up. Birdsong drifts down the ridge high and gay as playground noise. The wallaby blurs away the moment he moves.

While the billy heats on the fire, Fox climbs over the rocks to where the tide has receded again. The limestone buttresses of the cape trickle and seep. With a flat stone he knocks a few oysters open and sucks the meat and liquor out. He walks seaward through the puddles and freshets the tide has left. A mile out the sea is the weirdest milky blue.

In one pellucid tidepool he reaches down for a gorgeous blue-spotted stone but he hesitates when its markings begin to move. Blue spots morph into yellow dabs. The stone opens an eye and—fuck!—he recoils in shock. An octopus, a blue-ringed octopus, no less. And his fingers only a handspan from touching it. A bite would have killed him before he reached camp. Total nervous shutdown. Gone.

He hurries back to his fire, makes tea and eats a couple of muesli bars. The girl bothers him. Nora. He wonders what he could have done.

He's packing his gear when Horrie hails him.

Headin to Broome, right?

Yeah, says Fox. It's on the way.

Come with us. Didn't realize you were hoofin it. We're headin off after lunch. I want to fish this incoming tide. Like to fish?

Fox nods. He thinks about it. He wants to get going but by the time he makes it out onto the highway and waits an hour in the stinging sun they'll be by anyway. He pulls out his cloth hat and accepts.

Horrie and he fish the tide in the mounting heat. It's humid. The air is brothy. Fox casts with a borrowed rod. He sends a jig into the cloudy turquoise surge about the rocks.

Got an ambition? asks Horrie.

Fox shakes his head not quite truthfully.

Didn't think I did anymore either, says the old man. Except catch that fifty-pound barramundi every man comes north for. Been everywhere, I have. Merchant marine.

Saw the tattoos, murmurs Fox.

But somehow ambitions are shoved at ya. You probly guessed it about Bessie. Why she doesn't get up much. Abbreviation, eh? Gives you a new outlook.

Fox finishes his retrieve and takes the jig in hand. Looks blankly at the old man.

You got any idea what I'm talkin about, mate?

No, he admits.

She's on the way out, son. Cancer of the bowel. Like it's goin outta fashion.

Oh, man.

I'm all for circlin the wagons and takin every pill and poison they give her, but she's not havin any of it. She wants to go out with her boots on, give it the big Up Yours. You know, blaze of glory. She's a romantic. She wants drama. Wants to drive into the eye of the storm sorta thing. Somethin big. Cyclones, sunsets, mountains, red rivers two miles wide. Trees with cars hangin in them. She wants to sail off the edge of the world.

God, Horrie.

Russian bloke told me once. Said we all die. But you might as well die with music. Go out big. You see what I mean? She wants big music, Lu. And north is where you get it. The Kimberley, mate. Big weather, big fish, big distances—larger'n life. And that's my ambition. To get her there. Do her proud. Bloody drive right into it, whatever's out there, whatever's comin.

Fox can only nod.

She likes you. The poems and everythin. But just be...understandin.

Sure.

Taught me a lot, she has. More about music than poetry. But I'm glad she can talk poems with you. You like music, Lu?

Well—

Mate, those Russians.

Russians?

I can't get a bite. What say we pack it in, hit the frog and toad.

Out on Highway 1 the going is slow. The old Nissan Patrol is a roaring tin trunk. It slams and jiggers on its short wheel base, the suspension all but buggered and with the caravan in tow it barely makes it into top gear even on the endless flat plain. Bess natters about animal instinct, about birds and fish and ants and the way they think in groups. They hear each other think, she says. I believe that. A school of fish turns as one. Yes, and a flock of sparrows. They resonate. And so do we. Fox thinks of those termite mounds. And yes, he's seen the shoal of fish as one living thing. A thousand times. But Horrie has Prokofiev or some bloody thing on the tiny tapedeck. It sets his teeth on edge and blunts whatever it is Bess is saying about Wordsworth. Bess puts him in mind of his mother. She's more frenetic, and not beautiful as he always remembers her, but it seems that Bess looks for the links in things, not the gaps. What he recalls most vividly about his mother apart from her vanilla scent is the way she appeared to see the world as holy, joined, commingling. But he can't hold the thought with all this talk. And—God!—the sawing music.

When the old truck boils over, he takes it as a mercy. Horrie discovers they've blown a fan belt and Fox helps him fit a ragged spare. Outside, the heat is astounding, it seems to have intensified with every passing mile. While crows call in the glare overhead Fox and Horrie refill the radiator. Back underway, Bess asks for Bach. Fox recognizes the tune to an old hymn, and how it *eats* at him. He sees himself, a boy in his shorty pyjamas on the verandah. The smell of burning mosquito coils. He wills the music to end before it fucks him up entirely.

Bess plasters a handkerchief to her face.

The Patrol soon boils again and Horrie is

forced to cut the aircon to keep the old bus going. He decides that his old mate Shostakovich is the go. Piano quintet! he yells. Some *big* music!

Fox slumps back in the luggage space behind them, sweltering. The music is jagged and pushy and he for one just doesn't want to bloody hear it but the outbursts of strings and piano are as austere and unconsoling as the pindan plain out there with its spindly acacia and red soil.

Cars and roadtrains overtake in slams of wind. The dirt is the colour of food. This music feels like it's peeling his skin. He can't afford this shit. He needs covering, not stripping. Since that terrible night in which everything seemed to unravel in a series of jumpy, uncertain moments, everyone dead so sudden like that, all he's wanted is to be left alone, and music is a fucking bully—it's the last thing he needs; it'll rip him to pieces. There's simply not enough of him left to withstand it.

Bess is writhing now. Horrie pulls over. She staggers off into the acacias, but there isn't enough vegetation to hide in so the old bloke follows her out with a shielding blanket. Fox averts his head, swelters. Bess comes back in girlish high spirits but it's plain she's masking her embarrassment and discomfort.

How's your geography, Lu? Draw a line east of this very spot. Right across the country. Now name everything in the way of your line.

Fox shrugs.

Bess reels them off: the Great Sandy Desert,

the Tanami Desert, Tennant Creek, the Barkly Tableland, Mount Isa, Charters Towers, everything between them and the Great Barrier Reef.

He smiles as indulgently as he can.

She twists in her seat, looking feverish.

Now a literary litmus test, she says.

Bess, says Horrie, wiping at her one-handed with a damp cloth as he drives.

Virginia Woolf.

Fox wrinkles his nose.

And why not?

Never trust a non-swimmer, he says, glad that at least the music's off for the moment.

Would that account for Shelley?

Bad sailor, too.

Careful, she says. I married a bad sailor.

Oi!

Melville, then.

He nods.

But that shark poem, Lu—*pale ravener of horrible meat*—the sound of an anxious wader.

Fox laughs, bewildered by her antic talk. She goes on without him, jaunty as you like, answering her own questions with a quaver in her voice. Looking miserable and desperate, Horrie watches Fox in the rearview mirror. He slaps Mussorgsky into the deck and Fox squirms in his nest of luggage.

Twice more they stop for Bess. She squats behind the burr-specked blanket, cries out in pain.

Late in the afternoon the radiator boils again and they pull up to the thin shade of a solitary bloodwood. As he slides out to help

Horrie, Bess catches his arm. Swimmers, she says. Her breath is bitter. She declaims into his face:

> And what of the dead? They lie without
> shoes
> in their stone boats. They are more like
> stone
> than the sea would be if it stopped. They
> refuse
> to be blessed, throat, eye and knucklebone.

Geez, Bess, he says wiping her spittle from his cheek.

Anne Sexton. Christ knows, she had some swimming to do.

Beneath the hood Horrie is bawling. Fox stands beside him a moment, touches the old bloke's shoulder. Horrie flinches away. Fox feels the urge to drag his pack out onto the pindan and take his chances alone, but he fetches the jerrycan of water and helps fill the whining radiator.

For a blessed while Bess sleeps.

Stay a few days with us in Broome, says Horrie. For Bess.

Fox licks his lips. Night falls. They creep on. It feels like walking pace. Horrie goes searching for Arvo Pärt on the seat beside him. They yaw across the lightless highway. Out in the black distance the sky flashes. Campfires flicker beside the road. People hunker over meals. Their vehicles angle off into the scrub, some barely off the blacktop.

Like the Middle Ages out there, says Bess, reviving. Look at them all. Makes you think of pilgrims, traders, refugees, crusaders, lunatics. You half expect to see Byzantium appear round the next bend. Except there are no bends. Bend this road, Horrie. At once.

Settle down, love.

Arvo, she says in pain. I want Arvo. It's death music. Arvo in the arvo.

Bess, love—

Don't be shocked, Lu. Death's been round us before.

No, Bess.

Here's James Dickey. Used to call him James Dickhead but he redeems himself with this.

For Chrissake, woman!

The old girl yells:

I wash the black mud from my hands.
On a light given off by the grave
I kneel in the quick of the moon
At the heart of a distant forest
And hold in my arms a child
Of water, water, water.

Luther Fox flinches at this. He has to get out. Bess stabs the tape into the machine and slowly, tidally, the vehicle fills with the tolling of a bell and a descending string lick starts up. Something rolling down inevitably, compulsively, almost obsessive. Down. Diving. Skin-crackling. So beautiful it hurts.

That bell drones on and on, trapping him beneath a sky and a moon of his very own, on his knees, like the last man alive hearing the sound of the others lilting off into oblivion. He doesn't give a shit that it's beautiful; he wants it off.

Along the final punishing straights of the Roebuck Plains he covers his ears. The moment he sees the distant lights of Broome he's planning his escape. No plea, no weeping sailor will stand in his way.

four

THAT SUMMER Georgie's nervous cooking jag became a feverish binge, as though she was trying to cook her way out of uncertainty. Even Jim, who loved the food, began to wonder aloud whether she wasn't a little touched by the heat.

One night when she was cooking a risotto in her bikini and taking a bloodyminded pleasure from the endless, steamy stirring and folding, Jim came upstairs and just stood there and laughed. It startled her, broke her concentration. She'd been brooding about Shover McDougall.

Jim opened his mouth to speak and the phone rang. He walked around the benchtop and snatched it up.

Well, I'll be buggered, said Jim, delighted to hear from the caller. Long time, mate... *Second* cousins, don't get bloody familiar. Catchin a few bucketheads up there, are ya?

Georgie kept stirring her rice which had finally gone creamy from all that rolling around the pan and while it absorbed the last of the stock she thought of the surviving chives she might use on it.

He said *what*? What'd he look like?... Yeah? Well, that's interesting.... Yeah, too right. Glad you told me.

Georgie turned off the gas and folded the risotto round the skillet a while longer. Jim turned slightly away from her where he stood at the counter.

Maybe I will, he said. Yeah, I've got a pretty good idea... Okay, it'll be my shout. See ya.

He hung up with a delighted but baffled look on his face. He looked boyish and handsome like that. It made her smile.

Good news? she asked.

The far-flung family.

Georgie pursed her lips. His parents were dead and he had no siblings.

Didn't know you had any.

All over the state. Geez, some of the clan are major breeders. Look at that risotto, he said brightly.

Georgie turned back to the heavy pan. It was indeed a picture. She felt him lift her bikini strap and plant a kiss on her sweaty shoulder. He smelled of soap and, very faintly, of diesel.

I'll get the boys, he purred.

GEORGIE STARED at Jude's email. *Men are killing us, sis.*

Well, it made more sense than yesterday's. As she dumped the message and began trolling in the soft blue light of the web she made a note to call Jude tonight. Out beyond the plate glass and the airconditioning, it was a hot, clear midsummer day. Jim had given the boys a dinghy to use over the holidays and they were rowing it up and down the lagoon to set crabnets on the seagrass, each suspended from an empty milk container which bobbed on the surface. Daylight hovered like a headache at the edge of consciousness while Georgie tried to work her way free into that other milder world. She keyed in the word *medicine*.

A British woman desperate to be a mother. The miracle of fertility drugs. She is blessed with IVF triplets. And puts two children out for adoption... Australian authorities deport a pregnant Chinese refugee knowing that her child will be killed by a grisly, enforced late-term abortion upon her return... Keanu Reeves's spleen is listed for sale on eBay... South Africa's new president declares that HIV does not cause AIDS.

Georgie shut the machine down. She needed to get outside.

By the time the boys figured out who it was swimming toward them from the shore, their puzzlement had given way to alarm, as though her being abroad in daylight *and* encroaching upon their territory were cause for concern. Georgie sculled right up to the dinghy. Josh was shoving fish heads onto a baitpin and Brad rested at his oars. She saluted. She requested permission to come aboard.

There was a rapid exchange of fraternal glances. Permission was granted. Soberly and with unspoken reservations.

251

We're crabbing, said Josh.

Excellent. I'll be deckie. The three of them worked their way up the line of floats, pulling traps and rebaiting them quietly until the boys' wary politeness wore off. They let her row for a while. Not so long ago they'd been proud and voluble about Georgie's boating skills and her prowess with rod and reel. She couldn't think when she'd last stood at the point with them to cast for flathead and whiting. She'd become so disembodied, so abstracted in the last six months. She decided to view it as a digression. It was not indicative of the rest of her life; she wouldn't let it be.

All the crabs that came aboard were dun-coloured females. They were small and none of them were keepers. At midday she suggested they drift for squid, and their immediate success bound the three of them in a comradely warmth. They dangled bright jigs across the weedbanks and brought squid splashing and squirting to the surface. Soon they were giggling and teasing and stained with ink. They filled a bucket. They smeared each other's faces. When the breeze came in they lay back and drifted in a happy, cavorting uproar, and in the end they came so far down the bay that it was useless to try to row back against the wind, so they came ashore to walk the boat back up through the shallows. When they drew abreast of the house they ran the dinghy ashore.

Georgie was helping to turn it keel up on the sand when she felt her back go out. She fell to the sand with a cry. The pain was so sudden and intense; it was like having a piece bitten from the small of your back. The boys assumed she was still capering away in the spirit of the afternoon, but when Brad knelt down beside her, Georgie's tears surprised him. Immediately he assumed the calm authority of his father. He shaded her face, slipped his hat beneath her cheek to protect it from the hot sand, and when he thought her ready he supervised the wrangling of her twisted frame up the sand track to the house.

For a day and a night she lay in bed. Anti-inflammatories had little effect and the codeine phosphate brought on the sort of constipation that a few prunes will not remedy. It was misery.

While their father fished the long, trying days of the deepwater phase of the season the boys did their best to look out for her. From Beaver's they brought back the sorts of videos they imagined to be suitable for someone of her vintage. All she craved was Cary Grant or Hepburn and Tracy but she had to settle for Jessica Tandy, Michael Douglas, Kevin Costner. She was grateful they drew the line at Meg Ryan. The first day they did their best to watch companionably from the end of her bed, but they soon settled for looking in on her now and then. Before long, though, the outdoor world was too much to resist and they forgot her entirely.

After the best part of a week, with no improvement in sight, Jim suggested he drive her to the city for treatment. But she wouldn't hear of it. She told him she couldn't be responsible for keeping him ashore another day this season, especially not during the deepwater run, but in truth she just couldn't come at the agony of four or five hours wedged into a car. In the end she consented to being driven over to Rachel's. Word was that Rachel Nilsam knew a bit of massage.

When she came to the door that evening Rachel looked surprised. Stunned even. She recovered quickly enough and asked them in, but Jim demurred and left them at the threshold. The kids, he said.

Rachel took her through the modest house to a high bench with a batik slipcover. Georgie needed help to undress. It was awful. She felt like a child, like some frail old lady. She hadn't realized she would have to be naked. As she lay on the bench her face was hot. She turned her head to the wall. Rachel ran her fingertips down Georgie's spine. Elsewhere in the house there was music. All Georgie could think was that someone might come in.

Nice old spasm you've got there, Georgie. How long've you been like this?

I dunno. Days.

You should have called.

I didn't think to. Tell you the truth I was a bit stunned at first and then I just kept thinking it would sort itself out if I left it alone. How's that for a problem-solving action? Christ, what a summer.

Yeah, I was sorry to hear about your mum. Listen, I'm gonna put a poultice on this tonight. It's too inflamed to do anything with yet. In the morning I'll try and straighten you out.

I wish somebody would. What's in the poultice?

Oh, you know. Crab mustard, the testicles of a blowfish, the ring finger of a Portuguese deckhand and the sweat from Shover McDougall's brow.

The New Age finds its way to White Point.

Couple of old Croats in Fremantle showed me. Linseed oil, mostly.

I thought you did relaxation massage, said Georgie.

And go into competition with the Swan Brewery? Are you mad, woman?

Georgie laughed. I heard you were a social worker.

And I heard you were a nurse. Here. Push up. Keep your pelvis on the table.

Jesus!

Again.

You're kidding me.

I spose it hurts.

Georgie collapsed face-down with a fit of the giggles.

Something chimed nearby.

The microwave, said Rachel as she moved away. Then: Here, hold still. That too hot?

The poultice laid a steady suffusing warmth over the knot in her lower back and it was strangely comforting to feel Rachel binding

255

it to her skin with sticking plaster. Georgie let herself be helped into her clothes. The strapping reminded her of girdles, and she thought of her mother—again.

I'll take it off in the morning, said Rachel. Just lie flat tonight and don't bend for anything. You'll need to be careful.

Oh, I'm the careful type, said Georgie full of self-mockery.

Yes, Rachel said, unable to suppress a grin. That's what I hear. Bugger—I can't believe I just said that.

So what else have you heard? asked Georgie trying to seem unfazed.

And to think I have a degree in the social sciences.

The sociable sciences?

I'll stick to the back, Georgie. Your life's your own.

You might as well tell me, she said feeling jangly now and apprehensive.

Oh, it's just gossip.

In which case it's bound to be true.

Come on. I'll drive you home.

Next morning Rachel drove over to collect her. The Land Rover with its rigid suspension was purgatory. Rachel drove barefoot, her high forehead shining. Her hair was pulled back into a ponytail that still dripped from her swim.

You know, said Georgie, I've always wondered what it is that Jerra does.

Apart from basking in my love, you mean? Rachel said with a grin. He's a muso. A songwriter.

No!

Yes.

In White Point?

There's no law against it. Yet.

I see him down the beach with his surf-board, said Georgie. And I always—

Thought he was the local dope dealer.

Georgie laughed. She couldn't deny it.

Everybody does, said Rachel. What a laugh. Dope wrecked every band he was ever in. Drugs are his pet hate. Fancies himself a bit of a wine buff these days. That's success for you.

He does okay, then?

Georgie, you'd be surprised.

Well? Don't leave me hanging.

Okay. You're looking at a girl who's spoken to Van Morrison.

Jesus. What'd he say?

That's the thing, said Rachel steering them into her yard. I have no idea.

Georgie let Rachel help her down from the vehicle. They went inside slowly, like two old ladies. Rachel stripped her again and put her up on the bench. She ripped the sticking plaster off in two brisk swipes. Georgie was finding the patient-role something of a trial.

Jerra played with the Foxes a couple of times, said Rachel. Just for fun.

I never heard them, Georgie said flatly.

There was a sober pause between them now.

I've always wondered about you, said Rachel quietly. I've always wondered why you came here.

Georgie lay there.

And now I can't figure out why you stay. You know. After the dog.

Things aren't always what they seem, said Georgie. As you should know.

Okay. Sure.

But?

Sometimes they're worse than how they seem.

Meaning what, Rachel?

Well, he's been a scary person in the past.

Oh, it's all talk.

Rachel sighed.

Anyway, said Georgie. People have a right to leave their past behind.

I agree. Absolutely.

So what's the problem?

That everybody else remembers. Here, stand up.

Georgie let herself be stood at right-angles to the wall, one hip barely touching it, while Rachel leant into her. She felt her spine creak as the other woman pressed that hip against the wall and a blast of pain went right through her. Georgie began to sweat, thought she would faint or throw up, but the moment passed and the pain subsided, and within ten minutes there was just the mildest, residual ache. Most surprising of all, her back was straight.

How'd you learn that?

Like everything I know, said Rachel making them chamomile tea. I learnt it when I was supposed to be doing something else.

Jim didn't shoot the dog, Rachel.

So he says.

That's the word. Even Beaver says.

The word. The bloody *word*. Sometimes I hate this town.

So why do *you* stay?

I dunno. It's out of the way. And Jerra likes the quiet—well, actually so do I. It saved our bacon in a way. There *are* a few nice people about, despite the odds. And it's so damn beautiful—the beaches, the dunes, the island. Not even the...savages...can ruin it completely.

It was Shover who shot the dog, said Georgie. You have to believe me.

Oh, I'd believe it. Have you seen the flag he's flying in his yard these days?

Yeah. I don't get it. He's not a war vet or anything, is he?

Oh, you can't be that naïve, Georgie. It's about Lois.

What—the Australian flag?

Patriots. That's what these people call themselves now. Wrap themselves in the flag. Have you noticed the bumper stickers in this town? Notice many dark faces? Avis has *opinions* about immigration.

Oh, God.

What an irony, huh? Without Asia this town'd close down inside a week.

Georgie thought of Shover McDougall. So that's how he saw himself, as a patriot, a standard-bearer for the good ole days.

Through the kitchen window they watched

Rachel's son Sam while they drank their tea. Sun-bronzed and shirtless, he knelt solemnly in his long floral baggies to wax his surfboard. His hair fell in his face.

Sixteen, Rachel said.

He's beautiful.

Some days I can't believe he's mine. Come on, I'll drive you home.

On their way back, while Georgie enjoyed her deliverance from the worst of the pain, Rachel swung by the jetty and drove the Land Rover down onto the shore beside it so they could stare a little while at the lagoon which still lay flat before the fierce morning easterly. Georgie sensed that the other woman wanted to keep talking.

You know I only met Lu Fox a couple of times, said Rachel.

Yeah? murmured Georgie neutrally.

Jerra said his brother was kind of sly, said he had the junkie look, whatever that is. Didn't care for him. And he thought the woman, his wife, was a bit dim. Seemed an odd pair to me. But they could play. Like they were naturals. And they didn't actually play that often, not as much as you'd have thought, given how good they were. Wouldn't travel more than an hour in any direction. Could have recorded, you know—they were good enough.

And Lu?

Talked to him in the pub carpark. It was cold. Spring, I spose. He had the two kids under a tarp on the back of that ute. Those poor kids. I remember him leaning in, singing to them.

Later I saw him with the little girl. She adored him, I think. He was rocking her to sleep with this look on his face, that look you see on breast-feeding women. You know, that dreamy, satisfied, slightly defiant look.

Quite an impression.

Well, said Rachel sheepishly. I'd had a few drinks. I spose I expected something else. From all the stories, the way people talked about the family. I thought he'd be a bit of a dill. But he was funny and smart. He asked me if I knew the words to 'Amazing Grace'. I flunked, of course. We talked about growing asparagus. And some book he was reading. I forget the book... He's nice, Georgie.

Well, he's gone, said Georgie retrieving herself from this. And *you're* married.

Rachel squawked with laughter. Yeah, to a bloody drug baron!

WITHIN A FEW WEEKS, thanks to Rachel, Georgie's back had returned to normal. The school year began and she had the house to herself again. In fact, in many ways she felt restored to herself. As a gesture of gratitude and a stab at friendship she invited Rachel over for morning tea. She made madeleines and found some chamomile at the local store. She couldn't wait to give Rachel the latest installment in the Jutland family saga. Himself QC, recipient of a cruising yacht left to

261

him by his devoted ex-wife, had decided to give it to faithless daughter Georgie for old times' sake. Georgie really didn't understand her father. But she read the family uproar clearly enough. She was, of course, refusing the gift. He was asking her twice a week by snail mail to come down and see the boat but she was holding out against him. She was, she had to admit, beginning to enjoy it.

When Rachel arrived in leather sandals and a sleeveless summer dress of pale green cotton, Georgie brought out her little spread with a flourish but Rachel, who seemed edgy and pre-occupied, didn't seem to notice. Georgie wondered if it was because Jerra was in Los Angeles for the week. She realized that this was the first time in three years that she'd done anything as simply social as this—invite a friend over for a cup of tea. God, how isolated, how uncertain she'd become.

Have you seen Beaver lately? Rachel asked, smoothing down her frock with the palms of her hands.

Georgie shook her head with a pang of guilt and poured the tea.

Last night, said Rachel, I went over to rent a movie from him and there was a four-wheel-drive tour-bus pulled in at the pump. You know the ones. Full of carsick Japs. You know the deal. A day of bashing through the dunes thinking it's the almighty outback.

Poor buggers, said Georgie. All they want is the live rock lobster promised in the brochure.

Anyway, I'm on my bike. And the driver's

putting air in the tyres and I see these three kids, locals, about twelve, on their bikes in Beaver's driveway. And they're doing these big doughnuts. You know, circling the bus. And I get closer and I see these faces in the window, up in the vehicle, these wide eyes. And there's gobs of slag on the glass and nobody's getting out of the bus and the driver's just hanging the airhose up like nothing's going on. They see me, these kids, two girls and a boy, and they just look at me. Defiant. And there's Beaver and Lois in the office. Looking out. The kids ride off. And I get to the door and Beaver just says that they're closed. That's it. Won't even talk to me.

Georgie could see it, even down to the kids' faces, their sunsplit lips and she knew how it would be. They'd have those nasty white trash buzzcuts with rat-tails and BMX bikes rusty from being ridden through the shorebreak of the lagoon. Proud products of the community.

Why didn't he see them off? Georgie asked, appalled. Beaver's the size of a Kelvinator.

Rachel looked at her. Georgie felt she was being examined.

Georgie, he's scared. Wake up. He can't touch those kids. Think who they belong to. And Beaver's position.

What *is* his position?

Jim never told you?

Told me what?

He's got a criminal record as long as your arm, said Rachel. Armed robbery, mostly assaults.

Nobody told me this. Nobody.

So I see.

So what's his story, Rachel?

The biker mob, said the other woman. He turned crown witness. A pack rape. But the case failed. And now there's a lot of people with something on him or against him.

Nobody talks about it, said Georgie.

Not everybody knows. But the people who matter. They know.

Rachel, how do you know?

I knew him when he was in prison, she said. My other career, remember? I was—allegedly—a social worker for the Department of Corrections. But neither of us acknowledges our old life.

Jesus. Why does he live *here*, then? Wouldn't you bury yourself in a city somewhere? Here he's in the open.

His father was a fisherman here in the sixties. Maybe it's somewhere he's comfortable. And it's only an educated guess, but I imagine that Beaver knows a few things from the good ole days. Lots of nasty secrets in this town, Georgie. Knowing a few things about your fellow townsfolk—well, that'd be money in the bank, wouldn't it. That'd explain why he feels safe.

Well, you've thought about it a lot, I gather.

Hey, I've had the time.

The good ole days, muttered Georgie bitterly.

I don't think he pines for them. His old days or anybody's. I think he just wants a new life, a quiet life. Anyway, I doubt the good ole days are as far in the past as you might imagine. God, look at that view. Jim must feel like king of all he surveys.

After Rachel left, Georgie was restless and despondent. There had been something prickly about Rachel, something more than the lefty paranoia she suspected her of. The whole time Georgie had felt a mounting irritation coming off the other woman. The morning had not been a success.

She went down to the lagoon for a dip. The air was dry and hot, the water gorgeous.

When she got back to the house there was a message from Ann on the answering machine. Judith was in hospital. There had been a scene. Bob had taken her somewhere discreet. Georgie knew the place.

She called Jim first and then Rachel who agreed to collect the boys from school at three. Then she called her sisters but got either secretaries or answering services. She felt absurdly calm and it bothered her.

Beaver was short with her as he filled the canary Mazda with unleaded. She wanted to ask about the events of yesterday but his glare was enough to hold her off until he slapped the tank hatch home and brought back the keys.

Beaver, Rachel told me about those kids last night.

Gets better, he said. She pissed off.

Lois? No!

Shoulda known better. No way to get a wife. It's undignified.

Those little bastards.

Back to Mrs Palmer and her five daughters.

She was nice, Beaver. I liked her.

So did I, he said bitterly.

I feel so terrible.

Don't worry, he murmured. You'll get over it.

Georgie drove out stung to the edge of tears. Her recent calm was gone. She missed it.

The hospital was close by the river and, as Ann said, very discreet. It was the establishment that Perth's favoured families used for their elective procedures and their private weeks of drying out. After the mad, dysfunctional teaching hospitals that Georgie had trained in, the atmosphere of this place struck her as perfectly languid. There was no one at the nurses' station crying into a pillowslip, that was for sure.

When she was finally allowed into Jude's room she found her sister looking exhausted. Her skin was waxy, her lips chapped. When she hugged her there didn't seem enough of her.

Pumped me out, said Jude hoarsely.

Sorry? Georgie said pulling back a moment to look her in the face. Jude looked down at her own hands.

Pumped my bilge, Jude croaked.

266

You took something?

Everything. Throat hurts.

Christ, Jude, when?

Tuesday? Yesterday.

Georgie hugged her again. She felt dull with shock: the idea.

That's it. I'm officially nuts.

No, you're just miserable.

Weak.

No.

Weak.

Jude.

You're the tough one.

Georgie ripped a couple of tissues from the box on the bedside cabinet.

Been thinking of Mum today, said Jude. One time the both of them were all dressed up for dinner? Mum in this tight, pink dress, backless, you know. Us in our jarmies looking at her come down the stairs so beautiful. And Dad says, like a comedian, out the corner of his mouth: Lights on, nobody home; but such *pretty* lights. Georgie, did I imagine that?

Georgie shook her head, pressed the wet tissues to her mouth.

See, said Jude. I married my father.

Downstairs in the lobby thirty minutes later Georgie made a rash of angry calls. Why hadn't she been told earlier? What was all the secrecy, for Godsake? How did they plan to deal with this? But even as she barked and gestured futilely, she was thinking of herself, of her own inattention, her failure to read the plainest of signs.

Before she left she called her father; it was almost an afterthought. His secretary told her he was in Fremantle, that he was leaving for Rottnest Island in forty minutes and that Georgie could catch him on his cell phone. When he answered, the old man was earnest. He sounded so worried. Could they possibly meet?

It took Georgie half an hour to get down to the marina. Her father and Cynthia were on the dock in their poncey sailing outfits, all deck shoes and polarized shades on lanyards. Cynthia wore so much make-up Georgie figured she used it as sunscreen. The old boy's legs were white and scaly. The three of them kissed awkwardly.

Before Georgie could get to the point, which was surely Jude's immediate future, the old man placed a sheaf of papers in her hands. These were the registration and insurance details of a vessel called *Closing Address*. It was already in her name. Georgie looked up at him. His face nearly split with pleasure.

Take us out one day, he said stepping down onto a big, white Bertram, whose motors, she realized, had been running the whole time.

Cynthia pecked her on the cheek and, radiant with an emotion upon which Georgie could only speculate, cast off the boat's lines and stepped aboard. Stepmother. Cynthia waved, still beaming, and when the boat swung out and turned, Georgie saw the name emblazoned across the stern. *Summary Affair*. Good God. Why not *Billable Hours*?

Watching them glide from the marina Georgie had to face the fact of his love. She'd seen it in his grin. Along with all that manly hubris there *was* love. But of a kind that mystified her. Behind these years of hurt glances there was a hectoring persistence to it and yet it never felt intimate, or even personal. His devotion was, bizarrely, strategic. This past few weeks he'd tried to demonstrate affection with his gift and she'd rebuffed it. She could feel him straining for something; she almost felt guilty. But here it was, the cold nub of it: even at full stretch he had to plot, to ploy, and then win. Georgie knew that she'd been *served*. The gift bestowed the way you serve a summons or a writ. By canny entrapment. Even in fatherly love, the great game. To serve *upon*. That was his idea of service. This was love.

Over at the yacht club Georgie was directed to the hardstanding by a perky young boatman who kept eyeing her legs. *Closing Address* stood up on wedges and a frame, its keel blasted clean.

Jeanneau, the boy said. Pretty good for a production boat.

It was a Sun Odyssey; Georgie knew the design. Forty feet of glossy kevlar with lovely sheer and a sleek, low coachroof. The cockpit was ample despite the split pulpit and the twin helms. Mast, lines, brightwork—they all gleamed. It was everything you could want; you could sail this boat anywhere.

Hardly been in the water, said the boy. All the fruit. Interested in boats are you?

Only mine.

Got one, have you?

Yes, she said pointing.

Fuck me, he said. He made it sound like an invitation.

Georgie walked up to the offices across the tarmac, found a broker and sold the boat inside twenty minutes.

When Georgie saw her again not an hour later Jude seemed fogged in. Her earlier raw sadness was gone. She seemed to swim slowly up out of some happy reverie at Georgie's approach, but within seconds she was agitated. Georgie knew even as she was doing it that this was clumsy but she felt compelled to put the cheque on the blanket beside her sister's hand. Despite the discount for haste, it was still a lot of money.

You can leave him, Jude. With this you can buy somewhere of your own. Get a lawyer, do whatever you need to do. You're not stuck, okay? When you're feeling better you can leave. Take Chloe. Have your own life.

But it's stealing, said her sister, bewildered. It has your name on it.

I can fix that, sis. Jesus, it's simple.

We'll get caught.

Jude, I'll get you a new cheque. Forget you saw this one.

I can't forget! Jude bellowed.

A perfumed nurse appeared in the doorway.

Please, Jude pleaded with the nurse. Tell her I can't forget.

Georgie folded the offending draft and left without having to be asked.

TWICE THAT WEEK Georgie drove to the city to see her sister. She left at nine when the boys went to school and was home well before three each time. Jude was like a sleepwalker; it broke your heart to see it.

On Saturday she took Brad and Josh with her. They needed shoes. She took them to the science park for their trouble and afterwards let them wait in the hospital lobby while she visited Jude. It was a glum, bewildering half-hour. She didn't raise the issue of money— Jude's attitude had hardened irrationally with the passing days, and the cheque was now an unsettling figure in Georgie's bank account.

Heading back in the long drowsy afternoon she averted her gaze as they passed the fruit stand. Up around the bend a white plume rose above the trees. The boys stirred, pointing.

It was dust not smoke.

Rounding the bend they saw a child running barefoot along the road. There was a car in the ditch.

Georgie slowed to a stop.

I know who that is, said Brad.

Just stay here, said Georgie. Don't get out

271

of the car. You'll have a big job in a minute, d'you understand? When I bring her back you hold that girl and talk to her and keep her in the car.

It's hot, said Josh.

That's Charlotte, said Brad.

Georgie snapped on the hazard lights and chased the whimpering child along the roadside until she could take her hand and lead her back. There was blood on the girl's arm and on her clothes but it didn't seem to be her own. She looked about nine years old; she was cold with shock. The boys looked white-faced as Georgie opened the Mazda door.

G'day, Charlotte, said Josh timidly.

The little girl hiccupped. She sat passively between the boys, who stared at her. Georgie closed the door and took a breath.

The car across the road had rolled and come to rest back on its wheels. It was tilted in the limestone rubble of the ditch, warped out of shape. There was blood all down the driver's door. A head of black, curly hair rested upon the sill of the open window.

Georgie tried the passenger door but it was mashed shut. The window was open; she thrust her head in, sick with dread.

Hello? the driver, a woman, said.

Georgie wormed in through the window, across the glass and stones on the seat and took hold of the console to steady herself. The driver's face was distorted by gore and the way she was wedged with her chin against her shoulder. And there was the hair. The scalp was lifted back from the forehead enough to make those black curls seem misplaced. The woman's eyes were glued almost completely shut by blood and it pooled in the reservoir of her compressed cleavage. Her blouse was glossy with it.

She mouthed something Georgie didn't catch.

Tired, did you say? You need to stay awake. Can you stay awake for me?

The tyre, said the driver. Blew a tyre.

Georgie was right up to her, thinking that it wasn't so bad, just messy, when she saw the arm the driver was shielding from view by the twisted way she was seated. The right arm. Stripped to the bone. The muscle was a snarl of meat and tendon. It had been out the window by the look; she'd rolled the whole car over it. Already the hand upturned on her thigh was turning puce. Not good.

Charlotte? the woman asked.

She's in my car. She's okay. She's all right. Was there anyone else?

No.

You're doing fine, Georgie said, struggling toward the bright matter-of-factness, the casual confidence she used to be able to grind up for nine hours every day. She looked in dread at the arm, noting the steady loss of colour. There was no obvious spurting blood vessel. She looked for somewhere on that mess to tie a compression bandage, a tourniquet. Jack-knifed through the window like that, Georgie wriggled out of her bra and tied it above the elbow where the flesh was shirred like a puffy sleeve. The woman whimpered, stayed conscious, and as she shifted there was a squelch from the bucket seat beneath her.

A car seemed to approach and slow. God, thought Georgie, let this be someone who knows what they're doing so they can take over, so they can figure this out.

Reassuring the injured driver, promising she'd only be gone a second, she writhed back out.

A woman in a silver Pajero slowed to a stop. She was either stunned or wary because it took her a few moments to unwind the window.

Oh, love, she said. Are you all right?

As calmly as she could manage, Georgie told the woman to call an ambulance on her cell phone, immediately, to ask for the White Point ambulance because it was closer and to turn around and drive back to White Point with the kids in that car across the road. They would show her where to drive them. To the roadhouse, yes the service station and go now, now.

Climbing back through the window of the car Georgie saw that the driver was still conscious but shaking, and her arm was grey. She figured the ambulance was half an hour away at best, forty-five minutes if things went badly finding the rostered volunteers. From here it was ninety minutes to the city's nearest hospital. The arm was history. Georgie's only hope was to keep her going, that they might keep the patient alive long enough to make it to the city.

The Pajero left in a clash of gears.

Georgie thought about pulling her out now, making a dash for it in the bubble car. It'd cut half an hour from the wait. But every rule was against it. She knew the bleeding would start anew the moment she moved her and she'd probably arrest before she got her into the Mazda.

She pulled herself across the gear shift and craned around to look at the arm again. Right below the shoulder, at the joint, there was a seepage. A wound she hadn't even seen before. The driver's breast lay against it. The weight of the woman's body was against the door. That's where all the blood was from. She'd opened a major blood vessel and fallen back on the limb; the woman was holding herself together.

Cicadas beat away in the wattles beyond the ditch.

I write with my left hand, said the woman.

Well, that's a stroke of luck, said Georgie, wondering if a shoelace would do. If she couldn't keep the position then Georgie'd have to find the vessel and tie it off. She didn't fancy the chances.

You probly had the boys with you?

Sorry?

Joshie's in Charlotte's class.

She's fine, said Georgie absently. Really, she's okay.

Don't let me die, Georgie.

You won't die. The blokes'll be here any minute.

This road's a bugger.

Any road's a bugger when you're upside down in a car, said Georgie. Keep her talking, she thought.

It's unlucky, this road. That family. Those people.

Charlotte, said Georgie aloud trying to place Josh's classmate. There was nothing familiar about this woman's bloodsoaked and distorted face.

The dog.

You're okay.

He shouldna done it. I'm sorry.

It's all right. Help's coming.

The woman began to take deeper breaths. Oh, Lord, Georgie thought, here it comes, she's gonna die. Oh God. But the woman seemed to come to a crisper consciousness.

After Debbie died, she murmured, Jim lost pride, you know... My Gavin always looked up to him and his father, oh, Big Bill, *he* was a man... There's standards, Georgie.

I'm sorry, but do we know each other?

It's Avis.

Avis? McDougall?

Standards.

Georgie pulled herself up and sat in the seat across from the injured woman. God, the pain she must be in. It *was* Avis McDougall but you had to search for the features you knew her by. She thought of all the misfortune she'd wished upon these people.

Think about our children with no jobs while this country is...*Asianized*. That's what I mean... And there's no honour, Georgie. Not like there used to be.

Georgie sat there. She would listen to it. Whatever hateful bullshit Avis came out with, she'd let her go on. What was the point of arguing, and what right do you have in setting someone straight when they're dying anyway?

Those Foxes. They were low. And thieves. And druggies.

Avis—

But it wasn't right about the dog... You shouldna been with him, Georgie. You brought shame on Jim Buckridge.

Georgie thought of the night she got back from Lu's place. The white car pulling out of Jim's driveway. It was this car. It was Avis who was running to Jim.

I think you've been watching me, Avis.

My conscience is clear.

Except for the dog.

Yes, said the woman beginning to weep from beneath her mask of blood. Except the dog.

Georgie sat there watching Avis McDougall weep. She held her good hand. It was cold. The bad arm looked chalky now. She prayed that this woman did not die. She prayed for her own sake.

I'm sorry, she whispered. To Avis. Whoever.

The siren rolled down across the paddocks.

THAT EVENING Georgie was too shattered to cook. The phone rang incessantly. She let Jim field the calls. The boys were hyper from the afternoon's events; she sent them out to buy pizzas and the four of them ate on the terrace as the sun set into the sea.

From what I hear that was pretty slick work today, said Jim when the boys had peeled off to watch TV. He looked impressed but also amused. Avis McDougall had survived and the word was they might yet save her arm.

I've added to my reputation, said Georgie.

Yeah, the bra was the golden touch.

I had the tourniquet in the wrong place.

Saved her life.

People like Avis can't be killed, she said without conviction.

You look worn out. This thing with Jude. You're grinding yourself into the dirt over it.

It's not a *thing*.

And you really sold the boat?

Georgie nodded. The sky was a bushfire on the seaward horizon; another sunset, a lost day.

You must hate your father, he murmured.

No, she said. I love him.

I understand.

Tell me about *your* father.

Some other time.

In three years there's never been a time, Jim. You know, I thought it was grief the first year or so. Then I realized that I wasn't someone you wanted to tell things to.

Let it go, George. You've had a tough day.

I don't know anything about you.

I've been thinking about the end-of-season trip, he said. I've gone off the idea of the Maldives. Indonesia's a bloody mess. Fiji's a war zone half the time. Europe's—well, I can't be bothered. I've been thinking about Broome. Some salt-water fly fishing. I want that forty-pound barramundi before I'm too old to cast a fly.

Georgie sat there a while before the word even registered. She was busy considering the distance between them, this abiding silence. Broome?

Why Broome? she asked.

Like I said. Barramundi. You know, July in the north. Not too humid then. Sit on Cable Beach and drink daiquiris.

You don't drink daiquiris.

Besides, you can meet the cousins.

In Broome.

They're pearl divers, most of em. Half the family's from there.

But you never—

So now I'm telling you.

What brought this on?

Cousin of mine called the other day. Just an idea.

Georgie walked down to Beaver's. He'd locked the pumps and was sitting out the back in his wreckyard. His eyes and the beercan glinted in the light spilling from the back door but he was mostly a shadow.

Hey, where'd you learn the bra thing, watching *M*A*S*H*?

Georgie picked her way across to him. He was on the dimpled hood of Avis McDougall's Camry. You could smell the blood in the heat.

Shover wants this thing impounded. He suspects foul play. Sabotage.

Bullshit, she said with a laugh.

That's the word. Want a beer?

Georgie declined. She couldn't bring herself to sit on the Camry so she leaned against some other hulk in the gloom.

Is it because I'm self-obsessed and totally incurious that I don't know a bloody thing about anybody, Beaver, or is it just that nobody tells me anything?

Beaver's laugh was wheezy. You want my honest opinion or my shopkeeper's arse-kiss?

The truth.

Truth is, it's both.

Ah.

Nobody ever expected you to stay. Why blab to a blow-in? Anyway, you always kept to yourself. And, be honest, you come from a different life.

Georgie smarted at this but didn't take it up with him.

Avis reckons Jim's gone soft. That he changed after Debbie died. That true?

That's the theory.

Changed how? She makes it sound like he mellowed.

That's the word.

Georgie let a few moments pass in silence. She was fishing and Beaver didn't want to bite.

We all have regrets, she murmured.

Beaver crushed his can. Yes, he said. I wish I was William Powell. I'll bloody never get over it.

I'm serious, Beaver.

No, you're not. Someone like you, the past is just an awkward place to visit. That's how much regret there is. Some people... you can't even imagine, Georgie.

Because I went to a flash school? The silver spoon in my mouth?

And because you're a woman.

That's a load of crap and you know it.

Some men, he hissed, some men aren't *embarrassed* about things they've done, Georgie. They don't get *pangs* about their past. They're fuckin terrified of what they've been. And they're scared that they might be the same person they used to be.

You...you're talking about yourself, then?

Beaver laughed bitterly and tossed the can. It bounced off a wreck in the dark.

Actually, he said, I'm talking about Jim Buckridge. Go home, Georgie, you're givin me a headache. I've just finished my first day as an abandoned husband. There's no way I'm sittin here all night workin through your little problems. Thought you'd come to cheer a bloke up.

You think he's changed?

Give me strength!

Okay, I'm going.

Good thinkin.

But Georgie couldn't walk away.

No, she said. I have to know.

Shit! Ask yeself—can anybody change?

Just tell me if he has.

Well, Beaver said at last. Somethin's got up him. Like you said—people have regrets.

And that's your answer? she cried.

Gawd, Georgie. Why stay? Why'd you *ever* stay?

Same as you, I guess. Thought it was the quiet life. I settled for something instead of nothing.

Don't compare yeself to me, mate, he said hotly. *You* can go wherever you want. Right now I wish you'd go home and leave me alone.

I'm sorry.

There you go, your enormous regrets again.

That night Georgie's mind wouldn't settle. The sight of her sister, the ordeal by the roadside, the bottled fury in Beaver kept her awake and she thought of Rachel's exasperated prodding the other day and this creeping doubt she was stuck with. She was exhausted but she couldn't let go and she knew a few vodkas were not the answer they truly promised to be as she lay there in the dark. In the end, out of desperation, she relented somewhat and took a mild sedative.

By the time she woke next morning, Jim was long gone.

It was Sunday. She drank coffee while the boys prepared the dinghy for crabbing. They seemed only mildly disappointed that she wouldn't be accompanying them. When they were safely out on the lagoon she went to Jim's office and began to snoop.

It was a tiny airless room. The window which looked across town to the steep white dunes inland was never opened. Although it was next to their bedroom Georgie rarely went in there except to clean. It had, she knew, been Debbie's sewing room. Before Georgie came to White Point, Jim used the desk in the livingroom, but since then he'd retreated here. There was a pine desk, a filing cabinet, a port for his laptop and a few low book-shelves. The walls were bare. It was hardly the den she remembered her father holing up in. By comparison it was a purely utilitarian space. There had never been anything in the room to pique Georgie's curiosity. She sat in the beige swivel chair and looked at the shelves. Tomes on shipbuilding, fisheries management, meteorology. Almanacs, tide-books, a few novels like *Deliverance*, *The Bonfire of the Vanities*, *East of Eden*. Some war memoirs by Ray Parkin. Something called *The Knights of Bushido*. *Dead Men Rising*.

She felt strange going through the file cabinet. She was jittery just being in here. The files were the usual business stuff, bank and insurance records, correspondence of the Fishermen's Association. Nothing to get interested in. But she was surprised to find the desk drawer locked. She searched for the key along the windowsill and the architrave above the door but found nothing. She went next door to the bedroom and opened his bedside drawer. She had lived with him three years and never done this before, open his desk or his bedside cabinet. It struck her now as amazing. What discreet, discrete lives they'd been leading. It was as though she remained a guest in both their minds.

In a cut-glass bowl beside a roll of antacid tablets and a couple of small bullets was the key.

Georgie went out into the livingroom and scanned the lagoon. The boys were setting crabnets.

She opened the drawer. It wasn't much bigger than a shirt box. There was a white cotton blouse folded small. Size 10. It smelled only of wood. Beneath it was a green book. When she opened it she recognized it as the Anglican liturgy; a prayer book. There seemed to be no special markings in it. The breeze the pages made smelled of pine pitch; it rose in her face. Next she found two sheets of paper fixed by a rusty staple. Names ran down each page. The letters cut into the paper from the imprint of a manual typewriter. The names looked Japanese.

At the back of the drawer was a ziplock bag. Through the plastic you could see two teeth. Milk teeth, probably the boys'. Georgie smiled and set the bag back. Her fingertips rested on something wrinkled, more paper. Before she even smoothed it out on the desk she knew what it was. It had food smears on it from the kitchen bin. The boab tree stamp. The Broome postmark. Inside, the paper was still the colour of dried chilli. She put Luther Fox's envelope back in the drawer and locked it.

five

FOX HOLES UP at a boarding house in Broome while a cyclone bears down from the Timor Sea. The hot, drumming rain that began within an hour of his arrival has cut the road out. Lightning splashes through the storm shutters. Even with the wind mounting, the air is thick and wet. Fox sleeps. Now that he's stranded he's slain by fatigue. He wakes now and then to thunderclaps or the screams of fighting drunks, but the sleep is dreamless.

By the third day, though, he's restless. The cyclone veers away to expend itself in the desert but the coastal plain is flooded.

Fox walks through the fabled town with its Chinese shops, its corrugated iron storefronts and palm trees. The beaches are stained red from the run-off. Even in the downpour you sense the desert at the town's back. At low tide the mangrove creeks are little more than rain gutters. At their mouths, pearl luggers tilt on exposed mudflats. The tourists seem to be gone. The faces hereabouts are red, yellow, black beneath their hats. Children wade in the main street. There are smatterings of Japanese calligraphy on red-stained walls. Beyond the port jetty and the mocha bay the sky is black. He half expects to run into Horrie and Bess. They'll be stranded same as him. He dreads it.

He buys a sheaf of survey maps and spreads them out on the floor of his room. Inland there's the Great Sandy Desert. Further north the coast looks like a dropped plate, all island shards and crazed rivermouths, and behind this lonely-looking fringe is a profusion of converging ranges and seasonal watercourses. Country he can barely imagine.

Since Wittenoom he's had no goal, only a vague bearing. North. He could keep going right across the top—through the Northern Territory and into Queensland. Then work his way down the east coast, if he wanted. But the road has cured him of travel. What he wants is to slope off into the bush somewhere, do what he should have done more than a year ago instead of slinking around the edge of White Point like a feral dog. If you want to be left alone then clear out. Go somewhere clean. Some place with water and food so you're not skulking at the margins to keep yourself alive. A place where you can stand alone, completely alone. No roads, towns, farms—no bloody civilians. Just walk off into the trees. It's been lurking somewhere in his mind for days, beaten down by talk, by the frigging ordeal of other people and his own numbness. The idea of a place to be truly alone in—wilderness. And quite suddenly, there it is on a map beneath his fingers. He remembers it from the atlas, from the story Georgie told. This is the place. Somewhere to aim for.

He hitches out to the airport and finds a charter outfit. While he's waiting for someone to appear at the desk he takes in the massive wall chart of the region. Beside it some wag has pinned a map of Ireland which has a similar land mass. Next to this, the same character has laboured to produce a montage wherein the state of Western Australia is made up of multiples of France.

Makes ya laugh, dunnit, says a pilot appearing in the doorway. In his shorts he has the look of a whippet.

Fox reaches up, puts his finger on Coronation Gulf. Can you fly here?

Can't fly anywhere in this weather, mate. Everythin's underwater. Outta range anyway, unless we make fuel stops. And like I said, all the strips are wet. Be a few days yet.

Fox lets his hand slip from the chart. The airconditioner rattles.

What about a floatplane? he asks, jerking his head toward the photos of the company's modest fleet behind the desk.

In bits on the hangar floor, cob.

Fox purses his lips. The pilot looks at him, seems interested in his peeling face and scabby legs.

Flyin costs a bomb up here, mate.

Fox shrugs.

But if you're keen and don't mind waitin, we could bounce you up there in a few days.

I'll think about it, says Fox.

I'll bung your name on the sheet.

Well—

Just in case. You might get lucky. Where you stayin?

Fox gives him the address of the house above the bay.

Name?

Fox hesitates. Buckridge, he says.

That right? Jesus the country's lousy with em.

That's what they tell me, says Fox heading out the door.

That night he's eating a mango from the tree in the yard when he overhears talk of the road to Derby being open by morning. The smell of a clove cigarette wafts along the verandah. Fox packs his kit. Before bed he sits down to write a letter to Georgie Jutland. He feels the need to explain himself but with a pencil and paper in hand he can't make sense of his feelings. With her in the room, the smell of her in the air, he had a strange blaze of hope—a whole day of it. But it's gone and he can only fill the hole with the old determination. A plan, a strategy. And maybe, when he's settled, a routine. But how do you say this? How do you explain yourself?

He brushes dirt from his swag and looks at how it powders the floor like seasoning. He stoops and corrals the dust with the envelope. Takes a peck in his fingers.

Out on the muddy street he calls from a phone booth. He lets it ring in White Point until someone picks up. A small, hoarse voice.

Georgie?

But the voice is a child's. He hangs up.

• • •

In the morning he hitches a ride north on
Highway 1 with a mob of blackfellas in a five-
tonne truck. Fifteen people sprawl around
inside the steel cage amidst bedrolls and cardboard boxes full of supplies. No one says
much. The slipstream and the road noise
make conversation difficult. A couple of kids
give him shy, curious looks. A toothless old
fella offers him a swig from a warm bottle of
Fanta. He declines.

They cross the swollen Fitzroy River at
Willare Bridge. You can hear it over the sound
of the truck. Trees and dead cattle loll in the
churning pink current. The river is all over the
floodplain.

Out on some intersecting dirt road a semi
stands bogged to the axles, its driver out on
the bullbar rolling himself a smoke.

The land glistens yellow, orange, red. White
cockatoos rise into the charcoal sky. Thin
trees. Mud. Cattle grids.

As they close on the town of Derby boab trees
appear more frequently beside the road. Their
smooth flanks shine after the rain. They stand
fat and close, and to Fox they're prepos-
terous and lovely, like a crowd lining the
highway, hip to hip, all arse and head-dress
in the sun.

The old bloke with the Fanta leans in to Fox's
ear. Dis fulla, he says, pointing out a huge
knobbly boab with boughs like obese arms.
Same as my missus.

A ripple of laughter goes around the truck as though the joke's been told before. Up against the cab a woman wags a finger.

At the airstrip Fox finds an open hangar where a boy is shoving a two-seater into position. When he asks about a charter he's directed to the office. Chugger will fix him up. Chugger appears at the doorway, a silver-haired bloke in pressed shorts, a shirt with badge and epaulettes, and rubber thongs. He sucks his teeth when Fox asks about Coronation Gulf. They go in to look at the chart. The pilot points out the closest strip. It's high on the plateau inland. It's either that or a chopper and with half the inland cattle stations underwater there's not a machine to spare. Besides, says Chugger, he's not a chopper pilot.

How much? asks Fox. To the plateau.

A thousand bucks.

Fox peels off the notes.

Geez, yer keen, mate. Don't have to pay today, yer know.

I want to go today, says Fox.

Comin back when?

One way.

You're the boss, says the pilot, amused. Course there's paperwork.

Fox counts off another hundred dollars.

Squeaky! the pilot calls. Fuel her up!

I need some stuff in town.

Allow me. I'll shout you lunch.

Fox buys dried food, a waterbag, insect repellent, candles, sunscreen, lighters, mosquito coils, some first aid supplies to supplement his little box, a light machete, some thirty-kilo handlines, hooks, lures and a polytarp rolled tight as a newspaper. Then he chooses a telescopic fishing rod and a lightweight reel to match it. They look flimsy but everything else he sees is either too bulky or too heavy to carry all day.

You in trouble, son? Chugger says over lunch.

Only if you can't fly a plane.

Outside men and women push shopping trolleys stacked with beer. They're laughing and yelling. Some are swathed in bandages.

Pension day, says Chugger. They'll be tearin each other's throats out by dark.

Fox saws at the last of his roast lamb and works mechanically at the chips and gravy. He feels himself gorging. The bar smells of smoke and frying oil and underarms.

You got someone waitin for you out there, sport?

No.

Got an HF radio?

Fox shakes his head.

Well, says Chugger. Eat up.

They bank out across mangroves and mudflats. The great delta is webbed with rivulets and tide wrinkles and where the Fitzroy spills into King Sound the water is the colour of milk chocolate. Beneath the overcast they bear northeast into the interior and Fox sees how old and beaten-down the land is with its

295

crone-skin patterns, its wens and scars and open wounds. The plains, with their sparse, grey tufts of mulga scrub, rise into the high skeletal disarray of the sandstone ranges where rivers run like green gashes toward the sea. All rigid geometry falls away; no roads, no fences, just a confusion of colour. Out at the horizon the jagged, island-choked coast.

Get a better view, says Chugger through the intercom, if Squeaky cleaned the bloody windows. Coon grease.

Sorry? Fox says, holding the headphone tight to his ears.

The indigenous flier sweats it out like mutton fat, says the pilot. Have to scrub it off the perspex. Abos are the bulk of our trade. We bus em in and out from their settlements. They love to fly on the taxpayer's shilling. Orright for some, eh?

They climb above the thunderclouds into bright sun. After two hours they buffet their way down again and Fox sees the green swathe of the plateau above the long gulf. The airstrip is a pink cross. Chugger dives and cranks the machine over onto one wing to check the state of the surface. It looks wet at the edges.

We'll suck and see, says the pilot as they straighten out across the treetops and make a turn downwind for the approach.

So green, he thinks.

After they land it only takes a few moments to unload Fox's modest pile of gear.

Hope you brought yer umbrella, says Chugger. This plateau's the wettest spot in the state. Fifteen hundred mil a year—that's more'n sixty inches.

Fox sets his things out, considers repacking for the sake of neatness and better distribution of weight. Already his shirt is soaked through with sweat.

Spose I'll be comin back out for ya, says Chugger. One way or the other. Don't think I haven't seen a few of youse characters. There's always a search in the end. Doesn't matter who you are: boffin, fugitive, survivalist space cadet, God-botherer. It's all the same deal in the end. You want me to give anyone a message?

Fox shakes his head.

Didn't even get the name.

Buckridge.

Even that name won't get you out of the shit up here, sport. This is the dark bit at the back of the cupboard. You're on your own.

Yes, says Fox almost believing it.

He doesn't watch the plane taxi or take off. He kneels on the dirt and repacks his kit. His hands are shaking. He finds his hat and polaroids and carries everything toward the wall of trees. In the shade of a woollybutt he spreads the map. Already it's lost its crispness in the humidity, and the compass adheres to it.

On the chart there is a track from the airstrip down off the plateau to the sea. The contours are daunting.

He figures he has an hour or two of hiking time before he loses light. He takes a bearing and loads up.

Within five minutes he's half blind with sweat and the vehicle track he's following disappears beneath head-high canegrass. He's forced to gauge direction by feeling for the ruts with his boots and as he plunges through the vegetation, grasshoppers, butterflies and beetles blunder into him, snagging in his teeth and hair, filling his shirt, coating his pack and swag. Rising from the grass either side, livistona palms, cabbage gums and bloodwoods seem to spit birds as he approaches. The sky is creased with thunderheads.

In an hour or so he's nearly buggered. His skin feels flayed by speargrass. Ahead a sandstone spur promises the first change of elevation. The map had shown scores of ridges unfolding seaward. This rock might offer him a view. It's claustrophobic in all this jungly undergrowth. He gazes at the spur and bears toward it. And then a man appears on it. Fox keeps walking. The man is still there when he arrives.

Thought I heard a plane.

Me, says Fox panting. He looks up at the bloke. He's dark-skinned and barefoot. His shoulder-length hair is black with veins of grey in it. Army surplus shorts hang off his hips beneath a shiny hairless paunch.

Lost, eh?

No, says Fox wiping his face with his hat.

Sure?

Fox shrugs.

Science fulla, are ya?

No.

Guvmint?

No.

Adviser.

No.

Lawyer fulla.

Fox smiles and shakes his head.

Mine boy.

Not me.

Not a station boy, then.

Fox unslings a waterbottle. No.

Well ya not a blackfulla, he says with a wheezy chuckle. Thas for sure!

There's an oriental cast to this man's features but his accent is Aboriginal.

How long's it take to get down to the coast from here? Fox asks before drinking. He offers the canteen to the man who appears not to notice.

Good whole day if ya go the short way. You outta daylight, but. Better camp with us. Best spot.

Don't wanna be any trouble.

Look like you *in* trouble.

No.

Menzies, the man says, sticking out a hand whose palm is yellow.

Fox. Lu Fox.

Carn then.

Menzies looks at his load and seems to contemplate an offer of help but then he just turns and leads the way. Fox hesitates, but follows. The weight of all the gear on his back presses into his heels and it gets worse as they work their way down the ridge and stoop to pass beneath the boughs of trees.

Roots. Musty litter. Clay the colour of curdled milk. At the ragged edge of a red stone breakaway they climb down, holding vines and fig roots for support. They come to a clearing surrounded by cherty stone terraces, a small pan of dirt where a bough shelter stands surmounted by tarps like verandahs. Fox and Menzies approach the smoking campfire. A young, thin black man emerges from the overhang of the surrounding terrace. He wears a pair of blue football shorts and nothing else.

This me mate Axle, says Menzies. Shy fulla. He's a good boy.

G'day, says Fox writhing out of his load.

This fulla Lu Fox, says Menzies.

Flyin fox.

Don't be humbuggin im, Axle.

Djin bunambun.

Yeah, yeah. You see him. See him good. Get that billy on.

You got beer? Axle asks.

Sorry, says Fox. Some tea, coffee.

Tea we got, says Menzies. And you doan need any Emu bloody Export beer.

Axle's eyes dart in his partly averted face. He seems to be suppressing a smile. Menzies hauls Fox's gear in under the shelter while the boy fills a billy from a plastic jerrycan.

This is a good spot, says Fox.

The boy nods. His hair is matted. His knees are worn the colour of sandstone and his feet are wide and callused.

How long you blokes been here?

All time, says Axle. Everywhen.

Couple seasons, says Menzies crouching to stir up the fire. Come and go, you know.

Is this—?

Our country? Menzies shrugs dramatically. Dunno. Orphan, I was. Well, thas what the nuns said. Ever bin down New Norcia way?

Fox can't help but smile as he nods.

All them kids. Noongars, Wongai people. But you look at me. Half-Chinese fulla. Think my mother from Bardi people maybe. Who knows. Them nuns and priest fullas didn't hardly talk no English. Didn't tell me nothin! he utters looking more bemused than bitter.

Dis *my* country, says Axle.

Mebbe, says Menzies with a diplomatic shrug.

Too right.

Could be. Could be. You get that meat, boy.

Axle springs up and heads down a gully in the waning light. Fox studies Menzies wondering what it is that seems odd. And then he sees it—the man has no navel.

Interestin, innit.

Well.

Mebbe the skin growed over. Somethin. Them nuns didn't like it, thas for sure. Kept me shirt on all summer. And them kids? he says with a hoarse, joyous laugh. Nobody fight with a yellafulla with no bellybutton. Axle, too.

He come follern me like a puppydog when he saw it. Talkin rubbish.

Axel. That's a German name. He off a mission? Lutherans maybe?

Menzies squints. Spell it A-X-L-E way. Real particular about that. Only fuckin word he can write, poor fulla. Bit lost, ya know. Bit strange. Cut himself up to be like me. Nearly cut himself three bellybuttons! Found him up Kalumburu way. I was workin for cattle mob. He just walked in the outcamp from the bush—all wild and sick—talkin about bein in the islands and flyin up the coast lookin for the old ones, the old people. Proper heartbroken he was. Thinks they's old shy people still out there. In the old way, you know? Livin proper, hidin out still from the whitefullas. Reckon they's all *waitin* for im, poor mad bugger. Aw, Lu, he upset everybody. All this crazy talkin and gettin angry. Thought he's a petrol-sniffer. They didn't want no trouble, no church fullas or guvmint. So I took him orf. Out Karunjie way, Halls Creek. But he's a handful. All this language he talks, you know, little bit Wunumbal, little bit Ngarinyin, he learned it off some whitefulla. Makes it up. But he's not a proper Aborigine man.

Proper? says Fox.

Never bin through the Law, see.

Initiated.

Thassit. No people. No country.

And you?

Me? I belong to Jesus Christ. Like it or not. They wet you and get you. Anyway. No other bastard will have me.

Axle appears from the deepening gloom of dusk with a lump of bloody meat slung across his shoulder like a saddle. Fox drinks his mouth-puckering black tea while the two of them build up the fire and cut the meat into marbled slabs which they then roast on the coals.

They eat back from the fire where it's cooler and in the dark the flames are the only light.

Beef, says Fox.

Fresh killed this morning.

Pow, says Axle miming a rifle shot.

Fox considers the irony of having fallen among fellow poachers. Menzies explains how they live on bush tucker when there's no cattle handy, how Axle prides himself on his ability to hunt goannas and birds, to shoot the occasional crocodile and ferret out treats like sugarbag from the hives of the native bee. He knows the berries, has an instinct for it, though Menzies prefers beef and damper and tea, which is why they camp on the edge of the plateau. There's water nearby and the occasional four-wheel adventurer who needs rescuing from himself in exchange for precious supplies. Fox asks if they get lonely, and Menzies laughs. Axle, he says, doesn't care for girls but they both wish for some dogs to cuddle up to at night. Menzies confesses to being married once. He names all the prisons he's been in. He's more travelled than Fox by a good measure.

The older man gets to his feet and goes rooting around inside the shelter until a light grows and brightens and Fox smells kerosene. Coming out he stumbles on something that rings discordantly and he curses, almost dropping the lamp.

Special occasions, he announces setting the lamp on the dirt beside them.

What'd you kick in there?

Fuckin gittar thing.

Mine, says Axle.

He likes a strum, says Menzies. But he gets disappointed. Can't make a tune, not proper. Kills him. Awful.

I could tune it for you, says Fox. If it'd help.

Axle bounds to the shelter and brings out a cheap Korean thing grown smelly with mildew but still gaudy in its sunburst lacquer. He presents it two-handed to Fox who stands it on his boot and twirls it by the neck. He clamps it to his sweaty shirt and tunes it quickly. The strings are furry with corrosion. His fingertips feel virginal.

Play, says Axle.

Ah.

Axle and Menzies look at him expectantly, so open-faced and hopeful.

What music d'you like? he asks.

Slim Dusty, the boy announces.

Fox plays 'Pub with No Beer' and the others sing along with what sounds to him like apocryphal lyrics. It doesn't matter a damn to him; he hates the song. But the two of them croon on their haunches, eyes closed soulfully while lightning flickers in the sky. When they're done there's a huge sigh from Axle.

Nobody speaks. Fox tunes again for a moment before breaking into a mournful Irish air just to fill the silence, to mask his own discomfort. It starts out no more than a bit of noodling but the melody gets hold of him. He settles into the chord progression and feels himself begin to relax at the feel of the frets underhand, the way the tune offers itself up for elaboration at every turn, and when he completes the cycle he can't leave off, he has to go again, this time with confidence, with a little more tapestry. The air plays itself out but still he can't let go. He segues into a blues rag in the same key, just for a change of pace. Gets a little shuffle going despite himself, something that warms and loosens his tendons. The strings are like fencewire. Still, he bends and slurs. His wrist feels gritty with disuse but he manages a slim vibrato all the same. The guitar's tinny, toy-like tone rings in his chest. Music. And it's not hurting anybody.

He stops when the boy gets up and walks into the bough hut.

He okay?

Can't play. Little bit shame, see.

Oh. I didn't mean to—

Likes a strum, but. You teach him.

But I'll be gone in the morning, says Fox.

Pity, that.

Fox has an idea and de-tunes the instrument to open D. Tries it in the minor first but senses it'll be too mournful. He brings it to the major key and strums it one-handed.

Axle?

Won' come out now, Lu.

305

Axle. I've fixed it so you can play this chord, see?

He lets it ring. Look! One hand. Put a finger here and...listen. That's G. Easy. Up and down. Even with a bottle you'll do it. Axle?

The boy doesn't come out. Fox shrugs and puts the guitar down. It rings in D-major and Menzies smiles conspiratorially.

This land, murmurs Fox. Is this station property?

National park.

Ah.

And blackfulla land too. But all boxite, you know. Makes aluminiun?

Bauxite?

Everybody fightin now. Blackfullas, too. This mob, that mob. Lawyers. Awful.

What d'you think'll happen?

Menzies shrugs. Someone gonna kick us off sooner later. Boxite man, guvmint man, cattle man, Aborigine man. Too right.

I can't see it.

Too right. Blackfulla in a suit. Papers in his hands. Could be.

A distant toll of thunder rolls across the tree-tops.

You lost, Lu?

Not yet.

Where you *goin* to?

Somewhere quiet.

Menzies shakes his head, doubtful. A light rain begins to fall. They go to bed. Fox unrolls his swag beneath the outlying tarp and listens to the fitful patter.

In the night he wakes to find Axle hunkered beside him.

You *banman*? the young man whispers, staring fearfully.

Bad man? No. I'm just...just a bloke, Axle.

You take my *wundala*. For the music. Orright?

Um?

You paddle out there, out Widjalgur, past there. Find that mob.

Okay.

You fly. Like me, unna. In my dream I go. Fly out there on the sea. To Durugu.

Durugu?

Them islands. Long way. Where *djuari* go. All time. Gone people, *djuari*, spirit people.

Fox tries to understand him.

Axle, murmurs the boy patting his bare chest. Wheel turns on *me*.

Long after the boy has gone back to bed Fox lies there thinking of Axle's hot conviction that he means something, that he's central to something even if Fox or the kid himself don't understand what it might be. Even as a delusion it's attractive. He envies him. You can't help it when all you can feel is the wheel rolling *over* you time and again. It's why you get away, get out from under it for good.

YOU GOT one idea where you goin? asks Menzies in the morning as Fox prepares to pull his pack on.

Axle has disappeared; his blackened hunk of damper sits on the billy lid.

Fox unfolds the map to show Menzies the archipelago out along the gulf. He wants to work his way around the coast until he's close to the biggest island which is separated from the mainland by a narrow strait. He hasn't figured out how to cross it yet. He has the machete so maybe he could make a raft.

The older man purses his lips. Hm. Axle must have knowed already. True! Says he give you the boat. He's readin your mind, Lu.

He really has a boat?

Or you be walkin a long time. And then what? Swim? You take his boat. A present for the music, see. Here on the black beach. Wait for high stop tide. Paddle cross. You be right. Proper boat, Lu. Good one. But listen here. See this country? he says pointing out the western shore of the gulf. Doan go here, orright?

What's there?

Business places. Hidin from you. Not for you.

Secret, you mean? asks Fox. Sacred?

Menzies looks away.

What about you? Fox asks. You and Axle. You go there?

Menzies shakes his head. We's *wundjat* fullas. Lost people. We doan go there. From respec. You unnerstan respec?

I understand. I won't go there. But here, says Fox pointing to the island on the map, this okay for me to stay?

You can visit, says Menzies. That boat. You lucky fulla.

Yes.

Sometimes I think Axle's not so crazy. Like he dreamed you before, mebbe. Before the boat, you know, he did a dream and he tole me all about it. Little blue boat comin in from the sea. We go down to that black beach and bugger me! he says with a laugh. Washed up in the rocks. One canoe boat. Paddle an everythin! Ha!

Fox smiles and turns bodily to orient himself by the chart. He hears the jangle of the guitar as Axle comes smiling into the clearing. The smile drops. The instrument clangs to the ground as the boy comes running. He snatches the map and throws it onto the embers of the cookfire. Fox cries out in surprise. The paper ignites with a gentle *whump* and Axle is back in his face demanding the other maps, anything he has. Fox appeals to Menzies who advises him to give them up. The kid is trembling with fury. His eyes are startling, their yellowy whites right under his own. There's nothing Fox can do but pull the maps out and watch them burn.

Fuckin bastards, mutters the boy standing over the flames.

Shit, says Fox. That's torn it.

Got a thing about em, says Menzies. Just trouble, maps. You can't really blame him. Like

they suck everythin up. Can't blame a blackfulla not likin a map, Lu.

Go on the country, says the boy almost
pacified now. Not on the map.

And what the fuck does that mean?

Menzies shrugs. Then he smiles. Means, be
careful you don't get lost.

All day, he works his way down waterlogged
ridges to the sea, stunned by the loss of his
maps. Maybe it's for the best, he thinks in the
end. Another burnt bridge. Forces you forward.

Not an hour into his trek he hears a crack
and discovers that he's snapped the end off his
fishing rod. The thing is buggered now. It does
little for his mood.

From a long saddle of stone he sees the gulf
light up in a sudden grilling moment of sunlight, and in the distance, rising from the milky
turquoise water, the islands. There's nothing
behind him, nothing left now; it's all ahead.

Just on sunset he stumbles down to a tiny
beach of black stones. He searches the rocks
and thickets for a boat. Insects swarm at his
ankles and he begins to wonder if perhaps he's
been sucked in by some joke between Axle and
Menzies. But in the last light, beneath a mat
of vines, he finds a battered sea kayak covered
in logos and stickers from some geographic
expedition. It's a stubby polythene thing but
sturdy enough. The paddle is tethered to the
hull and in the compartments he finds fishing
tackle, a grapple and a coil of old nylon rope.

He lies awake all night beside a fitful fire, persecuted by sandflies and the spectres of crocodiles. Before dawn he rises to eat and prepare for the long paddle. In the first light he tests the kayak for leaks. It sweats a little but seems fine. He watches as the tide rises, bringing with it the flotsam of mangrove leaves, sticks and mud bubbles like foamed chocolate. When he senses the tide peaking he drags the packed kayak to the water and sets out. The sky is clear. The sun glazes everything.

With the weight of all his gear in it the kayak feels precarious. It takes him a while to get used to it and to find a paddling rhythm. He knows the gentlest nudge of a passing croc will put him over. The water is like shot silk and he barely raises a crease. It's so hot out there, so still and clear that the distances seem to expand until everything looks twice as far as it did on the map. He paddles with the great plateau in the air behind him. Works his way out along endless walls of mangroves. Across a rivermouth a mile wide. Toward the intermittent white flare of beaches on the farther shore.

At the corner of his vision, a flash. He swivels to see a mackerel fall from the sky and hit the water with a resounding smack.

Just as the tide turns he reaches the other side but the coast here is rocky. So he works his way along in search of a place to land. He begins to sense the tide sweeping him parallel. The kayak is sluggish. His anxiety rises. Where are the beaches?

By the time he comes to a white shell cove between sheltering headlands he's all but had it. He angles in through the current with the last of his strength, staggers out into the blood-hot shallows and drags the kayak up the beach.

First up he spreads his swag on the white shellgrit to dry in the sun. Then he goes in search of somewhere to camp. Within moments he stumbles on six red fuel drums hidden in a clump of spinifex. Forty-fours, all of them full. Immediately his excitement evaporates.

At the end of the cove he comes to a sandstone overhang whose shade is enhanced by a bough shelter of loosely thatched spinifex and within its shade he discovers a cache of weatherproof crates, two generators, a freezer wrapped in plastic, stackable chairs, PVC piping and a ten-horsepower outboard. Further back the cave has a maze of chambers like outspread fingers. In the darkness he hears water dripping onto water.

He fetches a candle from his kit and finds rock niches full of sportfishing tackle and canned food.

Even here, he thinks.

In the mouth of the cave he makes camp for the night.

He wakes with hermit crabs all over him and utters a silly yell. The sudden movement turns them into pebbles as they lie doggo. He laughs. His own voice sounds close beneath the stone roof. Down at the water's edge he splashes himself cautiously. He makes tea, eats his last muesli bar and goes foraging in the cache to satisfy his curiosity.

Sealed in PVC sewer pipe he finds graphite casting rods. Their reels are in a battered Igloo cooler, some still in their boxes and never used and others wrapped in old mosquito nets and bits of calico. There are tin trunks full of lures—jigs, spoons, plugs, divers. He sees spools of nylon monofilament leader material and high-tech gelspun fishing line. Some kind of professional set-up for the Dry season. All the more reason to go further, deeper up the gulf.

Fox packs his kit piece by piece into the kayak and straps the bulky swag across the top. From the cold pool in the darkness at the back of the cave he fills his canteen and waterbag, and, passing the stockpile of angling equipment on his way out, he hesitates. Unless he can fix it, and he hasn't yet thought how, his own rod is all but useless. He knows he can fish with handlines, that blackfellas favour them, but the casting power of a rod will make all the difference out here.

What else will you live on but fish? A good rod could save your life. He picks out a Penn rod and an Abu baitcasting reel. He fills a calico bag with lures and line and hooks, and jams it all into the kayak. Before he pushes off he goes back for the mosquito net the reel was wrapped in.

He paddles down the eastern edge of the gulf

past mangrove forests and rocky promontories and islets. The land this side is much drier than Menzies and Axle's camp. Sandstone breakaways rise from the spinifex and bleached acacia. Inland it looks desolate. The creeks are small with rockbars or sandspits at their mouths. He labours right through the morning. The water is calm. Sweat rolls off him. He sees the islands rise slowly from the sea, distinguishing themselves from the enfolding land by their splashes of green. He makes the high red blunt one his bearing and in the early afternoon, as the sky builds with monsoon cloud, he comes into its shadow and looks up at its mesa bluffs and strangling vines and clamouring trees. There are boabs on the beach. Birds flit through their web of shadows. This is it, he thinks. This has to be the place.

six

THE DAY AFTER she found the envelope in Jim's desk Georgie went walking to clear her head and make some decisions. The morning was hot and clear. Out on the packed sand of the point she came upon Yogi Behr parked in the company truck. Surfers were just visible in the distance; they sat like kelp bunches out on the reef where the crests of incoming swells peeled back as vapour trails in the northeasterly. Yogi had binoculars clamped one-handed to his face as Georgie sidled up to the window to say hello. One horny foot was up on the dash and the cab stank of ouzo. It took him a while to register her presence.

Ah, he murmured. Wonder woman.

G'day, Yogi.

Always wondered what bras were for. To keep ladies' arms on with. Me mum never told me.

I bet she didn't tell you a lot of things, Yogi.

Told me to steer clear of bad luck.

And did you?

See a lot of bad luck when you drive an ambulance.

And some good luck, remember.

But any fuckwit can pick a Jonah, Georgie.

She looked at him. He had the binoculars back to his eyes.

Are you referring to me, Yogi?

317

Yogi pursed his lips. Those Foxes, he said. Shit luck from go to whoa. The mother, you know, she was killed by an act of God. And the old man, Wally—Christ. He'd go out on a boat and they'd put him ashore before the end of the first day. Crayboats, prawners, sharkboats—he just killed their luck. Like a bad joke. You know one year he built a tree house up a pole in the front paddock. Lived up there for weeks. Bloody fishermen, they'd turn their head drivin past, look the other way so they didn't get touched. You don't whistle on a boat, Georgie, and you still don't take bananas out, but, round here, most of all, you don't take a bloody Fox on board.

What was he doing up a pole? Georgie asked despite herself.

Christ knows. Waitin for the end of the world, I spose. Fuck, he *was* the end of the world, the silly old prick. He was rubbish. They were all rubbish.

They're all dead, Yogi, she said with feeling.

Bar one.

Yes, bar one.

And what d'ye figure the odds are on that, all of em dyin in a rollover on their own driveway? I was there, love. You can't bloody imagine. And that last boy sittin in the ambulance like a zombie. You could feel it comin off his skin like electricity, just pure and simple shit luck. That's what you were foolin with. People did you a favour, love.

Well, thanks for the enlightenment, she said, pushing off the doorsill.

Community service, he muttered. That's me.

318

Ever think about luck? she asked Jim that evening.

He looked up from the weather fax. He seemed startled by the question.

No.

Jim, every fisherman lives by it. All of you.

He shook his head. Knowledge, he said. Seamanship. Experience. Good data and record keeping. A bit of lateral thinking and instinct maybe. Bad fishermen need luck.

You're no different, though. You ban bananas.

That's just to keep the deckies happy. They're superstitious.

And you're not?

No.

Hm.

What's this from, some movie?

There was a tone of dismissal in his voice that Georgie resented.

No. I was just thinking.

People are at the mercy of their own actions, he said. Consequences. But it's nothing to do with luck. Hey, I can't believe you sold that boat. Could have sailed around the world in that.

So you never had bad luck?

He gazed at her. No.

You didn't feel unlucky when your wife got *cancer*?

Jim's stare was cool and searching. He broke it off to look at the fax in his lap.

319

Georgie saw the anger in him. Debbie was out of bounds. Talk of her—even from the boys—caused him to shut down with a kind of instant fatigue.

He went to bed without speaking.

Georgie pulled in at the fruit stand. It was a forlorn structure. Much of it was held together with fencewire. Only a single sheet of iron remained on its one-sided roof. The tilted wooden uprights were weathered grey.

She drove on up the white ruts through the front paddock past the olive trees ghosted with limestone dust until she reached the yard between the sheds and the house. She parked in the shade of the casuarinas. A few feathers lay snagged in brown weeds but there was no other sign of poultry. Climbing out into the heat she got a whiff of tainted air, the sort you got passing a dead beast at the roadside.

With a stone she broke a pane beside the back door and let herself into the kitchen. There was a glutinous ooze at the foot of the fridge. She flicked a light switch. The power was out. She didn't like the smell. It gave her a spurt of fear, a charge of memory. Mrs Jubail.

Georgie didn't know why she was here. The boys were at school and Jim at sea. She just had to get out of town.

She figured the power bills hadn't been paid and the company had cut off supply. But then she remembered the generator droning out in the shed. They weren't even connected. Chances were the diesel had run out or he'd switched it off.

Georgie supposed that some last part of her had hoped he might have slipped back in under the radar. There was that much to admit to yourself.

As she got closer to the shed the smell got worse. By the time she entered the open maw of the workshop she was pinching her nose. Flies billowed in her path; they were a black crepe upon the freezers. An irrational dread took hold of her as she advanced upon them. She threw back the lid of the first and found bags of octopus an angry shade of foaming purple. They looked like shrunken heads piled there, warty with tentacle suckers. The second chest was big enough for what she dreaded most. She summoned a bit of nursely steel and hoiked the cover up. When she saw the writhing nest of feet and feathers she blurted a laugh.

It helped to think of the diesel generator as an overfed replica of the sort of motor she knew about. She had once laboured over a Yanmar marine diesel in the lonely tidal nightmare of Camden Sound. Here at least you had a stable platform and room to manoeuvre. You didn't have to hope the fool up on deck could keep you off the rocks while you worked.

The manual hung off the wall from a piece of string. The fuel tank was empty. She knew enough to realize that she'd need to bleed the lines. The smell from the other side of the asbestos wall was horrific; you could feel it on your tongue as you worked. There was a five-gallon drum of diesel beside the empty reservoir. She tipped it in and primed the thing as best she could. It took an hour to get it going but it gave her an absurd sense of pride, far more than she'd taken in keeping Avis McDougall alive.

She left it roaring and went in and cleaned the kitchen. As she worked she considered what Yogi had said about luck. She remembered her crossing of the Timor Sea. They did it without a hiccup, the original piece of plain sailing, and she knew it was undeserved. They had no right to be let off so lightly; they shouldn't have even been out there. She felt she was using up her quota. And hadn't it all come undone at the very last moment? Colliding with another vessel as they entered the anchorage at Senggigi. Screaming disaster.

Georgie had always assumed that an obsession with luck was the preserve of passive people, others unlike herself. Hadn't she been a great resister, holding out against all those limiting expectations? Trouble was she'd begun to see how little her resistance had brought her. Lately it seemed to her that she'd expended so much of her life's energy digging in her heels that she rendered herself powerless. There was a fraudulence about her rebellious spirit. She was drifting, had been for years. Even in the job. There's nothing like an institutional organization for dressing you up in an aura of action and hiding your aimless passivity. She hadn't *made* things happen for years. Things happened *to* her. Wasn't that simply, blindly, trusting herself to luck—without having the honesty to admit it? At least White Pointers owned up to their dependence on fortune.

Georgie made herself a coffee. She found a clothespeg and a shovel and buried the purulent freezer loads out in the paddock. Afterwards she tipped bleach into the chests and left their lids up.

Later she showered and lay on the dusty sofa in the library room while her clothes dried in the hot wind, and as she sprawled there she realized that her situation had altered again so quickly and in so many ways that she couldn't keep up. Whatever the hell Jim was up to she had a car now; she owned it. And there was enough money in her account to give her real choices.

This place, for instance. It was empty. It was somewhere, wasn't it? She couldn't countenance the idea of returning to the suburban blandness of Perth. And she had no desire to travel. This might be a short-term option. But how would she spend her time? Even if the White Pointers let her alone, how long could she seriously expect to last in a farmhouse hours from any suitable employment?

Still, she thought, whatever happens, however long it did last, it might be some sort of sanctuary. For a while. If she ever did make up her mind.

At her elbow a book of poems bristled with leaves, paper clips, twigs which marked the pages. She picked it up absently and opened to a heavily marked passage.

There were those songs, a score times sung,
With all their tripping tunes,
There were the laughters once that rung,
There those unmatched full moons,
Those idle noons!

Annoyed she clapped it shut and set it down.

She woke up with a start at two o'clock that afternoon. Naked and dry-mouthed and, for a few moments, quite befuddled. She stumbled onto the verandah to find that her clothes had been blown to the dirt below.

At the highway a few minutes later she got out of the car and dragged the farm gate to.

A FEW DAYS LATER, Georgie went back to the Fox place with two five-gallon drums of diesel. She tried to figure out the bank of batteries and how much fuel she'd need to keep the generator going. She cleaned the entire house, folded clothes and put fresh sheets on Luther Fox's bed. She stocked the fridge with a few things and added groceries to the cupboards.

On the third trip she brought the espresso machine from its box in Jim's garage. She made herself little lunches of ricotta cheese on Ryvita biscuits and sat in the library scanning the shelves. She flipped through the fruitboxes full of LPs. There were Australian records from the seventies—Matt Taylor, Spectrum, The Indelible Murtceps, Tully—and weirdo albums by the Mahavishnu Orchestra, King Crimson, Sopwith Camel, The Flock, Backdoor, Captain Beefheart. There was an entire box of blues records and another of bluegrass and folk. In a tin trunk she found a deep jumble of sound cassettes, most of them pirate dubs with names scrawled across them in biro.

She just picked out a name—Chris Whitley—and stuck it in the machine. She lay on the sofa and listened to the languid voice with its momentary looping falsettos. The guitar was wiry, almost harsh-sounding. Georgie didn't know much about music. She'd stopped being avid about it after adolescence and just bought stuff she heard on the radio. Yet there was once a time when she lay barricaded in her room lying on the bed with albums whose every song spoke directly. You could feel the singer pointing the words, the emotion, right at you. She lay here now staring at the water stains on the ceiling while these melancholy, enigmatic songs poured through the house. She'd never heard of this guy. She wondered what it meant to *get over to the big sky country* and *be kissing time goodbye*. All the words puzzled her and that strange wailing bottleneck guitar took some getting used to. But it stirred her. She lay back on the musty sofa and listened to the entire album.

When it was finished she got up and went room to room to open cupboards and drawers. In the main bedroom she tried on sunbleached dresses that were way too big for her. Lu's sister-in-law was, in Warwick Jutland's sweet words, too much woman for her. She felt like a girl trying on her mother's gear. You could make fists where that woman's breasts had been and Georgie had neither belly nor hips enough to give those frocks shape. She picked through underthings balled haphazardly in a drawer. In a trunk at the foot of the bed she found a wedding dress wrapped in cellophane. Beneath it, parcelled in the same material, was a mighty stash of old cannabis.

There was a shoebox of photos. The brother had a sleepy look about him. His hair was black and there was always some kind of knowing grin on his face. There was more grey than blue in his eyes. The woman was all hair and boobs and mouth. The mouth was sensuous, nearly ugly, always open. Her kids looked feral, their silky white hair askew, faces happy, dirty, weary.

Georgie looked through the kids' room but didn't linger. It was too sad.

And then somehow it was March with autumn in the air and a blanket on the bed at night.

The days were still warm—hot, even—but the sting went out of the day the moment the sun hit the sea. Georgie's father had disavowed her and, for some reason she couldn't get out of her, Jude refused to see her when she visited. The others maintained a frosty silence. At home Jim was getting irritable. He found fault with the boys at every turn. There was an ashen look about him and he seemed to be losing weight. He spent more time in his office at night. His conversation with Georgie was civil but distracted.

Beaver had gone into a funk. He filled her little diesel drums with barely a word. And with all the time she spent driving up and down the highway to the farm she hardly saw Rachel either. The one occasion they did have, one evening at the jetty, Rachel broke off the usual pleasantries to declare that there were times in your life when you needed to shake yourself off, drag yourself to your feet and bloodywell *act*. She sounded exasperated, as though this speech had been a long time coming, and Rachel looked so close to tears that if she hadn't immediately climbed into her Land Rover and driven off, Georgie might have hugged her and blurted it all out to her—that she *was* acting, that she already had a plan, that everything would be all right.

Georgie went every day to the Fox place. The trips energized her. She felt some confidence returning. The days she admitted to having been anywhere at all she passed off as trips to see Jude, but she needn't have bothered lying because Jim never asked. It seemed that his mind was elsewhere.

One of those days Georgie rolled an old drum down to the sandspit at the riverbend and began burning junk. It took her all morning and half the afternoon to incinerate Darkie's clothes, the wedding dress, the dope and all those summer frocks. She made herself burn the children's things, every stained tee-shirt and pair of shorts, the posters from their walls, the plastic toys and even their pillows. She spared Lu's room, but she re-organized it to suit herself. She dusted the library and scrubbed the kitchen. She emptied every drawer of its snarls of guitar strings, rubber bands, masscards, allen keys, thimbles and knuckle bones. She saved the stained pair of Levi's and the double bedspread until last. She'd figured out what the stains were. They were the only things she enjoyed burning.

DEEP IN THE BOX of pirate tapes Georgie found one marked FOXS. The label was a Band-Aid and the scrawl that of a child. She hesitated a moment but then shoved it into the player anyway and perched on the sofa to listen.

There was the raw sound of a room. A chair squawked on a wooden floor. A tap rushing on? Yes, and squeaking off. The kitchen. Georgie's mouth went dry. Someone, a child, asked something in the distance. Up close someone else breathed.

A guitar began to pick out a melody. It was simple and melancholic. A mandolin and violin joined in. And then someone began to sing. Georgie knew instantly that it was Lu. It made her chest tight to hear it. She didn't know the song but it was some Celtic-sounding air, the story of a king whose queen lay dying in childbirth after nine days in labour. It was beautiful but there was something savage and unbearable about it. Hearing his boyish tenor only made it harder.

When the song ended there was a long silence. A sigh.

Geez, I could murder a beer, said a man. Georgie figured it was Darkie.

That's the saddest song in the universe, said the little girl close to the microphone. So— they were *her* sighs, her breathing before. Her proximity was startling.

That's why we need a beer, Bird, said Darkie.

Instruments clunked. Somebody tuned a string. The chair scraped and there was the suck of the fridge door.

Did he do the right thing, Lu? asked the little girl. She does ask him: *Open my right side and find my baby.* But he won't. Queen Jane— she dies. And it's so awful.

Go on, Bird, said the mother. Be tea soon. Go out and play.

Lu? the child persisted.

Well, mate, said Luther Fox. I dunno. The

old king, he's frightened, I spose. Would have been pretty radical in those days, doing an emergency caesarian. He says, *If I lose the flower of England I shall lose the branch too.*

I hate that, said Bird.

Never mind. The bub gets born. And it's just a song, right?

Too sad.

If you squeeze the Queen of England, Lu sang impromptu to the same tune, *you can seize her ranch too, you can seize her ranch too.*

Lu! howled the girl amid laughter.

Sorry, Bird. I'm a republican.

Tell me!

Tell you what, love?

What you'd do. If it was you.

Me?

Doesn't have a queen, said a little boy with an adenoidal honk.

Fair point.

Shut up, Bullet.

Bird.

Tell me? the girl asked.

You don't always get a choice, said Lu, between a right thing and a wrong thing.

Oh, Bird said sounding confused.

Oi, turn that thing off, Bullet.

The boy farted. The tape jolted into silence.

Georgie ejected it from the machine and dropped it back into the pile. She stood at the window beside the ruined piano. She felt that she'd trespassed, but she also felt trespassed upon.

That afternoon she walked up to the stones

on the hill and pulled out that tea tin to examine the contents. There was nothing remarkable about them. The little single-word notes were odd. The tin smelled of boronia and of tea or just dust, maybe. She replaced the cache in the rock's side and stood there for a time to listen to the hum of insects and the endless note of wind through the fronds of the grasstrees.

Georgie went to Beaver's to order a delivery of diesel and bottled gas to the farm. Before she'd even told him where to take the stuff he was rolling his eyes and throwing a rag at his feet.

Mate, you've got shit for brains. He's not comin back.

She shrugged.

Oh, the shrug. It's so Jennifer Jason Leigh.

I'm gonna miss you, Beaver.

You bet your pert little arse you will, he said without smiling.

She took to playing 'Kumbayah' on Luther Fox's tarnished steel guitar. From the sheet music in the library she taught herself the chords to 'The House of the Rising Sun' and doubled her repertoire. She liked the feel of the instrument, the way it zinged and jangled on her legs.

She lay for hours in the bathtub. The pasta lunches she made for herself filled the house with the smell of garlic. She read novels on the sofa or swinging in the rocker and some days she took a bricklike poetry anthology down to the shade of paperbarks at the riverbend. Wordsworth, Blake and Keats were bruised with underscorings. Robinson Jeffers, Heaney, R. S. Thomas, Les Murray and Judith Wright bore asterisks and exclamation marks in various hands.

Some mornings Georgie did nothing more than try on Lu's many fingerpicks. She lay on the sofa flexing her hand while the sunlight flashed off brass and plastic and tortoiseshell. They made her feel like a different creature, those glinting claws.

Each day that autumn Georgie collected the mail with a surge of anticipation. It took time to admit to herself the fact that she had begun to expect a sign. Nothing seemed to happen but the conviction grew. The only letter addressed to her was from Avis McDougall, who announced her imminent release from hospital after weeks of surgery. Her emails were all from demented strangers or marketing sharks who'd bought her details from other businesses. Silence from the family, though she tried to call them.

Jim barely spoke.

Georgie decided to move her stuff down in stages.

HE WHEELED THE CRUISER into the sorry-looking farmyard with the jerrycans gulping in the back. The old unpainted house was dark and above it the night sky was blank.

He grabbed the bottle from between his thighs and took a gulp. The beer was almost warm now. Lightheaded with fumes he wound the window down to get a draught of clean, dry, dusty air. He wanted to get out to stand clear of the stink of petrol but he would not allow himself—he was afraid of what he would surely do.

Torching the joint wouldn't cauterize bad luck the way you wanted it to. Nor would it free you of that sensation of being watched and judged by whatever seething, hateful purpose was at work in the world. But, by Christ, it'd have its satisfactions.

If he got out of the vehicle—under any damn pretext—he knew he'd probably go ahead and do it, he'd light up the fucking night, he'd put stars where there were none and it wasn't as though a man didn't have cause.

And yet within the first few seconds of being there he knew he wasn't going to. Hadn't he proven a point to himself? Just sitting here wild as fuck, with the means and the inclination and *not* doing it, wasn't that proof-positive you weren't doomed to repeat yourself forever?

He finished the beer and steeled himself for the drive back. So bloody tired.

◆　　◆　　◆

SHE SAW LU FOX kneeling in a urinous haze. The sun was a penny. He dug in the earth with the bushfire sky behind him. He paused a moment and beckoned. Georgie squatted alongside him to see the black steel pipe beneath the surface with its rash of valves and taps. Saw him twist each in turn. One spewed numbers, another laughter. There were little jets of every odour: your mother, the smell of the back of your arm, food, shit, decay, soap. She heard the cries of children, saw photosynthesis. Chunks of information spurted out like sausage meat. From one tap there was just salt and from the next the smell of fresh-minted money. Lu went forth like a dog digging, with a spray of dirt fanning from between his thighs, until he revealed an infernal network of pipes beneath the earth that seemed to leach and store and ferment every moment of time and experience from beneath their feet. Everything that ever happened was there. She didn't understand why or who did this or what became of it.

She began to cry from bewilderment and anxiety.

And then he looked up, took a peck of dirt, spat on it and rolled it into a yellow pellet. He pressed it gently into her ear and smiled. It sang. Like the inside of a shell. Like a choir on a single, sustained note. Like a bee in her ear.

♦　♦　♦

GEORGIE SLIPPED back into town each day before three o'clock when school got out. Today, easing the little Mazda into the garage, she wondered whether anyone had begun to notice the extra space since she'd begun taking a carton down the highway every other day. She doubted it. Jim was preoccupied. She was gone most of the week now. She did her domestic duties in frenzied bouts in the morning before the boys went to school. Nobody seemed the wiser.

Upstairs there were five messages on the machine. Most of them were incomprehensible squawks of excitement and congratulation and it was only Jim's curt voice at the tail that enlightened her. He sounded tired and flat but you could hear his deckies whooping and shouting in the background.

We'll be in just after three, he said. When we've unloaded we'll go straight to the pub. Bring the boys.

Jim didn't go to the pub anymore. There could only be one reason for the visit—the traditional requirement of shouting the bar at the end of a killer day.

Georgie switched on the VHF and caught the vibe on the air. Clearly he'd found the mother lode; he'd killed the pig. You could hear it in the urgency and awe of the radio talk, the admiration tinged with bitterness and the cagey enquiries about co-ordinates.

While she waited for the boys to get in from

school she took up the binoculars and picked *Raider* steaming in across the bank and into the passage through the reef.

At four the pub was pandemonium. Georgie had seen it once before and heard stories of other big catches and celebrations to match. In White Point you paid homage to peaks in luck with the same seriousness you employed in ignoring the troughs. You partied for fear that such good fortune might never return. But on a day like this, with a haul so mind-bogglingly huge that it seemed almost supernatural, you had to expect that they would run amok.

By five Georgie had retreated to the grass outside to spare the boys the worst of it. They were hyper and happy but they didn't need to see barmaids in g-strings having their tee-shirts sprayed with beer from water pistols. The pool tables were like paddle pools, their felt tops spattering under dancing feet. She wondered if this was the kind of gathering the Fox family had ever been called in to entertain with mere guitars and fiddles. Christ, it'd be like being thrown into a bear pit. As it was the jukebox was killing itself to deliver AC/DC and ZZ Top at the volume required. A bare-arsed deckie dived over the bar and returned so fast you'd swear he'd hit a trampoline on the other side. There was shouted laughter and the sound of breaking glass. She saw Yogi in there and Shover McDougall. Beaver had closed early. He seemed miraculously able to avoid her gaze. She recognized a dozen scab-lipped surfers, parents from the schoolyard, faces from the supermarket. A few had neighbourly smiles for her but none spoke. Everyone was there except Rachel and Jerra.

Jim came out in a wave of back-slapping, looking solemn for a man who'd just made a nurse's annual salary in a day. His polaroids swung from his neck. The boys shook his hand soberly and the four of them moved across to sit on the grassy edge that gave onto the beach. Gulls hung over them. The sun leaned toward the sea and in its glare the boats toiled at their moorings.

How many? asked Josh. How many crays?

We ran out of crates, said his father. We had to bag them like the old days and put the deck hose on them. We had to empty the ice hold when we ran out of bags.

Good luck or good management? Georgie asked, teasing.

Neither.

Enjoy yourself. I'll take them home and feed them.

Wait up for me, he murmured.

Just then Avis McDougall stepped outside holding her arm like a newborn. Georgie grabbed the boys and slid onto the beach just as Avis laid eyes on Jim.

About nine that evening Jim came up the terrace steps from the beach and sat down heavily beside her. The boys were asleep. The air was cool. She needed a cotton windcheater in order to sit outside. Jim kicked off his deck shoes.

Quite a day, said Georgie.

They're still at it, he murmured in a bewildered tone.

Spose you have to hand it to them. Go hard or go home, huh?

Well, I'm too old for it.

It was quiet for a while. Jim smelled of sweat and beer.

You asked if it was luck or brains, he said in the end. You know, right away, before we'd even finished pulling the first line I knew it was something else. It was too weird. Come noon, I was sure of it.

Sure of what?

That it was some kind of sign.

Sign?

I'm pulling the pin, Georgie. Boris can see the season out from the bridge. I'm going away for a while.

What are you talking about? she asked with a nervous laugh.

I've enrolled the boys in a boarding school for next semester. I want you to come with me.

God, Jim, you've had a few drinks. Maybe we should talk tomorrow when all the excitement's worn off.

Debbie's sister is collecting them on Saturday.

Do they know about this? The boys?

No.

You mean you've been planning it?

Weeks, he murmured. But today confirmed it.

A *sign*. I thought you weren't superstitious.

I'm not. This is different.

But the boys, Jim.

They're my kids. You know I was gonna do it eventually. And you, you're halfway out the door; they don't need to see it. This past few months've been a ragged bloody mess and it's time to make some decisions. It feels clear to me.

Georgie's throat was suddenly tight. She thought of that bloody envelope.

It's Broome, isn't it? she said. You're going to Broome.

Yes. And I want you to come. It's important.

You know where Lu is, don't you?

As good as.

Why? Why should I go?

Jim sighed. Why move into his house? Why pretend you don't want him?

Answer me, Jim.

I can't. Not here. Not tonight.

Then I won't go.

You'll go.

Don't threaten me.

Jesus, Georgie, I'm not threatening you. Look, he said twisting toward her in his chair in a manner so earnest it alarmed her even more. Haven't you ever felt the need to make amends?

For what? she said defensively.

You know, things you've done in your past.

She hugged her knees. The southerly rattled in the cotton palms.

No, she lied.

Well, some of us do.

Jim, you don't have anything to make up for. Not to me.

It's not about you, he said in exasperation.

Then tell me what the hell it's about!

Christ, he muttered. It wasn't supposed to go like this. It was meant to be something gracious.

Georgie stood up and looked at him. In the light spilling from the doorway he was haggard but his eyes were wide open. He looked like a child struggling to swallow something too big for him. The sight of it dampened her anger. Such a long time since she'd seen that look of fear on his face. She believed him. It wasn't about her. He was in the grip of something he could neither understand nor control and she found herself intrigued and repelled.

Go to bed, she said.

Yes, he said. I need to.

Georgie stayed out on the terrace in the chill evening air. Down the bay the pub was jumping. It made her feel old. She went to bed late but only slept fitfully in a profusion of dreams. Before she woke she was on a white shell beach. There were boabs under moonlight. The water was flat and laddered with reflections. Above the beach there was jungle and it smelled rich with decay. At the edge of the sea there appeared a silhouette. It billowed fabric like a Sunday school Christ. It beckoned with outstretched arms. When she reached it she found Mrs Jubail with her brain on her face, her breath a tropic foetor as she whispered, O Nurse, O Sister, and held her arm. Georgie pushed away. There was a steel spade glinting in the moonlight and she took it up and swung it. Mrs Jubail's head opened like a sliced melon. She toppled into the shallows. There were people suddenly behind the trees. Georgie threw the spade but did not hear it land.

STILL NONE OF Georgie's family returned her calls. The staff at Jude's hospital said she couldn't come to the phone. On Friday afternoon she took the little Mazda over to Beaver's to ask whether he'd store it until she returned. He'd barely spoken to her all week. She parked in his wreckyard. He emerged from the back door beside the reeking toilets and they stood beside her yellow bubble.

I've figured it out, he said kicking the front tyre with a toecap. He's got religion.

Well, something's up him.

The fear of God, he said with a snagtoothed grin.

You really think so?

Somethin close to it, George.

Said he wants to make amends, she said handing him the keys.

What, havin your wife die not enough?

She shrugged. It's something to do with her, isn't it?

That's my thinkin. That and you, George.

341

What the hell is he on about, though? He's talking signs and omens, and I can't tell if it's luck he's worried about or God Almighty.

Maybe it's the same thing for him.

Well, it scares me, said Georgie. This kind of talk, the trip to Broome.

So why go?

Well, she murmured, there might be something in it for me.

Fox, said Beaver with a laugh. Now *there's* a name to conjure with. Always made *him* jump, too.

Jesus, you know more than you let on, Beaver. I bet you know every bloody thing about him.

Nah. Still, I've got shit on him and he's got shit on me.

And, let me guess, you won't tell me the goods you've got on him.

Correct.

You his therapist or his priest?

Beaver laughed and nudged her little car with his hip, and his belly jounced around in syncopation with the vehicle's suspension.

So, Beaver, as a friend. Tell me if people change.

As a friend? I don't know. Tell you one thing, though. Things were simpler in the old days. Jim Buckridge included.

Afterwards she walked with Rachel along the lagoon and they stopped at the point to watch her son Sam drop down the face of a distant wave out on the reef. Rachel knew it was him by the colour of his board but to Georgie he was just a squiggling wake across the wave's surface. When they walked on in a kind of fraught silence they came upon a small turtle on its back surrounded by pecking seabirds. They picked it up and washed it off in the shorebreak and saw that it was still alive, but it had a gross-looking stalk growing from its head at the end of which grew a mussel of some sort and as they rinsed it and felt a faint revival, a tiny crab fell from its arse. Georgie recognized the species of turtle. She'd seen hundreds of them in the tropics. It was a loggerhead, a thousand miles out of its way. She imagined it lying exhausted in the southbound Leeuwin Current with other creatures attaching themselves as though to a piece of flotsam.

You believe in signs, Rachel?

Nope, said the other woman testing the root of the mussel.

I figured you New Agers saw them everywhere.

What's this New Age stuff? I rub your back and I'm a bloody crystal-gazer. Mate, the only sign I associate with the New Age is the dollar sign.

You old cynic.

You got me.

What'll we do with this?

Sam and Jerra'll nurse it. Someone's bound to take it north come winter.

It's a long swim to land on the beach right at our feet.

Rachel laughed.

You think I'm mad, said Georgie. About this. About going with Jim.

The other woman held the loggerhead and scooped some water over its shell.

You know, said Georgie, usually when I do something stupid it's impulsive. Frenzied even. I don't feel like that. I feel calm. Almost resigned. It's just a few days. And then I'll be back. He doesn't know about me moving to the farm yet. Will you drop by when I'm settled in?

Of course, said Rachel, as the turtle tried feebly to swim from her grasp.

As they walked on beyond the lagoon the creature stirred itself now and then to scull the air. They walked the whole beach and never saw a soul.

seven

Fox MAKES a fine camp beneath an overhang at the base of the island's mesa bluff. There's a long ledge here powdered with rosy dirt and a little way along it is a freshwater pool that forms where rain spills down the cliff in the afternoons. He sets his swag beneath the sandstone awning and makes a fireplace out on the open ledge. From this position he can see across the treetops down to the belt of boabs and then the beach. From here the whole gulf spreads out in the direction whence he came. In the distance the vast plateau lies in its variegated layers of red and black and green and in the afternoons the monsoon rains spangle it with waterfalls that look no bigger than sequins. He chooses his camp primarily for its proximity to drinking water but he recognizes its defensive virtues. After he's built the bough shelter across the mouth of the overhang you can't see it from the beach at all. It blends beautifully with the fringing fig and vine tendrils.

In time he beats a discreet track through the remnant belt of rainforest to the beach, where he chips oysters and casts lures for fish. One end of the white cove ends in boulders and rocky scree. The other is thinly belted with mangroves through which he passes at low tide to the stony

347

edge beyond that gives out onto a sandspit. From the spit you can see the mainland not half a mile away. Even in the monsoon season it looks dry over there. The ranges inland look rough and treeless.

His days are lived according to the tide. From the spit he casts for queenfish and trevally and now and then he takes a spanish mackerel. Amongst the rocks he jigs for mangrove jacks, fingermark, bluebone and pikey bream. He gathers driftwood as he goes and he carries it strapped to his back when he returns to camp. He grills fish whole in the coals or makes soup in the billycan. Early on, out of excitement, he catches too many and is forced to smoke them on greenwood racks. Some days it's just too damn hot to cook so he eats fish raw by the water and saves himself the trouble of carrying anything back but rod and reel.

He learns to eat green ants for the lemony fizz on the tongue and the way they spice a chowder along with a bit of chilli. He proceeds cautiously with mangrove snails whose blue flesh alarms him and he tries figs and berries with his mouth puckered anxiously. The pandanus nuts are almost tasteless. He has no luck with the pith from boab gourds but he likes to walk through the shadows of the trees where the shellgrit crunches underfoot. He spends entire days satisfying himself that he has the best camp on the island. He clambers his way around until it's impassable and he labours all one morning to make the mesa's summit and traverse its windblown gutters to look out oceanward and see the archipelago backed up like a jack-knifed train in the gulf below.

For some days he suffers a kind of restless disbelief that you could find a place like this. But in time he settles to the comfort of a routine. He tries to forage in the cool of the morning or evening. In the torpid, rainy midafternoon he retreats to the cave to weave pandanus leaves for his shelter or just lie there panting in the timeless heat.

The nights are sticky and mostly calm. Quolls rustle about on the rock ledges. Bats flit from crags and the stars roll by on their wheels. Strange cracking noises reverberate in the rainforest and birds chime chaotically up in the bluffs, but the most constant sounds are those of the tides ebbing and flowing in a nearly incessant murmur.

In the daylight he feels safe in a way he hasn't felt since early childhood. There are perils, of course. He climbs rocks and wades through mud at low tide with ponderous slow-mo caution for fear of cuts and falls, and he never swims, never even takes his morning and evening douches on the same piece of beach for fear of crocodiles, whose log-like passes he sees offshore now and then. Yes, there are simple dangers but he has nothing personal to protect himself from.

On the island there are so many unexpected pleasures, like the hot warm boles of the young boab trees he brushes with his fingertips in passing. The shapes of those trees delight him. Leaners, swooners, flashers, fat and thin. At the edge of them all is one huge ancient tree, festooned with vines and creepers, whose bark is elephantine. There's a glorious asymmetrical splendour about it; it makes him smile just to catch a glimpse as he passes. When he climbs it he finds an ossuary on its outspread limbs where some hefty seabird has hauled mudcrabs aloft to feed on. The broken hulls are thick and white as china plates.

He finds that if you sit still long enough the bush or the sea will produce an event. You wait with trancelike patience until manta rays begin to roll in the shallows or baitfish form like stormclouds along the spit. A beetle big as a golfball will fall from the woven pandanus. A turtle ups periscope in the stillness. A sheet of lightning scours the brainpan.

Fox begins to grow expansive. There's no one to keep your thoughts from so he begins to think aloud. He utters observations in the direction of the sea eagle that has its eyrie in the bluffs above. Every morning he greets the beautiful brahminy kite when it hunts abroad from its mangrove nest. As he shits ankle deep and facing seaward at the water's edge, he mutters Not today Mister Crocodile, not today, not today.

But as he walks on the shell beach he becomes acutely aware of the sound he's making. There's a curious reverberative lag, an overlap, as though someone else is walking too, someone behind him. Now and then, unable to help himself, he spins around to check that he's alone. Even the slop of his waterbag does it to him. Sometimes the sound of his breathing. The sensation is more potent than the usual tiny gap between his being there and the sound of him being there.

Shells and rocks turn the soles of his feet milky with calluses. He saves his boots for hard treks. His shorts and shirts bleach with sun and salt and his cloth hat has concentric sweatlines like the growth rings of a tree. His new beard itches but it gives him some protection from the sun. In the mornings he wakes with raw patches of skin on his chest and shoulders from it. The humidity irritates the beard-burn into a broken rash. It adds to the discomfort of the gouges and stakings he sustains from fishing and from generally living by his hands. In the steamy rain one afternoon he slips on vine-strewn rocks and plunges down a sandstone slope to land in a bed of leaf mould. He knows he's lucky not to have broken an arm or a leg but his polaroids are shattered and his leg is grazed from knee to ankle. He limps down to the water's edge and rinses it absent-mindedly in saltwater. The next few days he wades through mud in search of crabs. He fishes in the shallows and searches for relief from the heat in rockpools and his graze begins to ulcerate. He keeps the worst of the festering at bay with his precious tube of Betadine and is careful from then on to wash his wounds only in freshwater. Even though the regular monsoon overcast spares him some of the glare, he feels the loss of his glasses. He often climbs into his swag at night with headaches and the feeling that his eyes have been scorched.

At rare low moments he takes comfort in sharpening his knife, in the simple, useful repetition of the stroke and the rhythm of blade on steel.

Now and then Fox feels agitated for reasons unknown. It causes him to throw stones or break tree limbs to no purpose. He runs along the beach to kick up sprays of shell like a mischievous child and he yells until his throat is sore. He still can't believe that he's managed to arrive here without a single book. He revisits every opportunity on the road, considers the poetry volumes crammed into old Bess's caravan. He thinks wistfully of every novel he's ever turned his nose up at or given up on, every hyphenated Englishman and triple-barrelled American who's ever put him to sleep. Come home Gertrude Stein and Jean-Paul Sartre—all is forgiven. Fox would content himself with a phone book, a shopping list.

One afternoon he's filleting fish and throwing the heads and backbones into the water when a pack of sharks glides in across the shallows. The tide is high and the water a little murky but he sees them clearly enough as they swim figure-eights at the shoreline, their double dorsal fins and high tails out of the water. He picks them as tawny nurses; their shovel-like heads are bronze and ochre and the way they swim is a kind of dance, a fluid movement from nose to tail. Out beyond them two sleeker sharks make passes. Lemon sharks. Skittish, aggressive, more the whaler type with all that lunging paranoia.

Fox throws out a few morsels and the sharks roll in a welter of spray to get at them. He drops hanks of skin and guts closer to shore and the lemon sharks bullock their way in so fast they wet him. The sight of it makes his heart thump. He drops his meal almost onshore and the sharks rush it in a wild scrum of fins and tails. Two sharks find themselves beached in all the mayhem and Fox gets down on his haunches and laughs as they writhe back into the water. He feeds them, applauds and taunts them until dark when he heads up to his camp facing a hungry night.

Next day the sharks return with the tide and the sight of them cheers him. They come back every day after that and he looks forward to their arrival. Despite his croc anxiety he cuts tidbits for them and teases them in closer until they're snatching meat from his hands. They stand on their pectoral fins, heads clear of the water, and he strokes their bony, flat pates as they lunge forward. From camp he brings down his coil of rope and ties plate-sized fish heads to it to play tug-of-war. The bigger sharks haul him off his feet or drag him heels-first to the water's edge before snaffling the prize or gnawing through the rope. Emboldened, they chase treats right up onto dry land and roll and writhe their way back down to water, and the games escalate until Fox is manhandling them and they're bumping and passing him in the shallows. He loves the sport of it, the mad, reckless play, but it's the bodily presence of them that he treasures most, the weight of them in his arms, against his legs, the holiness of their power, the carnal sociability of the buggers. Every day they come like a bouncing, bickering pack of dogs, and after they're sated with food they tug on an empty vine until Fox laughs so hard he gets hiccups.

THE CYCLONE catches him by surprise. Preoccupied with shark play, he barely registers the two dark days of solid overcast which precede it. The afternoon of the third day is black but it feels no different from the usual diurnal build-up until he notices fish jumping madly amongst the flooded mangroves and when he looks down the gulf he sees the irritable state of the water beyond the island's lee. The air smells suddenly electric and his ears pop. A chill wind comes ripping through the treetops.

Fox carries the kayak higher up into the vegetation beyond the boabs. By the time he's up on the ledge, securing what he can at camp, the air is deliciously cool. Huge black toadstool clouds bank up across the water and thunder rolls in. He moves his gear back in under the overhang and lashes his bough shelter down with the sorry remains of his rope. Lightning bleaches the trees and a waterspout rises like an angry white root from the dirt-coloured sea; it comes hissing and spitting across the water sucking small dark objects into the air. It bears down on him but then veers suddenly toward the mainland and is lost from view.

Before dark the wind comes from the sea and the island's bluffs protect him from the worst of it, but as the light fades he feels it begin to angle in more from the west and waves begin to pound the beach. He doesn't like the feel of the storm. Anxious about the precious kayak being washed or even blown away, he scrambles down to haul it all the way through the trees and up the rock terraces to camp. He shoves it back into the confines of the overhang as water begins to fall in sheets from the bluffs above.

In the early evening the bough shelter begins to break up. The wind screams in the vines and the fig tree seems to strain at its very roots. The rock face becomes a waterfall and during the night the rock above his head begins to seep. By morning there is a stream running through his little cave. It issues from the base of the bluff behind him and forces him up onto narrow niches where he crouches with his gear, unable to keep a candle alight.

The storm continues to intensify. The shriek of the trees terrifies him. The kayak butts against the rocks beneath his feet. Fox wraps himself in his sodden swag and tries not to think of his mother. He begins to hum to block out the sound. He blocks his ears with his fingers.

Tuarts. Tuart trees on the sandy coastal plain. In the days before the old man sawed them down and ground out the stumps vengefully, the house was encircled by tuarts. His mother loved them. Graceful, and grey-barked, their shade cooled the yard and brought birds and from the largest hung a tyre swing that Darkie and he rode until their feet ploughed a four-way furrow in the dirt and the tree bore a shiny patch from collisions.

The broad crowns of the tuarts roared with the unceasing wind of the midwest coast. On summer mornings it sounded like a mob up there high off the ground and in storms the tuarts made the wind sound like an advancing army.

It was just a trip to the chookyard. A northerly gale was blowing, the kind of warm mealy blast that preceded the passage of a big winter front. His mother's hair streamed back across her shoulders. Her laugh was musical. They squatted to gather eggs. He held the wire basket. They headed back for the house; he remembers the feel of his hand in hers and the bummy smell of eggs.

They were under the swing bough, leaning on the wind, when a gust wrenched the tree with a noise like a slap round the earhole. She swept from his grasp. Half a second later a storm of foliage yanked him off his feet. He lay there a moment staring up through the leaves at a fishscale afternoon sky. A birdnest hung above him speckled with foil and feathers. The very earth beneath him seemed to vibrate with the struggle of trees against the wind but the blanket of gumleaves felt like protection. He felt dreamy, safe. When he did get up to find his mother, there was no blood on her that he could see, just spilled yolks and the sinister, glistening albumen smeared up her bare legs. The sheared point of the bough was in her chest but he didn't yet understand that she was dead. He would be ten in a few days.

Tonight every flurry beneath the rock feels like the breeze of her passing. It buffets him all night; he knows it too well. All his life it seems he's been walking in the slipstream of the dead and he hates it.

Always that slap of wind. Left behind.

And here he is again bringing a snakeskin in from the creek to show them. She holds up the papery tube and smiles.

Look, Wally, she says. Look how good the world is, look at the things it leaves us. It means us no harm.

The boy senses he's stumbled into a debate in progress.

Doesn't count, mutters the old man hardly looking up. It's an illusion, a dream we have to pass through.

But look!

Things. Stuff. Just things.

And the smile on her face as she sits back in her chair with the book open on her lap and the hair shining with each happy shake of her head. Holy, she says with a hint of teasing. Holy, holy, holy.

Shit and gristle, that's all. It doesn't matter. Holy. Tell him, Lu.

Standing there openmouthed between them, wondering if bringing it home has been a mistake.

Holy? He always wanted to believe it, and it felt instinctively true from a thousand days spent dragging a stick through the dirt while crows cleared their throats benignly at him and those stones whined gentle upon the hill. But there she is in the end with a tree through her. And the old man all that time dying with those blue fibres in his lungs. God's good earth. Tilting away from him time and again, stealing from him. Sliding beneath the tyres of that old ute and then suddenly catching, biting enough for it to roll and send the kids out into the paddock like flung mailbags. The world is holy? Maybe so. But it has teeth too. How often has he felt that bite in a slamming gust of wind.

At dawn he crawls through the run-off and stands on the scoured ledge to see that the worst is over. There is the smell of brimstone in the air. From there he can see slagheaps of shell and the log ramparts thrown up by the sea. On his way down he sees his freshwater pool overflowing. The track is a rivulet through the chaos of strewn rainforest. He picks his way until he comes to the great asterisk in the beach where the giant boab used to be. Within the lightning crater coals still glow. A few amputated limbs lie smouldering beyond it but most of it's ash now, ash and fire-glazed shell. A few nearby trees are scorched but the fire hasn't spread back into the belt of green below the bluffs.

There are jellyfish in the trees. They glisten in the sudden sunlight.

Fox chips oysters and throws them into the hot coals of the tree until they bubble and hiss and open their mouths.

In the wake of the cyclone the season wanes and the days become clear and hot, the atmosphere drier. Fox senses the beginning of a contraction, a scarcity of berries, a browning off of grasses. He works harder for his daily catch and he sees that the basin at the foot of the bluff, although wide and generous in its supply of drinking water, may not get him through the Dry season.

On hot, breathless days he paddles around the spit toward the mainland and heads up mangrove creeks to search for water and maybe a camp spot. He finds the remnants of the creeks' freshwater sources in shrinking billabongs, but the hikes are brutal and the sources unlikely to last. He heads north into the archipelago and finds lovely places but none more practical than where he already lives. In a week of day trips he moves through the islands without success until he's forced to consider the mainland coast enfolded by them.

Coasting back toward his island on the early change of tide he comes upon a white hummock at the side of a tiny mangrove creek. Beside the hummock are slim boabs and a sandy cove. He paddles in for a quick look, puzzling over the shelly mound. It's the size of two Landcruisers parked together and it's not until he's stood on it a while that he realizes that it's a midden. Within the pearly surface are veins of grey and black, bits of charcoal, mussel shells, cockles, oysters.

Behind the midden is a wide flat area dotted with pandanus palms. Curious, he goes down and finds a steady trickle of fresh water winding its way seaward across the field of crushed shell. Beyond is a thorny vine thicket and the sound of frogs. Fox works his way around until he comes to a sandstone breakaway. There's a promising overhang here. Yes, a good camp, an alternative should the water ever dry up completely on the island.

Fox climbs up the little escarpment to get a view and on the next ridge he finds a wide-mouthed cave shrouded with rock figs. On the ledges outside the overhang are tiny dancing figures the colour of dried blood upon the yellow rock. He gives a little grunt of surprise. He examines the dynamic images, most smaller than his hands, and marvels at their tufted head-dresses and skirts. Many are weathered into obscurity.

Inside the cave he sees other paintings in a different style. He stoops to look, but hesitates. On the rear wall a large mouthless face stares at him. Rays stream from its head. Fox feels green ants dropping onto his shoulders from the fig. He thinks what the hell, and goes in crouched.

The ceiling is taken up by a huge ochre figure in red and white. Its head is the size of a turtle shell, the eyes big and dark, and it too is mouthless. Arms like plucked wings. Between the splayed legs a strange trunk reaches down.

Fox lies on his back to see it better. Such a fierce, staring face. Like a stormcloud.

Hello, he whispers. Just visiting.

The weathered face is twice the size of his own.

Dirt creaks beneath him. The cave smells of charcoal. He thinks of that kid Axle and wonders if he's seen this. Insects have daubed mud nests across this fella's knees. Parts of him are fading altogether but the face is bright enough, the eyes still fiery.

Halfway out into the light Fox catches himself making the sign of the cross and he stifles a laugh. Hasn't done that for a while.

Fox holds the midden camp in reserve. Meanwhile he looks for food, measures it, ekes it out, thinks about it. His dried fruit is gone now and with it his rice and precious chilli powder. He gathers pinches of salt from rock dimples at low tide. He finds himself scrounging longer and longer every day. He can ill afford to spare fish carcases for the sharks.

In the end the thought of all that stuff

cached down the other end of the gulf is too much for him. On a day of modest neap tides he strikes out in the kayak at first light.

Even with a light breeze at his back it's a four-hour paddle. He goes ashore at the headland and lies among the rocks a while to make certain the fishing camp is still deserted. But there's no sign of anyone. The cyclone has knocked the bough verandah down and torn its spinifex thatch.

Inside the cave a few crates have tipped as though water's been through and stuff has spilt on the shellgrit. There's quoll shit every-where; the hardy little marsupial buggers have been at everything. The generator and freezers seem to have endured inside their plastic wraps, and beyond them, in foam and PVC boxes, Fox finds candles, cigarette lighters, antiseptic cream, a carton of beer from which he takes a six pack, curry spices and black pepper, weevilly flour, bags of rice, tubes of sunscreen and repellent. With persistence he finds freeze-dried vegetables and even raisins. He piles it all into a plastic drum and lashes it to the kayak.

He searches in vain for a book or magazine. He consoles himself with an iron skillet and a tiny jar of paw-paw ointment. He has no luck replacing the insect net he's ruined catching prawns, but he makes off with a thrownet he wishes he'd seen last time. He stuffs it into the kayak and hopes the disarray from the storm might cover his pilfering. He seals every con-tainer and before he goes he rakes the floor of the cave with a dead branch. He goes back on the tide in high spirits and makes the island well before sunset. The sharks are waiting but he has no time to play. He plunges the six pack into his dwindling freshwater pool to let it cool while he stashes his haul. He cooks rice in his skillet with peas and dried apricots and while the new moon gets up he opens a can of beer. He's surprised at the unearthly sound it makes when he rips the top and how sour it is and how quickly it makes his head spin. It goes down in three swallows and he fetches up another. He lights a candle just for the novelty of it but blows it out again, wishing there'd been a book; anything to contain his mind, direct his thoughts, feed him.

He sits on the smooth warm terrace looking out across the treetops. He drinks the entire six pack and falls asleep in the dirt.

FOR DAYS AFTER the six pack Fox feels persecuted by thirst and heat. He's listless and in his afternoon stupors he fantasizes about refrigeration. Beaded cans, foggy plastic containers of lettuce, sweating bottles, red dripping tomatoes, snowy ice shavings and the trickle of chilled liquids. The torment ruins his new plenty; it sullies the luxury of soy sauce and chilli and the soothing balm of paw-paw cream on his many wounds. The evenings lag. He lights a fire just for something to watch. Something is building in his head; stuff fizzes and flickers, bloated pictures and half-thoughts that run into one another and cancel themselves out. Even simple, physical tasks no longer organize and pacify him. He believes he's going mad.

Lubricating his reel with precious cooking oil one afternoon, Fox plucks the taut-strung leader tied to the last runner of the rod and hears something like B-flat. He twangs it again and laughs. From the spool in the cave he reefs off a couple of metres of nylon line and strings it between two limbs of the fig tree shading him. The slack old note it gives isn't much of a sound but when he tightens and reties it he likes it well enough. It makes a nice drone, a sound just outside nature but not dissimilar to it. He clears his throat uncertainly and hums the note. He thinks of Darkie's little hairless bum sticking out of the piano as he pulls the strings. His heart races; it feels dangerous, listening to this, giving in to the sound, but his thumb whacks at the string out of reflex. How many times in the past year has he walked past that steel guitar and seen his face distorted in its tarnished steel curves and just kept on going by? God knows, music will undo you, and yet you're whacking this thing into a long, gorgeous, monotonous, hypnotic note and it's not killing you, it's not driving you into some burning screaming wreck of yourself—listen! Within the drone, all those sweet multiple timings there to embroider with, the gaps and fills, the hot gurgle coming to your throat. The sudden groove you're in—damn, just listen to that! You're humming and stamping and chanting nylon bloody B-flat and it's good. *Whang-whang-whang-whang, wucka—whang, whang!*

He growls out a chant, his throat burning with pleasure, and begins to hyperventilate to sustain it. His body fizzes. Bubbles on his skin, twisting strings of bubbles in his vision; they dance across the gulf before him while his ears chirp through the pressures of descent and his collarbone aches. There's an inward glide in the drone. Like the great open spaces of apnoea, the freedom he knows within the hard, clear bubble of the diver's held breath. After a point there's no swimming in it, just a calm glide through thermoclynes, something closer to flight. Within the drone, sound is temperature and taste and smell and memory, *wucka-whang*.

And when he surfaces from it, the sun is down and the mosquitoes are upon him. The sound of the world is raw. At his ear, in the fig tree beside him, a leafball of green ants chickers a scratchy gossip and beyond it he hears the wingbeats of outward-bound bats and the frothing mandibles of crabs at feast amongst the mangroves.

He rubs paw-paw ointment into his hand and sits up in the dark feeling sated, stunned, excited.

In the following days, whenever he's not gathering food, he plays the drone. At first he plays for the liberation of it, as rebellion against the discipline that he's maintained so long, and the return to music is sheer physical pleasure, a kind of relief-in-relenting which is more than sensual. But when he has exhausted plain musical playfulness, the hide and seek of improvisation, he finds that within that long, narcotic note there are places to go.

He beats a path south, across deserts and mountains to the coastal plain of the central west. He strides across the parched, alkaline paddock to the verandah steps and down the dim hallway to the library and hour after hour he swims into books. Their covers creak like doors. Sometimes they give up the tiny gasps of split melons and he moves through their lines as a man walks through home country. He scrambles up through the crags of *The Prelude* and *Tintern Abbey*, across hot, bright Emily and into the spiky undergrowth of Bill Blake. The lines come to him. He chants them in B-flat, in a kind of monofilament manifold monotone that feels inexhaustible, as though it's a sea of words he's swimming in, an ocean he could drink.

With this fullness, this ecstatic sense of volume, there's only one regret and that is having no one to share it with. He thinks wistfully of Georgie and her playful prodding, her curiosity about the books, and his stunned inability to say what he felt. God, the things he had wanted to tell her. Fox doesn't know what you're supposed to make of Wordsworth and Blake, how you might speak of them if you'd been taught by experts, but he knows he would have tried to explain this sense of the world alive, the way they articulate your own instinctive feeling that there is indeed some kind of spirit that rolls through all things, some fearsome memory in stones, in wind, in the lives of birds.

After some days of chanting, he finds he can travel beyond the library, move through the house with exquisite intimacy, an almost painful vividness of presence. He smells his own bread baking. And there he is at the sink, beside himself in his own kitchen, barefoot in Levi's. Before him, the window needs washing. There's a riverstone on the sill and Bullet's front tooth in a butterdish beside it. The sound of the kids somewhere in the house. When he turns, Sal looks at him from the dust mote cascade of the doorway and scratches herself with the rosined bow as though he's no more present than a dog under the table.

Out in the laundry he's small and pressed against the whirring Hoover twintub which threatens to launch itself into space. But the *whor-whor-whorr*, the sound of it!

And the sleepy sound of the rip saw in the jarrah log, *sheet home, sheet home, sheet home*, while his father's sweat shines in the sun. Standing beside himself, Fox rocks on his dimpled infant legs to the rhythm, puzzled at his father's wry grin.

Bird wrapped in his denim jacket, her milky breath upon his face as she sings hymns in his arms. *The north wind is tossing the leaves, the red dust is over the town, the sparrows are under the eaves, and the grass in the paddock is brown.* Christmas, then, it has to be Christmas, and her head no bigger than a runty cantaloupe.

Fox walks out to himself hunkered in the noonday paddock amongst watermelons at picking point. Hot Christmas. The sun on the back of his neck. And he looks up to see them, Darkie and Sal, sprawled on the verandah steps watching him work.

Standing behind Bird in the shed. She's paralyzed at the sight of the old man's sign.

Christ is the head of this house,
The unseen Guest at every meal,
The silent Listener to every conversation

The day after the poor old bugger's funeral Darkie tore it off the kitchen wall and here it lives. Bird gives it a wide berth on her way out into the glare of the day. She knows when you're there. The way his mother knew if you were there, or when one of you was hurt. A sudden hand across her chest. You saw it yourself.

In the afternoons the sharks cruise the shallows but he plays the drone. His thumb is callused now; he can go for hours.

Fox sings himself down sheep pads and yellow washaways to walk up the dry riverbed toward the farm. Paperbarks are shrivelled spindles of themselves. The silicate soil of the high paddock squeaks underfoot and where the house should be there is no house. His trees are dead and not even a silver filigree of dead melon vine remains on the ground. He expects at least a mound of ashes, a lightning crater, but there's nothing. Only the bones of rock up there on the hill. When he gets up among them, the pinnacles' shadows are treacly. The air smells bitterly of sweat and piss. The monoliths lean on the wind but even the perennial southerly is no more. Fox stands there beside himself and slips his hand into the stone fissure for the tea can, and the limestone stirs against him, its hip on his as he leans in. It's hot and damp inside and slippery on his arm as though felted with wet moss. The tin is just out of reach. When he strains deeper, the rock moans and cries out in his ear and right beneath his leaning weight it grows a bluish bark, a smooth, fleshy covering that causes him to recoil so fast that when he rips his arm from it there follows a gout of blood and water.

Fox stops playing. The night sky is purple now and red stars spin earthward. There are crickets in the trees and a nightjar whooshing by. Back in the rocks quolls scuffle. He's awake. Not drone-stoned but conscious and present; his knees are sore, he needs a leak, but the sky is wild with red falling stars as though he's dreamt them or sung them up. They're like windblown embers pitching out toward the mainland for minutes at a time until it's just purple night again.

He lights a candle for the comfort of light and to eat some rice gone sour in the heat since

369

noon. He dabs hanks of cured fish in chilli dust and eats, troubled by the image of the stones. It's not a memory. It's something else and it frightens him. He resolves to give the droning a rest.

Next day he's tired from broken sleep, and he gathers oysters feeling woolly-headed and abstracted from things. Hunkered amidst the burbling rocks at low tide he chips the big black-lips from the boulders with the back of his machete. There's a tune in his head as he works, a repeated descending phrase. He opens shells with the bladetip and eats his fill, puzzling over the music. It's the same over and again, like a tree endlessly dropping its leaves. Each note floats inexorably, almost unbearably, to the ground in its own time. Cellos and a bell. The unravelling thread of it is familiar. He tries to bring his mind to bear. The music makes him queasy with its familiarity. He fills his calico bag with oyster meat but the signature phrase rises through his heels; it chimes in his spine, and resonates in his neck. And then it's gone, fading like the rush of a vehicle passing distant upon a highway. Bess, he thinks. That's the music. Bess's music on the torturous Roebuck Plains on the way to Broome. Death music. Arvo, she said, play Arvo in the arvo! Our little Estonian mate! He knows! And Fox is certain that he's just felt the old lady's death. Right here, right now. He stands there a while and then he lifts a hand palm outward. Can't decide what the gesture means; doesn't know what else to do.

He takes up his bag and heads for camp. The dead, he thinks, it's always the dead. I'm hearing dead people and singing their words. I'm dreaming of them, that's all I do. All my people are dead people.

When he gets to the boabs on the beach he squats in the shade a moment and opens the bag to smell the clean, briny flesh. Georgie Jutland. That's who it reminds him of, that pure smell. The smell on his hands that day, those days, that one night. Even the scent in her hair after swimming—like clean seagrass, shiny against your lips. Well, that's *one* live one, he thinks.

He bolts for camp thinking in flashes and hot arcs and he blunders into a low branch that nearly takes his eye out. Lying sprawled in the dry litter he berates himself for his carelessness. He gets up shaken and bathes his face at the shallow pool on the camp ledge. No more singing. No more music. Or you'll go insane. You always knew it. Since the day you came back alone to the farm with that awful static in your ears, you understood. For weeks it persisted, that stuffed sensation in your ears; it was like the hiss and fuzz left in your head after a rock gig, the half-deafness of bombardment. And it protected you, numbed you a little. But when it wore off you were naked. You had to put yourself out of reach. Of music first, and also memory because one lived in the other, but people too, because they could say anything, do anything, bring anything out at any moment and do you in without even noticing.

For a treat he fries oyster meat in precious oil and a handful of crushed ants, drizzles in some soy and sprinkles chilli pepper across it and feasts. He savours the physical fact of it, the meal's every detail. This is what's required. Attention to now.

FOX WORKS on his rebuilt bough shelter and thatches it with spinifex and palm leaves. He weaves himself a pandanus brim to fortify the ruin of his cloth hat. He stockpiles pulpy mangrove wood along the ledge and goes searching for birds' eggs. Some days he plays fitfully with the sharks but he's cautious about it now; it seems like a waste of energy. The taut nylon drone hums in the afternoon breeze but he doesn't play it anymore. And yet memories flash at him, persistent and chaotic, like creatures spilling through a torn fence.

The image of the old man pulling down all the icons and snatching the candles. The cold fury that came upon him the day he got shot of Rome for good. And no idea why. Only their mother knew. Old Wally went into Protestantism like a hard man into a cold bath. Had Fox been born a few years later he might have been a Calvin and not just a Luther. But then, one day before they carted him off to die, the old boy sat up in bed and made the sign at the empty doorway, then crossed himself absently, methodically, the way a man shuts down a machine or locks a vehicle.

He thinks of Bird climbing in beside him smelling of pee, of her crouched in winter sunlight over the cat's cradle, and those little message pellets—SORRY. And Bullet asleep—asprawl on his bed, cupping his little dick and mouthbreathing. He considers the big-hearted *chang* of a dreadnought guitar ringing up your arm, in your lap, down the heels of your boots. And the three of you out on the verandah in the evening, feet up on the rail, swinging some smoky J. J. Cale thing, knowing that *this* was it, you were blessed, that they had real music in them and you could only be glad, for without them you were nothing. Those evenings you knew what was holy. Just the smell of the night and the smiles on their faces and the chords slipping each to each.

But he remembers, too, way before then, the ugly orange pumpkin of the school bus pulling up on the highway with Dogger Dean at the wheel. The smell of Brut 33. Sal with her suntanned cheek pressed to the glass as they climbed up out of the shade of the fruit stand. The old Leyland hawking into gear as they lurched down the aisle to where she waited on the long back seat. Those mornings she and Darkie kissed and passed Juicy Fruits tongue to tongue, their hands all over each other. They made feeding noises right there beside him. Darkie tugging at the nipple pressed up in her white blouse. With him, his brother, right at the end of his elbow. The lowing sound in her neck sent a charge through his body. The paddocks blew by. His bag crushed into his lap. The blood and bone smell of her that rose every time she shifted her thighs. He's guilty about the memory, for having it at all, for letting it back. It dishonours the dead. It shames him.

Down around the rocks where the water comes in deep, a great school of spanish mackerel rises to storm a ball of baitfish. He snatches up the rod, ties on a chrome lure and goes down to cast for one. He picks his way out across barnacle-crusted rocks, wishing he'd thought to pull on his boots, but the sight of those spaniards mauling bait is too much to resist delaying for footwear. Birds shower the water and snatch up the wounded anchovies. The surface boils with silver and black flashes. Fox lands a cast outside them and winds for all he's worth and gets an instant hook-up. The reel screeches and he spits on the spool to ease his burning thumbs. The thing feels bigger than him; it slams the rod over, bends it to the very butt, and takes line so fast that the steel base of the spool begins to show through. He has to stop it. He cranks on the brake and suddenly he's sliding down the rock across oysters and barnacles sharp as broken glass. Rod and reel fly from his hands. He skids into the water with his feet shredded. He scrabbles back on hands and elbows, sees blood in the water, looks out to see the rod skipping across the bay.

He tries to limp back to camp but completes the trip on all fours. He rests a while at the remnant waterhole and washes his feet to see how bad it is. There are gouges and lacerations every which way. Pieces of shell are embedded like shrapnel beneath the surface.

He crawls along to camp and pulls the tweezers from the bottom of his pack. He washes his feet again and sets them on a clean piece of driftwood. Then he takes the tweezers and begins to dig. The pain is terrible but the sensation of the steel so deep in his skin is worse. He gouges and probes and fishes, willing himself to keep at it for fear of lameness and infection and God knows what else. When he drags out the first inoffensive-looking skerrick of black shell, his hands are shaking and he doubts he can go on with the rest. The longer he procrastinates the worse his dread becomes. He tries a little ditty to distract himself a moment and that's how he goes on, in a kind of humming, groaning, wincing trance, never letting go of the riff longer than a second or two lest he give up again altogether.

It's nobody's fault but mine (no sir!) *Ain't nobody's fault but mine* (fuckin shit!) *if I die and my soul gets lost, it's nobody's fault but mine.*

And the tune takes him off a little way into thoughts of Darkie and Sal. Hard thoughts in the pain. Disloyal thoughts.

That sideways look that Darkie had. He never *looked at* you. You loved and loved him and always wondered and despised yourself for your wondering. Yes, you did. Hated yourself for it secretly. But he barely glanced.

It was slant, like a bullock sizing you up. And Sal's laugh—*heh, heh, heh*—from girlhood onwards, the same snicker, from behind the hair and all that glossy skin, as though she was laughing at you, not with you. Neither of them—you might as well bloody admit it—neither of them ever lifted a finger. It was always you out in the melons, you at the fences and up to your elbows in the generator, you in the kitchen and at the bloody school parent nights. Jesus, you bought the Christmas presents, you did all the saving for housekeeping. And mostly you didn't mind; you were happy to be along. Wasn't it their place, wasn't Darkie the eldest son? Besides, there were the kids, there was the music and you were your brother's brother. He was your hero, wasn't he? The boy could play a wet string bag. It was what saved you all from complete disgrace. It made you battlers, not losers; it was what earned you that last grudging shred of respect in the district, and in your heart you always believed that it was because of *them*, not you.

And yet, when you let yourself think it, what a pair they really were. Their need for one another was ravenous but it didn't extend to anybody else. They were fond of you and they loved the kids in their distracted way but there was no passion, no sacrifice in it. What they loved was playing; it was the best of them. For years you thought the music was *in* them, that it came from them. You knew your own instincts were good, that you felt the music deeper but that your playing couldn't match it, didn't reach their level of virtuosity. Didn't you tell yourself three thousand nights of your life that you forgave them the rest because of what they could do? Because of the music? But that only held when you believed in them as creatures inspired, as sources of the music. Now that they're dead, though, you're just *willing* it to be so; you don't really believe it anymore. You always wanted them to be so much more special than they were; you needed it in order to keep yourself in line, to make living with them bearable, so you wouldn't lose the kids. But beaten down like this, with nothing to protect you, with a piece of shiny steel going halfway into your foot over and over again, you just don't have the energy left to convince yourself anymore, you're down to the bare wires here. The music wasn't *in* them. They barely felt it. They just liked playing. They loved performance and riffing off one another and being good at something and squeezing a reputation out of going hard and fast to raise themselves out of the old White Point contempt. But they were just players, people who knew their licks. Darkie was an inspired mimic. He loved playing but was only fond of music. Both of them were as careless with it as they were with their children.

There it is, he tells himself in a cloud of pain, you've thought it.

There, like your suffering prick every morning on the school bus. Like Darkie sliding his finger under your nose so you could smell her. Why do that to your brother? And why after those first, mad gigs, why drive out across the Buckridge tracks to the coast with the radio spitting the Ramones so they could park on the beach and go at it like you weren't even there? Why climb out and lie all over the hood and leave you there watching her hair all over the windscreen while the car pitched and the keys swung and jangled in the ignition? Why do that? Was that just carelessness, too, or did they enjoy the cruelty of it? You might have murdered them for that, for years of it. And then when they *were* gone? You and those jeans. Is that what it was really all about? Revenge? Did you imagine yourself getting her in the end to spite him? No. That's too much, that's not how it was. It was just a shape he was responding to, the outline of a woman, not Sal, not someone with her voice, her blank pauses and her strange domineering needs. She was one-dimensional, like an adolescent's idea of a woman. He wanted something more intricate, more animated. He wanted some wit, some memory, some kindness, someone who saw him, saw through him, saw the music of him. That's what he conjured up night after night like an alchemist in their bedroom, like some opium-addled poet going again to the darkness for what couldn't live in nature. God knows, it's shaming enough to remember but there's a shred of solace in the knowledge that he might have wanted something better than to be his brother and to have his wife. The kids were the best of them; that's what he did have. The rest was desperation and unholy Romance.

If I die...

His hands shake again now and his feet have stopped bleeding. *Soul gets lost.* His throat is sore but he doesn't relent from his growling chant. *Fault but mine.* There's nothing left. The fragments of shell lie on the driftwood and he douses his feet in antiseptic and binds them and stuffs them into his boots to keep them clean. His whole body is slick with sweat. He crawls deeper into the shade and lapses into silence.

Shadows morph across the dirt as the day wanes. He lies on his swag in a fugue of shock. It's as though he's robbed himself of something. And now, in addition to everything else, he has to mourn his idea of them. It leaves him more diminished than liberated. All he can do, while he lies there with his feet throbbing, is to wonder why he stayed, why he persisted. Why he's lived this past year in homage to these people even after their death.

Why? he asks himself in the falling dark. Because you loved them. You did it out of love. And owning up to what they were really like won't change that.

THAT NIGHT Fox dreams that the boy Axle comes up the beach under moonlight. He emerges from the solemn mob of boabs with

379

gills in his chest, horizontal slits that give out thin bands of light, and as he approaches, labouring somewhat across the million white shells, he drags a wing like a wounded crow and calls out, teeth flashing, in the chord of D-major.

Fox makes himself walk. The moment it's light enough he pads his feet in an extra pair of socks and hobbles about to prove to himself that he's not lame. Within minutes he has to sit down again but he knows he can get back up and walk if he has to. With no rod and reel now, it's important to hold onto the knowledge that he can still walk. Lameness is death.

Within a couple of days he realizes that the only way he can fish successfully with handlines is to troll up and down the deeps in the kayak trailing a lure as he paddles. It's hard going but it saves his feet and hours of fruitless casting. He catches mackerel that tow him so fast he fears a capsize. When he fillets them out on the beach the sharks fight over their football-sized heads and their two-metre backbones.

He cleans his feet twice a day until his antiseptic cream is gone and all he can do is dab paw-paw into the puffy wounds and hope for the best.

Some days he thinks of nothing but the hairs on the back of Georgie Jutland's arm. He remembers lying there like a dog while she pulled ticks out of him. Her breath on his skin. The feeling of calm. Funny to think it but those few hours with her he was unafraid. Maybe he was too tired to be afraid. But he begins to think that it was more than that. At the centre of Georgie's wildness there was a calm. You could feel it in her hands. There was a competence, an authority, a seriousness. Yes, and passion. Almost despite herself she was a person of substance. He trusted her. And when he woke in that house and she was gone he was just plain scared. Before he met her, Fox was furtive. He was cunning. He was never scared.

He begins to plan another raid on the cache down the gulf. He needs another rod and reel and there's food there and tools he could do with. While he's down that way he'll go the extra distance to the plateau and hike up to visit Menzies and Axle. The dream has stirred him and he fools with the idea of playing that cheap little guitar again. Yes, when his feet are completely healed, when he can manage the walk.

He's on the beach one morning stepping gingerly in his boots when he hears a confusing drone. It sticks in his ears but it feels like something outside of him. The plane bursts from the island bluff so suddenly, with such glossy redness, such a toothy-faced radial engine and shattering noise, that he stands there like a stunned mullet for a second before diving into the shade of the boabs. The shadow of it splashes across the beach and Fox rises on his elbows to see it bank out across the gulf and shrink to the size of an insect. It disappears behind a headland at such low altitude that it seems to be seaborne. Less than an hour later, while he's still crouched uncertainly in the shade, the thing reappears down the gulf and rises from the water to list out across the mainland with its white floats flashing in the sun.

Next day he sees the white streak of a boat wake way out on the water. He rakes the beach clear of footprints and gathers up anything that might give away his presence. He waits up at camp for the inevitable and by morning it comes in the unmistakeable form of a bow wave.

Lying in the shade of his rock shelter, and hidden by the lattice of the fig, he watches the boat skate into the island's lee where the mackerel are. It's a solid beamy thing. Aluminium plate, maybe eighteen feet. Open, with a casting deck like a bass boat or a barra punt. Three men. They troll for a while, making parallel sweeps only a stone's throw from the beach. One at the rear tiller. The other two holding rods. Fox smells fumes. Now and then the helmsman's face flashes pink and Fox senses him looking his way. They have strikes and break-offs. The motor goes silent and they drift a while, jigging with white lures. Now and then the silver flash of a jumping fish rises above the water. He hears men's laughter.

The tillerman points out something on the beach. They're looking at the remnants of the lightning-struck tree. Fox sees the guide's face again, just a fleshy dab. It looks his way so long that Fox's skin begins to creep. He senses the guide searching the bush for something. For him. And he knows that his island camp is history.

While their wake still fans back toward the other end of the gulf Fox begins to gather his modest belongings. He leaves the heavy skillet and the stick figures and favourite shells, breaks the shelter and smoking rack and throws them off the ledge into the trees below. He packs every compartment and crevice of his kayak and with all the water he can carry paddles north.

THE MOON WAXES and wanes and takes a whole cycle of tides with it and for much of that time Fox feels disoriented. The midden camp is a good one but he misses the drama of the island, the lush patches of vegetation, the glorious bluffs of the red mesa, the panorama from the ledge and the company of the sharks. The seaplane comes and goes every seven days or so and though he only sees it those rare times when it wanders north of its track he's forced to stay tight to the mainland coast for fear of being seen. He paddles in the shade of mangroves and rarely walks on open ground beyond the shell pad of the camp.

The new spot has its compensations, though. He finds that on high neaps the shallows out front of the midden are clear enough to swim in. Anything big and toothy will be visible at a good distance so he has the impossible luxury of lying fully immersed with his face in the water. With the passing of the Wet the sea has lost its bloodlike heat and he often lies there just to feel the cool passage of water across his ravaged skin. He lies face down with his eyes open to see the sleep-waves of the sandy bottom. He watches the shadow of his own head as it travels across the white sand in its aura of radiating ripples. He holds his breath, sees himself winged, fluid, twice the size he feels.

Without rod and reel he catches most of his fish with the thrownet. On the incoming tide, mullet and whiting come foraging in shoals across the flats while he stands stone-still in the shallows, staring into the glare, ready for a shot. It's murder on the eyes and an ordeal of patience, but he gets by. Some days he stalks the shallows with a sharpened stick to spear shovelnose rays. It's all lesser fare and harder work. But he has water, a tiny steady stream in which he bathes his sores and his raw eyes, and he drinks his fill.

He likes the slender boabs beside the midden. After sundown their skins are still warm against his cheek. In the evenings he keeps a smoky mangrove-wood fire to ward off the worst of the mosquitoes and he sets up another drone in the plum-like tree beside the rock shelter. Out of restlessness he goes back to singing. It consoles him, takes his mind off the feeling that he's confined here now, almost a captive. From the midden the archipelago looks like a floating boom, a chain corralling him against the mainland.

His first efforts at reprising the nylon string are disheartening. His thumb hurts and the tone is flat and dreary, without nuance. It's noise but not music; it's worse than silence. And yet crows do their monkish improv all day beyond the ridge and the creek tinkles a layered monotone and the first baler shell you find after the spring tide kicks you into action with its endless *whorrrrrr* against your ear.

He bangs away until he finds a sound. An E, he thinks, but it's only a guess. Gets himself a four-four beat with a bit of shellgrit footstomp for colour and suddenly there's a groove, a little room in there for feeling. *Boom-boom-boom-boom.* It's the righteous one-chord boogie of Mister John Lee Hooker. It's Long John Baldry. It's Elmore James and Sleepy John Estes. It's a jaw harp whanging down the tree into the sandstone just begging for bottleneck and banjo. Okay not bluegrass but browngrass at least and the rest of you has to sing to it; there's just no way you can't. Makes you laugh, dammit. Gets your teeth buzzing. *Boom-booma-boom-boo!* Just one note. One, one, one, one. Yes Bill. You Bill. *One command. One joy. One desire. One curse. One weight. One measure. One King. One God. One Law.* One, one, one, one— you go up and down your note like a pup up and down a dune until you don't feel your festering bites or your oozy eyes or sun-scoured neck, until you're not one moment empty, nor one bit lost or one breath scared. You're so damn far into ones you're not one anything. You're a resonating multiplication. You're a crowd. You're the stones at Georgie's back and the olives shaken to the dirt at her feet. All the hot sweet night you're the hairs on the back of her arm.

eight

ON THE FLIGHT NORTH to Broome and for two days thereafter Jim and Georgie barely spoke. Jim slept all the first night and half the next day before leaving her in the palm-shaded bungalow while he drove into town to see family. Georgie sat, listless and heat-stunned, by the resort pool while on sun-lounges all around her, fellow guests tinkered with laptops and spoke into cell phones. Everyone wore strange hybrid clothing, the sort of tense holiday get-ups that her sisters called Smart Casual. Lots of pastels, plenty of pasty urban flesh on show. She walked down through coconut palms to the beach where red soil faded into white sand. The water was opaque, turquoise. There was no wind. Down here it was all camel rides and thong swimwear. White boys and girls played didgeridoos. Someone in orange shorts dangled from a parachute towed by a speedboat.

Georgie felt bewildered by the crowds and the sudden change of climate. She still smarted from the leavetaking and the knowledge that the boys held her responsible for their banishment to boarding school. And she was confused within herself about being here. One moment she was suspicious of Jim and berating herself for her stupidity in having agreed to come and seconds later she was scanning faces, expecting any moment to see Luther Fox walk blue-eyed and bare-chested through the crowd. In her day-pack she had a handful of his pirate tapes and when she climbed into the town bus between some Americans in Birkenstocks and a woman who looked Aboriginal-Japanese, she pulled on her Walkman to blot out the possibility of conversation. Mandolin, guitar. John Hiatt's strangled voice. Songs about drinking and car wrecks and ruined love. She turned it off and tried not to smile back at the Americans.

Georgie had always liked Broome. Didn't everybody, deep down, want a louvred house with a mango tree in the yard? When she was nineteen she'd taken the hell trip up here by bus. In those days hippies and backpackers slept on Cable Beach and the locals all seemed to be delightfully hyphenated. Everybody you met was half-something-or-other. It was like Queensland without the white-shoe brigade. To Georgie it was *the* tropical dream town. She supposed it was still a nice place to live, but even since her last visit four years ago when she and Tyler Hampton anchored inside Gantheaume Point the place had taken on an air of self-parody. There were so many palm trees, so many brand-new old-timey corrugated-iron shopfronts. In the town centre Landcruisers were still angle-parked and she didn't imagine you'd ever see the park without its bandaged drunks. But the building was as frenetic as the tourism. Out on the red dirt, shopping malls and carparks and subdivisions had gone up. It was becoming a suburban outpost with a hokey pearl-diving theme.

For fifteen minutes she trod the two or three dusty commercial streets like a sleepwalker. She didn't know what it was—the heat, the disappointment, the lack of purpose—but she felt sapped. She went back to the resort and turned on the airconditioning and lay in the bungalow till sunset.

By the end of that day Georgie knew that Luther Fox wasn't in Broome. He wouldn't be. He might have been here before Christmas but he was long gone. He could be anywhere across the north by now. It was hopeless. She'd fly back south tomorrow; this was stupid. And she needed a drink.

When she got to the pool she pulled up at the sight of Jim with two old men at the bar. Their faces flickered in the light of tiki torches. They were faces ruined by sun and drink. Each wore elastic-waisted shorts that clung to his hips below a beer belly. They were shirtless and wore rubber thongs on their feet. Amidst all the resort wear they were a jarring sight.

Jim saw her, hesitated, and waved her over.

Georgie, he murmured. This is Tiny and Merv. My cousins.

Her surprise must have been all across her face.

His dad was married twice, said Merv.

Pleased to meet you.

They smiled and looked into their beers.

Their hair was silver and Brylcreemed. They were brothers. They seemed stricken with embarrassment at her presence.

A mate of Tiny's is a pilot, said Jim. I'll tell you all about it at dinner.

Georgie gathered that this was a dismissal. She bade them goodbye and walked through the scented gardens to the restaurant. She'd only had the one glass when Jim arrived.

Your cousins are older than my parents, she said as he sat down.

We're leaving, he said.

But I haven't eaten.

Leaving town. We're going to Kununurra in the morning.

Oh, she said looking along the verandah hung with bougainvillea, where romantic dinners were under way. Well, I'd pretty much decided to call it quits and fly south.

We know where he is.

Jim, you realize how much country there is out there?

He pulled a map from his shirt pocket and unfolded it on the table. Georgie looked at the airstrip beside his fingertip and the coastline below it. Her heart jumped. She looked up at him. He seemed genuinely excited.

There's a lot of country, Georgie, and not many people. When somebody passes through people notice. Someone flew him here during the Wet. Before Christmas. A good description. Plus, he used my name. The dense prick.

Georgie considered the map, the spill of topographical contours into Coronation Gulf.

She felt an absurd thrill of pleasure at the idea that Luther Fox should remember, that he'd paid attention to her whimsical memories of the island. Few places were as remote and as difficult to reach. It hardly seemed possible that anyone would go to all that trouble simply in order to be found. Unless, consciously or not, there was someone in particular you wanted to be found by. The idea was mad but it wouldn't leave her.

There's a floatplane outfit in Kununurra, said Jim. A couple of their pilots have been talking about seeing someone up here around this little chain of islands. People have been treating it as a bit of a joke. I've booked a charter out there. Tomorrow.

Ah.

A waiter finally came and took their orders. The air smelled of citronella. Georgie filled her wineglass with water.

What? said Jim.

She shrugged. Christ, she didn't know what to think.

Just sudden, she said.

You look panicked.

I spose I am, she admitted, feeling the energy and confidence of the past week ebb from her.

They sat in a stranded silence until their food arrived. Both had ordered barramundi and the single fish arrived whole. It lay between them, steamed on a bed of shoots and lemon grass. Its skin still looked metallic. The eye was opaque.

I want to catch one of these babies, said Jim with a sad stab at lightening the mood. A fifty-pounder. I'd like to see it jump.

You know, murmured Georgie, it suddenly strikes me that you and Lu Fox have a lot in common.

Jim put down his fork.

I mean, she said, you both lost your mothers when you were young. People view you both through some weird lens of luck. Very differently of course. And you live...well, in the wake of some kind of disaster.

What is this? said Jim with a quiet fury. Some high school essay you're writing?

What is it with you and them, Jim?

Curlicues of steam rose from the fish between them. Jim drank off his glass of sauvignon blanc and poured himself another.

My mother killed herself. There's nothing at all in common.

But I never knew that! Georgie cried. Christ, in three years you'd think I'd find out basic things like that. That and the fact that you have cousins on the old-age pension.

We never went that deep, Georgie, he said, looking as though he regretted it immediately.

And why was that?

Jim drank half his glassful and tried to recompose himself. He had that earnest look from the night out on the terrace, a nakedly searching intensity that was unsettling.

To be fair, he said carefully, you were never very curious. And that suited me because I wanted to be left alone. I've always, *always* kept things to myself. Still, there were a few times when I got close to...well, not spilling my guts so much as...well, saying a few things. About Debbie and how things were. The good ole days. But I always held back.

Because of something about me? Georgie asked, wondering whether she really wanted to know.

Most of it I hadn't even said to Debbie.

And you *loved* her.

Well.

It's all right, she said.

Always liked you, Georgie. But I just didn't have room, you know? I was never really there, not present.

Still, said Georgie without managing to suppress her bitterness, the way you describe us we were a perfect match. One mute, the other deaf.

Jim stuck his fork into the fish and the bright foil of its skin seemed to slip.

Look, I never went after you, Georgie. On Lombok I didn't even see you, even after we met, wouldn't have even noticed you if you hadn't come bounding up to play with the kids on the beach like that.

You made love to me, she said with what breath she could muster. The second day.

Yes, he said, peeling white flakes of meat from the fish's shoulder.

I guess you needed something.

He nodded. But I didn't beg you to come to White Point.

You asked me.

I was being polite.

You're saying I attached myself to you like some opportunistic infection?

No. Jesus, we just felt sorry for each other. I helped you get home. You were stuck even when you did. And me, well you pitied me.

I wanted to help, she said. I thought I helped.

You did. I don't regret that part of it. Hell, I was cooked inside, totally stuck. The kids were cute. Nice big house on the water. You were unemployed, recovering from your American and the voyage. There we all were.

Did you think I was after your money? Georgie asked, feeling the tears come.

Don't be silly.

God, you must have been appalled when I showed up in town with my backpack.

Jim filled his plate with fish and meticulously picked out the roasted flecks of chilli.

Well, he admitted. It didn't look good. But I couldn't turn you away. You'd been kind to us—

And I was good in bed.

And I was lonely and trying to fix myself up so I decided I didn't care what they thought. That was part of what I'd decided I had to change. This idea people had of me, the way they saw me.

Georgie watched him carefully. That grave, almost frightened intensity had overtaken him again. It fascinated her. She had an inkling that just beyond this point was the secret place where he really lived.

Do you mean, she asked, their image of you as their talisman, the lucky one, the Golden Boy?

No, he said impatiently, not that. Not *just* that.

And how is our meal? said their waiter, a svelte young woman with a stud in her navel.

Dead, said Jim pointing at the fish. You want me to check?

They finished eating in silence and Georgie watched Jim's face as he chewed and drank in complete withdrawal. She couldn't tell if he was summoning some kind of will to go on or if he'd shut up shop for the night.

They walked for a while after dinner on the broad, dimpled beach. A yellow moon hung over the resort and the scrub country beyond it.

Miles down the beach a light shone on Gantheaume Point. The air was warm. Jim walked beside her with his shirt open. She couldn't really see his face despite the moonlight, but after a while she decided to press him.

Are you talking about the family reputation? she asked. Is that what you meant? About changing.

Yeah, he said, sounding almost relieved.

Why bother trying to change that? Small towns, legends spring up. It's usually bullshit.

Well, in our case it wasn't all bullshit.

Your father?

The war fucked him up. Before he met my mother he had a son from a previous marriage. This is the Second World War I'm talking about. I guess that makes this boy my half-brother. He was a prisoner of the Japanese. Tortured to death. Think that's what turned the old man, made him so hard—he never got over it. By the time I came along that was all I knew, this scary, vicious bastard. That's what they miss in White Point. This prick I hated. I couldn't even tell you the things he did.

And your mother?

Well, you can imagine why she did it. He was a monster.

But this legend, this reputation you have to live under—

Jesus, sometimes I can feel him in me like some kind of poison. You can feel it's passed on—

Oh, Jim, you can't say that.

And *you* don't have a fucking clue what you're talking about.

Georgie walked for a while, angry, chastened, fascinated.

Beaver thinks you've got religion, she said at last.

That right? he said dully.

You were frightened of being like your father?

I *was* like my father—that's the point, he said exasperated. And Beaver knows it. The fucking good old days. I wasn't a nice man. I was a spoiled, wild kid, untouchable because of the old man's power. I could do anything I wanted in that town, and don't think I didn't try. That's how I grew up. That's how I was.

No bloody grammar school was gonna polish that off. What else does Beaver have to say?

He won't say anything, said Georgie.

Can't tell if he's loyal or scared.

He saw something, didn't he?

I imagine he saw plenty. But...yeah, he saw me...out of control.

Jim stopped walking. He stood with his hands in the pockets of his loose cotton shorts. In the moonlight his chest looked flaccid. He was aging—his breasts had begun to slip on him. In the lee of the point Georgie could see the masthead lights of anchored yachts.

There was one night at the pub, the day Dirty Herman killed the pig. Everyone was off their faces. I was hammered on rum and speed, like a Catherine Wheel, I was. Staggered out with a woman and we ended up in Beaver's wreckyard. I knew who she was—I'd had my eye on her for a long time. She was blasted, too. Anyway we were screwing on top of some old car when Beaver came to the back door. We were making a lot of bloody noise. He had a torch. He just opened the door and flashed the light around and saw us out there. This girl's hair all over the hood of the car, our clothes everywhere. And I didn't even stop. That light was in our eyes and I just kept at it, just grinning into the glare until he gave up and went inside and I kept going until I was finished. I was untouchable, Georgie. That's how I was. That was the night Debbie had Josh. Nineteen-hour labour. The girl on the car, she was from the band. It was Sally Fox. And at the time I didn't give a shit, never gave it a thought. I'd been daring myself to score her for years.

Georgie looked at her feet on the sand. He couldn't seem to stop now but she wished that he would.

And then the day comes, Jim said, and it's like a saw taking the top of your head off. You look at the x-ray they've done of your wife's breast and it's like you can read your whole life in it. Geez, there were plenty of other things but all I could think of was me and that girl. That particular girl. That one night. Like I could see it in the tumour. And the next tumour. All the operations, everything. Jesus, I wasn't even thinking of my wife, you know, I was thinking to myself, *you've* done this, you've brought it on yourself. Sometimes I thought it was the way the others would see it, that the Fox luck had rubbed off, that I'd caught it from her like some disease. The sort of thing a good fire will always fumigate. But I spose deep down I knew it wasn't true. It felt like judgement. Not just for that but every other mongrel thing I ever did to my wife, anyone. Some kind of judgement that wouldn't let up until I changed.

You can't possibly *believe* that, said Georgie with a shudder.

But I do, he said.

It's vile.

I'm not proud of it, he said.

I don't mean that, I mean the way you're seeing the world. Like some vengeful balance sheet.

I reckon that's how it is.

Then haven't you paid? Hell, you lost your wife.

No, I think you have to make amends yourself. Give something, not just have something taken off you. It's the only way to call the dogs off, I reckon—prove to yourself you're changed.

Like, what...doing some sort of penance?

Maybe. Yes.

And that's what this is about? Delivering me to Lu Fox like some kind of pay-off? Who does it make amends to? His family honour? Two dead women?

Georgie turned on her heel and began walking back, her mouth dry, her lips all chalky. Jim caught up, his shirt flapping as he drew up beside her.

No, he said, but I've been thinking about it a long time. About you and me and him. And it's like a test. Christ, I've tried to make myself over and here's the situation. Prove to myself that I'm different—and get free. At least in my head. In White Point, no matter what I do, I'm still my father's son. Half the time I think it myself. You need a moment, something that defines you.

And what am I, the witness to your symbolic moment?

Won't we both get what we want?

Georgie didn't answer. She was repelled by him now but she wanted to believe that it was possible.

THE MOMENT FOX WAKES in the cool blue light of dawn he goes to the drone. He greets every day with music and likewise bids it goodbye at sunset. Hunting and eating become diversions. His technique develops the better he understands the flexibility of the tree until, by leaning hip and shoulder against the trunk, he can alter the string's pitch and slur notes gently or wildly in a smooth, fretless sound that's not quite Eberhard Weber or Stanley Clarke but superior to any jug band tea-chest bass and subtler than any bottleneck slide he managed in his playing days. Early on the droning was exuberant but now it's wistful. He sings the gloss of Georgie's skin, the hot rush of her laugh. His digressions from the plangent monotone are like meandering treks in a minor key, embroideries he can barely manage to return from. In trying to match it, his voice becomes thin and birdlike. The music develops a pattern whose order just eludes him. He knows it's there, feels himself always at the brink of comprehending it the way he stands at the shore with a scallop shell seeing its patterns repeated in the sandy-ribbed bottom and in the fluted shoreline and the sandstone ranges. He sings until he's hoarse, until he wonders whether the tree isn't bending him now, if he's the singer or the sung.

At night the stars wheel ever westward. Mostly they're just texture. But sometimes he stares so hard and attains such crisp focus that he sees them as the places and bodies they are. They lie there in sheets, before and beyond each other, interleaved in their bronze, gold, silver, pink, blue facets, in mosaic overlaps like the scales of a fish. At moments like these the sky has an awful depth of field, an inwardness that makes him afraid that he's falling out into it, about to be inhaled like a dust mote. He digs his fingers into the dirt either side of his swag as he lies there overcome with vertigo. He holds to the earth by his nails and his clenched buttocks for fear of tilting out into space.

Some mornings he has to unglue his eyes by bathing them in fresh water. One of them feels lumpy and his eyelid irritates it every time he blinks. He lubricates it with soothing drips from his dwindling tin of olive oil but this leaves a cloud over his eye and he feels his peripheral vision shrink. Paddling the kayak through mangroves one afternoon he doesn't see a croc until it's almost at his elbow. A couple of mud bubbles on the shadow-latticed surface are transformed in a second into the snout and eyes of a great saurian bastard not a metre from his hip. Fox slams the paddle blade so hard between its eyes he nearly tips out. As it rolls and flees in surprise, all flashing pale belly and armoured tail, he sees it's bigger than the kayak and the surge of displaced water shunts him sideways, cocked to the verge of capsize. It ploughs through the trees to leave him shaking.

But he persists in the mangroves despite the fear of crocs because the tree canopy offers

shade and camouflage and his hunger grows
more nagging. He catches small barramundi
on handlines and lures mangrove crabs from
the mud. The crabmeat is rich and he savours
the cheesy orange roe.

Sometimes he finds himself floating through
the trees doing nothing at all. Thinking of the
orange blossoms of the Christmas tree, for
instance, or the scalloped ridges on Georgie's
fingernails.

He loses his voice. A fever comes upon
him. For a few days he just lies on his swag,
shivering. Now and then a quoll looks down
on him from a crevice in the rock shelter.
Like a big, handsome, red rat, it appears
osmotically from the sandstone, its ginger
fur starred with white spots, one five-toed
forefoot splayed on the ledge. Fox likes its glistening protuberant eyes. If he even breathes
the quoll disappears as though inhaled by
the stone itself, and he almost cries every
time it goes.

The air shimmers. Georgie Jutland breathes
into his mouth. She tastes of food that he's
cooked for her. She lies hot across him, her
hipbones creaking against his. Those sad,
changeable green eyes. When she leaves with
her shining steel guitar, a train of silver fishes
follows in her wake. Now and then he sees her
at the shore, sees himself there, too. They're
like trees. They *are* trees. All morning they reel
their shadows in from the west only to troll them
ever eastwards across the shell bed in the
afternoon.

At dusk he gets up and shuffles down to stand beside himself. He touches her, breathes in her nutty odour, shudders as his hip brushes hers. He presses his brow against her bark and puts one clear eye against her, thinking, this is a tree you moron, and slinks back to his swag. But he comes back in the moonlight to hold it anyway. It's warm-blooded even after dark and its skin so smooth, its clefts so sculpted. He watches himself looking on from lower boughs. He sees a naked creature swimming up against a tree, holding its slim hips and pressing himself to it. A ragged man with flayed shanks whose sudden tiny cry in the night is no louder than the gasp of an opened oyster.

THE PLANE FELT as if it would never fly. It roared across the listless river while the barefoot pilot rocked and cajoled the thing and finally levered it by stages into the air. The dam wall flashed beneath them. Irrigation channels caught the sun. The plantation town of Kununurra was a weird, virescent swathe in the ochre landscape, a few moments of rigid geometry that fell away in seconds and afterwards seemed imaginary. The aircraft's shadow rippled across the Carr Boyd Ranges. Over the country beyond—the parched savannah, the yellow floodplains, the spare khaki blotches of acacia, the spinifex and red dirt and the dry snakeskin rivers—hung a veil of smoke. It looked to Georgie as though the entire Kimberley was smouldering, and the haze only added to the madness of the distances, the disorder of the view.

The cabin air was hot and tainted. The harness felt heavy on her, its buckles and latches daunting. The headphones hurt her ears but the engine noise was worse. She sat amidst styrofoam boxes of food and watched Jim's head swivel from window to pilot to the dials in the dash. He'd been tense and anxious all morning. At the hotel he'd shoved a man aside when he staggered clumsily into their luggage. His lips were chapped from being licked. About an hour into the flight he snatched a foil-lined bag from the floor and shoved his face into it. From behind she watched his neck convulse. Last night he was drunk and sullen. He'd wanted sex. She held him off with talk. She knew he hadn't slept then, that he'd stayed up drinking, that something wasn't right with him. And now she wished they could just arrive and be there and have happen whatever would happen so she wouldn't be reduced to interpreting and rethinking the spasms in his neck. The seaplane felt suspended; its only perceptible motion the horrid upward lunges in the heat. The scale of the land below stole any sense of progress. She closed her eyes in order to endure it.

Another hour passed. The gulf emerged from the haze as a blue gash in the land. Georgie saw the archipelago, she picked her island without a moment's hesitation but there was no shiver of recognition as before. True, she felt relief, but also a pang of disappointment.

The plane skidded and skipped across the water. Spray beaded on the windows, and then they taxied around a headland into a white shelly cove where a man stood waiting.

Red Hopper brought them into the shade of his thatched shelter, sat them at the table and poured two tin mugs of iced water.

He was the same big ginger bloke that Georgie remembered. His features were pugnacious, you could easily imagine him with his dander up, but his face was brightened by a steady sardonic amusement that rendered him instantly likeable. He wore a long-billed cap that was stained with salt and he had the wide, crusty feet of a man who rarely wore shoes. The shorts and tee-shirt were bog-standard western male get-up but the red bandana round his neck was close to flamboyant. His fingers were scarred and blunt and his nails were bitten to the quick.

White Point, he said with a rueful laugh. I know it. Got me head kicked in at the pub when I was nineteen. They take no prisoners in that town. So much for the temperate zone, eh?

The water tasted sandy and sweet. Georgie saw the two men size each other up.

The camp was an open-sided bough shelter built at the mouth of a wide, low cave. Red

Hopper ran an orderly outfit. There were kitchen benches, a steel sink, fridge and freezer, plenty of stacked utensils and the loose shell floor was raked and clean. Overhead a brace of baitcasting rods and a bewildering array of lures hung within arm's reach. Along the swept rock ledge, beside bottles of sunblock and insect repellent and a serious-looking medical kit, were the two HF radio units that Georgie presumed were the only link with the world beyond. Next to the radios were books and magazines whose pages were curled and wrinkled with humidity. The books were mostly about tides, birds and fish but they included what looked to be the entire oeuvre of Hunter S. Thompson.

Not a bad set-up, said Jim.

Well, if you're a fisherman, anyway, said the guide.

I am.

That's right, the guide said mischievously. So you are.

I'm afraid we've met before, Red, said Georgie. She felt Jim's head swivel. It was a few years ago. You towed us off the spit out near that big island.

Hopper thumbed his cap back and looked frankly at her for the first time.

You probably don't remember, she said.

I thought you were Americans.

Well, one of us was.

I'll be buggered. How far'd you get?

They sank it at Lombok, said Jim.

Well, said Red diplomatically. He was a character, that fella.

Georgie could only smile.

Listen, said Jim. About this week.

You've paid for the week. Doesn't mean you have to stay the seven days. And like I said, I'm used to finding fish, not people.

I understand that. But you know the country.

Well, the coast. I know the gulf and the plateau. This bloke doesn't owe you money or anythin, does he?

Jim took a gulp of water.

I mean, I'm assumin this is some sort of rescue mission and not somethin...untoward, as they say.

He's someone we need to make contact with, said Jim.

About ten years ago someone tried growin dope way the hell back in the islands out there. I found tools and irrigation pipe—

It's nothing like that.

Which is what makes me wonder, Jim. About why there'll just be the three of us lookin. You could've had choppers and boats, a full-scale search. Black trackers, the whole circus.

It's a private thing, said Jim.

Yeah, I gathered. But a bloke can't help but be curious. Spose that's why I took you on.

Not the fact that I tripled your usual fee? asked Jim with a mirthless grin.

And how can that douse a bloke's curiosity? By the way, I took the liberty of havin your bags searched in Kununurra. Not polite, but there it is.

What the hell for? asked Jim rearing upright in his chair.

And I don't spose either of you carried a firearm on you when you boarded the plane?

No, said Georgie who felt herself turn to Jim.

Course not, he muttered.

A bloke has to take a few precautions, that's all.

We understand, said Georgie.

You think this guy wants to be found?

She shrugged.

He's a white fella?

What difference does it make? Jim asked.

Well, for a couple of years pilots've been sayin they see someone up and down this country. You know, right back in the rough stuff, places you never see people. But he's a blackfella. You have to take what they say with a grain of salt. They're mostly young blokes. They like a story.

Well, what would be so remarkable about seeing an Aborigine up here? said Georgie. Most of it's native land anyway, isn't it?

I'm no expert, said the guide. But for one thing, you couldn't fill a Japanese car with the number of blackfellas who still have the bush skills to live out in that sort of wilderness for years at a time. And of that carload, most of those blokes'd be too old to walk or see anymore. And for another thing, it's not very common for blackfellas to go out and live alone for any great period. In my experience they don't have a passion for getting away from other people and *communing* with nature. They like each other's company.

What's this got to do with why we're here? asked Jim impatiently.

Because those reports from earlier in the season were of a white bloke.

He's white, said Georgie. His name is Luther Fox and he's thirty-five years old.

Makes sense. You know, I didn't believe em, not at first. But I know he's out there. He's been here.

You mean you've *seen* him? said Georgie.

No. He's been flogging stuff from the camp.

That's our man, said Jim with a bitter laugh.

How's that?

Family tradition. God helps those who help themselves—to what belongs to somebody else.

Red Hopper grinned. Georgie could see the way he looked at Jim, as though he was trying to decide something about him.

Could hardly blame a bloke, the guide murmured. Whatever he took has probably kept him alive. If he is still alive.

I think I know where he is, said Georgie.

It was a thirty-minute run in Red Hopper's aluminium barra boat. There was a mild chop on the water but the occasional bit of spray came as cool relief. She watched the way the guide took his polaroids off to lick the blurring salt from the lenses while continuing to steer. Jim looked uncomfortable with someone else at the helm.

The full light of afternoon lay on the island's orange-red crags. It lit the crowded treetops of its vegetation. The glare from the scalloped shell beach was punishing. The guide pointed out the ruins of an ancient boab destroyed by lightning and he led them up through the rainforest toward the base of the bluff.

He's been here, said Red. Look at these trails he's made.

And you told him about this place? Jim asked Georgie.

Told you too, she murmured.

I don't recall.

They climbed from a snarl of vines onto a stone ledge that ran along the foot of the mesa. They came to a stagnant puddle of water and, further along, the remains of a camp. Ash from cooking fires was mounded on the dirt of the terrace. There were shells and pieces of stick bound with gelspun line. A few bits of bleached coral, some tattered palm weavings. In the fine dirt beneath the low rock overhang was a long depression, the imprint of a body. Georgie knelt beside it. It felt strange to be there, to see his outline. There was a dull twang behind her. Jim stood at the wizened fig tree with his thumb on a bit of nylon leader tied between two boughs.

It's him, she said.

He's long gone, murmured the guide.

That your skillet?

Yep, Hopper said with a smile.

They looked out across the treetops. Behind its levee of mangroves the nearby mainland was spiky and dry.

So few trees there, said Georgie. And it's like jungle here.

Fire, said Red. You get patches of rainforest over there, too, but only in the lee of big
breakaways where the wind can't blow the fire.
Funny thing is, there's more water over there
than here.

Which is why he's gone, said Jim.

That and he saw us coming. You can see clear
to the plateau from here. He's probably been
gone since I first showed up this season.

Jesus, he could be bloody anywhere, said Jim.

Anywhere there's food and water.

Somewhere on the island?

Nah. No water.

My guess is he's camped along a creek or on
the coast where he's found a spring. Some place
he can fish. He's got himself a boat somehow.
He's no idiot.

Georgie thumbed the string in the tree.
Oh. Oh. She felt the guide watching. Even when
it stopped vibrating the breeze soughed over
it enough to make her smile.

So what now?

It's nearly beer o'clock, said Red. And I have
to catch your dinner on the way home.

We can catch our own dinner, said Jim.

Well, said Red, that remains to be seen.

That evening they ate panfried fillets from
the barramundi the guide had boated in the
last of the light. Both of them had lost fish,
Georgie from preoccupation and lack of conviction and Jim from uncharacteristic impa-
tience. But the sight of Red's fish leaping
into the air with its gillplates flashing and
rattling had stirred her. The fishing guide

413

laughed as though it was the first fish he'd caught in his life; there was no need to ask him why he did this for a living.

After dinner they sat out under the stars while the tide burbled up the beach.

Tomorrow, said the guide as they sipped their beers, we'll start working through all the fresh-water spots. That's all we can do, really.

What are our chances of finding this bloke? asked Jim.

If he doesn't wanna be found? Nil. Might find his camp but all he's gotta do is hide. He's smart enough. He'll hear us coming for miles.

Jim stirred. Bloke's stealing your gear and it sounds like you admire him.

Hopper laughed. Well, you gotta hand it to him. Besides, it keeps you guessin. You should hear my clients talk about him. The pilots get em all wound up. Half the punters are lying in their swags at night waitin to get their throats cut. Seven days of freedom and safety and they're fangin to get back to Sydney or wherever. They appreciate it, though. He gives em an excuse to be scared.

That didn't make a lick of sense to me, said Georgie with a self-conscious laugh.

It's like this, said Red. Half the people who fly in here for a week's mad-dog sportfishin— at iniquitous cost, as you now realize—spend six nights lyin awake terrified. Now, they're mostly from the city, so you expect a little cul-ture shock, but I guarantee that if you took every spider, snake, shark, box jellyfish, wasp, sandfly and crocodile out of the equation—

just wiped em out at the touch of a button—
they'd still lie awake all night.

Well, there's the heat, of course, said
Georgie. And look how bright the moon is. And
all the new smells and noises.

They're shit-scared, if you'll pardon the
language. People are terrified of the wide,
brown land.

And *you* have to reassure them, said Jim.

Mate, these are big beer-swillin *blokes*. You
know, lawyers and surgeons and kick-arse
CEOs. I don't reassure em, I rip the piss out
of em.

Jim had to laugh. It must eat into your
return business.

Jim, they love it. They're back every year for
more.

Ritual humiliation, said Georgie.

I figure I'm just doin my bit for the nation,
you know?

All three of them laughed and Jim's prick-
liness subsided minute by minute. The guide
had been puzzling over them all day, she felt,
and now he'd decided how Jim might be managed. He was no fool.

About nine they called it a night and Georgie
and Jim walked up to their insect domes a little
way along the ridge. They were separated
from the beach by a belt of spinifex. Georgie
lay a while wondering if Lu wanted to be
found. There was something special about him,
not just because she had become obsessed
by him and conferred importance upon him
by simple investment, but because there was

415

a thing about him she'd been trying to define for herself, and it struck her right there as she zipped herself in and Jim scrunched around on the shells to get comfortable. It had something to do with music. The string in the tree had confirmed it. So many other men were mostly calculation. Jim Buckridge, even Red. The chief impulse of their lives was management. It wasn't exclusively a male thing but, God knows, men had it in spades. Most of her life she'd had it, too, just living by will, achieving and maintaining control. But Lu was pure, hot feeling. Emotion cut off and backed up. She'd felt it the instant she pulled at his shirt in the hotel room. His startling tears. They'd shocked her briefly; she found it all a bit off-putting. For her it was just an impulse, but she'd started something she hadn't counted on. He was a man trying to live like a man, by force of will. But it was against his nature. And in that moment of need or mischief she'd broken into something. You could see the relief in him as he cried, even before they made love. Music wants to be heard. Feeling wants to be felt. He'd always wanted to be found, even if he didn't know it. She had found him once. And that was in the dark. She'd just have to find him a second time.

Georgie sat up in a ship's bunk and slid dazed to the thrumming deck. The bulkheads groaned in the swell. She wore a starched white uniform that was stained and wrinkled and on stockinged feet she stumbled down corridors and up companionways in search of clues as to her purpose here. It was as though she'd woken from an almighty bender that had fried her memory entire. The fob watch bounced so painfully on her that it felt pinned to her very breast. Flakes of paint fell from riveted steel panels. She felt the ship twist and flex on its keel. She came upon a man in a wheelchair whose hospital gown was askew. His cock and balls lay against one flaccid thigh and a line of sutures divided him like a ragged zipper. As the deck tilted he crashed into the bulkhead and fell across another man who seemed to be riding a bedpan in the swell. A surgical trolley spilled bloody implements and wadding and the whole ship seemed to hesitate a moment as though suspended. A solitary groan issued from the silence, a woman's voice, chillingly familiar, and then the deck slammed up beneath Georgie's feet and doors burst open left and right to spill men and women like rubble across her path, people mechanized by traction pulleys and naso-gastric tubes, by bone braces and monitors. The voice from behind propelled her. She began to pick her way through the confusion of limbs and apparatus but ended up just scrambling over as though they were one inanimate mass until she came to a companionway on whose lowest step sat her mother. Vera Jutland had the doll-like rosiness of complexion that only a mortician could supply. There was an uncharacteristic look of concern on her face. In one hand she held a shard of mirror. The fingers of the other hand lay on the wattles of her neck. As Georgie came close she looked up a moment without recognition.

I don't feel anything, she murmured.

Water began to spill down the companionway and a smell like the mud of mangroves rose from somewhere below.

Georgie sprang up in her swag and blundered against the gauze of the insect dome. The sky was oceanic. She lay back and felt the shells grind softly beneath her.

Orright? murmured Jim in his dome nearby.

Yes, she said.

In the moonlight Jim's head was cradled in his arms and she knew he hadn't slept yet. She sensed that he wanted to talk. She fell asleep waiting for him to speak.

STEEL GUITAR. It's across his knee. He sees his face distorted in its undulating surface as he plays right there on the verandah step with the bottleneck glissing up the fretboard and the slow vibrato shaking the loose muscle of his arm. Such an old, old lick he plays, the first he ever learned, and its physical pattern is as sweet as the sound it makes. Like an old woman's voice. A shadow falls across his feet. He lifts his head and she's there, her hair grey, her mouth twisted into a grin.

That dirty music, she says. Someone'll hear.

Behind her the land is thick with trees. Even the birds stir at the sound of her.

The moon comes to earth in his camp. The midden and the beach and the boabs are pearlescent. His hands, his feet, are lunar. He's washed in cold light. Transparent.

By dawn the fever is gone. His limbs feel heavy on him and every movement is a kind of wading. The air is laced with currents. His skin prickles as though he's being watched at every point.

He stoops to drink at the tiny, shrinking stream and knows in an instant that he can't stay. He's exhausting the food around him; the only way to keep this up is to continue moving up the coast to new reserves of water and fish. Staying only a few days at each place, goaded on by hunger. But he just can't see himself doing it. He's not a nomad, he can't even imagine such a life. It's not just exhaustion that disqualifies him but his instinct to linger, to repeat, to embellish. A way of living isn't enough. Fox has to stay, to inhabit a place. It's as though his mind can only settle when he's still. He feels he's dragging a life and a whole snarled net of memory across foreign country. None of it lives here; it doesn't spring from here and it will neither settle nor belong. However good the fishing farther up, no matter how clear and fresh the waterholes, he knows now that he'll die out here; he'll eat himself alive like a body consuming its own wasted muscle.

AT BREAKFAST RED HOPPER presented them with a survey map and a number of likely campsites and before there was any heat in the day they set off down the gulf. They worked their way up creeks and poled through mangrove everglades. They climbed out at rockbars and sandspits and Georgie felt Jim's mood slip from his early neutrality into a sullen silence. As the day wore on and the colder the trail felt to Georgie, the more dogged Jim became. Each miserable spring and puddle had to be covered thoroughly and he stormed through the undergrowth of the hinterland until he was speechless with fury.

At the landward end of the gulf, beneath the great striped plateau, they entered a rivermouth a mile wide. Red steered up muddy switchbacks, scattering birds in their path, until the mangrove ramparts became stony banks and the river petered out at a sandstone wall. In the Wet season, the guide told them, this was a cataract and the country above a series of rapids. They climbed up the terraced stone and came to a chain of billabongs whose clear water was dimpled with tiny, brazen fish. There were shady gums here, and pandanus, but she never expected any sign of Lu Fox. It was a long way from the sea, and the surrounding country felt hemmed in by high ground. The sun was pitiless now. She sat in the smooth stone basin of a waterhole until even Jim conceded that it was hopeless. The three of them sank to their chins in the cool water while fingerlings nipped at their elbows.

BEFORE HE LEAVES, Fox realizes there's nothing he wants to take with him but a waterbag and the pack into which he stuffs boots, socks and some sunscreen. He pushes off from the midden and paddles until the glare off the water gouges his eyes. He makes it level with his old island before he pulls up a creek, drags the kayak to high ground and lies in the shade a while until the pain recedes. Even as he lies there the tide peaks. Before long it will begin the run-out and he'll be paddling against it, and he realizes he's begun his trek too quickly; he hasn't thought it out. He'll have to lie here for hours or press on by foot. It pains him to leave the kayak after all this time, but he's anxious to get on so he stashes it safely out of sight.

He pulls on socks and laces up his boots. With the waterbag in his pack and the pandanus fringe of his hat clamped low, he sets off. Straight away he's glad of the boots. The ground is hot and stony and the spinifex sharp. The country is riven with washouts and escarpments. Trees are sparse and their shade miserly. Several times he comes to impassable gullies from which he must turn back and beat his way round.

The tide is well out when he comes to a delta whose grey mud is veined and wrinkled. The river's mangrove barrier looks bereft of water.

From here the sea looks a mile away. He works his way down to where the mud looks dry enough to cross but the crust breaks at the first step so that he plunges thigh-deep into black stinking ooze from which he has to haul himself with sandflies swarming and biting. The hell with that. Shaken, he heads inland, and crosses at an oystery rockbar. He makes his way to the shade of a sandstone bluff.

He sits there a time to compose himself. He drinks deeply from the waterbag and gathers his bits about him again, but he starts at the sight of two handprints blown in red ochre on the yellow stone above him. He stretches his own hands over them and sees how much smaller the painter's are. Although he hasn't meant to touch anything a thumb comes away with ochre on it. He's surprised to find it so fresh. There's something not quite right about the whole set-up, an obviousness that makes him think of Axle. He brightens at the idea that the boy might be about, that they might sit down and talk, bang on the guitar, laugh about those maps and how much easier today might be if he had them. Thinks of the kid out here making himself up as he goes along. Wants to return the kayak. Wonders about Menzies.

Just past midday he makes the ridge above the fishing guide's camp and hears the petrol generator wailing away down there like a stranded lawnmower, and his resolve founders. He thinks of all the stuff he's nicked. What kind of a bloke is this guide? Here he is again, exposed, outnumbered, isolated. His mind wheels in all directions. He lies there in the sun with sweat in his stinging eyes until he works up the nerve to take it slowly, to watch and see.

He comes down in stages, until he reaches the cave roof where a bank of solar panels is tilted. From here he sees the empty beach, the boat gone. He worms his way down a cleft into the cool black shade of the cave and stands in water to his shins. A breeze runs through the cave; it smells of animal fat, LP gas and insect repellent. A long time he stays there, hearing nothing. In the end he creeps out into the light with his heart racing—and a sudden movement causes him to cry out. A big gingery quoll plunges across the bench in a bebop flourish of tin plates and lids and cutlery before disappearing into the rock ledge.

Several seconds pass before he can move. He looks at the plastic tables strewn with bits of tackle and dirty plates. Towels hang from the edge of the shelter. He goes to the cooking bench and sees the pans loaded with leftover sausages, chops, fried eggs and bread. He reaches in disbelief and shoves two sausages in his mouth. He tears meat from a lamb chop and sops bread through the skillet drippings. He goes at it hand over hand until he's wracked with hiccups. With an egg on the palm of his hand, the yolk all grey and powdery, he sits in a plastic patio chair to savour the sensation of having his arse off the ground and his feet free.

The fridge whirrs. He wolfs the egg between spasms then cracks the door to look at lettuces in Woolworths bags and cans of beer, tomatoes, carrots, apples. He hooks out a plastic jug of orange juice and slugs it down in cold, shocking gulps that he can't stop. Drinks the entire two litres. He stands there like a moron with the empty container and just stuffs it back in the door. The cold air tingles on his legs while he pulls off his pack and stuffs it with bacon rashers, apples, oranges, a whole lettuce.

At one end of the camp is a nook partitioned by a sandstone pillar. The guide's lair. A bed. A few steel boxes. A plastic tub of clothes. Above the bed, in a rock niche, beside some candles and a shaving mug, is a toothbrush whose scruffy bristles lie awry, like canegrass in which some beast has been sprawling. Fox feels the coatings of fat and fur on his teeth. He has to have it. But as he reaches for it he gets a glimpse of himself in the shaving mirror and stops dead. His hair is a dirty spinifex snarl and when he steps back involuntarily he sees the colourless rag of his shirt. He looks more closely at the scabs and scales of his brow, at the festering beard and those wet, red eyes, and he feels himself searching out his own face in these features with a desperation that soils the pleasure of all the food in his belly and the feeling he's had that this could be it, the day he might come in out of the bush and make peace. But this. You can't come in as this *thing*.

He hears the outboard motor and wheels around, knocking the mirror from the rock. It falls to the bed, bounces, and settles back, leaving a crescent of light on the sandstone over-hang. Fox snatches up a shirt and some elastic-waisted shorts and blunders through the camp for his pack. From the kitchen bench he grabs a bottle of olive oil. The guide boat spurts from behind the rocky promontory and wheels into the cove while Fox crouches, stuffs the pack closed, pulls it on. At the last moment, as he bolts for the darkness of the cave and the shaft up to the ridge, he filches a book from the ledge and goes like hell.

GEORGIE HELD THE COLD bottle to her fore-head while the fishing guide laughed. He rested his freckly arms on the kitchen bench. He shook his head till his cap fell into the sink and his ears went crimson.

He's playing with us, said Jim.

Maybe we're playin with ourselves, Red murmured, still grinning.

Georgie maintained what composure she could. All day her spirits had been sinking. The heat and Jim's darkening mood sapped her. Only moments before, she'd arrived flat, and now her hopes were up again and her head and heart were pounding.

At least we haven't imagined him, she said with feeling.

So what now? Jim asked.

Well, you know the bloke. It's your call. He's either pissed off back to his hideout or he's hanging back in the breakaways behind us. My guess is he's hungry. Why not have ourselves a monster cook-up and see if he comes in?

Or we could call him in, Jim said. We could walk up into the escarpment and call his name.

Red Hopper pursed his lips doubtfully and looked Georgie's way. He raised his eyebrows at her. She set her teeth while Jim spoke.

You know the Christmas tree from down our way, Red? *Nuytsia floribunda*. Big orangey-yellow blossoms on it—they flower in summer, you see em all along the sandy country. That's what this prick's like. All colour and nectar. The bees come swarming. Everything else around is just low scrub or dry banksia, a few tuarts and grasstrees. You know, your hardworking dull grey western scrubland. The wattles flower, I spose, but there's nothing like the Christmas tree. That's him.

Jimbo, you've lost me, said Red still looking at Georgie.

Thing most people don't know, said Jim, is that the Christmas tree is a parasite. The roots suck the juice from all the trees around, they travel a distance you wouldn't credit. Just to get at what the others have got.

Bit of a botanist, are you, Jim?

Like I said. I'm a fisherman.

Like you said.

Georgie should call him in. He'll come if she calls him.

There was a smouldering anger in his voice. Georgie knew she wouldn't do it. The way he was talking you couldn't let yourself.

I think, she murmured, that Red's idea is best.

Just go up there and show yourself! said Jim.

She shook her head.

Don't you want to find the bastard?

Let's have a cook-up, she breathed.

He's probably still close by, said Jim. You mightn't get another chance, Georgie. You know you'll regret it if you don't. It'll eat at you. You'll be thinking about it all the way home. You'll be sitting in that house wishing you did.

She looked at her hands.

Christ, he muttered, after all this.

Who's for a cuppa, then? said the guide.

Georgie felt herself stitching her lips between her teeth.

Jim stood up.

How d'you have it? said Red, bluff but watchful.

I don't want any fucking tea, said Jim. I want this sorted.

Hey, Jim, settle.

The guide was still grinning but alert now, poised. Throughout the long day he'd been pepping Jim up, joshing him along, managing him, but beneath the jokey bonhomie there was an edge. Georgie sensed his mounting distrust of Jim Buckridge, even dislike. Until now Jim had seemed so preoccupied as to be oblivious. He stood with his hands on the bench between them. Christ, she thought, even he doesn't know what he wants to do when he sees Lu Fox. He can't even decide what to do with himself this very moment; he's possessed by rage.

I bloody hope you have a teapot, she said.

The guide looked at her askance.

I won't drink anything made with tea bags.

Georgie, Hopper said with a smile that looked like relief, nobody likes a snob.

Jim walked out into the hard white light. The gas ignited with a tiny *poof*. The guide pulled his hat from the sink and wrung it out with a flourish.

Neither of them spoke for a while. It was hot in the shade. There was no breeze.

This bloke you're lookin for. He your brother or somethin?

She shook her head.

This whole thing's pissing me off, you know. Somebody better cough or I'll have to call the plane back.

He needs it, said Georgie. For his own peace of mind. He's frightened for his children, she said realizing it only as she said it. Jim has the idea that his past is catching up with him and that the world or God or whatever will keep taking revenge on him and his family if he doesn't put things right.

And that means findin this bloke?

In *his* mind, yeah.

And that's why he's got the shits, then. No result.

I guess. I'm struggling to figure him out.

And you believe that stuff. You know, God and revenge?

I think Jim believes it. But *I* don't think the

world is like that. Without some mercy, a bit of forgiveness, I reckon I'd prefer it to be completely random—meaningless. In a sick way I envy the fact that he believes in something. D'you believe in anything?

Three square meals a day, said Red. And the sound of a screamin reel.

What'll happen to him, you think?

Who—your wildman? He'll either die or come in. By September there'll be so little water out there he'll be out of his mind. He knows I've got food, water in the cave and tank storage... You reckon he wants to die?

Georgie thought about it. All that longing for the dead he had. He could have killed himself any time. You don't swim the ocean and trek the land if you don't want to live. There were moments when she told herself that he wanted *her*. She couldn't get through a whole day being certain of it but some stubborn part of her clung to it. That was as close to faith as she came.

Red pulled a leg of lamb from the fridge and laid it on the sink.

We'll cook up a whole poultice of food tonight, he said. God's own picnic.

Yes, she murmured. That's what we'll do.

FOR HOURS HE SQUATS up there in a paralysis of indecision. He's wedged between baking rocks that scald him at every point. He realizes that he's skylined himself, that he'd be visible the moment he tried to worm out over the bare rock to get across the ridge. Back there he might have found a bit of shade in which to think it out, to work up nerve enough to take his chances and face them, whoever they are, but he's caught out here in the crucifying sun where you can barely think straight.

Three people. That's all he had time to count before he bolted. Two bigger than the third. Big enough. And yet what can happen? There should be nothing to fear. It will just be awkward, that's all.

He pulls his tattered hat low. Against the stones his gut is churning.

Fox tries to imagine the picture he'll be—this ragged creature, a shambling beast come suddenly into their midst. Slinking in like a feral dog.

He pulls the bright blue tee-shirt from his pack and sniffs it. Fabric softener. In white letters across the back it says I'M WITH STUPID. When he smiles his lip splits. He tastes blood. His own shirt comes apart in his hands as he tries to reef it off while lying low. The sandstone grates him and the old rag smells like something dead. After he wriggles into the fresh shirt and shorts he splashes his face with the last of his day's water to sluice off some of the grime. He tries to smooth his beard which is full of twigs and grit. The sun eats at him, radiates from every direction. Even through the lids of his eyes it lances him. When he blinks involuntarily the movement is audible.

His gut really hurts. Feels like he's swallowed acid.

But he hasn't shanked it all this way to sit here in the murdering heat and do nothing. Thinks instead of clean sheets, cold sweating mangoes, the potent bodies of living people. The bus they'll put him on. The road south to the sand country. Verandah step. Yes.

The cramp comes over him just as he pulls himself up against the rock. A downward rolling spasm. He presses against the sandstone to wait it out but it only gets worse. He drags his shorts down and shits across the back of his legs, his boots. It splashes the pack, flecks the waterbag even while he's leaning miserably away. When it's finally over he wipes what he can with the old shirt. The fresh shorts are history. He hasn't water enough to clean up. He lies there exhausted in the heat and hears himself weep. Not like this. Not like this.

And then there's the impossible sound of water on the rocks. He levers himself up to a crack between stones and peers down toward camp. There is a man there backlit by the sun. He's standing on the roof of the cave more or less, taking a leak with his head down. Finishes up with a comic shiver, gives it a shake, slips it back into his shorts and looks up. Right this way. Fox knows it's the sun. It has to be the sun. He squats there, reeking and spent, and watches this man scan the ridge, the shell beach, all the rugged gullies of the country beyond. He's looking right this way. Big square face. Hair with a bit of steel wool about it. Kicking at the stone with a deck shoe.

Jim Buckridge.

He's saying something but you can't catch it. And then he's gone and you're asking yourself, feeling yourself limp and roasted, smelling yourself, putting together your sorry bundle and, no matter what, breaking for the ridge the best you can.

IT WAS ONLY EIGHT O'CLOCK but it had already been a long, tense evening by the time Georgie helped Red clean up the remains of their gargantuan meal. They'd stuffed the leg with garlic cloves and baked it in a camp oven dug into the hot shells beneath the fire on the beach. Even now the cave stank of caramelized onions, of potatoes and sautéed mushrooms, of damper and burnt sugar. Georgie felt a surprising equanimity. The food had fortified her; she felt revived by it. They drank shiraz at almost body temperature. She savoured its jammy flavour and the tannic feel of it on her teeth.

The guide lit himself a little something which he offered wordlessly, but she declined. They stood out under the moon while he smoked.

Tomorrow, she said, we'll head back up into the islands.

You're the boss.

I'll pay for anything he's stolen.

The guide shook his head. Nah.

A bird flapped by in the dark.

What'd you do in your other life, Red?

Real estate.

And?

Found it was a contradiction in terms. You?

Nursing.

The life you save may be your own. Who said that?

Georgie shrugged. That your motto?

The guide laughed and expelled a column of smoke that rose in the moonlight. Fish are where you find them, he said. That's my motto.

And now you're a fisher of men.

Why'd you quit nursing?

I lost my way, she said.

You woulda been a good one.

I was.

Hermit crabs tottered in their thousands across the beach.

You can radio in a plane whenever, before the week's up? she asked.

Just say the word.

Jim was awake when she got to her swag.

Fox dies out here, he murmured, you think it'll be my fault?

Go to sleep.

I want to know if you'll blame me.

Jim, I'll hardly think about you. Either way.

He bolted from White Point for a reason. Because he thought I was coming for him.

Well, apparently you weren't.

Christ. It's like the past keeps at you. Whatever you do, however you change.

Georgie lay there a while.

You could leave White Point, she said. Why not start over? Sounds a bit wet, but maybe you need to forgive yourself. All this talk about change. Why not change all of your life? Quit. Sell the boat and take the boys somewhere nice. You could live in Broome. You're loaded, Jim. Why not live with your own kids while they're young, if you're so concerned? Don't repeat the family story. Don't *be* the family story. Cut them out of the pattern. Hell, you don't need to work, but if you want the structured thing find another job, something fresh.

Jim scrunched around inside his insect screen.

Jesus, Georgie. I'm a fisherman.

Right.

HE WALKS INTO THE DARK. Follows his moonshadow. The night is noisy with the grub and scrape of his boots and the tittering of bats and some owl's low query from the black mass of a tree. Fox scrapes at his eyes and stumbles on. Rockrats, quolls, a dingo. Everything scritches and murmurs and yowls about him.

If he stops, the rocks sigh with a spinifex hiss. He falls and starfish leap up; they spin red beneath his eyelids. And out there someone is singing.

He sees trees as men walking, as women tearing their hair.

The tune is familiar. He halts to cock his head. It's from behind a scree slope. Rising into the bleached sky. A hymn. A tune both of them liked. Bach. His mother and father. He recalls them on the verandah, all combat suspended. Singing quietly.

As he scrambles up the rise the pack hammers him. Down in the next gully there are five, six figures. Walking. You can hear the jolting in their voices. He slips and skitters their way. Their calico shirts and dresses glow in the light of the moon. They look too big, distorted. And then he sees the chairs and clocks and trunks strapped to their backs. One of them plays a wheezy organ. The straps cut her almost in three. A sour smell of sweat comes off them, dust too, and furniture polish. They're singing in German, it seems to him, and he follows for as long as he can but can never quite catch them.

He wakes in the sun, his cheek embossed by stones. His eyes are gritty. He looks quickly about to get his bearings and sees on one side the eastern horizon and, on the other, the blue strip of the gulf in the distance and he understands that he's come way inland. Within moments his eyes are no good. The light pierces his head but it hurts to close his eyelids. He remembers the oil in the pack. It's beneath him; he's lying on it.

The oil is hot and heavy on his eyes but it soothes them a moment. As he lies there it trickles back into his ears. He digs out an apple and sucks the juice from every bite. It's a Fuji. God's own sweet apple.

With the landscape glistening and smeary, he walks on. He comes to a low escarpment and sees something daubed on the stone. A keyhole? A lagoon ray? A sperm? Just a body with an upstanding tail—or neck. And one dot on its back. It's a bloody guitar.

Fox wheels about, peers through the oily haze. Axle. He hears bees or flies. Along the break-away a solitary tree. He cups his hands to his temples to make out the bundle nested up in the thin foliage. It's like a rolled swag and he's too far away to tell but it seems tex-tured, as though made from dry palm leaves or paperbark. The pool of shadow beneath the tree rises as a man and tilts his head upward.

Axle? he calls.

Something falls from the tree. Fox registers the flash of bared teeth, the figure's mouth open as though catching dark sap from up in the boughs.

Axle?

The face turns. It sings the sound of a thou-sand flies and Fox's ears burn. That face is only a mouth, nothing more. He turns away and walks seaward, doesn't look back until the sound is gone and he can smell the festering mud of the delta.

436

Out on the gulf the comet streak of a boat wake.

He stops to pour more oil on his stinging eyes. Everything is glazed now and indistinct. He thinks he's found the rockbar he crossed before but it's suddenly slimy underfoot and he flounders into mud, falls and claws himself upright again in a hot rash of insects. All about him the mud bubbles and farts. Oh, well done, he thinks. I'm with stupid. Before stupid was, I am. A life writ in mud.

A smear of colour ahead. He wallows toward it hearing the saurian creep of the tide coming slow across the muck, and to keep afloat he churns forward, arms and legs, grinding through the slurry like a machine. The mud is peppered with cockleshells and sharp twigs that score him. Skippers or worse writhe across his belly.

Hears the ragged panting he makes.

The great silhouette form is a mass of mangroves. He stumbles against the coiling roots, begins to drag himself through the lowering forest where the water sluices and the trees burble and fizz. Fiddler crabs flee from his path and hot white birds. The sludge beneath him is mined with a tangle of limbs. The slippery, upstanding pneumatophores across which he writhes become agitated by his passage through them. They feel slimy and animated, like horrid gothic fingers all over him. Even stumbling, shitcaked and blubbering, into the fishermen's camp would have been better than this.

◆ ◆ ◆

BEHIND THE MIDDEN they came upon the tiny stream and a billycan. Oystershells, fish-bones. In the shade of the rocky overhang, a rancid swag. It was a good situation but there was an air of misery about this camp.

There's me old thrownet, said Red.

Jim kicked the fire-blackened billy across the shellgrit. At the wizened fig tree he wrenched the nylon line from between the boughs. When he hauled the swag out and began ripping the filthy sheets from it, the fishing guide laid a hand on his arm, but Jim elbowed him away. Red Hopper staggered a moment and hesitated. Jim tore a grey sheet into shreds; it seemed to fall to pieces without any force.

Leave him be, said the guide.

Red, said Georgie. I want you to call the plane in. Today.

Not till we find him, Jim said.

This tour's over, said Red.

I paid for a week.

Mate, you can shove your week fair up your date! said the guide snatching at the rag in his hand. Jim stepped into his space.

And you call yourself a bloody professional.

Sport, you need a holiday by the look of you, and I'm not it.

They were in each other's faces now. Jim's cheeks were mottled pink and grey and his eyes were sunk so deep that she doubted he'd slept in days; the last time she'd actually seen him asleep was in Broome. She backed into the shade. She wanted to get back in the boat and leave them here.

We need more time, said Jim strangling on his anger.

No, Georgie said. No more.

This isn't your charter, Georgie, Jim said, still fronting the guide whose jaw was set in a mocking grin.

When could they come, Red? The plane.

It'll be the middle of tomorrow morning, said Red nose to nose with Jim Buckridge. By the time they got here today it'd be late afternoon and they're not licensed to fly in the dark. It'll have to be tomorrow.

Go if you want, said Jim. But pay your way. I'm staying.

The guide shook his head slowly. They were almost touching now.

Beside the ash mound of the fire was a machete. Georgie felt alone out here. Once something started it would spin out of control. She wasn't afraid so much as enraged by the prospect. The sight of their heaving chests made her sick.

That's *it*! she said with a quiet ferocity that startled them. Back off, the both of you. Get the fuck back.

Each of them looked at her, hesitated, and stepped aside.

That's all, she said. Please. Go back to the boat.

Red Hopper licked his lip and pulled at the bill of his cap. Jim Buckridge snatched the Ray-Bans at the end of their lanyard and stuck them on his face. A last scrap of sheet fluttered to the shells.

Georgie rooted around in her little day-pack for a pencil and paper with which to leave Lu Fox a message. But there was only sunblock, lifesavers, tampons, the Walkman. She jacked the tape out of the player and laid it on a stone beside the firepit. It was all she could do. Red dragged the swag back under the rock and brushed dirt from its wizened foam mat.

Jim, the guide said through his teeth. Last chance barra. You copy?

What the fuck's he talking about? said Jim.

We have one good tide left, said Red. It's beginning to run as we speak. Call me unprofessional but I thought you might like to catch yourself a barramundi before you leave.

Jim was silent. They walked up and over the midden. The boat lay in the still, clear water before it.

Doesn't sound like I've got any choice, does it? Jim muttered.

I'll make a fisherman of you yet.

Don't push it.

Georgie got into the boat between them.

HE COMES LOLLOPING OUT onto firm ground and lies there a while just panting and grateful. He gets up and goes on through the jumbled broken country of boulders and trees and dry canegrass until he senses it falling away toward the creek where he left the kayak. He sees the island across the narrow strait. He smells smoke in the air. Tobacco smoke. And voices.

He clambers up to a cleft in the rocks and thinks he's seeing Georgie Jutland standing on the rockbar not fifty metres away. She's casting a fly across the water and stripping it back across a submerged snag. In sandy-coloured shorts with pockets all over them and lace-up boots. Her shirt is sweated through and you can see her shoulderblades. A daggy cotton hat shades her face. Sunlight lives in the down of her arms. On her calves the sheen of perspiration or sunscreen. Thinks he smells Johnson & Johnson baby powder and some creamy lotion.

Her posture is all intensity. There is such angelic float in the line as it ripples and rolls in the air above the creek. He understands it isn't real but he won't move until it's had its moment, so he lies there like a dog on a full belly thanking God for whatever it is working along that tongue of rock like something his poor sorry being has conjured from the blurry bush.

Then she gasps and braces, straightens up on a strike. Line rips through her hand and soon she's palming the reel to slow the fish. The fly rod bellies out over the water and her boots scrape and skid across the barnacle crust. He can't see the fish jump but he witnesses her upturned face and the look of awe as the shade falls from her. The splash is mighty, as though a steer has fallen in, and men are shouting somewhere around the bend. As it cuts through the water the line spits a little spray. She's bent at the knees now, getting leverage on the fish, gaining ground, and suddenly it's in the air where he can see it, a huge barramundi, shaking its head in a red-eyed frenzy, hanging there bright as a thought. He sees the hook come free and the line worming back. Watches its gills swimming at the air, its upturned mouth shut. Georgie Jutland staggers a moment. She stares as the fish crashes back into the water. Then she straightens up and laughs. The men are there with shouts of consternation and laughter.

Fox rises on four points but can't move. It's Jim Buckridge. They seem so real, so crisp in his smarting vision as they walk across the bar to the boat. He makes himself get up. The boat rears onto the plane. He plunges and skids his way down but they're gone around the head-land. He bashes through spinifex. The pack snarls and slows him. By the time he gets there the long white train of their wake comes slapping at the rock below his feet.

ON THE RADIO people from Aboriginal communities hundreds of kilometres apart made travel arrangements and checked on the whereabouts of various individuals. Their exchanges were hesitant, repetitious, mean-

442

dering, and their voices high. There were long, potent silences. At the close of one communication, news came from Kununurra that a plane might be available for Coronation Gulf in the morning. Probably. Definitely.

Red Hopper turned the set down and opened a beer.

Looks like leftovers, he said.

Fine with me, said Georgie.

The guide began to laugh.

What? she asked.

That barra was twenty-five kilos or I'm a wanker.

Well, you said it, muttered Jim.

Fifty bloody pounds of buckethead.

It was a beaut, she conceded.

Georgie, it was a horse!

Just a fish, said Jim. And she didn't land it.

You would've given your left nut, said Red.

Mate, I would've given me left nut only it's already bin given.

Georgie didn't mind the loss of the fish, in fact she was glad of it. Something like that you wanted to share. For the rest of your life you'd need someone with whom you could bring it to mind with nothing more than a raised eyebrow. That thing shining there, like something between you.

The men got drunk.

She thought about the tape she'd left back in the lee of the archipelago. It was a compilation he'd made himself, various blues players young and old. Mississippi Fred McDowell, Son House, Ry Cooder, Bonnie Raitt, Dave

Hole, Keb Mo, Ben Harper, Kelly Joe Phelps. It featured the whining bottleneck style she'd come to love. The more she listened the more she was convinced that this was as close as an instrument got to the human voice. Not as brilliant as the violin nor as mournfully rich as the cello. It was something humbler. No graces, no airs. It was as rough and plain as the voice of a crying child.

Would he see it? Would he understand?

The moon got up like a broken biscuit.

She woke to the sound of Jim falling into his swag. He was hammered.

Trouble with you is you can't bide your time, he said. Even with the friggin fish you screw it up. You can never pick your moment, Georgie, you never could. I spose it's a woman thing.

Spose away, Jim.

He began to snore with his feet out and the insect dome unzipped.

FOX DRINKS at his stream till he's ready to burst and then he just wallows in the trickle of it. He knows they've been here. Someone's kicked the crap out of the place. He doesn't care. She's there. It's her.

He limps through the amorous boabs with the net and makes a couple of weak throws.

He fills the billy with whiting on the last of the tide. He pulls up some spinifex and lays it over the oystery rocks at the end of his cove and when he lights it the stuff flares and crackles. With a few more sticks thrown over the flames oysters begin to heat up and spurt and open. When the blaze dies out he blows the embers onto the wet mud and sucks the meat from the rock itself.

By the stream he grills whiting and mullet. He peels his final orange, savours every segment.

He soothes his sunburnt limbs with olive oil, rubs it into his lips.

The book is *A Field Guide to the Birds of Australia*. It's too little, too late. He flicks through stilts, plovers, sandpipers, recognizes the gorgeous Northern Rosella and the Brahminy Kite, the brolgas and fairy terns. But it's the owls that he lingers over: the Rufous, the Masked which is rarer, the Grass Owl and the Barking Owl that screams at him some nights. Those big, ghostly watchers' faces. The earlike eyes. They remind you of a houseful of sleepers, of boobook nights, cool, mopoking winter nights.

He feels her out there now. He knows she's real. He'll have to go in because every poor tree and turtle, any bird, every creature will end up having to be her if he stays.

Dark falls. The air quivers. He oils his eyes and feels the sound in his throat. Feels every living thing, each heating, cooling form lean in on him. His skin crawls with things that were and with those pending. They hang there in the steady note of his song, in his matted hair, in the oil on his cheeks, and when he opens his eyes the quoll is right by him on the rock. Its black eyes shine and it carries moon-splashes in its ruddy fur even as it withdraws into the dark crevices to watch him. He feels himself within himself. There's nothing left of him now but shimmering presence. This pressing in of things. He knows he lives and that the world lives in him. And for him and beside him. Because and despite and regardless of him. A breeze shivers the fig. The rock swallows the quoll. He sings. He's sung.

GEORGIE WOKE with a start in the gauzy light before dawn. Jim was snoring across from her. The sky was blank but for a solitary star across the gulf. She lay back to think about the dream that tipped her out of sleep. In it she was on this very beach with her back to the sea and something was crunching across the shells from the water's edge. She couldn't move. She couldn't turn around. Something had slipped from the water and was coming for her, so slowly, deliberately. Georgie knelt on the beach with her fists at her sides. She couldn't get up to run. Her skin tightened at the presence of a body right close behind, there was a foul smell and a voice at her ear saying, Sister, Nurse, thank you. I thank you.

• • •

At breakfast there was a spent atmosphere, a weariness between the three of them. The men were hungover. They ate their bacon and eggs without pleasure. Georgie looked at the bites and welts on Jim's legs with grave disinterest.

Sorry you didn't find your bloke, said Red.

He'll come in, she said, feeling unaccountably peaceful about it. Tell him I'll be at the house, will you? He'll know what you mean. You can bill me for whatever it takes to get him out in one piece. If you could just be kind to him. Just tell him I'll be at the farm.

For how long? said Jim.

She shrugged. Just have them all leave us alone. That's all I want, Jim. That's all you need to do to prove anything to anyone.

He nodded curtly.

Sorry you didn't get what you wanted, she said.

Did you?

Something. I got something I think.

The guide scratched his chin and watched them. The HF radio squawked his call sign and then his name. The operator's voice seemed to bend and stretch within the fuzz of static. The de Havilland was booked out. Would the Buccaneer be all right? Red Hopper answered that beggars couldn't be choosers but that he himself would rather walk. Nine o'clock, said the radio voice. Hopper said, Roger that, and signed off.

They took turns to shower discreetly beneath

447

a water-bag. The men shaved. Georgie shampooed her hair. She couldn't help but think wistfully of how she might have helped Jim had she known him better all this time. But if she'd known him better would she have stayed? She doubted it. And she wouldn't have had what it took to save someone like Jim. She'd lived by force of will the same as him. They'd just cancel each other out the way they had already. She realized now that she didn't like the man and she was afraid of his need to wrestle virtue from himself and meaning from the life around him. He wanted to bring things to heel somehow and it wasn't working. But however you felt about that, whatever you thought about him, you had to pity him now. This morning he had the face of a man condemned.

Georgie towelled off and dressed and when she came out she felt clean and fresh for about five minutes.

The HF sputtered the news that the Buccaneer was still on the river experiencing fuel problems. It would be late.

Georgie watched a manta ray flounce about in the cove while the guide gathered up their linen and made coffee. She asked Red about the next party which wasn't due to fly in for several days. He pointed to his Hunter S. Thompson collection to indicate how he'd been spending the downtime.

The morning dragged. The conversation, which had been stilted before, dried up altogether. She resolved to take a separate commercial flight from Kununurra. The plane out of here would be the last time she'd ever share a space with Jim Buckridge. She wondered what it might be like to live in his mind, in a world without forgiveness. She thought of the Fox place and of decent coffee she might make for herself there, of the still flatness of the paddocks and the dry heat of the south.

And finally the plane flashed across the water, green and beetle shiny.

Ugly bastard, innit, said the guide. I'll be thinkin of yez.

Looks more like a boat than a plane, Jim said.

The floatplane came in fast to land. It did look like a watercraft, a sleek hull suspended beneath a single engine, but it sounded whiny as a power tool. As a conveyance it was altogether unconvincing. When it hit the water, spray rose in sheets and the plane feinted and rocked until it slowed and taxied their way.

Jesus, said Jim. This looks promising.

Before he leaves his camp for good Fox finds the tape on the rock. He's slept like the dead and got up and probably passed it twenty times in the dawn before the first light hits it and causes the plastic to flare and shine. He knows every track on it. He knows what kind of day it was when he dubbed it, how the light slanted through the library. He's not the same creature. The world itself has changed. He stuffs it into his pack, walks

449

down past the boabs and the midden and pushes the kayak into the shallows.

He's sore and weary but he knows he can make this last effort. There'll be no more treks now and the knowledge of it lifts him a little, gives a bit of sting to his paddle stroke. But the tide is still on the outrun. His progress is slow into the current. Out across the gulf, beyond the island chain, the high secret country lights up in the morning sun.

By the time he draws alongside the big red island the tide is slack. Most of the morning is gone. He hopes a breeze doesn't get up at noon. He's tired and sticky with sweat and his eyes are playing up again.

When the green plane rises from the water he just stops paddling. Down the gulf a way it lumbers up like some frightened marine creature whose frogleaps have unaccountably got it airborne. Sun flashes along its green fuselage and as it climbs toward him water spills from its tail.

He's in the strait between the island and the mainland. Adrift now, the paddle heavy across his knees. The plane banks. Its shadow races across the water behind it. She's on it. Georgie is in that plane.

As the shadow comes at him he raises the paddle and bellows. He howls at the engine whine and paint dazzle, at the blur of the prop, at the wings and animal-pissing-stream from its belly. He howls at its rushing, trailing, fluttering shadow, and the moment it passes over like some hateful angel, Fox is just a hot, raw, hurting sound that's swallowed in a rush of wind and noise as though he never was.

As soon as they were free of the buffeting water Georgie became conscious of the island which loomed into view on her side of the plane and at this final sight of it she felt the same queasy jolt of recognition that she had experienced the very first time. But there was no delight in it now, no tantalizing wonder— just the miserable fact of her incomprehension. There it was, like some bearded, featureless head rising, perennially and pointlessly from the water.

From her position in the rear she saw Jim and the pilot turn their heads in the same moment toward the other side of the plane. They began to speak and Jim gestured vigorously but the pilot shook his head. Georgie held her headphones in her lap.

The island fell by and the shimmering gulf was gone. Below them lay the yellow broken land.

Georgie looked up to see Jim still speaking. His finger jabbed the air near the pilot's cheek and the sinews of his neck stood out. With downcast eyes the young pilot spoke to Jim or to someone on the radio. He appeared to be hesitating, though the plane was still nosing up, seeking altitude.

The cabin smelt faintly of puke.

Georgie saw the young man's lips stop

moving at the same instant the engine's note faltered. She saw him mouth the words, *You bitch!*

He suddenly had his hand on one gauge after another as though his fingers might clear the plane's choked throat. Then he gave up and pumped the plane higher.

She felt him physically levering the thing up in steps, while the engine sputtered and gagged overhead. He put them into the gentlest of turns. Georgie began to see the blades of the prop becoming distinct. And then there was just whistling quiet and the prop fanned into a lazy windblown turn and they were gliding.

Jim swivelled in his seat. His face was grey.

Georgie saw the blue strip of water ahead. She saw the island. So this was the shimmer of recognition. You saw this day. But not this comic resignation, nor the whistling emptiness of the air around you. Somehow it'd always felt like a future, not the end.

She heard the pilot talking to himself. Jim breathing deeply. From behind he had the weathered neck of a turtle. He began to writhe in his seat. She was sorry for him.

When the plane chokes and goes silent, Fox feels his gut fall. He's killed it. With a shout, with that owl scream he's killed them all.

It turns back toward him losing altitude, chasing its shadow toward the water, toward him. A breeze springs up. At first he thinks it's slipstream but the whole gulf ruffles around him. The plane tips down at him, with the wind behind it, as though it's searching him out. Green now, shining. He feels himself cringing on the water as it shrieks over, towed by its own shadow, close enough to feel in the air around him. Too steep, too fast.

Before it even hits the water, he's paddling flat-out. He feels the seam in his collarbone as he digs toward it. The plane is suddenly a white cataract, a storm. The port wing shears back, flutters skyward, and the whole machine goes over in a cartwheel of spray and noise while he paddles.

Already there's the flare of a bow wave from the direction of the guide's camp. He smells kerosene and hot metal. Air hisses from the fuselage as it lists and settles. Voices. A khaki shirt comes up, a man bloody-faced and yelling. Fox almost runs him down as he ploughs up against the gulping aircraft.

A door shoots two metres into the air and the entire hull shudders. Another man swimming.

Fox claws his way along the ragged wing-stub. It's upside down, windows submerged. With his feet he finds a sill, an opening, and he hyperventilates as hard and fast as he can while there's time. The fuselage shudders and he soaks his bones with air. With a final breath he plunges under. He gets a hand-hold as the plane tips away. His hair and beard stream back in the current. His ears pop as he plunges through the milky deep with his eyes burning and his breath aglow like a coal in his chest. You can do this, he thinks with a bright, mad flush. This is what you do.

Air cheeps from his ears again. The water vibrates against his skin as he rushes all the way to the pale sandy seabed.

Georgie hung upside down against her harness with her whole weight against the clumsy latches into which her fingers could not fit. Air burbled and boiled somewhere in the cabin like the sound of a human voice. You could feel the weight of the motor dragging you down. Spritzing bubbles. Everything blurry. Ears hurting.

The doorway was just a rectangle of pale blue light now. She watched it as passively as you would a TV or a computer screen. She was calm, so calm—and then not calm.

The thud of the plane hitting the bottom kicked the air out of her; she felt her last breath run up her chin and across her breasts and she saw the shadow coming for her like any ordinary saurian nightmare. She lashed at it, fought it off while it clawed at her. Such a hot darkness and so insistent upon her. It pressed itself furry against her face. She saw red eyes within the black wavering blur. Georgie could feel it snapping her free from herself; she sensed her last awful unbuckling, the yanking sensation of coming unstuck.

But air against her lips. Hotter than water. It boiled through her teeth and into her throat.

It blew her open. It was like an electrical charge. For a moment she thought she saw his face in that hoary mass before her eyes. She felt his lips pressed against her. Luther Fox.

She felt herself come unglued, felt the grip of his hands upon her arms. She was floating into that pale blue screen, into the soft world outside. Georgie Jutland drank his hot shout and let him swim her up into the rest of her life.

HE LIES with his head against the deck and does not breathe. The sky is behind her. She's real. She's not real. The others have faces they don't seem to own yet. One of them looks as though he's still waiting to be rescued.

Georgie looked at the martyred jut of his hip-bones, the twigs in his hair, the livid ulcers all down his thin legs. The boat was moving now. The sea behind them was glossy with fuel and a final coil of bubbles that twisted on the surface. The pilot shook. Jim Buckridge held his head in his hands. The fishing guide worked the tiller and licked his lips as though lost for words.

She looks in from the sky. Eyes wide as a fish's. Real or not, he should breathe. He feels his lips split in a smile. Soon. There's plenty of time for that.

Georgie saw his eyes roll back and his hips lift toward her. My God, he was blue. The bleeding pilot drew his legs back in horror and Jim Buckridge bellowed. Georgie froze. She was as stuck as she'd ever been in her life. Luther Fox began to convulse.

Well, said the guide. You're the nurse.

Yes, she thought. This is what I do.

She fell on Luther Fox, pressed her mouth to his and blew.

She's real.

acknowledgements

I would like to thank Robert Vaughan for his generosity and his friendship and for the many days and nights on One Tree Beach where this story took shape.

For editorial advice I'm indebted to Jenny Darling, Howard Willis, Hilary McPhee and Judith Lukin-Amundsen.

I thank my children for the years of encouragement, for the little notes in the drawer and for their gentle patience.

This book is for Denise who endured it and made it possible.

There is no town called White Point in Western Australia, nor a place by the name of Coronation Gulf. This is a work of fiction and its characters are imaginary.

permissions

Excerpt from 'The Lifeguard', from *Drowning with Others* by James Dickey. Reprinted with permission of Wesleyan University Press.

On page 385 Luther Fox quotes from 'The Book of Urizen' by William Blake.

Excerpt from 'The North Wind Is Tossing in the Leaves'. Music/lyrics by John Wheeler/William G. James (W/C 100%). © 1968 Chappell & Co. Ltd., London/Sydney.

The lyrics quoted on page 375 are from 'Nobody's Fault but Mine', by Blind Willie Johnson.

While all efforts have been made to contact copyright holders of material used in this work, any oversights will be gladly corrected in future editions.